The Prince of Leroy

The Prince of Leroy

Brian T. W. Way

First Edition

Hidden Brook Press
www.HiddenBrookPress.com
writers@HiddenBrookPress.com

Copyright © 2018 Hidden Brook Press
Copyright © 2018 Brian T. W. Way

All rights for story and characters revert to the author. All rights for book, layout and design remain with Hidden Brook Press. No part of this book may be reproduced except by a reviewer who may quote brief passages in a review. The use of any part of this publication reproduced, transmitted in any form or by any means, electronic, mechanical, photocopied, recorded or otherwise stored in a retrieval system without prior written consent of the publisher is an infringement of the copyright law.

This book is a work of fiction. Names, characters, places and events are either products of the author's imagination or are employed fictitiously. Any resemblance to actual events, locales or persons, living or dead, is entirely coincidental.

The Prince of Leroy
by Brian T. W. Way

Cover Design – Richard M. Grove
Layout and Design – Richard M. Grove

Typeset in Garamond
Printed and bound in Canada
Distributed in USA by Ingram,
 in Canada by Hidden Brook Distribution

Library and Archives Canada Cataloguing in Publication

Way, Brian T. W. (Brian Thomas Wesley), 1951-, author
    The Prince of Leroy / Brian T.W. Way. -- 1st edition.

ISBN 978-1-927725-53-5 (softcover)

    I. Title.

PS8645.A915P75 2018   C813'.6   C2018-905565-0

for Tai

Acknowledgement

I am indebted to several people who helped in the revision and development of this novel. It has been a long journey. A heartfelt thanks to Dr. Miriam C. MacCormack who thoroughly read and offered critical suggestions on an early version of this manuscript; to Dr. Cornelia Hoogland who also waded through this book in an early form and provided invaluable feedback; and to Ona Gutauskas, Sally Panavas, Alexandre den Broeder and Hannah Renglich for their beneficial help in the creative process and refinement of various things along the way. And of course, to Richard and Kim at Hidden Brook Press, without their publication of *redirection*, and assistance here, *The Prince of Leroy* would not exist.

Every day I see people in Tokyo handing out handbills to other people. This is the way they make their living, by standing on the street handing out handbills to total strangers, wanting them to spend their money on something they may or may not need.

Most of the time the strangers don't make use of the handbills. They just throw them away and forget about them. I also see men holding signs that want other men to spend their money in nearby massage parlors and cabarets where there are women for the purposes that men use women and that women get money for.

Often the men are old and wear poor sloppy clothes, standing there holding erotically promising signs. I wish the old men were not doing that. I wish they were doing something else and their clothes looked better.

But I can't change the world.

It was changed before I got here.

Sometimes when I finish writing something, perhaps even this, I feel as if I am handing out useless handbills or I am an old man standing in the rain, wearing shitty clothes and holding a sign for a cabaret that is filled with the beautiful and enticing skeletons of young women that sound like dominoes when they walk toward you coming in at the door.

Richard Brautigan
The Tokyo-Montana Express

The best lack all conviction, while the worst
Are full of passionate intensity.

W. B. Yeats
"The Second Coming"

T of C

Acknowledgement – *p. ix*

Chapters

1. Logos rising – *p. 1*
2. A cup of Rainy's – *p. 9*
3. All that glisters – *p. 18*
4. The Stump and the Saint – *p. 21*
5. I hear what you're sayin' – *p. 26*
6. As if they had never existed at all – *p. 29*
7. Another cup of Rainy's for the road – *p. 32*
8. Marlboro, man – *p. 44*
9. Fly on, my beauty, fly on – *p. 49*
10. So now everything's ready for Burning Day – *p. 56*
11. Time to go to war – *p. 61*
12. Time for a bit of Geography and History, but not too much – *p. 63*
13. Me and America – *p. 66*
14. War brings out the best in humans – *p. 69*
15. Hey little girl, is your daddy home? – *p. 75*
16. Neither like hawk nor wolf – *p. 80*
17. That's all right, mama – *p. 85*
18. Who'd you think you was fuckin' with? – *p. 90*
19. A long time since Placid – *p. 95*
20. The Gardens of the Leroy – *p. 98*
21. Down to the river – *p. 103*
22. This land is my land – *p. 105*
23. A bleedin' mess – *p. 114*
24. Not enough cannibals – *p. 117*
25. *News Centre Now* – *p. 126*
26. Hello, Mr. Dalco – *p. 130*
27. A place called Leroy – *p. 135*

28. The games are over – *p. 140*
29. Some stale bread to feed your chickens – *p. 145*
30. Do Re Mi – *p. 149*
31. Antebellum paramours – *p. 153*
32. Have you nothing to say? – *p. 157*
33. The eternal freak-out of being – *p. 165*
34. A right gude-willie waught – *p. 168*
35. A large coffee to go but no meatloaf – *p. 175*
36. Rats and cockaroaches – *p. 180*
37. Time for a bit of Sociology and Psychology, but not too much – *p. 185*
38. The salt taste of blood fills his mouth – *p. 195*
39. A helluva thing – *p. 199*
40. The Leroy sounds fine to me – *p. 203*
41. Let's go, Larry – *p. 206*
42. Ah, shit! – *p. 208*
43. Waiting in the dark – *p. 209*
44. Nature commits no errors – *p. 213*
45. What the hell's the matter with these people? – *p. 221*
46. Any quadruped can get a degree in those – *p. 225*
47. A knight without armour in a savage land – *p. 228*
48. Something's coming, don't know when – *p. 231*
49. Our brother's keeper – *p. 237*
50. A mad jigsaw puzzle – *p. 241*
51. Fruit goes before the fall – *p. 244*
52. The hydro man – *p. 249*
53. Corvid scarlet – *p. 252*
54. Above us only sky – *p. 253*
55. Tom and Dick Grill – *p. 258*
56. You know I always like seein' youse too – *p. 261*
57. The road goes on forever – *p. 263*
58. Beyond the gift of reason – *p. 265*
59. That's a lot of Pérignon – *p. 268*

60. Another bug on the windshield – *p. 270*
61. The phantom slips away – *p. 272*
62. On a foggy night – *p. 274*
63. Holy shit on the sepulchre – *p. 276*
64. When hens are made of clay – *p. 277*
65. Holy Mother of God – *p. 280*
66. Rat in a trap – *p. 282*
67. Bird and fish and stone – *p. 284*
68. Everything's been quiet, Mr. Prince – *p. 285*
69. Taking charge of change – *p. 288*
70. The heart of the problem – *p. 297*
71. *Assez propre* – *p. 303*
72. You can check out any time – *p. 306*
73. Back on the saddle – *p. 323*
74. The prosaic detritus of the day – *p. 326*
75. One toke over the line – *p. 329*
76. On the road again – *p. 335*
77. Let me see your gun – *p. 343*
78. Time for a bit of Meteorology and Archaeology; some Mythology too, but not too much – *p. 348*
79. She is loud and has a tongue like fire – *p. 352*
80. Hurricane Angel – *p. 357*
81. The fox is trapped in the hen house – *p. 361*
82. If his brains were lard – *p. 366*
83. The soup was good, man – *p. 368*
84. *Je ne suis pas fait de sucre* – *p. 371*
85. Magic carpet ride – *p. 376*
86. Jesus – *p. 381*
87. Silent as lightning, stoic as thunder – *p. 385*
88. The implacable weight of knowing – *p. 388*
89. A beautiful friendship – *p. 391*
90. Yes – *p. 398*

- 1 -

Logos rising

The sun is searing the horizon. The large white cross on top of the old department store begins to surrender to darkness, then suddenly staccatos into light under the command of its wary timer—this light from above illuminates the ragged store front and a dilapidated parking lot beyond. Once a K-Mart, this old building is showing signs of wear and neglect, its vast space now only rented out to *The Holy Shrine of the Simple Church of Bleeding Jesus the Almighty Provider*. This is a religious splinter sect that formed a couple years ago when local Catholic and Anglican Church societies had mistakenly double booked Harris Thorn Park for their summer picnics. Churches always seem full of disgruntled people and so it came to pass that some of the unhappy ones from each congregation had met by accident over the bowl of heavenly hash potato salad and, in a stroke of divine intervention, one might say, decided to form their own holy conclave. The naming of their mutual sect had taken almost a year to negotiate but now they met every Tuesday, Thursday and Sunday in the old K-Mart, the best and cheapest place they could find in Thornton. They congregated near the back of the cavernous building where the Auto Shop had been and where the roof didn't leak so much. The eternal smell of grease merged with that of grace, at least of incense and molten candle wax, and everyone was careful not to get too close to the oil change well, although one devotee had suggested filling it with water to make a splendid baptismal font, to which someone else had made a Baptist joke and the sermon began.

It is dusk. Near the side of the building, which had quickly come to be called the *Church of the Holy K.* by the locals, a grey, older model Mustang stops, angling itself across the lines of two faded spaces—there are no rules in parking lots. Two men get out and disappear into the shadow on the west side of the building under the cover of shade and overgrown bushes. What re-emerges is an orange 1970's vintage Dodge pick-up, the two men pushing it out across the lot, one from the rear, one from the side with a hand on the steering wheel. They stop and, their tasks obviously preordained, one man, a short fellow in a tan wind-breaker, gets in the Dodge; the other, a tall lanky man wearing a black long-rider coat, returns to the Mustang. He starts it and manoeuvres around the pick-up, gently bumpering it from behind. He leans his long-haired head from the window and shouts:

"Ready, Gabe? Here goes nothing, man. Hi Ho, Silver!"

Slowly, but with certainty, the Mustang nudges and grunts the pick-up forward and the vehicles gain speed; then there is a jolt as the truck's clutch engages, a sputter, and the Dodge fires to life.

"Hi Ho, Silver. Away."

Both vehicles move across the cracked, weed-festooned parking lot toward an access road, and along that road between the remnants of a long-ago burned-out building and another small square brick structure. They turn left onto a main city street and head east toward the freeway—there is little traffic at twilight on this Spring Monday.

Just behind them as they turn, a great sign rises into view. Sitting at the front of a parking lot, supported by two large poles cemented in asphalt like a pair of modern-day excaliburs, the sign is large and old, of metal and rust swathed in chipped yellow paint, in the shape of a great crown with five points, each supporting a round white light like five opalescent pearls. The red neon on the crown, it too a bit weathered and arthritic, reads *Le Roi Motor In* and, in a smaller font below, *La Reine Resta rant & B r.* Lower down, a red **VACANCY** sign stretches between the poles. As the vehicles pick up speed out of town, a second sign rises in contrast diagonally across the road. This shining beacon is much more modern than the first with the image of a large blue canoe and two crossed paddles cresting up into the evening sky. *Voyageur's End* arcs across in golden letters.

The Dodge pick-up and Mustang speed out of town and pass the intersection with the freeway. The four lane city street soon turns into a two lane country road, lined by a few farmers' fields but mostly acre after acre of abandoned farm land, once ploughed and sown, now replenishing itself with frost-risen stone and new growth brush and trees. After some fifteen minutes or so, the vehicles move up a long hill and begin to slow down. The Mustang, well before the crest of the hill, swings out and passes the Dodge, heedless of the risk, it seems, then slows, stops, and backs into a gravel side-road. The pick-up does the same, jockeying itself in front of the car.

Lucas Burrell, the tall, moustached driver of the Mustang, gets out and pops open its trunk. He wears cowboy boots, blue jeans, a black t-shirt and his treasured black long rider coat. From the trunk, he retrieves a couple empty liquor boxes, a pair of binoculars and another object which he tucks in his trousers. Then he turns and gets into the passenger side of the pick-up.

Gabriel Black, a short man with a ruddy complexion and a slight limp in his gait, gets out of the pick-up. He wears green work pants and work boots, a grey sweatshirt and a well-worn tan windbreaker. He quickly removes the licence plates from the pick-up—they are loosely wired on—tosses them into the back seat of the Mustang, retrieves a bottle of liquor and returns to the pick-up. As with their actions in the *Holy K.* parking lot, these tasks are obviously rehearsed.

"You ready, Lucky?" Gabe speaks casually to his partner.

"Hot to prance, Gabe, like a nun on her first vacation. I'm kinda amazed this old crate made it this far."

"You and me both, buddy ... it was always a trusty old thing, though. Years of lugging fruit and stuff off the farm. And then in my brother's carpet business. And now, one more small job to do. See anything comin'?"

"No ... nothing. And I can see all the way across the valley, past the marsh. As long as it hasn't gone by already...!"

"Jesus, I hope it hasn't. Stump would fry our asses if we missed it."

"Ahh, don't worry, man, we're prime. We'll get it done. Like always! Hand me that Comfort ... you're driving. You shouldn't be drinking. And here, take this box. I figured these might cushion the blow in case there's a collision. This old baby don't got no air bags."

"No shit—just a steel dash. But I hope there's no collision. We're just plannin' to cut 'em off, right ... not hit 'em! At least, that's my plan." Gabe squeezes the empty cardboard box between his chest and the wheel. "Hey, you know I had to laugh. I heard you givin' it the old 'hi ho silver' back there. That takes me back a few years."

"Yeah. Don't it! Some things stick in the head, pardner. Last forever. Never change. Never should."

"I don't think we ever missed an episode, did we? That and the Stooges."

"Yeah. I used to come over to your house pretty much every Saturday morning, 'cause Mom didn't have a TV, couldn't afford one, what with the cost of booze, and all."

"And remember, all the adventures the Ranger and Tonto got into, and then just rode away without anyone ever knowin' who they was ... and the Ranger, he had that code to live by..."

"Yeah, and we memorized all of it, mostly—we each got half of it anyways and then used to say it back and forth. Other kids thought we was nuts. I don't think I remember any of it now. You, Gabe?"

"Nah, not really—there was something about for a man to be friend, you had to have one—something like that."

"Yeah, that made sense. The only one I really remember was that God made firewood but you had to take it and light it yourself. That didn't make no sense but it was part of the code. Oh, and sooner or later every man gotta settle with the world. That was always my favourite."

"Is that a new tatt?" Gabe gestures to some blue markings near the back of Lucky's left wrist.

"Yeah. Got it last week. Korean or Chinese or something."

"Cool. So how many you got now?"

"Fifteen, sixteen, give or take."

"And all words in different languages, and you don't know what any of it means?"

"No. I ain't got a fuckin' clue, man. It's like I'm a walking, talking mystery ... to myself, to everyone I meet. It's like a bunch of different dictionaries blew up and they landed on me.

Remember, I got the idea back in Grade 7, before tatts became popular like they are now; got it from that book old Rivers read to us…"

"I remember him. Wise-crackin' asshole."

"Yeah, that's the dude. But remember the story about a tattooed guy and everybody looks at him and sees their future, good or bad? Well, that story stuck, except anyone who looks at me sees nothing they can understand one way or another. I am the end of futures, man."

"No shit. I believe that, Lucky."

"And that movie they showed us in stir, the one about the whale and the guy with all the tattoos. He didn't know what they meant either. I tried to get people to call me Ahab after that but they wouldn't. 'Lucky' had just stuck by then."

"It's a fine name buddy … it's got you this far."

"I guess it has … both of us, you know. Lucky and Gabe. The Lone Ranger and Tonto. Quite a team."

"Maw always said we was both named after angels. All of us, my brother, Mike, too. I always thought that was cool."

"Well, just in case the angel thing ain't happening tonight, I brought this along." Lucky reaches behind and pulls a large, nickel-plated automatic pistol out of his jeans.

"Jesus, Lucky. I hope we won't need that. This is just gonna be a straightforward jack, I hope. No firepower needed. Right?"

"Yeah, I hear you, but you never know. Better to be safe than you know what…"

"I suppose. Where'd you get it?"

"Taber. You need it, good old Taber can get it."

"It's huge. What is it?"

"It's an 80 calibre Glock, I think that's what he said. It's the best thing I ever bought, man. Automatic. Packs a helluva wallop. Pretty accurate for one shot, but when you hold the trigger down, it's like pissin' with a hard-on."

"Well, I hope we don't need it. We're just hittin' a book truck, right? And nobody'll be packin' on a book truck. And we want to keep this cool, not lose it like … other times."

"Yeah, I know, that old house job was a mess. I told that kid just to keep quiet but she ran for her phone. To this day, man, I don't know what kind of parents would put a phone in a kid's bedroom … I mean maybe today when everybody's got cell phones, but not back then…"

"Well, we did our time; and we were true to old Duff and that's why we got this gig today. Loyalty pays, you know. … Still, I'm a bit jumpy. If Liz knew I was out here, she'd tear me a new one."

"No shit," Lucky smiles. "She scares the hell out of me and I'm not even married to her. Just remember, though, Liz and little Jimmy, that's the reason you're here. You ain't goin' nowhere in that dead-end job, man, puttin' in cable. Cable's done for. Every place that needs it, already got it, and they don't put it in new places anymore. The world's moved on. It's all wireless. Blue balls and wiffee, and whatever."

"Yeah, maybe. But Smitty said they might even be expanding. That big job we just did rewiring the old Voyeur's Asshole made some money for him, I'll tell you that. He can sure afford to expand."

"Yeah … hey, there's some lights. Gimme the glasses." Lucky sits the boxes and bottle on the seat, opens the door of the old Dodge, and uses the binoculars to peer into the twilight. Far down in the valley headlights pierce the gloom. He hops back in the cab. "White truck. **LOGOS TEXT**. Yep. That's them. Ready or not, man, time to get at 'er."

7

Lucky pulls and releases the slide of the Glock, and takes another quick swig. Both men re-position the empty liquor boxes in their laps. They sit, still and tense, as the sound of an approaching truck gets louder. It groans up the hill. Logos rising, its headlights shoot up at the stars and then flatten out as its white snout levels. Gabe pumps the gas once, twice. The engine sputters, then stalls. Dead silence. He turns the key, pumps the gas—after some hesitancy, a spit of fire leaps from the tailpipe and the truck comes to life once more.

"Now, Gabe, now. Pump it, man. Like our fuckin' lives depend on it—Hi Ho Silver. Away."

- 2 -

A cup of Rainy's

Two men amble down Victoria Avenue. One is short, wildly gesticulating with his arms and hands, and continually talking; the other is huge, still and never seems to say anything. This is Dom and Deed, never employed but always at work; they are the inheritors of this particular piece of earth.

"Yes. Just like I said. I dreamed I was dead and when I woke, for a minute, I didn't know who or where or what in hell I was. Do you know what I mean, Deed? Know what I mean?"

"Hmmm?"

"Well, it was the strangest feeling I ever had, man. Like, fireworks were going off, but there was no sound or light. Nothing. It was like I was asleep inside of my sleep, and then I swear I woke up and I was still inside. The darkness was visible. And I was inside it, Deed. Inside of nothing. And I knew that the world was still going on but beyond my touch or feel— beyond me. My only thought, how d'you wake from bein' dead, man? Finally, I just surfaced and sat on the edge of my bed and didn't know who or where I was. Whether I was awake or still dreamin'. Sittin' there, and wonderin'—do the dead dream, man? Do they remember? It was the strangest feeling I've ever had, Deed."

"Mmmm."

"Like, how do you wake from being dead?"

"Mmmm?"

"C'mon, let's step it up, my brother. I really need a cup of Rainy's. And right now."

The two men continue down Victoria Avenue and turn east on Dundas. The weather is warm on this late Monday afternoon in early spring. On they go, down the four lane street for a block and a half drawn toward the great crowned sign of *Le Roi*. They choose a gap in the traffic and cross to the north side.

"I wonder if the Prince will be back by now. Did you hear the latest, Deed? They say he's got some kind of big score goin' dow—errands as he always calls them—some guy from Philadelphia showed up last week and him and the Prince talked in one of the booths at the back for over two hours, sometimes quiet and slow, sometimes fists pounding on the table and fingers jammed in each other's faces. But nobody knows what the score's all about—Fruitfarm thinks it's some new kind of computer chip—micro ones that hold a gazillion bits of info. Man, would I like to be in on that—'cause with the Prince, you know you'd get a fair deal. He's a straight shooter—the most honest guy I ever knew. Ever!"

"Hmmm?"

"Yeah, I know—present company excluded. 'Course, you know the Prince only runs the Leroy because he inherited it from his uncle and made a promise to keep it going. It's only like a hobby to him, something to do while he makes his real coin other places. That's the only way it stays open anyways, what with *Voyageur's End* all new and bright right across the road, flashy rooms and that big sign. Look at that thing floatin' in the sky over there—that big blue canoe and two gold paddles. Their sign should be a big blue French ass stuck up in the air with a couple breadsticks poking out. Man, Deed, do I need a cup of Rainy's. That dream's got me spooked. Being dead'll do that to you! Trust me on that!"

Along Dundas Street the two men reach their destination—it is a motel and restaurant of the old fashioned kind, straight from the fifties, a quaint mix of drive-in charm and whorehouse desolation. The grey clapboard Motel Office sits to the east, a small vacancy sign lit in the window, with its stretch of 24 rooms, each marked by a door and window, forming a great 'U' back and around to the west. Faded parking spaces creep out in front of each unit and breezeways cut through the corners to the lot behind, once used for overflow parking, now covered in soil and destined someday to become the motel's "Gardens." The restaurant is a square, two-story building with rectangular, tinted windows stretching east from the office. And at the front of the parking lot near the street, the great sign with the five pearls rises into the air announcing the place that all the locals simply call the Leroy.

Dom and Deed enter the restaurant as they have done so many times before. As they do, an old orange truck and a grey Mustang emerge from a rarely used service road and head east out of town.

The two men glance around as they amble to the counter. Rainy's spills out about them, red vinyl booths flowing along the windows and back into the receding light of the eastside 'L'. The floor space back there is crowded with small round tables and bamboo bar chairs, and a black riser leans against the back wall where local bands sometimes play on the weekends. Blue is behind the lunch counter, a tousled but attractive woman in her mid-thirties with bobdylan-hair that hints in faded hues of all the colours of Joseph's coat. She looks up from a magazine she is reading, nods at the two men and turns to the kitchen serving window saying something indistinguishable to the unseen short-order cook known as Grease. She fills two thick diner mugs with coffee from a spigot.

"Hey, Dom, Deed! You guys are here late today. What'd you do, have a rough day wakin' up?" Blue inquires in her own welcoming way.

Dom and Deed sit at the counter.

"Hey, gorgeous. Yeah, somethin' like that. Had some late night business that got in the way of sleep. You know how it is," Dom replies.

"Maybe I do. Maybe I don't … Or maybe I really don't want to know, do I? So what can I get you, boys?"

"I'll have that coffee and some toast. What're you having, Deed? The regular? Coffee, and some corn flakes?"

"Mmhmm" is all the big man says.

"There's your coffee, gents. And the rest of your order's already in. You're so late today, Dom, your best friend's out with Oz…"

Deed offers a quizzical grunt.

"Sorry Deed … I mean your other best friend, Dom, the four-legged one. Angus is out for a van-ride. He loves riding around … that and usually Oz makes a stop at the pet store and loads up on treats. So what are you two breakfast-for-supper boys up to this fine spring day?" asks Blue whose name in an earlier life was Suzie Greenway but who, like so many others, has been baptized into the world of the Leroy with a new eponym, one that stuck.

"The usual, Blue ... a million things on the go. Sorry to have missed my boy, though," says Dom. "Maybe he'll be back before we go. Anyways, here we are. Couldn't let the day go by without a coffee. Rainy's coffee—you know, the nectar of the gods."

"Old Jake's special blend—and only the Prince knows how to mix it now."

"And of course, I wouldn't want a day to go by without seeing my favourite girl."

"O! Haven't you heard? She doesn't date men she has to bend low to kiss."

"Well, there's a solution to that, gorgeous."

"And you keep dreamin', Frodo. There's your toast and your corn flakes. Now Deed, now there's a man I could look up to. A true knight in shining armour. Every lost maiden's dream. Right!"

Deed's huge shoulders shake as he suppresses his laughter.

"Now that you mention dreamin', the main thing on my mind right now is just that, the dream I just had. I been tellin' Deed about it. It really spooked me, Blue. You see, I dreamed I was dead. Dead! It was the strangest feeling I ever had ..." and the story of the dream of being dead is retold, as it will be retold again and again in the next few hours. And days. And then, well, then there'd be strange accidents and actual dead bodies and crazy professors and wild shoot-outs and other stories to replace its immediacy. But it was a dream that would continue to hover in the background for some time. At least for Dom.

"Wow, Dom, that is one strange dream. Weird, man. Maybe it comes from sleeping too much. Or too little! The big sleep got mixed up with the little sleep, you know! But dreams are all supposed to be about something, aren't they—I wonder what that could mean?" Blue spoke casually, but gave thought to each word. Whenever you listened to Blue, it seemed as if she cared. You know, I don't think I ever met anyone who didn't like Blue.

"I hope to hell it means nothing, girl. I ain't planning on being dead real soon, you know. Trust me on that!"

"From what I've heard about dreams, Dom, it's most likely connected to something in your past, not your future. Like, did anyone you know die recently, or have you had any near death experiences? Nearly get run over crossing the road, or anything?"

"No. Not lately anyways. Seen a movie the other night where some mobsters got whacked! But they had it comin' though they didn't see it. I guess they hadn't read the script."

"Well, they say you never see it comin', Dom, otherwise you'd be somewhere else. Dreams are funny things, aren't they. You remember, old Jake used to have a lot of strange dreams."

"Yeah, that's right, too. I remember Jake and his dreams—he was always talkin' about 'em, wasn't he? Always around and always talkin' about his dreams, when he wasn't talkin' about the Leroy."

"Yep, in some ways they were the same thing, Dom," replies Blue.

"He pretty much did everything here himself, didn't he, at least 'til the Prince grew up. But yeah, I remember old Jake talkin' 'bout his dreams."

"Well, he'd been in the war, of course, and had recurring bouts of malaria for years afterwards, and I think a lot of his dreams came out of that. There was one in particular, though, I remember him telling over and over—d'you remember it? It really stuck with him. Something like your dream of being dead, Dom. Jake said that he'd be asleep in his dream and wake and hear something outside and he'd go out and there'd be this dark shadowy figure—at the first he could never make out the face—but this person would have a knife and he would start to chase Jake and they'd go running and running around the house until old Jake would wake up in a cold sweat screaming. And Jake said this dream happened over and over for years after the war until one night—it was a night one spring—Jake claimed that, finally, he just said to himself, 'to hell with 'er, Clem'—that was the nickname he had in the war, bein' from a farm and all—so one night he said 'to hell with it, Clem' and stopped running. And the dark figure stopped too. And then, Jake said, he turned and started to scream 'to hell with it' over and over and started to chase the figure, and he awoke and never had that dream again. Strange stuff, eh?"

"Yeah, well I hope I don't have my dream again. Gawd, it really spooked me, Blue. I feel like I haven't slept in a week."

"Well, you could try goin' to sleep before five o'clock some morning."

"What! And miss the best part of the day. A lot of business gets done after midnight. And, you never know, there might be a song or two there, Blue!"

"I know all about your kind of business, little man, and it's not my kind of song. But, you know, talkin' about Jake's dream ... the strangest part of it, the part that Jake said he could never understand. He said that, just before the figure in his dream turned to run, he saw its face clearly for the first time, and you know what, Jake said it was like looking into a mirror. The figure with the knife that had been chasing him for years looked just like him, like he'd been chasing himself. Strange stuff! Anyway—'to hell with it, Clem' old Jake said one spring night after the war and he ran that shadow right into oblivion. So maybe you'll figure out some way to deal with your own dream, Dom. Maybe just say 'to hell with it' ... maybe that's what we all need to say to our dreams? Good or bad? Maybe that's the song."

"'Cept in my dream I'm dead, I'm already in oblivion, Blue. There ain't nothin' to talk to. Or sing to! Nothin' to chase. And nowhere to chase it—hell or anywhere else. I mean, how do you wake from bein' dead? So I don't think that Jake's dream is gonna to do me any good."

"Well, I know what you can do then—talk to Benny, the Professor. He just went off shift but catch him tomorrow—he's probably read stuff about dreams and what they mean..."

"Yeah, that's an idea. He'll know something, university guy and all. I'd toast you for your good idea, Blue, but I'm afraid my cup hath runneth dry..."

"I hear you big guy. Refill on the way."

"Thank you ma'am, and thank God for Rainy's and the Leroy. I don't know what I'd do without this place, girl. You know, I don't know how you do it or what the Prince puts into it—this coffee is great. Best in the world. And this place, it's just kinda perfect, too. Always so easy here. Comfortable. There's nothing like it any time of the day, any day of the week. It's so calm here, cool and settled—like the eye at the centre of a storm. You know, I always feel that, like if you never had a home, or if you were so far away from your home that you couldn't remember where it was, you could come here to Rainy's and sit down and have a coffee and feel like you'd found something maybe you never even knew you'd lost. And even bad dreams would start to seem better. You know what I mean!"

"Yep, I know Dom. You're preaching to one of the lead singers in the choir. It's why I've hung around here so long, I guess. It's home away from home. Or maybe it's my real home? I don't know. But sooner or later, everybody comes to Rainy's, or should."

"What about you, Deed? You know what I mean?" asks Dom.

"Mmhmm," comes the reply.

"Ah, Deed, a man of many words?" He slaps the big man on the shoulder. "'Course if there was anything wrong, Johnny would get it fixed pronto. Right?"

"Well, Dom," Blue replies, "Just remember our slogan, 'if the service is slow or the steak's tough, speak to Mel.'"

"Yeah, I know, and Mel don't exist! But, hey Blue, speakin' of Johnny, is the Prince around? He mentioned last week he might have a job for me and Deed sometime this week or next."

"No, I haven't seen Johnny since late Thursday. I guess I told you, didn't I? He had this long meetin' with some guy from Jersey a week ago—it was a real serious meeting too, and he disappeared for the last few days—down to Atlantic City, he told me. Nothing unusual, in that, of course. Living his life in jacks and queens."

"Yeah. Staking his soul on the rattle of the bones."

"And disappearing for a couple days every now and then, especially after one of those meetings, that's normal for the Prince. But he never stays away from the Leroy too long—as you know, like his Uncle Jake before him, Johnny and this place are really one and the same. One breathes in and the other breathes out. Never apart for long. Besides I know that he'll be back sometime soon, by Thursday at the very latest…"

"Why's that? He tell you?"

"No … 'cause Thursday's Burning Day. Remember?"

"Oh, hell yeah, I had forgotten; it'll be the 21st, won't it? Burning Day. And the Prince never misses Burning Day at the Leroy!"

- 3 -

All that glisters

"Ride 'em, cowboy," roars Lucky.

Instinctively, Gabe releases the clutch and slams the gas, and the old Dodge leaps into life, spinning stones and dust from the dirt side road where it is parked. Springing across the road, the Dodge t-bones the white two-ton van marked Logos Text directly below its sign. The sound of screeching tires and folding and ripping metal ensues, and there is a metallic bounce as the universal joint of the van snaps and its drive train dislodges. In the impact the van rides up on the hood of the Dodge, hovers, then goes overbalance, tipping to its side and sliding forward with the barbaric yawp of flailed metal. Its back doors break open, a pile of boxes and books spills across the road. The Dodge, once moving due north, now spins to the west and, caught in the undercarriage and wheels of the van, slides along with it, front tire popping and windshield and passenger window shattering amid a fireworks of spark and steam and dust. Then, all is silent. Eerily quiet.

"Holy shit! What fuckin' truckin' a ride! You ok, Gabe?"

"Yeah. I think."

"Wow ... I thought the plan was to side swipe the cab—force them into the ditch."

"Yeah, it was. I sorta missed. The tires spun in the gravel too much. But the box idea worked pretty good, didn't it? Cushioned the blow."

"Yeah. Not too bad, 'though I got a helluva bump on my head."

"Ahh, you'll live, buddy. It's a long way from your heart. We better get moving. You'll have to get out of my side."

Gabe's door creaks open and he and Lucky scramble out. The darkness is deepening. They move cautiously toward the cab of the overturned van, Lucky carrying his Glock and the Southern Comfort. There is a groan and a figure hoists himself through the broken window on the driver's side. Lucky steps closer and hits him hard with the side of his pistol and the man collapses back into the cab. The men retrace their steps around the old Dodge to the rear of the van where one of the large doors has flopped open to the roadway. They unhook the other and throw it up over the side. Inside there is a chaos of overturned boxes and loose books. Gabe holds a flashlight and the Comfort while Lucky steps on and through pages and covers and spines.

"Make for a good night's read, wouldn't it?" says Gabe.

"Make for a good bonfire, if you ask me?" comes Lucky's reply. "There. There it is. An orange box marked Shakespeare. That's the one we're lookin' for, isn't it Gabe?"

"Yep. That's what Stump said. Bring it here. I'll open it." Gabe lifts his right arm and when he brings it down he is holding a six-inch blade. Lucky slips and slides back through the strewn words of the van and drops the orange box of the Bard at his feet. Gabe carefully slits the plastic tape that seals the box. In the arc of the flashlight there are shimmering bags filled with powder.

"Yessir, that's what we're after. Good old Shakespeare! All that glitters is gonna make us rich as shit. Didn't he say that, Lucky?"

"I don't know what the fuck he said. But I do know one thing. Let's get the hell out of here before somebody shows up, or that driver wakes up again."

Gabe and Lucky move back across the road and put the orange box in the trunk of the grey Mustang. They climb into the car. Lucky drives. The engine and lights come on simultaneously and the rear wheels kick gravel. The car moves onto the main road past the overturned van and the crumpled Dodge and picks up speed heading west into the early night and back toward Thornton.

- 4 -

The Stump and the Saint

"Yeah, this is Malley. Come on up."

Jerry Malley, a short, stump of a man, eases back in a leather Queen Anne behind a large red mahogany desk. He replaces a black phone in its cradle, snaps his fingers a couple of times—a compulsive habit—and continues his reading of a computer print-out. Wearing brown khakis, blue shirt and yellow tie, and a company windbreaker, Jerry inherited this company, involved in trucking and other varied enterprises, from his father Duffy. And like so many sons who inherit their father's substance and sin, Jerry has the desire to prove his worth but not always the aptitude.

The room is large, with an expanse of drape-enclosed windows along the side behind the desk and a variety of book shelves and cabinets and tropical plants around the other three. A dark burgundy leather sofa sits against the far wall and two matching chairs face the desk. In the centre of the orange hardwood floor, there is a large multi-coloured Persian carpet, an absolute showpiece, plush and carved and covered in a labyrinth of lines and swirls—reds and blues and greens and violets.

A double knock at the door and the stump-man presses a button beneath his desk. A buzz follows and one half of a large oaken door swings open. Paul "the Saint" Corrino enters. Sharply dressed in a dark Armani suit, Corrino is slick and quick but careful, furtive in his movements, ready to leave as soon as he has arrived. He is a member of Frederick Dalco's family, an east-coast syndicate that, like Malley's local company, is involved in many kinds of businesses, legitimate and otherwise, but on a much larger scale.

"Hi there, Jerry. How are you doin'?"

"Not bad, Paul. Not bad at all."

"Is that a new rug? Pretty plush! Amazing carpet, Jerry. Too nice to walk on." Paul stands to the side of the carpet.

"Yeah, almost. It's an import. Direct from Paki-land. Worth a lot of bread. They say it's a very unique pattern, too—it tells a story of some kind. About some old facker of Lahore who robbed from the Rajah's treasuries with a magic word and some trained monkeys. There's a whole other story, of course, about how it got here, but that's not why you're here, is it?

"No. You know it ain't. We're safe here, ain't we?"

"Safer than your Momma's soul, Paul. Things are right on track, I assume?"

"Yep. The truck got hit last night just like we planned. Or, I should say, sorta like we planned. Instead of just cutting it off, those lackeys you hired drove a truck straight into the van. They crashed right into it—it's a wonder they didn't kill themselves! Turned the Logos' truck right on its side. It's like a disaster scene. But they got the box. I gather They haven't showed up here yet, eh?"

"No. I told them to wait a day to make sure they weren't followed. Didn't want someone tailin' them straight to me.

They'll be here after midnight. But you're right. They ain't the brightest stars in the sky. In fact I never told them what they was after—just an orange box. But they was happy to get whatever chicken feed they could and didn't really ask no questions. They both served a lot of time for my father and never sang. So they're faithful. Like a stray mutt you take in and feed. I trust them as much as I trust anybody. And they usually get the job done. One way or the other! So Dalco don't got any idea who hit him, right? You're still sealed on your end?

"Yeah, Jerry. Frederick trusts me. I'm his golden boy. Saint Paul Corrino in our 'hood, you know. Yesterday night, after I confirmed the hit, I called him real quick with all the bad news. He went ballistic, Jerry. Started to blame the Asian boys almost immediately, Ng's gang. First thing he did was to order an interrogation of the driver. That poor sucker, he don't know nothing and he'll kiss the sky that way. Dalco's gonna come to Thornton right away, to have a first-hand look at things. He filled me in on a lot more of the details. I mean, like I told you before, I knew it was gonna be big, but not how big. It's a helluva hit, Jerry. Dalco told me that the stuff, after its cut, will be worth nearly six million on the street."

The Stump and the Saint glance at one another in silence for a second.

"Holy shit! That's a lot of cake." Jerry's frozen stare shows his disbelief. He snaps his fingers several times.

"You know it. And so you know Dalco's gonna pull all the strings he can to get it back. And to get the ones who took it. Add to that, he now owes the Rummies nearly a mill. So the heat's on. Eighteen kilos…"

"Eighteen bags?"

"Yeah. Eighteen kilos of raw, uncut China White—each of

those suckers should be worth about three hundred grand after they're milked and dimed. That's quite a haul, Mr. Malley. We need to be damn careful."

"Yeah, no shit. I didn't think it would be that big. Some luck, and some stupidity on Dalco's part. To risk an open run like that. Sometimes the big boys think they're bigger than they are. As you say though—careful, careful with a capital 'C'. You can't spend nothing if you're worm food."

"So what are your plans for it?"

"I'm not going to move any of it here, Paul. There'll be too much heat on the local scene. I'll send some of it to the big smoke, some west, some over the border, probably through Rabbit on the Rez. Make our killing bit by bit. And our split. You'll be rich and your boss'll never know, Paul. And maybe, when he's unlucky and has to answer to the Rummies, you may end up in his shoes, as boss. Then we'll really be able to do some business. Just keep out of the line of fire, though. Right?"

"Yeah. I'm planning to. You too."

"Got my head down already, Paul! Or should I say Saint Paul? Would you like a cigar, and a drink? Toast to our good fortune."

"Thanks, I'll take a cigar for the road, but a rain check on that drink. I just wanted to check in like we planned, in person. Low key. But I gotta get back in the loop real quick. Get ready for the boss to get here. Things are about to boil, Jerry. So, if you have any problems or updates, here—it's the real reason I wanted to touch base in person." Paul reaches in his coat pocket and takes out a small cell phone, still in its package, "Use this, and call this number," Paul gives Jerry a piece of paper with the phone. "That'll put you straight through to the burner I have. And if I can't talk, it'll just be turned off." Jerry takes the phone and piece of paper, glances at them and places both in the top drawer of his desk. "And remember, Jerry, from now on, no names on the phone…you're 'P', I'm 'Q'."

"Ps and Qs? Ok! Good. Thanks, Paul. So far so good. But you sure about that drink? You're missin' out on some smooth Glen on the rocks."

"No, thanks anyway. I need to hit the road. We can celebrate a bit later, when the heat to melt that ice has let up a bit."

"Sounds like a plan, Paul, uh, Saint Paul, or uh, 'Q'."

Jerry holds out a sleek wooden humidor, Paul takes a cigar, nods to Jerry and then briskly turns and exits. Malley smiles, shakes his head and settles back in his chair. He presses the lid of the humidor closed and snaps his fingers several times.

- 5 -
I hear what you're sayin'

Lucky's apartment is sparsely furnished and dimly lit. In the low light that shines on Lucky's kitchen table eighteen plastic bags are laid out that look like eighteen bags of flour. But they are not.

"So here's the deal, Gabe. Old Shakespeare there had six criss-crossed layers of three bags each. Eighteen bags in total, right? But young Malley, he don't know how much was in the Logos shipment, right? He told us that himself. So we bring him the box with five rows of three. He ain't never gonna know a row's missing. He pays us the grand he promised, he gets his Shakespeare and we get our money plus three bags of Romeo and Juliet to boot. Pretty good, eh? Romeo and Juliet! We can unload them easy, probably make an extra thou each. Think of it as a kind of tip. I tell you, it can't miss."

"Yeah, I hear what you're sayin' Lucky. Do you really think we should be messin' like this with Malley, though? I mean, Stump can be one dangerous dude, and he's been pretty good to us since we got out, since his old man died. Givin' us these part timers and such. And he's also connected pretty good. He takes care of people he likes, and them he don't, people who cross him, even people who try to."

"What he don't know, man, he don't know. And he won't know a thing about this. How could he? Besides for a job like this, we shoulda been paid three times what he's givin' us—easy. He owes us, Gabe. He owes us. And you, do you want to live in that shitty apartment all your life. Your kid deserves better, man—you should be puttin' together a down payment on a nice little house somewheres. Maybe outside of town in one of those new subdivisions. Maybe back in the country, down near the Valley. A house with a yard. Little Jimmy deserves that. Don't you think?"

"Yeah, as a matter of fact, Lucky, I do…"

"You're damned right you do, man!"

"Ok! All right. You're right. Fuck it. Let's do it. You can get rid of the three bags through Taber, can you?"

"Yeah. Should be no problem. He's still dealin'. And nobody knows the business better than him."

"Yeah, I guess. That's sort of how we got to know him, wasn't it? Through his deals, and drugs?"

"Absolutely, partner. My first memory of Taber … he was the English kid who came to Thornton High, and he was high most of the time. Remember, he was a wiz at soccer. He could roll through any of the other teams; the coach worshipped him. Then came the game he was too stoned, out of his gourd in fact, and scored twice in his own net and cheered for himself each time. I think it was the cheering more than the scoring that did him in. The coach booted him off the team and then the school threw him out. He never went to many classes anyways. But he's done ok around town ever since. He knows his business."

"All right, then. Let's do it. Where's that bag of shavings that you bought. Let's give old Shakespeare here some padding, and put the bags back in place. Most of them, anyways, right?"

"Fuckin' 'A,' man. Now you're talking, just like the old Gabe I used to know. I can just tell, man ... this is the beginning of something good! Something real good!"

-6-

As if they had never existed at all

Ten minutes after midnight. The buzzer sounds and the oaken door of Jerry Malley's office opens. Lucky and Gabe stand there for a moment cautiously waiting for Malley to invite them in, and then they enter. Lucky is carrying a green garbage bag that obviously contains a heavy box. He places it on one of the chairs facing Jerry Malley's desk and joins Gabe who is fidgetably standing on a lovely Persian carpet in the centre of the room, arms by his side. Neither of the men seems to notice the rug, their eyes fixed on Malley.

"Well, very good, boys. Congratulations on a job well done. No real problems, I trust."

"No problems, Mr. Malley. It went off like a piece of clockwork," says Gabe.

"Good. Good, glad to hear it, boys. Anyways, here, take this for your good work."

Malley steps forward from behind his desk and gives each man a thick white envelope which each takes and simultaneously pockets.

"And here, do you boys smoke?" asks Malley of the intrepid

pair, retrieving a white cardboard box, not the fancy humidor, from an upper drawer of his desk. He passes each man a short fat cigar. Both Lucky and Gabe accept their just desserts.

"Thanks, boss," each says in unison.

"Anyways, boys," Malley's timbre now switches to a serious tone. "I guess I don't have to remind you that nothing that happened Monday ever happened. Right? You know Logos Text is part of Dalco Corp ... they own Regent Construction and the *Voyageur's End* chain and Cassidy Trucking and a bunch of other stuff. And you know, of course, that Frederick Dalco is their main man, and you know he's nobody to mess with. Right? So don't say a thing to noone. Even your wife and kid, right, Gabe?"

"Yeah, we understand, Mr. Malley." Gabe responds. "I was home all night Monday night, and Lucky, he was there with me. We did nothing all night but watch TV. Right, Lucky?"

"Yeah. Hockey."

"Baseball." They say in unison.

"Hockey and baseball," Gabe corrects.

"Yeah. That's it, Gabe. Hockey and baseball."

"Ok, that's fine. Good. ... I'll be needing some drivers next week, so I might have some more work for you if you're around. That sound ok?"

"Sounds good to me, Mr. Malley," Lucky utters.

"Yeah. Good for me too, as long as I ain't doing cable. ... So, anyways, if that's all, we better be going. I got an early morning, you know."

"Ok. Thanks again, boys. But for Christ's sake, keep a lid on this or we'll all have an early morning."

"We hear you, boss. Nothing happened ... at least nothing that we know about. C'mon, Lucky. Let's go. We'll be in touch, Mr. Malley. Good night."

"'Night, boss. Take 'er easy, but fuckin' take 'er. Right?"

"Sounds like a plan to me, Luke. G'night, boys."

Gabe and Lucky move to the door, open it and disappear into the early morning. Jerry "Stump" Malley watches them go and snaps his fingers, three times, quietly. Then his eyes move to the multi-coloured carpet and he observes the fibres of the Persian inexorably re-assume their original form, intractably erasing all imprint of those who had just been there, as if they had never existed at all. Next he turns to the garbage bag and begins to examine the haul.

- 7 -

Another cup of Rainy's for the road

A quick word about Angus. He's on his way toward the counter in Rainy's right now and will show up here and there in the events that follow; and while he does not do too much for this narrative, like most of us, I suppose, he is still worth knowing.

He was Angus the moment he wandered in. No reason was given, that was just who he was. Some, more formally, declared him Angus, *Dauphin de Leroy*, and the name stuck. So did the dog; as many suggested, he knew a good thing when he saw it. Angus seemed lost but friendly, wild but house-broken, and was probably only a year or so old when he arrived a couple springs ago. Since then he has taken over the place as dogs often do to places and, ubiquitous as this may sound, he can be found almost anywhere at any time, although he stays out of the motel's guest rooms as if he knows that would be bad manners. You can see him casually hunting mice in the Gardens or greeting the arriving worshippers over at the *Church of the Holy K.* or tail wagging the customers at Rainy's or sleeping almost anywhere, in the kitchen or Office, behind the counter or in Johnny's apartment upstairs or in the dark cool of the 'L', where he has a bed. He likes certain humans; others he avoids or growls at. Dogs often seem to possess an uncanny ability to judge human character often better than we humans do. Most of the time, he does his bathroom business in the ruins of Bowlie's so no-one has to worry about that and, in keeping with his ways, Johnny has purchased yearly dog tags for Angus and orchestrated regular visits to the vet so he is as cared for as all of the other refugees around the place. To help the financing, a Vet for Angus jar sits on the counter right next to the Tips for Waitresses jar. On many occasions, Angus's jar fills more quickly than its twin which sometimes brings a gentle scowl from the working staff and the derisive conclusion that people just can't read.

As to what kind of dog he is, what breed of *canis lupus familiaris*, well even Angus is not too sure of that and, on most days, does not really seem to care. In my experience, he is like most dogs in that, from Westminster victor to slum pariah, they are content in just being dog. He is medium-sized, big enough so that you know he is a dog and not some guinea pig on a string, mostly short-haired, black with some white and some merling and brown spots here and there, and brown eyebrows. His ears are floppy and some of his toes are webbed and, when he lets select people have access, his belly is revealed to be quite pink. The pads of his paws used to be pink but have darkened over time. A variety of customers have earnestly identified him as part, never full but always part, Lab, Retriever, Cattle Dog, Hound, Shepherd, Beagle, Shetland, Border Collie, Husky, Pointer, Terrier, Wolfhound, and so on, a dog for all seasons, if you will. Angus usually loses interest as soon as this quest for his canine pedigree commences; he finds another adventure to pursue, or retreats to some quiet place to sleep. To be honest, not many around the Leroy know too much about dogs or dog breeds and, sometimes, when they get to the process of etymologizing Angus and making their case for one breed or another, in all likelihood they have had just a little bit too much to drink, or not enough.

And so as not to ruin the spirit of the discussion, or intercede and reduce sales of nectar at the Leroy, let the debate rage on. And wherever he may be let Angus have his sleep, that wondrous sleep of dogs. Let him twitch and growl and dream and lead the gypsy pack across that ceaseless silver tundra under the stare of the cold moon's light. You have now been formally introduced to Angus, *Dauphin* of the Leroy, and that is all that really matters at this point.

Incidentally, the Leroy has no cats.

Dom and Deed sit at the counter in their usual places and Blue attends to a few of the other lunch-time customers, most of them regulars like the shaggy fat man with the greying beard and thick glasses who downs endless cups of coffee at the counter or the pair of love-sick hipsters in the third booth along the side who are going to change the world of pop music with their new-age country zoot-rap. Angus lays on the floor between Dom and Deed, having helped Dom consume a piece of his toast (actually an extra piece placed on his plate by the cook) and finishing the milk left over in Deed's cereal bowl.

"So, Blue, the Prince still hasn't shown up, and it's Burnin' Day."

"Haven't seen him yet, Dom, but the day is young. You're just not used to being awake with this much daylight to go."

"Tell me about it, girl. To be honest, I ain't slept much at all, day or night, since I had that dream of bein' dead, almost afraid to."

"Ah, you'll shake it off. You got nothing to worry about, 'specially with the mighty Deed around to protect you. More coffee?"

"Never turn down a cup of Rainy's, right Deed?"

"Mmhmm."

"And when Johnny gets back, he'll have that job for you and Deed and that'll get your mind off your old dream."

"Yeah, maybe. I wonder what the Prince wants us to do. He's always up to something, you know. Just look at the floor tile in here. Remember those guys were puttin' new floor down across the road, what was that, four, five years ago, and the Prince convinced them that the Leroy was just an Annex of the End and, before you knew it, Rainy's had a whole new floor. God."

"You are a walking mad man for the Prince, Dom," smiles Blue.

"Hey, you got to know whose got the butter for the bread, sweetheart. Remember that time the City Controller's Office threatened to withhold a liquor licence and, a day later, the Mayor himself shows up for lunch and brings that licence with him. Gave it to Johnny, personally. Shook his hand. And then there was that mattress deal. Remember that?" Dom nudges Deed.

"Mmhmm!"

"Yep," says Blue, "and that big concert with Siobhan and the O'Shaughnastys who played their gig here by mistake. Three nights in a row!"

"Ahh, the Prince rules the world. No doubts about that!"

"Sometimes it seems that way, doesn't it? And I know I've heard you say he only runs this place as a hobby, that it's a kind of game for him, but sometimes I think it's really the life force that keeps him goin', saving others from the kinds of things he's been through."

"Maybe, but trust me, Blue, mostly it's his hobby, he makes his real coin other places. That's the only way it stays open anyways, what with that flashy Voyageur's ass over there."

"But, whatever you think drives him, to his credit Johnny's also put a lot of time and effort into this place. Old Jake had really let it get run down; it was grubby and there were all kinds of seedy characters camped out here, drug dealers and hookers and worse. And then when Margaret died, Jake was hopeless and then he got real sick that last year, the year Shonagh was here. After Jake died and Johnny inherited the place, he really tried to fix things up."

"Yeah, I know. Like I said, all those free 'home repairs' courtesy the End. And, even the bums that were living here, he didn't just kick them out. He found other places for them, jobs, brought in those Agencies. He gave them a fair shake, a chance to do something better with their lives."

A new voice joins the assembly.

"And that made room for an entirely new kind of bum to land here, a bum such as I."

"Hey, Professor. Haven't seen you in ages." Dom spins on his stool to greet the new arrival. "And, you know, I got something I need to talk to you about."

Benny Alamo is a slight young man who moves about the world with ease and wears a white or yellow shirt (whether it had been white and was now turning yellow, or had been yellow and was undergoing a transmigration toward white was difficult to say). Benny had been a graduate student in Literature Studies at Thornton University but now he has achieved the new status of student emeritus. He has worked at the front desk of the Leroy for the last six months as the Day Clerk. Like so many before in the more or less hallowed halls of academia, he has not, as they say, so much dropped as faded out, losing himself in his thesis research and writing, seeking now to find himself at the Leroy.

"How you doing, Dom, Deed? Blue, I caught a scent of that supernal Ambrotus from the front desk and just couldn't resist its Siren call. May I steal a cup, please?"

"Sure thing, Professor ... comin' right up."

"So Benny," Dom hijacks the conversation. "You're the educated guy around here. I want you to tell me what you think. You see, I just had this dream ..." and the dream of being dead is told once more.

Angus twitches in his sleep and emits a slightly audible growl.

"That is a curious one, Dom. For what it's worth, you're probably not alone, at least in being upset or curious, dreams routinely unsettle all of us, you know. Some of the experts say it's because, in our dreams, we're put in a position of being spectators of our own selves, watchers as our own lives unfold, and there is little we can do. What we think of as ordered and rational, in dreams we come to see as out of control, random, fragile. Chaos."

Blue interjects. "Like I told him, Benny, maybe we all need to do what old Jake did with that dream he had, wake up inside it and take control. 'To hell with it' said Jake and chased that nightmare right into daylight."

"Yes, you told me about Jake's dream, I remember, Blue," adds Benny. "Turn and face the abyss of our own dark subconsciousness. Face down the blameless consequences of our own randomized existence."

"Ask a college guy a question and get a college answer, I guess, right!" says Dom, smiling. "That all sounds good, Benny, but what if you wake up and you're dead, pretty hard to be in control of anything, to face down anything, when you're dead. Trust me on that!"

"I guess that does complicate things a bit, Dom. I'll give it some more thought and let you know. I've got a book somewhere on interpreting dreams. I'll see if it says anything about your kind of dream, dreaming that you're dead. Blue, have you seen Johnny around? He told me last week that he wanted me to put a bunch of that lost stuff from the safe onto a rolling cart, the stuff from six months ago and earlier. That's done, now I need to know what to do with it."

"That stuff's probably for Burning Day, Benny. I haven't seen Johnny yet, but he'll be here to take care of that for sure, and before the day is done. Count on it."

"Ok, I'll just let it sit then. I've heard about Burning Day, of course, but I've never been here for one. The last one was just before I was hired. I gather Johnny is around here most of the time anyway, and always for the burning?"

"Oh yeah, Professor. I keep forgetting. You fit in so regular around here I forget you're a Leroy virgin. And there ain't many of those around." Dom glances from Benny toward Blue, who lightly tosses a dishrag at him.

"No-one's talkin' to you, shortstop," Blue replies. "Yep, the Prince stays pretty close to this place, Benny. As you know, he lives in the apartment upstairs and doesn't stay away on any of his trips too long. He came here right after his parents died in a car wreck; it rolled and caught fire and Johnny got out but couldn't free his parents. He tried … you can still see the scars on the back of his hands. He was six or seven and watched his Mom and Dad burn to death."

"Christ … talk about disturbing dreams and nightmares; that's not something you'd ever get over, is it?" Benny's eyes wince.

Blue reaches across and squeezes Deed's hand who nods his head.

"No. Losing your parents is always tough; the younger you are, the tougher it is, unless you're just a baby. To this day, I've never seen Johnny go to a funeral; he avoids the dead at all costs. And sometimes I think that's why he's hung around the old Leroy all these years; here, he's saving things from dying, bringing life to things."

"Yeah. Remember little Angie, one day when she was just three or four? She saw Johnny's hands and said they looked like a broken river. It was spring, like now, I guess, and she had seen the ice breaking up on the Moira."

"I remember that, Dom."

"And Blue's right, Benny. The Prince wouldn't go to his Aunt's funeral, or even his Uncle's, though after the accident Jake was like a father to him. But Johnny just refused. And I don't think he's ever even visited his parents' graves," adds Dom.

"Really ... but he's not afraid of fire, right? He's here for Burning Day?" asks Benny.

"Hell, he invented Burning Day," Dom says in a vaunting tone.

"Well, yes and no, though ... he always makes sure it's set up," Blue corrects. "But it's always someone else who does the actual burning. Usually Oz. Johnny just walks away."

"I guess I can understand that," Benny replies. "The actual fire would bring back a lot of memories, a lot of pain. What a curious idea for him to come up with, though; of all things, a Burning Day!"

"Well," Blue begins, "it's a time of cleaning up around here. You know all the left-behind stuff that's collected from the rooms and stored in that old walk-in safe—from socks and underwear to rings and ruby necklaces, the stuff you just put on that cart—every six months the previous batch is taken out and burned in the crematorium behind this joint. Used to belong to Bowlie's Abattoir but that went under when the place was torched. You've heard the phrase Bowlie burger around here—that's what happened to old Max and his son when he ended up in a fight with the mob. Anyway, if you leave something at the Leroy, you get six months max to claim it; otherwise it goes to the flames. And nothing is ever opened or kept—Johnny says it has to do with legal stuff."

"'Cause if it's opened or taken or disappears," rejoins Dom, "a Timex turns into a Rolex. A rhinestone becomes a diamond. With law-suckers and -suits to follow."

"Exactly. So we have the ritual of Burning Day every six months. Part of it, I think, like I know you're thinkin' Benny, is a kind of penance, a memorial of sorts to Johnny's past. It keeps him rooted, rooted in fire and ashes."

"Well, that sounds like the stuff of princes, doesn't it!" says Benny. "Anyway, I better take my coffee and get back to the desk. Don't want my job to disappear like the smoke of some distant fire, you know. Have a good one, everybody. Blue, if you need anything, just let me know. And Dom, I'll try to look up something on that dream of yours. ... Hey Jackie. *Bon jour.*"

As Benny returns to the front desk, Jacqueline Savard enters from the kitchen. She is employed at the Leroy on double duty, as a maid to clean the rooms each morning, and as a waitress to help with the lunch hour rush and other restaurant duties when necessary. Originally from Newcastle, New Brunswick, Jackie is a very attractive woman with raven-dark hair who can be tough or tender as the need warrants—she is a survivor. She has one daughter, Angelique, who is pretty like her mother, but dangerous like her long-gone father, Ray; Jackie, though, does not see this in Angie any more than she had seen it in Ray.

Angus's tail slaps the floor in greeting although he does not arise from his comfortable sleeping position.

"*Salut*, Benny. And *allo*, boy, good to see you too." Jackie rubs Angus's back with her foot. "Blue, just wanted to let you know that I'm done for the day. All the rooms are ready, and all the dishes are loaded in the washer. I'm off to the gym."

"Thanks, Jackie. Have a good work-out."

"*Et bond jourez, ma belle-icious* one. What's a doll like you doin' in a dump like this?" interjects Dom.

"Oh, *mon petit un*, it is not a dump when someone like me cleans it. And your French wouldn't get you very far in Quebec, and it won't get you anywhere here, *certainement*. How are you doing Dom, Deed?"

Deed nods and smiles at Jackie; Dom replies.

"Ah, princess—when beauty enters the room, we are always doin' better. Can't hurt a man to try, you know what I mean?"

"Oh, you're always trying, *ma petit* Dommy, always trying ... and we wouldn't want it any other way. Has anyone seen Angelique? She said she might come over here for lunch today. She has her basketball practice tonight and the team is going out for pizza. She said she might need some cash."

"I haven't seen her at all today, Jackie, although she's been around quite a bit lately," Blue responds in a slightly incredulous tone.

"I know. I know. You don't have to tell me. She's been hanging around with that Walker kid from the End. I don't know what she sees in that moron."

"Well," says Dom, "... it's spring and young love, you know."

"Oh yes. *Oui*. I know all too well. Spring, and worrying. A mother's lot, I guess. Anyway, I might as well work some of that worry off in the gym over at Caxton's Spa."

"Ok, Jackie. If I see Angie, I'll let her know you were looking for her. See you tomorrow. And that might be your bus now," says Blue glancing out across the parking lot.

"*Oui*. It is. *Au revoir*, all."

Jackie turns and quickly exits, moving across the parking lot toward the bus stop, just under the shadow of the great sign.

"I hope she's in time to catch it."

"No worry, Blue. The bus always waits for Jackie. But that daughter of hers…"

"Dynamite looking for a match, Dom."

"Yeah … I just hope the pieces don't fall on me!"

"Our poor little Angie, you know … she has grown up real fast."

"Too fast, my dear. Scratching on the door to Hell's cathouse, if you ask me. Like a hormone at a mink farm."

"Well, she's trying to find her own way. I know she got that big tattoo without even asking her mother."

"Her tramp stamp."

"Yep. Jackie was furious for weeks."

"The kid is certainly livin' her dream, whatever it is."

"Yep. What'd Jackie call her, jokingly, *ma belle petite salope!*"

"Well. It is quite a tatt."

"Yep. Big dragonfly done in a lot of colours."

"Really, shines like a frickin' lighthouse, doesn't it? Probably attract lotsa sea creatures, of one kind or another."

"No doubt! But, ups and downs, Jackie still sees her as a golden kid and I am not going to be the one who tells her any different. She's like most parents, I guess, know their kids too good ever really to know them at all, if you know what I mean!" Blue says with a shrug of her shoulders.

"Yeah. Jackie's lucky that the Prince is around. If Angie gets in any real trouble, you know he'll be there! Like last year when she got picked up smokin' weed at the park, and he got her out of the cop-shop before any charges had even been thought up. He's been like a guardian angel for her. For Jackie, too ... with this job and all."

"For all of us at one time or another, Dom." Blue says pensively. "Just think about it!"

"Yeah, I guess you're right there, girl. Every time me and Deed seem out of coin, another mysterious Leroy errand seems to pop up. Hey, you wouldn't have another splash of that grand beverage, would you? Me and Deed are both dry."

"Well, I don't know, now that the 'doll', or was it 'the princess', has caught the bus, there may not be anyone left in 'this dump' to serve you..." Blue's sarcasm drips.

"Oh no, no, let me explain, gorgeous. You see, there are princesses, but, but they pale before queens. And I bow before the Queen of true beauty, you know, the one and only Queen of the Leroy..." Dom comically tries to cover himself. Deed's body shakes in suppressed laughter.

"Keep talkin', Dom. Keep talkin'. And while you're at it, here's some joe."

Angus stretches and then farts in his sleep to the winced laughter of the Rainy crowd.

- 8 -

Marlboro, man

The rooms on the third floor of the *Voyageur's End* are pretty much like the rooms on every other floor, decorated in rich shades of blue and gold and large enough to seem ample, small enough so that each floor holds enough rooms to turn a maximum profit. The drapes are pulled shut across a wall of windows, bathroom and closet doors are closed, a full length dresser fills one wall and, opposite, a large king-size bed is in disarray. Three large factory paintings of faux-natural scenes are securely attached in various places on the walls and a desk, a couple chairs and a small round table complete the furnishings. I'm pretty sure that you have been in enough mid-scale motels to know what these rooms look like.

Bobby Walker sits on the side of the bed. He is the nineteen-year old son of the manager of the *Voyageur's End*, Charles T. Walker, and is newly employed at the End as a security guard. He is about to come on shift at two o'clock but has not yet changed into his uniform. Bobby is a pleasant looking young man who, in his life, has attended more to the coiffing of his hair than the developing of his intellect.

Next to him is Angelique Savard, the sixteen-year old

daughter of Jacqueline Savard who, as you know by now, works as maid and waitress at the Leroy. Angelique is tall for her age, with straight black hair and dark eyes and, as is often the case with young women of her age, an unnecessary coat of dark make-up over beautiful skin. Like her mother, she is pretty. Like her absent father, she is dangerous in a migratory way even she does not understand. She wears a tight t-shirt and short skirt and is edgy, dissatisfied with her current life, always seeking something new. The two are in the process of finishing a session of heavy necking.

"O Angel," Bobby soothes. "I really like being with you. Wow. You are an angel, baby. You are the best."

"Get me a light, will you, Bobby? I need a smoke," comes a terse reply.

"OK. Sure. I got a pack of matches right here in my pocket. There, there you are. I can light it for you if … well, ok, light it yourself."

"These are great beds, Bobby. So big. You wouldn't be able to fit one of these into my whole god-damned bedroom in our shitty place."

"Oh, hell. I just remembered. This is supposed to be a non-smoking room. Do you mind if I open the window."

"Ah, there's too much light and noise out there, traffic and stuff. Don't worry about it, Bobby. One cigarette isn't going to make any difference anyway. You said the room's not rented tonight. You can leave the damn window open when we leave. By tomorrow morning no one will ever know. No one will ever smell a thing."

"Yeah, well, I like my new job and want to keep it," Bobby responds petulantly.

"Your old man's not going to can you for some smoke. Not for anything, probably. You worry too much *ma petit oiseau*."

"Yeah, ok, I guess you're right. Want to watch some TV? There's pay-per-view."

"No, let's just lay back here. Talk about something. Do you like being on security here or, hey, I know, Bobby, what's the earliest thing you can remember? The very earliest thing?"

"Wow, Angel, where do you get these ideas?"

"C'mon ... the earliest thing."

"Well, I'm not sure. Let's see. I think I can remember my Mom crying. And ... I know. I remember going to see a zoo in Waterville. I was so excited."

"A zoo?" Angel is incredulous.

"I must have been three or four. I'd seen zoos on television; I remember, there was a TV show with an old man who talked a lot—it was sponsored by some insurance company or something. The old man's zoo was huge with wide open spaces and animals wandering all over the place, like you would see them in Africa or wherever they was from. A whole world of animals all in one spot, safe and happy."

"I don't think we got that channel."

"We set off in the morning and it was a long drive on a really hot day. The car had no AC or anything. And we finally got there, and we went through the front gates and mostly I remember the smell. It smelled real bad, worse even than the animal barns at Thornton County Fair, and it smelled that way all over. Even the soda pop and the hot dogs we ate had that smell. And for weeks afterward I could smell it on my clothes and in the car. And the zoo itself was rows of concrete bunkers, sticking out of the ground like the way they bury the dead in New Orleans. And each bunker had a cage door and you could look into the darkness and see some small and mangy and uninterested animal curled up in the back corner. It's where I guess I learned that real lions aren't really anything like they're supposed to be, that there were things in life that lied to you, and I got sick. I threw up everything I had eaten for the last two days, and more it seemed. And Mom and Dad argued all the way back in the car about whether or not this or that was a stupid idea. And I don't think their arguments ever stopped after that until they got divorced, then Mom got cancer and died and I got sent up here to Thornton to live with Dad."

"Quite the zoo!"

"And, you know to this day, I never think of zoos or circuses or anything with wild animals that I don't think of vomit and cancer. That real lions aren't real. ... There. How's that? That's one of the very first memories of my life. Not so wonderful, is it?"

"It don't exactly sound like no Disneyland. Is that a tear? You ain't crying, are you?"

"No. No. So. How about you, Angel? What's your very first memory?"

"TV, I think. Being left in an apartment with the TV on all day long 'cause *maman* couldn't afford to hire a sitter or dump me off at a day care. And we only got a couple of dumb grainy channels. I watched all those old reruns they used to show. You know, Lucy getting into trouble day after day, and the millionaire and his wife and all the rest never getting off that stupid island, but most of all, I think, I remember Jeannie in that bottle and Samantha, the witch. You remember them?"

"Yeah, sort of. Some of them were made into really bad movies."

"And whenever anything went wrong, and usually without anyone knowing about it—especially all those stupid men who lived in their lives—they'd twitch their nose or blink their eyes and everything would be perfect again. No matter how much anyone screwed up, no matter how much everything went wrong, twitch, blink, and it was all okay. In fact, for a year or so, I insisted everybody call me Sam. I thought, I guess, if everybody called me Sam, then sooner or later my witch powers would kick in and I'd become Sam. Pretty stupid, eh! But I was a kid and didn't like the life I was leading. I never knew my father—did I tell you that? He hit the road before I was born. I think, someday, I'm going to try to look him up. Track down those who knew him, find out where he was from, what he's like, talk to him, if he's still alive! Discover my roots, I guess, like that old TV show about them slaves. And make connections with all the people on that side of my family—they got to be more interesting than my mother's relatives."

"Why, what are your Mom's relatives like?"

"Hah! You want to know anything about fish—just talk to the New Brunswick Savards—how to name it, catch it, clean it, cook it a thousand ways, and then cook it again tomorrow. Eat it for breakfast, lunch and supper. And talk about fishing all day long. Oh my God. I need another cigarette."

"Yeah, well, Angel, it's almost time for my shift to start. I need to get going…"

"Oh, you got lots of time. Light me up … or do you need me to light you up…?"

Angie slides her hand along Bobby's jeans.

"Well, I guess … oh, Angel."

"Oh. *Qu'est-ce que nous avons ici?* That's some Marlboro, man! Let's see, maybe I can take a puff or two."

"O yes. You can really make me smoke, baby. Angel, you are the best."

- 9 -

Fly on my beauty, fly on

The bus stop is near the corner only a half a block from her apartment. The entire block is made up of similar nondescript buildings. Jacqueline Savard eases along the sidewalk carrying her heavily-filled nylon gym bag, bright purple in colour. She pulls a gaggle of keys from her purse as she walks up the sidewalk that leads to the doorway of her building. It is a so-called walk-up, a twelve-plex with four apartments in the basement, four on the first floor and four on the second. Her apartment is 302. She opens the mail box, takes out two fliers and a telephone bill, and walks up the stairs. She slides a key into the lock. It is a typical two-bedroom apartment, a short front hall leads to a living room with balcony; to the right a centre hallway with a partitioned kitchen and bath on one side, two bedrooms on the other, a small storage space at the end. Everything is quiet. Angie has a late basketball practice and then pizza with her team—she won't be home until 8:30 or 9:00. Jacqueline drops the gym bag on the floor of her bedroom, changes out of her cleaning clothes and puts on her old maroon track suit. Ugly—*laid comme un pichou*, her father might say. Ugly as last year's valentine—that's what her mother would have said.

Ugly, yes, but comfortable, and Jacqueline needs some comfortable right now.

She puts the kettle on to boil, slides the balcony door open and sits heavily in the white wicker chair that she had moved up from storage just last weekend. It has been unseasonably warm this spring and, although it is cooling off right now with the onslaught of darkness, Jacqueline feels she needs the fresh air. Conversely, she also needs a smoke. The first hit of her cigarette takes away some of the weariness of what has been another long and repetitious day. The apartment is on the northern edge of town. While the balcony overlooks a parking lot below and a big box office supplies store to the right, off to the western horizon, across the river, there are farmers' fields and woodlands and the sun setting into earth and trees every night. It offers an habitual consolation of a sort. Like exercise routines at the gym and cigarettes.

A bright light traces along the far tree-line. Thornton's parochial county airport has been expanded in the last couple decades to reach international status so now all kinds of aircraft come and go, even military jets and transports from time to time. So now you never know what odd lights you might see in the skies above the city.

Jacqueline returns to the balcony with a cup of tea and a white shawl. The sun is cut between earth and sky and red as blood. Jacqueline remembers her mother's casket hovering on frayed green straps over the dark grave before they let it down with the wind stirring the dying roses she had placed on top. And her father shrunken more than she had ever seen him before. He seemed to be smaller and smaller each time she had journeyed home and she knew that he wouldn't last long after *maman*. And then she remembered Ray, and for a moment, for a brief moment, wished that Ray were here. Seventeen years ago next summer it would be. He stepped into the Newcastle Bus Station like a rock star. Black hair and blacker eyes. Black leather coat. What's the best thing on the menu, he'd asked her and then sat on it. And she was in love with him from that first moment. Ray, full of all the faraway charm that could conquer the heart of any lonely and lost adolescent. He was driving truck for Cassidy Castings, a factory, located in a southern Ontario town named Thornton, that distributed specialized machinery parts throughout the country, and she was eighteen, two years after dropping out of high school, she served the lunch counter at the Bus Depot in Newcastle, New Brunswick, located on the mighty Miramichi as her Grandfather always called the turbulent little river that divided town. And two weeks later, when Ray passed back through town on his return trip, Jacqueline found herself sitting beside him. The next thing she knew they were living together in Ray's bachelor apartment in Thornton and Angie was on the way. And six months later, one cool November morning, Ray went out to get a pack of cigarettes at the corner store and never came back. She never saw him or heard from him again. The castings firm he worked for phoned a couple times wondering where he was and then phoned a third time to tell Jacqueline to tell Ray that he was fired. And the police took down some information but didn't seem too interested. Ray had a record as a small time felon and was known for disappearing. He had done four months at the Minimum Security Farm over in Ridgeville for smuggling booze and cigarettes across the border, and a couple other nights in the local lock-up for some brawls he couldn't get himself out of in time. That was always Ray—trouble with time. Showing up in the right place at the wrong time or the wrong place at the wrong time or not showing up in any place at any time. It was all wrong thought Jacqueline, not unfair, just wrong. She had gone through the process—dismay, disbelief, denial, grief, remorse, anger, fury, resignation, and then just not thinking about it anymore. Were there any other stages you could go through? And why was she thinking about it now? Why, after a relatively routine day such as this, would thoughts of Ray come back to her? Why? She knew why, she knew the reason deep down, the inconsolable knowing a day like today sometimes raised to the surface. *Ma mère est mort.* Ray's gone. Hell, even Newcastle doesn't exist anymore. She knew why. She knew. Even though about all of Ray that was left now was whatever genetic part of Angie could be blamed on him, and that old fire extinguisher in the front closet, brass and cast iron and long since emptied of the chemicals that once made it work when you turned it upside down. The Guardian brand, Ray's old family fire extinguisher. The only thing they managed to save when my parents' home burned down he used to say and laugh and laugh. The only thing left of Ray. The Guardian. The only thing. And why Jacqueline kept it, she couldn't say, perhaps didn't know.

The next thing Jacqueline knew was the sound of the door, and someone shouting. My love. My love. I'm home, at last. Ray. Ray. Ray's strong face. I took a wrong turn looking for cigarettes. I got lost in time and space, but now I'm home. Home at last. I'm home. My love. My love.

"Mom. Mom."

"Ray. ... Angelique. Angelique." She must have fallen asleep. She looks up into Ray's eyes and they are Angie's.

"Hey, Mom, it's freezing in here. It's like a meat locker. What'd you do, fall asleep out there?"

"Hi, *chèrie*. I guess it is a bit on the cool side." Jacqueline steps into the apartment and slides the heavy balcony door shut. It is cool but she doesn't seem to feel the cool at all. One could certainly be a lot cooler she thought.

"How was the practice, Angie? Are you goin' to get to start next game?"

"Maybe, I'm not sure." Angelique opens a closet door and puts her bright yellow jacket away, a glistening vinyl thing, opens the refrigerator, takes out a diet Coke and moves down the hallway towards her bedroom door.

"Hey, you aren't still mad at me because I haven't been able to get to your games this year, are you? You know I've been doing that extra waitressing at work—if I can save enough in our petite safe, we'll be able to go on a vacation together next winter. Wouldn't that be cool?"

"Yeah Mom, that'll be cool. I'm not mad, just tired. I'm goin' in my room, ok. I've got some math homework I've got to get done for tomorrow. I'm going to phone Donna—she's a math wiz. Talk later." The door is brushed shut with that kind of adolescent nonchalance that makes a parent's heart lose a sacred beat to time.

Jacqueline notices the time. Trouble with time *comme son père*. It is nearly 10:30. That is a bit late to be getting home on a school night, even from basketball and pizza, but she would not raise the issue now. There is enough chill in the air right now. She would eat a bowl of cereal and some yogurt and go to bed, and talk with Angelique in the morning, or maybe tomorrow night. Yes. That is the plan. She fills a bowl with some Cheerios and milk, and gets a small yogurt container from the refrigerator. She takes a second cereal box from the cupboard and dumps a large roll of cash out of it. Then she takes a few more bills from her purse, adds them to the trove and returns the box to its place. That is her secret safe.

After her quick meal, Jacqueline lays on her bed, turns out the light and drifts off very quickly. She no longer dreams. When she was young, as a child and teenager, she used to have very vivid dreams, curious dreams—some from which she did not want to wake, others that puzzled and fascinated her for many years of her life. One she always remembered was of a great meadow and a picnic spread out on blanket after blanket, every kind of food imaginable, great green salads with red tomatoes and crunchy golden croutons (which she liked best), dark marbled slices of beef and shanks of ham and bowls of crisp fried chicken, pitcher after pitcher filled to the brim with every beverage imaginable, from kool-aid to coconut wine, and the desserts, oh all the desserts of the heart in all the colours of the rainbow. And in the dream, she would wander from blanket to blanket and each would be surrounded by her relatives, some living, many dead, many long since dead, going back and back into her past to ancestors who wore strange clothing and spoke a dialect she did not fully understand. But all smiled upon her as she passed and offered her the bounty of their blanket. And the sun shone on and on and the warmth of the day never ended. And there were other dreams, some more troublesome and frightening. One inspired, she always thought, by stories her aged *gran-père* told her, those few scattered tales really the only thing she remembered of her mother's father who died when she was very young. Her *gran-père* and she in a great sleigh pulled by two massive horses reeling through the winter snows, flying against drift after drift, and the sound and the scent of ferocious wolves getting closer and closer. Closer and closer, until the sound of the howl was at the level of her ear and the hot foul breath and the yellow eye of the wolf were upon her and her *gran-père* standing up in the driving snow and lashing with his whip at the beasts that were pulling them and at the beasts that were chasing them. And then her *gran-père*, desperately forcing the reigns of the team into her hands, crying to her, "fly on my beauty, fly on" and letting himself slide from the side of the sleigh. And the screams of the wolves and the tearing and crunching left behind in the wild storm. And waking in the dream to a crisp day of winter sunshine with the horses walking slowly on the laneway toward home. Shaking the snow off and seeing her mother waving from the porch and smiling on her daughter who was safe now from the wolves and the weather, the bright cottage ahead, welcoming and warm in spite of the dark news she brought. But now, no, Jacqueline no longer dreamed. She had willed herself in the last decade to stop dreaming. What was the point, she told her friends. And while mostly all of her friends said that it was impossible to stop dreaming, emphasizing the point by telling her their own dreams, Jacqueline would listen patiently and when they were finished, she would say: "'Isn't that lovely,' or 'Wasn't that horrible.' I remember when I used to dream, but I don't anymore."

And, as always happens, the dreamless night turns all too quickly toward morning and the inevitable buzz of a relentless alarm.

- 10 -

So now everything's ready for Burning Day

Bright shafts of morning sun cut through the windows of Rainy's, capturing a galaxy of dust motes swimming in their swath. Dom and Deed sit in their usual places with Blue nearby making some fresh coffee. Angus is finishing a piece of toast.

"So, how's the corn flakes, Deed, my man?" quips Dom.

"Mmhmm," is Deed's iconic reply.

"Hey, Blue. How about a refill, now that the new stuff is brewing? How long've you worked here anyways? Been a while, hasn't it?"

"Yep, Dom, I guess it has ... I guess, nine years this summer—a couple years before Jackie, but years after Oz—the old wizard's been here forever. As you know, he was one of Jake's men. Like Grease back there. Jackie came in just before Shonagh. And of course, Benny's only been here six months and Trace a couple weeks."

"Trace seems pretty shy, doesn't she? And pretty beat down."

"Yep. She's had the habit, big time. You can still see the

tracks. But to her credit, I think she's really making an effort. Johnny's letting her do the night shift this week. Alone. That's really her first big test."

"But, if I know the Prince, he won't be too far away if she has trouble."

"You're probably right there."

"Is Jackie around today?"

"Yep, she's over on the far side, I think. It's only Sundays she takes off. A religious thing, I think ... French and Catholic and all that."

"Really? God, Blue, she never struck me as exactly the religious type, you know! Like, I've seen her down shots with the worst of us! And she smokes like a wet chimney. And if you say the wrong thing to her, she can spit rust. She ain't no choir girl. But when she dresses up, she can be a real knock-out. How come she hasn't hooked up with someone?"

"Well, mostly, I think, she's got her daughter. And that uses up a lot of her time and energy. For a lot of single mothers, that's probably enough. As for anything else—well, she did go out with big Charlie a couple times, but that just blew up. Sometimes I think that Jackie's still waiting for that guy who left her—what was his name ... Roy ... Ray? Still got a torch in the window for Ray."

"And how about you, gorgeous? You got any torches lit for anyone?"

"Yep, I do, I got one lit and I know just where to shove it, Dom. Actually, truth is, I'm waiting for some larger-than-life hero like Deed, here, to propose to me."

Deed chuckles.

"Well, as they say, you and Deed would make a fastidious couple—one fast and the other hideous. And I ain't sayin' which would be which..."

"Whoa ... big word, little man!"

"I always thought maybe the Prince would hook up with Jackie. One night I even saw her make a move on him. She was PWA, if you know what I mean, pissed, willing and able—but, he wouldn't take advantage. He just sent her home in a cab. And I know he ain't walkin' the wild side ... what with all those crazy times with Shonagh and the boarding up of Room 12 and all of that."

"Yep ... Johnny and Shonagh really hit it off, didn't they—they finished each other's sentences for God's sake. But she was only here that one year. Disappeared on the day old Jake died. ... And that is all I am going to say about that! The last person who talked about Shonagh and Room 12 around here was that punk-ass handi-man, Ricky Howatt. Remember him? Ricky made some smart comment about it and we never saw or heard of him again. Shonagh O'Mara is not a topic for conversation around the Leroy unless it's Johnny himself doing the talkin'. And that is that! Sealed up just like Room 12 itself."

"Yeah, I heard about the mysterious disappearing act of Rappin' Ricky."

Seen through the windows of Rainy's—an old blue Econoline slides out from behind the restaurant and backs deftly in front of the great Leroy sign, its back bumper resting just against the inside pole. Blue smiles as the driver gets out, face unseen, and walking, retraces the van's path out of sight.

"Hey, Blue," Dom continues, "did I tell you, me an' Deed are headin' over to the university tomorrow."

"Why ... they hard up for some new professors, or something..."

"Close ... we saw an ad for a new program they're starting ... to get groups who have been disfran-something, to get outsiders into teaching. And there's nobody more outside than me and Deed. And it's fully paid, and in eight months we would be fully qualified teachers. What do you think about that?"

A voice speaks from the recesses of the 'L,' "I think nobody would be better…"

Everyone's gaze shifts to the darker part of Rainy's where a man stands, frozen briefly, half in shadow and half in light. And then he steps forward into the sunnier space and toward the cluster at the counter. It is the Prince of Leroy, Johnny P. March, wearing a red shirt beneath a worn, bronze-coloured leather bomber jacket and blue jeans and dark brown loafers. He is over six feet tall, solidly-built with wavy brown hair, a moustache and squared, seductive features, age-wise, somewhere north of thirty—more or less just what you would expect of a modern-day Prince.

"One of your schemes or not, Dom, with the experiences you guys have, you'd be good for a school. You're cut from a different cloth than most—you'd bring a different point of view to the kids and that would be good."

Angus explodes from his slumber and with the joy only dogs can know runs tight circles around and around Johnny while the Prince mutters hellos and strokes the whirling dervish. Angus finally settles and sits, leaning against the Prince's leg and looking up with a doggy kind of unabashed adoration.

"Yep, I can only imagine what you might teach them, Dom."

"Hi, Johnny … long time," says Blue.

"How are you, Blue? Looks like things are still on the rails here without me. Took a bit longer this time than usual, but I got several things sorted out. Speaking of that, Dom and Deed, I need someone to take the van and run an errand in a few days. You two up for that?"

Dom nudges Deed: "Absolutely, Prince. Count us in."

"Good. I'll let you know the details when I know 'em myself."

Benny Alamo steps into the doorway from the Office.

"Hey, Prince. Good to see you back. We were all starting to suffer some separation anxiety."

"Hi Benny. I can imagine—it's almost the end of the week and the cheques aren't signed."

"There is that, but I got the cart loaded. And you're here. So, now everything's ready for Burning Day."

"Good. Benny, can you step out and give Oz a shout? He's around the back. Tell him to meet me at the van."

"Will do."

"Thanks. In the meantime, Blue, a coffee on the house for our two new teachers-to-be. And I'll be back in a bit—I want to hear the details—but I've got a couple quick things to do first to make sure everything's ready for Burning Day. You know, a couple errands to run."

Angus follows close at his heels.

- 11 -

Time to go to war

"C'mon, Oz. Time to go to war."
"I got you, Prince. Let's get to it."
The men meet at the rear of the blue van, quickly open the doors and climb inside. Angus watches sadly from the door of the Office—this escapade allows no country for young dogs. Austin "Oz" "Wizard" Peters (it had been thirty years since his grandmother died that anyone had called him Austin), in his early sixties, is lanky, spry and goateed, the oldest member of the Leroy gang having been hired many years before by Johnny's Uncle Jake. He has become Johnny's right hand man.

These daylight raids were always the riskiest, but sometimes you had to make hay while the sun shone, as the old saying went—today was a busy day at the Leroy but supplies were low, so a soldier's work had to be done. Inside the van, Johnny and Oz kneel in the back and work a metal cotter key loose on the floorboard. They lift up a large piece of the floor, fixed on hinges, to reveal a sewer cover in the asphalt directly beneath. Each man picks up a metal bar in the shape of a 'T', suited with a hook on the long end, and in unison reach down and lift up the metal cover, as if they had done this many times before. Then

Johnny, one after another, drops four large, stuffed duffle bags into the hole, then slips in himself, vanishing out of sight. Oz follows suit.

- 12 -

Time for a bit of Geography and History, but not too much

Thornton is a medium-size city in the near mid-west. The Leroy and the End are both situated on Dundas Street on the eastern outskirts of the city near the freeway, a landscape that has recently been drawn and shaped by a variety of similar commercial establishments, the kind that people regularly drive to and, shortly after, drive away from. This area of Dundas has turned into that stretch of pavement which every town of a certain size now seems to have, unevenly lit and lined with gas stations and garages and fast food joints and slightly run-down discount stores. It's that city landscape where summer weeds grow around utility poles and bus stops and along the pavement curbs and are never trimmed. Like self-fulfilling prophecies, Liquidation Barns keep coming and going. And behind this commercial phalanx, a set of square factories and small retail businesses on boxy roads with names like Industrial Court and Enterprise Avenue. The Sunshine Laundry sits next to a chain link divider to the west of the Leroy; to the east, beyond a little used access road, the Regent, a discount movie theatre, then Walts' Gas Station and Kwik-Mart (for those concerned with the decline of modern-day punctuation skills, I know!); then Valhalla's Massage Parlour and, at the end of the block, Sharad's Tattoo Emporium. Behind the Leroy, there is ruin and open fields and, in the far distance, you can see a white cross attached to the roof of what used to be a K Mart Department Store (you remember, where this story started). It was now *The Holy Shrine of the One and Only Church of Jesus Christ the Almighty Provider.* But you know about that too and, to be honest, it plays a bigger role in a different version of this story than it does here. So for now, and here, I'll just tell you about the geography and history of what you might need to know.

Directly behind the Leroy is a cracked and weed-drunk parking lot; it belongs to the Roosevelt Dance Hall which has long since closed and fallen into ruin, its stucco walls cracked and tin roof rusted and bent. A tall chain-link fence encircles it. Some claim the Roosevelt is full of ghosts and on hot and muggy summer nights, particularly if you have consumed just the right blend of Rainy's magic and mix, you can hear mostly unknown bands play their jitter and jive and you can eavesdrop on laughter and lies from eighty years ago. Adjacent to the south, more recent but no less abandoned, is Bowlie's Meat Packers—or, more exactly, the foundation of what used to be Bowlie's. Max Bowlie and his oldest son, Leo, had perished one winter's night in a blaze that consumed his business, and the foundation walls have since stood as a playground for two generations of kids juking out their games of hide and seek and destroy. Max has become a popular dyphemism around town, "Do what you're told or you'll become a Bowlie burger"—not at all a positive divination. Unlike the Roosevelt, no one reports the sounds of ghosts at Bowlie's—I am guessing that they are far too real. What does remain of Bowlie's, though, is a small brick edifice, eight by twelve, next to the Roosevelt's devolving pavement and just behind the east breezeway of the Leroy. It is the abattoir's crematorium and, repaired and maintained by Austin Peters and Johnny P. March, it is still in perfect working order.

Across Dundas Street—as you know, every town in this area of the world seems to have a main street named Dundas—across and slightly east from the Leroy stands the *Voyageur's End*, large, newly renovated, with bell hops and door men and endorsements from all of the travel and credit card organizations. Its foyer is a utopia of plush carpet, weighty chandeliers, polished mahogany and faux-marble surfaces. Its conference hall and meeting rooms are regularly booked and regularly situated at the epicentre of momentous decrees announcing the advent of earth-shaking plans and iconoclastic visions, at least of the local sort. The clandestine affairs carried on in its wonderful rooms (with their wonderful king-sized beds) are carried on in general only by Thornton's best. And when this grand edifice was constructed some forty years ago, many thought that it would mark the end of the lowly Leroy across the street, but the Leroy endured. And twenty-five years ago, when this grand hotel was entirely remodelled with pay-per-view movies, a mini bar and free telephone service in every room, many thought that the poor Leroy would certainly vanish, but the Leroy endured. And a decade ago, when the grand establishment changed ownership, fell into Dalco Corp's greasy hands, and a gymnasium and dance club were installed and all the rooms again remodelled, many thought that surely the demise of the Leroy was at hand, but the Leroy endures.

- 13 -

Me and America

Dave Bryden III steps from his vehicle. It is a red 1985 Omni with a white roof, the model that Dodge Motors Corporation had christened America. It is too old to be on the road, but here it is. The interior upholstery is a dark blue and has seen more than a few tired bodies scuff across it. But Dave has kept the car in vintage shape with hours of labour and it has passed all the requirements needed to keep such a vehicle legally on the road. Dave reaches into the back seat and pulls out three sample cases, two of carpet and one of laminates, Tecumseh Flooring's newest line. Dave walks around the car and enters the front door of Elliot City Carpet, Mid-Western Distributor of Tecumseh Flooring. It is nine o'clock on this unseasonably warm spring day, Thursday March 21 to be exact. An advertisement taped on the door reads: "Saint Patrick's Day SALE, ends and remnants, all week long". Dave hasn't thought of Saint Patrick's Day, just a few days past, until right now. He remembers the celebration that it used to be, though he doesn't really mark it any more. When he was younger, fifteen, twenty years ago, before he was married and mortgaged, a buddy and he would always light out for Lake Placid around this time of year, about a day's drive away. They would drink their way there, stopping off at a score of little Adirondack Mountain beverage holes as they climbed up to Placid, itself a town of about 2,000 or so with, at Dave's count then, about 44 bars. It would be the off-season in Placid so the motels were cheap but the bars stayed open and they were cheap too. One year Dave and his friend even wore stupid little bowler hats made of green plastic, his friend's idea, travelling from bar to bar, speaking a fake Irish brogue and collecting free drinks here and there as they went. But that was ancient history. He hadn't been in touch with that friend for a long time and, now, he really couldn't afford to take any days off work, let alone weeks. He was even briefly bemused that such a thing as Saint Patrick's Day celebrations still existed. Especially given that saint's recently diminished reputation as a torturer and killer of women and children—such were the witchy snakes he drove from Ireland.

"Hello, Eddie. I'm just about ready to hit the road. I'll need that cash for expenses, and the samples. Anything I need to know?"

"Dave, I wouldn't know where to begin there!" Eddie DiGenero steps out from behind the cash register. He is a thin, well-conditioned man wearing a blue cardigan over a pristine white t-shirt and, with no customers yet in the store, he is sucking religiously through a straw on some brown, no doubt healthy, concoction in a plastic Starbuck's glass. Eddie, inheriting this business from his great uncle, is actually younger than Dave and has yet to lose his illusions of fame and fortune, maybe never will. "Kidding aside, thanks for taking this on, Dave. Arnie came down with the flu, and Cece is tied up with that Pierce Avenue job. And I gotta be here for the quarterly Business Association meeting this Saturday—I'm vice-chair this year. I know that this was supposed to be a weekend off, but, trust me, I'll make it up to you. I laid out the samples that you need there—two carpet, two laminate and that bag full of accessories. Here's 400 bucks in cash—that should be enough to cover you for gas, sleeping and meals until Sunday. You should be able to make it back by Sunday night. You can have Monday off but drop the samples by sometime in the morning if you don't mind. And remember to keep your receipts or I'll want that 400 back, right. Oh, and if you get a chance, slip away from Tom and Mike's and get around to some of the other carpet stores in Thornton—here's a list and addresses. I put some flyers in there for you to drop off—show those other stores some of the new Tecumseh stuff and remind them that we're the exclusive mid-west distributors. I can't think of anything else. You got any questions?"

"No, I don't think so, Eddie."

"I hope that old crock of yours will make it."

"Oh, never fear, Eddie. It's the most dependable car I ever had. I'd drive it anywhere, to the gates of hell and back. I trust it … it's faithful as that old hound I used to have. You know, don't you, it's America. Like I say, when I'm drivin', I'm driving America. Right! And America's never goin' to let me down, now, is it, Eddie?"

"Well, as long as Dave Bryden doesn't let me down, that's all I'm concerned about. And don't forget to get receipts. And don't lose those samples. See you on Monday."

"Yeah, don't worry, boss. You can count on me. Me and America!"

- 14 -

War brings out the best in humans

Beneath the earth the walls are made of large blocks of limestone and create a passageway about three feet wide by six feet high. On occasion, the tunnel-walls curve sideways, often near intersections with other passages, creating enough space to allow you to pass by anyone you might chance to meet in this subterranean labyrinth. Johnny and Oz, each carrying two duffle bags, hump awkwardly along. Each manages to squeeze a flashlight in one hand offering an oscillating glimpse of the darkness into which they are proceeding like an old episode of *The X-Files*.

"Let's rest here for a minute," says Johnny. "We're pretty close to Hell's Boulevard."

"Okay by me, Johnny," came the reply. "I guess I ain't as young as I used to be."

"Sad to say, Oz, none of us are. It just don't work that way."

The two men rest their burdens and lean against the stone, letting their lights illuminate the uneven brick floor.

"I am always amazed whenever we come down here—what a set-up."

"Yeah, it is kind of amazing, Johnny. Of course, I guess if you think about it, almost all cities have a maze of tunnels and passages underneath them. Cities are built as much on air as rock, on gateways to the underworld."

"When'd you say all this was built?"

"Quite a while ago. And over time. There was a pioneer fort built near this site, near the forks of the river, nearly two hundred years ago. And this whole area of town, from here to the train station, was a military staging area for the first World War. And a barracks and training area too. They practised building trenches, ten, twelve feet deep, then they built covered tunnels, then near the end of the war they built an entire network of these experimental trenches, twenty feet deep, brick floors, stone walls, cement ceilings. Not that it was a new idea, mind you, the military had been using this kind of thing for hundreds of years."

"Yeah, Oz. You know, I told you before, eh, I saw one like these in that old fort you can go through down there in Kingston—from the war in 1812. A long underground tunnel goes from the courtyard of the fort, out under the walls, to an outpost near the water. It's amazing. A thing of genius."

"Yeah. I guess there are military tunnels that have survived since the Dark Ages, over in southern France."

"And they're still used in warfare—Charlie had them all over the place in Nam, and they used them in the Gulf wars. It's where they caught old Saddam. Like I say, things of genius, I guess."

"Yeah ... I suppose. You could say that war brings out the best in humans."

"Well ... that's one way to think of it, Oz. Helluva price to be paid for that kind of smarts, though."

"Always is ... for almost any kind of smarts, my young friend."

"I suppose. I still can't believe that these things here have survived though."

"Well, as you know, a couple sections have caved-in—from water damage, mostly. When the city was having trouble in the thirties and forties with spring floods from the Moira, they hooked their storm sewers into this system. The water would overflow back into these passages and sit in here until the river went down and then it would flow out again. The floods softened some of the mortar in the walls, took their toll like floods always do, I guess. 'Course it's also because of those floods that we can get in here through the sewer grate. Since the water control damns and levee systems were put in on the river in the sixties, it's been as dry as a desert in these tunnels—almost too dry even for rats. Even us rats, right Johnny."

"Good to know I keep movin' up in the world, old man."

"When they built the End some forty years ago, as you know, they dug below Hell's Boulevard and didn't even have to worry about any water seeping in. They just put that big steel grate in like a doorway, with a drain below. As you know, it's their furnace room now. Good for us, of course."

"Back door to the country store."

"You know it."

"Anyway, I suppose if we don't get going again, we're never going to get our shopping done, are we? We've rested here long enough, old fellow. Let's get at it. Let's go silent from here on though—we don't want to get the attention of any other rats. Right?"

"Right."

The two move on. In less than a minute they arrive at the

intersection with Hell's Boulevard. Although constructed in the same fashion, the boulevard seems spacious by comparison; it is six feet wide and nine feet in height and runs in a north-south direction directly beneath and perpendicular to Dundas and, as the faint light to their right shows, directly into the nether regions of the *Voyageur's End*. Perhaps most unusual and out-of-place, the erratic beams of their flashlights reveal a cluster of coaxial cables fastened along the ceiling, seeming to run the length of the boulevard.

"Time to be especially quiet, Oz. Easy does it. Let's go."

The two men, walking more easily now in the more ample space, move stealthily toward the light of the End. A large iron grate, like the kind that teases freedom to desolate prisoners, blocks the entire end of the boulevard. Through that grate, Johnny glances into a dimly lit room whose ceiling is a menagerie of air and water circulation pipes and electrical conduit; the room houses four large furnaces, two of which are earnestly humming on this fine spring day. With a dexterous move and a minimal squeak, Johnny lifts and spins a huge chunk of the grate back into the tunnel, something those desolate prisoners cannot do, at least not without great preparation and risk. The iron has been invisibly severed and is now held in place only by concealed brackets. The two men drop three feet into the furnace room and pull their duffle bags behind them.

"Almost there now, Oz. Time for action," Johnny whispers.

"The usual battle plan!" is the quiet reply.

The back door to the main storage room, an auxiliary entrance to the furnace room, is cracked open very slowly. Along one side of this room are great wire racks set on wheels; about one third stand empty, the other two thirds are laden with freshly laundered sheets and stacks of clean, white towels. In the middle of the room are great canvas carts positioned carefully beneath two dark chutes in the ceiling, diurnal receptacles to all of the dirty laundry that plummets down from the luxurious rooms above. Along the other wall, storage shelves filled with all of the minutiae that make visitors want to return again and again to such places of repose: box after box of tiny bars of soap, dwarfish bottles of yellow shampoo and ivory hand lotion, score upon score of shoeshine cloths and shower caps in plastic bags and packets of instant coffee and cheap tea and complimentary toothpaste. At the front of the shelves, boxes of toilet paper piled to the ceiling. And toward the back wall, all scripted with the hotel's name, *Voyageur's End*, and embossed with its logo—an empty canoe and two crossed paddles—large boxes of stationery and envelopes and postcards and pens without caps.

Without a word, Johnny and Oz move to work. The usual battle plan. Each opens his duffles, pulls out a full garbage bag and dumps the contents into the central canvas carts—used sheets, pillow cases, towels and face cloths. Then they move to the last full wire rack and transfer a wealth of cleanly laundered sheets and towels and such into the duffle bags. That done, Johnny pulls two of the plastic garbage bags inside out and places various quantities of the soaps and shampoos and the like in the bags. He takes no stationery, no toilet paper.

Within two minutes, the gate is reset and the two soldiers are marching back down Hell's Boulevard, another small battle won in this secret and everlasting civilian war. It would not take much to imagine bold strains of "Dixie" or the "Battle Hymn" filtering through these hollow tunnels. And beyond the noise of the present motion, an acute intuition might easily feel the unquiet silence of forlorn ghosts. But Johnny and Oz push on, reaching the passage to the Leroy and they are soon beneath the van. Fired by elation and relief, the fallback always seems quicker than the foray out. In moments, the blue van fires up and moves back to its parking space behind Rainy's. An invisible armistice in place for the visible moment, the ghosts at ease once more.

- 15 -

Hey little girl, is your daddy home?

Little Davy steps back from Dave Bryden III's hug and crisply salutes—he had seen pictures on TV, after a retrospective on the plane crash of JFK Jr., of little John-John saluting as his father's casket passed by long ago and, for some reason that only the misfiring neurons in the brain of a four-year-old can divine, Davy has started to salute his father every time he leaves the house. Unlike the casket of the dead president, Dave salutes back.

"You take care of everyone here, ok Davy? You're in charge now 'til I get back Sunday night."

Dave turns from his son to give Barbara a hug and a quick last kiss. "Our boy never quits surprising, does he?"

"Yeah, from Superman to saluting—who knows what'll be next?" Barbara says with a small smile. To his parents' relief, at least Davy had recently surrendered that old blue pyjama top scattered with Superman symbols which he had insisted on wearing for the past year until it was little more than a rag. By the end, it hardly honoured those familial Kryptonian hieroglyphs it purportedly celebrated.

"I'll probably be in pretty late on Sunday—so don't wait up.

Eddie's giving me Monday off, but he wants the damn samples back in, so if I'm still groggy in the morning, maybe I'll have you take them in, or maybe Davy and you and me could go out for a big leisurely breakfast on Monday. We'll see."

"Ok Dave. We'll play it by ear, see what you're feeling like on Monday. But take it easy. Drive carefully, ok? You know on these trips, I really miss you. I really am tired of you not being around…"

"Well … we've been over that. Eddie has promised me an in-store job when they open that carpet and drape store across town, and the long days and nights on the road will be over. It won't be long."

"I hope so. Davy needs you around more. He really misses you, too, you know."

"I know. I know."

"Anyway … I need to get Davy in and maybe down for a morning nap. We'll see. Drive safe."

"No problem. There isn't a safer, or slower, car on the road. See you Sunday, or maybe Monday if I get in too late. I got my cell so if there's any problems, I'll call, ok? Bye. Bye." Dave gets in his car and, with a wave of good-bye, backs onto the suburban side-street then heads out toward the freeway which has never been far away in his life.

Shortly after, a blue Chevy SUV with labels on the doors that read Elliot City Carpet, slithers around the corner and pulls into the Bryden driveway. Eddie deGenero gets out, slips his cell phone into his pocket and moves assuredly toward the front door of the house. It is not Dave or Davy Jr. that he has come to see.

In a matter of minutes, Dave Bryden III eases America out of the freeway merge lane and into the sparse Thursday traffic. It is nearly noon—he had hoped to be an hour or so along at this point. Checking in again at home had cost some time, but it was time well spent—any time with Davy and Barbara was time well spent. He flips the radio on and an old bluesy Bruce Springsteen song cuts in: "Hey little girl, is your Daddy home?" Dave pushes the accelerator slowly to the floor—50, 55, 60 miles an hour. There, that is about right. America can take that speed and be in Thornton in about five, maybe five and a half hours. Time to check in to a motel in the late afternoon, and be at the carpet store by six o'clock for the Thursday evening crowd.

The traffic thickens in a half hour, as expected, after the Ridgeville cloverleaf. Continually, now, flocks of cars and transports migrate up and fly by him, but that is okay, that is as it should be, the democratic declaration of the freeway. America can travel whatever speed she wants—she passes a few, a few pass her, and Dave imagines, if you could look down from some satellite soaring in space, or if you were able to fly above it all like Davy's Superman, the majority really move along at a constant speed, in a constant rhythm over the rivers, past the hills, through the cities and towns. It is the life of the carpet salesman, independent, interdependent. The rhythm of the freeway, of America. And the glorious "City upon a Hill" is surely just ahead, always just ahead.

THORNTON

POPULATION 789 000

12 MILES

BUSINESS EXIT 79 SOUTH

(DUNDAS STREET WEST)

"Damn. What did that sign say?" Five hours and forty minutes driving, with only one brief pit-stop, has taken its toll. Dave claws back from that twilight zone of freeway ontology—giraffish gas and food signs and garish billboards for parks and attractions and fireworks and beer and cigarettes and souvenirs and lodgings and restaurants and towns and cities and all the scruffy bifurcated land in between and the rest. So many signs with so much to say that, finally, signifier and sign become nothing. You stop comprehending, stop seeing, and the sign you were anticipating for five hours and forty minutes sweeps by like another sad tree, like another splayed and beaten highway pulp that used to be some kind of living thing. The tenacious cost of the freeway, deadening life and language in all directions.

That's when America hesitates. And hesitates again. And then lurches, as if her pistons and valves have just gone out the front door on a wildcat strike. And Dave comes to full consciousness as his speed plummets and vehicles rise up from behind and start to hit brakes and horns and swerve around him. Dave pulls his coasting car to the right, onto the paved shoulder, joining the pop cans, the newspapers, the strips of diesel rubber, and all of the other cast-off things of this moving world.

America is still. Dave opens the hood and stares at the motor. Like most humans, he really does not know a hell of a lot about these vehicles that propel us from place to place. But staring at a bunch of wires and tubes and engine protuberances seems like the necessary thing to do. He only knows that the engine is hot, that the car does have a half tank of gas, that the tires are ok, and that the horn, lights, doors and radio all work. Dave squats. He can see some hot red liquid pooling on the shoulder beneath the engine—it looks like America is bleeding, maybe to death, and he has no tourniquet or transfusion.

However, just as he fishes his cell phone from the glove compartment, a police car stops, a tow truck is called and, within a half hour, America is on the last leg of its journey to Thornton, Dave sitting nervous in the cab of the truck.

- 16 -

Neither like hawk nor wolf

"**So, how's the corn flakes,** Deed, my man?"

"Mmmm."

"Hey, Blue. How 'bout a refill here on such a beautiful day. Tragically, methinks my cup hath runneth empty."

"Well, some kind of rough magic, no doubt. And me thinks me was just reading your mind, Dom—got the pot right here. We wouldn't want you to succumb to some kind of strange spell—you might lose track of who you are, become a stranger, or a jackass."

"Oh, that could never happen, my beauty. I will always return to this haunted wood and its beautiful creatures and strange charms. ... Oh, and speaking of strange creatures, look who should appear. Look Blue, Deed, there—coming across the road and heading straight over here—if it isn't the great jackass himself, the plump old grand general of the End, Mr. Charlie T. Walker."

Charles Thompson Walker, by anyone's account, a large man, clothed in a bulging charcoal grey suit, white shirt, and blue tie with a prominent *Voyageur's End* logo, pushes open the door of Rainy's and robustly steps inside.

"Where's March?" he barks toward Blue.

"Right after February, you dumb arse," replies a large voice from a small man sitting at the counter, without turning in his seat. And even from behind, you can see a convulsion of laughter being held within the body of his huge, stoic companion.

"I don't need any lip from a stunted dwarf like you, Domino, a queer reject from a Snow White poster."

"Well, Hi, Ho. Prince Charming you certainly ain't."

"No I'm not, but I don't do zero like you. Hi or Ho—you've made doing nothing into an art form," snarls Walker.

"You may be right, but I am good at what I do," Dom spins on the counter stool. "No need to be jealous, though. You can always ask me for advice."

"I'll ask for that when … when hell freezes and you skate over it, when you manage to find a job somewhere and, as we all know, that'll never be."

"Why, Charlie, I was just going to apply for a job at the End. I hear that the manager's job may be up for grabs if business don't pick up soon."

"No chance, friend. We're doing just fine. But you, well, stay to hell out of my way or you're likely to become a Bowlie burger, if you know what I mean?"

"Oh, yeah, I forgot. Who gets hired at the End is a touchy subject. I hear that you only hire relatives, don't you, Charlie?"

"And you, my friend, will thankfully never be one of those."

"I don't know, Charlie. That boy of yours is pretty cute. And when he's in that new uniform you got him waltzing back and forth in over there, with that big shiny gun sticking out, I could just end up as family after all."

"On that day, Dom, there'd be a wedding and several funerals, just like the movie. Trust me. Where's March, Blue?"

"I don't know, Mr. Walker. I saw him a bit earlier today. He's around."

"Well, I want to see the bastard."

"Something I can do for you, Charlie Walker?"

Everyone's gaze shifts to the office doorway where Johnny easily emerges, Angus like a Doberman at his side, breathing a slight growl with every breath. Johnny rubs behind the dog's ear to ease his tension. "Easy, boy."

Charlie hesitates for a moment, as if all of the bravado of his visit into enemy territory has, for a moment, leaked out of him like a balloon after the parade. Then he regains a semblance of his composure and his mission.

"You're damn right there's something you can do for me," he waves a crumpled paper in his pudgy fist in the air. "I got a bill here from Pete's Paving People for repairs to the parking lot…"

"Try saying that real quick three times in a row," Dom quips.

Charlie ignores him and plunges on "… and *Voyageur's End* never had any repairs done to its parking lot—the asphalt's brand new two years ago for Christ's sake. It's a helluva lot like that bill we had two months ago for roof repairs and we never had any roof repairs done. I fired our bookkeeper then, but this is too damned suspicious, March. Especially when I'm coming here and there's a newly paved entrance off Dundas and I'm walking over a bunch of fresh asphalt patches."

"Why don't you have a seat at the counter, Charlie, and have a cup of Rainy's. It's on me, ok? The Wizard and me, we did that patching with a do-it-yourself kit a couple weeks ago. It was easily done. Talk to Oz, if you want. Ok?"

"No, dammit, it's not ok. Do-it-yourself kit, my ass—the only do-it-yourself kit was labelled Pete's Paving and somehow you got the invoice sent to *Voyageur's End*."

"Let's see that bill, Charlie." Johnny takes the crumpled paper and glances at it. "Why, Charlie, that's your signature on this piece of paper, right there, where it says Authorization, right there, it's signed Charlie T. Walker. I don't know what to say, big guy, it looks like you signed it yourself. Maybe you forgot?"

"Like hell, I forgot. I don't know how you're doing it, March, but I know you're doing it. And I'm going to find out how; it's like you've got some kind of pipeline right into our data base or something. But I'm warning you, March, I'm going to get to the bottom of this, and get you, one way or the other; and when I do, I'll sue this dump right out from under you. I've called Head Office—you know who that is, that *Voyageur's End* is a Dalco Corp operation. So they're on the case now. And they're no chumps. They're looking to buy up this whole tract of land—if they take my advice, a year from now the Leroy'll be a parking lot. You and your crappy little hole here are in deep trouble, March. 'Cause Frederick Dalco's comin' to town, and when he gets involved, the shit's gonna hit the fan, and you're the fan. Oh my, my. Mark my words."

"Does that mean that Dalco's the shit, Charlie—I must tell him that the next time I see him?"

"Yeah, and is he makin' a list and checkin' it twice?" Dom pipes in.

"Anyway, I'm sorry Charlie. I don't know anything about your paving bills or your roofing bills or the cost of your furnace repairs. You know, I really think that you need to learn to keep better track of your accounts." Johnny hands the receipt back. "With bookkeeping like that, like Dom just said, you could end up out of a job, if you're not careful."

Dom, in the middle of a sip of coffee, breaks into laughter

The Prince of Leroy

and spits the hot liquid back into his cup, mostly. Charlie's whole body winces at him and glowers at Johnny.

"I'm going to be watching you like a hawk, March, and you make one slip from now on and I'll be on you like a wolf." Charlie T. Walker turns to the door.

"Sure you wouldn't like to stay for that coffee, Charlie? It's on the house."

"Like a wolf, March." He spins out of the doorway and starts across the parking lot. Then he stops and, his face red, he stares back for a moment at the darkened windows of Rainy's. Even audible to those inside is the phrase he utters: "Furnace repairs?" Then he storms off across Dundas toward the End, quite frankly, in his rolling, stocky gate, looking neither like hawk nor wolf. Perhaps he was beyond hearing the chorus of laughter that had erupted inside the restaurant; perhaps not.

- 17 -

That's all right, mama

Blue sits a cup of coffee on the counter for Johnny. Angus has curled up in the Office doorway—nothing will pass, even in sleep, without his knowing.

"So, it sounds like big Charlie has a real hate on for this place. And you, Johnny."

"No. Not so much for me, Blue, I don't think. At least not personally, not yet anyway. No. The End's probably not doing as well as it's supposed to right now, especially in the off-season; our lot's almost as full as theirs many nights. And as all of you know, Charlie was trying to get close to Jackie. Sent her flowers and asked her to dinner a few times, offered her a job at the End with all kinds of perks—so she said anyway. But a couple of weeks ago, as Charlie might say, the fan got hit. Jackie blew up at him and, in no uncertain terms, I gather she told him where to go, and worse, and in two languages. There must have been something happened—I'm not sure what—cause quite frankly I thought they were on the verge of sort of getting along. But since then, big Charlie has been on a rampage. Right now, he hates all things Leroy."

"Oh," Dom reacts, "Now wouldn't that be terrible way to

spend your life, eh? Hating all things Leroy. There's some mystery there that needs revealin', Prince."

"Well," says Johnny, "the universe unfolds in its own way, Dom. You know that. Like bad dreams! Sometimes, certain things are just beyond our control. Of course, sometimes the universe needs a bit of a kick-start too. A little mystery ain't always a bad thing, but putting a light bulb in the dark can do a little magic too. We'll see. Refill my coffee, will you Blue? Let's drink to the mystery of things. And the magic too."

"Well, knowing her, I imagine that Jackie could really make a guy disappear if she got pissed at him, and that wouldn't take no magic!" Dom responds.

"No doubt, Dom."

Oz enters the restaurant and nods to all as Blue retreats to fill a cup for him.

"Any truth, Johnny, to what big Charlie said?" Blue asks as she gives Oz his coffee. "Could the *Voyageur's End* people buy all the land around here and put everybody out of business. Frederick Dalco is a pretty powerful guy, I hear—kinda walks both sides of the law. We'd have to fight them. And that would be a rough fight, wouldn't it? Dangerous too?"

"Well, Blue, I don't think I've ever met anyone who doesn't walk both sides of the law, even the law. But no, there won't be a fight. The Roosevelt took care of that."

"What do you mean?"

Benny enters from the office and takes a seat at the counter. Blue pours him a coffee, as well.

"Well, the best person that I know of to talk about the Roosevelt is the only one of us here who ever danced at the place. Right, Oz?" Johnny turns with a nod toward Oz. "Why don't you tell all the youngsters here about the old Roosevelt, Oz?"

"Wow. You danced there, you old devil?" says Blue with a smile. "I bet you were a slick dancer, Oz. Tell us about the old place."

"Well, old it is, I guess, just like me. And yes, I did some dancing over there—I could cut a rug in the day, if I do say so myself. And the Roosevelt used to be a great place, even though it's a dump right now. But, about thirty-five years ago, it was declared a national historical site, really international if you can believe it."

"So why was it considered so special?" asks Blue.

"Well, take a look sometime, there's still a plaque on the wall near the front entrance that explains a bit of it. When the Roosevelt was built in the twenties, it was actually just outside of town limits, to be near the old army base and train station and to be away from the law and all the moral do-gooders downtown who didn't care for dancing and booze and Blacks. I'm gonna sit down." Oz settles on one of Rainy's counter stools. "But during the construction, a train full of architects and designers on their way to a Chicago exposition got stuck in town for a couple of days because of some track trouble over in Miller's Hills, and as coincidence would have it they looked over the plans for the Roosevelt and several of them made suggestions that were later used and signed a document to authenticate their contributions, and to authenticate the fact that they were contributions, if you know what I mean—so they might get paid, 'tho I don't think any of them ever did? That great curved glass-brick bar, the square columns on each side of the stage, the inlaid dance floor, the triangular designs pressed into the ceiling-tin—all of those were ideas of these famous architects—I can never remember all the names—Frank White, Walter Grouper, a guy named Proove, I think—the names are on the plaque. I don't know much about that kind of stuff, except that the Roosevelt was built in a style they call deco under the influence of all of these famous international designers. And then, add to that the fact that some of the greatest musicians of the century played there—Lombardo, Satchmo, Shaw, and, of course, as you know, the greatest of them all—at least the greatest story of them all—that one night in '55, just before he hit it big, the King took the stage. Elvis sang "Mama It's Alright" and "Houn'-dog"—he blew the roof off the place and people couldn't believe he was a White kid."

"Wow," says Blue. "Elvis just next door. I didn't know that."

"Yes ma'am. Then when the Roosevelt was being reopened for the last time—just about the time the End was being built—the owner contacted some politicians and it got a huge amount of publicity and a small grant. A bunch of important people showed up for the unveiling ceremony—and it became a national historical site. 'Course what that meant was that when the new owner tried to make some renovations some twelve or fifteen years later, a new sound system and disco floor and so on, he wasn't allowed to because of the historical designation and so the Roosevelt went out of business. And into receivership, and a couple of years ago the bank donated it to the city and the city has had a committee trying to decide what to do with it ever since—museum, art gallery, drop-in centre. Except it's not in the right area of town, is it Johnny?

But it's protected. By law. And a fence. That's why that ten-foot fence was put up. So who knows, maybe someone will open it again someday, maybe even as a dance hall—and by God if it does, I'll dance there again whether I'm alive or dead"—there are some smiles from his audience—"but they'll never be able to tear it down to build a parking garage or anything else. So, joined as it is to the Roosevelt property, the Leroy's pretty safe in spite of what Charlie may think. The Roosevelt ain't going to be anything but the Roosevelt. And, you know, as far as all those ghosts over there are concerned, I imagine that's just fine with them."

"I've heard people talk about the ghosts of the Roosevelt, especially after they stumble out of here late at night." Blue pipes in. "If they get close to that old joint, they claim to hear bands playing swing and blues and they swear to have heard people talking and laughing from years and years ago. It sends a chill down my spine."

"And so it should. Hey, Oz, here's to the ghosts of the Roosevelt. May their dreams be peaceful." Dom lifts his cup. "Well, I would drink to them, but I guess I'm out."

"Fill everyone up, Blue," Johnny speaks and slaps Dom on the shoulder. "The house owes one to the world this morning. Especially to the ghosts of the Roosevelt. And I gotta be on my way. Errands to run before the day is done. See you later, folks."

A ripple of farewells and thanks follows the Prince as he steps over Angus and exits the restaurant. Despite his best laid plans, Angus continues a deep sleep.

- 18 -

Who'd you think you was fuckin' with?

A new, bright yellow Mustang shoots around the curve and levels out on the empty boulevard. It slows and reels sharply on to Bleeker, then picks up speed again.

"God, Lucky. Does this car ever take the turns!"

"Yeah. It hangs cool. Best thing I ever bought, man. The old one was getting pretty tore down. I didn't get much for the trade but with the score we just made and the cash from Malley, the down-payment was easy. I got a good deal. And Malley said he might have some work coming up later this month, so things are really looking up, Gabe. I just got a feeling."

"Yeah! I got a good feeling, too."

The Mustang shoots passed a slowing school bus, its lights blinking.

"Whoa. Ain't you supposed to stop for school buses?"

"Naw. Not if they're still coasting, man."

"If you say so, buddy, but you're the one gonna pay the ticket."

"Ah, you know me, man. I don't pay tickets!"

Gabe smiles. "You know, Lucky, I'll never forget my first ride with you. Remember, back in high school, the Yonie pony?

"Oh yeah, that was my last day of school, man. Forever! I was downtown skipping classes and borrowed that Aimless buggy—had to toss a sleeping kid out of it."

"And then you came gallupin' up to school. I never seen nothin' like it, man—that shaggy old glue stick'd never run so fast. You drove that buggy right around the track and everyone stopped what they was doin'; classes just froze 'n everybody jumped up and stared out the windows. Nobody knew what in hell to do."

"Yeah, it was quite a ride. Quite a way to say good-bye to all that high school crap. The old principal, what was his name…?

"Fat-ass Brown…"

"Yeah, old Fat-ass tried to stop me and he ended up suckin' on a mud-puddle. Then you hopped on and we road right out across the country over to your place. That was one of the best days of my life."

"Yeah … 'course it was also the day my Mom died. Set herself on fire."

"There was that too. A good time can turn to a tough time real quick, can't it! Shit can happen. Real quick."

"Anyways, things are going too good right now to think about the past. And this is a great car. So, Taber's took care of all the powder."

"Yeah, he says the less we know the better. But he sold one brick east and bagged the rest around town. We each got our $1500 so I'm happy—that's more than I thought we'd get."

"Me, too. And I put it away without even telling Liz. We really need to get out of the dump we're in. There was another big fight across the hall last weekend. And puke on the stairway this morning. It's not a fit place to live, to bring up little Jimmy. He deserves better. And Liz too. We're goin' out this weekend to look at a few houses over in the east end. So, things really do feel like they're changing for the good, man. And speakin' of the dump, here we are."

The Mustang slows in front of a rose-coloured apartment complex on Rolph Street and pulls into a driveway that curves in front of the main doorway.

"Why don't you park over there and come up for a beer, Lucky? You haven't seen Liz and the kid in quite a while."

"Ok. I guess. As long as the car will be safe."

"Yeah, it should be. It's still light out, for another hour or so at least. Nobody'll touch it—not until after dark, anyways."

The Mustang eases to the side of the lot parking on an angle, taking up three spaces. There are no rules in parking lots. Lucky and Gabe get out of the Mustang and the locks click with a chirp from the press of a key fob. They move toward the three story walk-up, enter and climb a flight of stairs. They saunter along a dim and greasily matted hallway toward Gabe's apartment. In front of apartment 7, the two men stop.

"What the hell?" utters Gabe.

In front of them, the dark green door is slightly open, a fresh green splinter of wood around the latch visibly absent. Gabe pushes the door and quickly steps into the apartment, Lucky and a sense of dread close behind him.

"Liz? Liz? Jimmy?"

There is no answer. A couple cushions rest on the floor and a kitchen chair has been overturned.

"They should be home by now. Liz was off work by three this afternoon and was going to pick up Jimmy at Kindergarten. By 3:30. That's only two blocks down the street."

"Maybe they went for a walk."

The men begin to search throughout the apartment although they already sense that it is lifeless as a tomb.

"Maybe. Maybe they went for a walk. But it's nearly 5 o'clock. They should be here by now. Supper should be on."

"What if someone tried to break in, or when they came back they saw the door busted. Wouldn't they go somewheres else? What about a neighbour, Gabe?"

Gabe retreats to the hallway and pounds with urgency on the door across from 7. There is no answer. Attempts on doors down the hall bring chained responses—'No. No I ain't heard nothing' and 'Naw, I just got in a couple of minutes ago.'

A telephone. From the hallway, they hear it. A telephone ringing.

"Hey, man. That's your phone."

As in the unexpected burst of all telephones, an abrasion cuts along the nerve. Doubts. Fears. You know the sensation. The invasive ring, then, thoughts that end in dark clothes and umbrellas in the rain. Of course, in more recent time with more expensive contracts, well, praise to the Lords of Bell for the illusory balm of Caller ID. But no such luxury exists here.

"Hello," Gabe, slightly winded, somewhere between bewilderment and dread, speaks.

"Gabe. That you?"

"Yeah. It's me."

"The shipment that you and Lucky delivered, it was light, you know what I mean."

Gabe recognizes the voice of Stump Malley.

"I don't know what you mean, Mr. Mal…"

"Don't screw around with me. The time for screwin' is over. Look, today's Thursday—you got one week. I want those three bags back, or a million bucks. That's what they're worth. Your choice. And don't even think of trying anything, or goin' to the cops. Not if you know what's good for your kid, and your wife."

And you. Got it? Three bags or a million. By next Thursday. I'll be in touch. You stupid bastards. Who 'd you think you was fuckin' with?"

Silence. Click. Then dead silence. And then the indifferent buzz of all the telephone lines webbing out from Rolph Street. Across the city, the country, the world. And an emptiness, a void deep inside that did not allow Gabe to move a muscle for what seemed like eternity. As if a vacuum had sucked away his insides.

"What is it, Gabe? What's up, man?"

"It's ... it's Malley. He found out, Lucky. He knows. He's got Jimmy and Liz. He's holding them until we give him back the drugs we took. How the hell did he know? He wants the three bags of smack, or a million bucks. That shit couldn't have been worth that much, was it?"

"Oh! That son-of-a-bitch, Taber! He screwed us."

"Shit, Lucky, what kind of mess am I in? What can I do? Liz and Jimmy!"

"That son-of-a-bitch!"

- 19 -

A long time since Placid

Dave Bryden III does not know Thornton that well so he instructs the tow truck driver to take him to a garage not too far away from Tom and Mike's Carpets. The garage, Walts' Gas Station (one hopes that Walt understands cars better than he does punctuation), is right next to a large motel chain that Dave has heard about but has never stayed in, the Voyageur's End. By the time that he gets settled with the tow truck driver—it eats up about a third of his expense allowance—and talks with the garage manager, it is early evening and Dave is feeling tired and downcast. It looks like America has some serious engine problems, and he and Barb have already talked about getting a newer, if not new, car. Maybe an SUV. So he takes all of his personal items out and puts them in a plastic grocery-store bag, and drags out the bag of accessories and the Tecumseh samples and asks the manager to park the car for a day or two at the rear of the garage; he will let him know what his plans are by Monday at the latest. After he settles down a bit, gets finished with the weekend's work. After he talks to Barbara. And as Dave takes one last look with the sun low in the sky, it is a starkly cheerless and melancholy sight to see America, once proud and dependable, sitting at the rear of this wretched garage amid a bunch of other rusted and cannibalized machines. Somehow, almost, Dave feels that he should salute like little Davy, that twenty-one guns should be fired, that America deserves at least that much, but he also knows that he has always avoided such rituals, made excuses as to why he couldn't attend. As he has been known to joke, he plans to skip his own funeral. So, quickly, he turns away. Damn the expenses, he thinks, he will stay at the Voyageur's End—it is off-season, so it shouldn't cost too much.

He turns from the check-in counter—one night at the End has used up another third of his expense allowance. And it is only after he turns that he sees another motel right across the road, one that would probably have been a lot cheaper because it looks a lot dumpier. Declining assistance from two swarming bellhops, he rides the elevator to the second floor, and with carpet samples, the accessory bag, his own suitcase and the plastic bag of personal articles from America all in hand, he trudges down the hallway and finds his room—221. Inside, his first duty is to phone that carpet store, to tell them he'd had car trouble and that he would be in tomorrow, not tonight, and then take a long warm shower. Maybe later he would visit the bar or maybe have room service send up a big steak and a six-pack, and order a pay-per-view movie—what the hell, in for a penny, in for a pound. He had spent two-thirds of the boss's money already, he might as well blow the rest. And tomorrow, well tomorrow he would go back to being Dave Bryden III, 42, starting to go bald, getting a paunch, selling carpets for a living, driving a car that was older than God. It had been a long time since he had taken a night to eat and drink and relax, a long time since Placid. He is due. Here's to you Saint Pat and all the snakes you crucified.

And tomorrow when he awakes, well, he would find a way to make America be like new again and he would get back to work with energy and ambition; tomorrow when he awakes, he would really impress the owners of Tom and Mike's Carpet and blow away all of their customers; and tomorrow when he awakes, he would rise up and go forward open and easy into the sun and conquer the carpet world as if he were living the last days of his life, maybe even skipping his own funeral. Which, of course, is exactly what he would be doing.

- 20 -

The Gardens of the Leroy

The red sun is setting and the *Church of the Holy K.* is as still as Roosevelt's. Johnny slits open another bag of charcoal and dumps it into the fire chamber of the crematorium. He throws some wood shavings from another bag on top, then glugs some lighter fluid over the coals from a gallon can, sits the can aside and closes the metal double doors. Johnny then closes a larger set of metal doors on the top of this oblong bricked furnace and sits a box of matches on the surface. The day is ready now for fire but no smoke; with the triple damper system and the wet carbide filters there is almost never any smoke—nothing at all to alert the locals or upset any fire codes.

Behind him, there is a rolling rack, the kind normally used for storing towels and sheets. Instead, the rack is filled with the flotsam and jetsam of travelers' neglect and haste. There is a large blue suitcase, a light-green carry-on case, and two small overnight bags, one purple with a TU on the side, another maroon. In various plastic bags there is an assortment of toiletry items—five toothbrushes and three tubes of toothpaste, three nail-files and a pair of nail-clippers, a yellow hair net, an electric razor, two safety razors and a package of blades, five unopened, three condoms, two packages of tampons, four hypodermic needles cautiously double-bagged, two plastic combs, two hair brushes, four cans of hair spray, six lipsticks, and a package containing an additional menagerie of small and sundry make-up items. And further on the cart, seven single shoes (four female, two male, one child), one pair of shoes (brown loafers, male, with an American penny in one), twelve mismatched socks, one man's corduroy sports coat, four pairs of underwear (two female, two male), three pairs of panty hose, a wooden cane with a silver grip, a straw sun-hat with a red bandana, a brown fedora size seven, an empty picnic basket with the top missing, three travel mugs of different sizes, two cassette tapes—one, an anthology of the best songs of the 1970s, the other, Who's Greatest Hits—an old Simon and Garfunkel CD sans case, a CD ROM offering free access to the Internet, one thumb-drive with NOVEL-PL scribbled on the side, a wind-up alarm clock, three pens, one set of hand-cuffs, a '38 revolver with the chamber missing, three bullets (Johnny isn't sure how these will incinerate but he thought it might be interesting to find out), a pair of false teeth, two pairs of eyeglasses, three pairs of sunglasses (one broken), a journal full of elaborate entries in beautiful green handwriting, five computer disks, nine notes on post-its or paper scraps (four written in foreign languages), a Keystone vest-pocket New Testament and five books—a Danielle Steel novel, a harlequin romance, a book containing the world's greatest poems, another small book of poems with a red maple leaf on its cover, probably never opened, and an illustrated children's version of Sleeping Beauty.

 Oz has prepared the site earlier in the afternoon, scooping a couple wheelbarrows of mulch and ash from a large recycling bin near the crematorium, to be used as potting soil in the

Leroy's window boxes and flower beds, the rest spread over the so-called Gardens of the Leroy—the garden idea is part of Johnny's grand vision for the site. Stretching from behind the Leroy to the ditch that separates it from the Roosevelt's rugged lot is a field of broken asphalt, once intended to serve as a space for overflow parking. Johnny, using an industrial drill, has perforated this parking strip with dozens of holes; then lined the area with old rail ties and had four truckloads of topsoil added over a load of gravel. It is to be the Gardens of the Leroy, providing a flowery panorama to any who gaze out through the bathroom windows which line the back of the motel and serving as a source of fresh herbs and vegetables and cut flowers for Rainy's. But there never seemed to be quite time enough to tend the site and, even when given some attention, the Gardens of the Leroy never seem to thrive anyway; they are always somewhat sparse and barren, in effect becoming a perfect liaison between the motel and the shambled landscape that lies beyond. After spreading the mulch, Oz has refilled the recycling bin with the cold ashes of the incinerator's last burning; thus all is made ready for Burning Day.

Alice Tracey "Trace" Walters arrives on the scene, pushing a second cart up to the first, this cart half full of items similar to the first. Trace is the newest member of the Leroy staff. From a more than troubled background and less than stellar street-life, she is thin and fragile both in body and in spirit and is about to begin her first full night-shift all on her own.

"Thanks, Trace," Prince nods to her.

"No problem, Mr. Prince," Trace replies in a paced monotone.

"Why don't you call me Johnny, kid! We like to keep things low key around here."

"Ok, Mr. Prince. ... That's a furnace."

"Yes ... it is ... it comes in handy. That old ruin back there was Bowlie's Meat Packers—this was their crematorium where they burned up all their garbage, the bones and offal that couldn't be sold."

"No smoke. No fog."

"No, when the city sprawled out here Bowlie's installed a system of dampers and filters so there is almost no smoke—no smoke or fog at all. Keeps everyone happy. And Oz—you've met Oz, right—Oz keeps it up and running to perfection? Very useful to get rid of all this stuff. ... Is this everything?"

"Yes. According to Mr. Alamo. You burn all this?"

"Yeah, it's one of the few policies we have here. We never keep or even open anything we find. It stays for six months in the big safe, then it gets destroyed. And so nobody can get blamed for theft or anything."

"Cool."

"And then we take the ashes, sieve out the metal bits, and mix what's left with some mulch and fertilizer and spread it around on the ground over there. Going to grow a garden, herbs and wild flowers—the Gardens of the Leroy, Trace, all from the lost and neglected of the rooms. How's that sound?"

"Cool."

"And springtime, too. March 21st. The equinox, a time of balance in the year. A perfect time to renew, to level things out, to start again. Plan a kind of redirection. Don't you think?"

"Cool."

"That's a good word for it, I guess. Anyway, thanks for the help here, Trace. If you have any questions tonight, I'll be upstairs. Just shout. Ok?"

"Ok, Mr. Prince. I'm going back to the office now."

"Good. Benny will be wanting to get home. He'll have some new poems to write or more books to read or something. And here comes Oz to get things started."

Trace leaves quietly as Oz comes ambling toward the crematorium.

"Hi Trace. Banquet for the beast ready, Prince?"

"Yeah. Feeding time, Oz. Time to kickstart some flowers for the Gardens."

The Prince turns and leaves. Oz opens the metal doors but holds the matches for a moment, waiting for Johnny to disappear through the Leroy's breezeway. Then, a quick flick of his wrist sends a lit match spiraling through the open rack; flame erupts, blazes for a moment, and then relaxes toward a crackling, hissing choler. The light of the hungry flames shines upon him as he starts to load the random leftovers into the pit.

- 21 -

Down to the river

The radio in the blue and white squad car crackles and the two occupants balance their coffee cups carefully. The driver is Frank Elliot who has been on the Thornton Police Force for twelve years and has settled into the routine of a police officer's life. He has a wife, two children, a golden retriever and a house in the suburbs with a lawn to mow. His partner is Laura Santolin, a rookie officer just in her fifth month of active duty and still very much sorting out her relatively new identity. Her origins are in an inner city Hispanic culture so, while she has already seen many of the things she is now encountering, she is now engaged with them in a much different context.

The two officers casually attend to the squawk of the radio; it may not concern them.

"Probably another lost cat or dog. Or another dead junky," Frank quips.

Dispatcher's Voice: "Five Zero Seven. Wilson Hall, Thornton University. Perp being held by security."

"I guess that's for us, partner," Frank sighs. "Only a couple blocks away." His voice changes to one of business-like authority. "T-town 210. Responding to five zero seven. Our GPS is still on the fritz. Could you provide exact directions?"

Dispatcher's Voice: "Wilson Hall is ... at 23 Athena Avenue. Enter the main gates off Dundas, follow Hestia Crescent about a half a kilometre and then turn left down to the river. The location is marked with a sign."

"Copy. 210 out. ... I thought I'd better check. University's a maze. Hang on. We'll make it a light show."

"Sounds good, partner. Wake up all those students who've been out all night partying, maybe even wake the ones that made it to Friday morning class."

"Most likely ... wake a few anyway, Laura."

The lights begin to blink and flash sharply as the squad car pulls into traffic and the morning awakens with its howling siren's song.

- 22 -

This land is my land

The front doors of Wilson Hall are flanked by full floor to ceiling windows lined with sets of low naugahyde-upholstered benches, purple in colour. A blue and white squad car, lights flashing, can be seen through the windows; it pulls up behind a brown sedan labelled Campus Security. Two police officers get out, put on caps and move toward the doors. Inside, three individuals wait.

Henry Douglas MacLean, Dean of the Faculty of Education and president of Maclean Insurance and Real Estate, is a tall man in a tailored grey suit, with glistening white hair, a deeply tanned complexion and vivid blue eyes. (If this were a science fiction story, these are the kind of Martian eyes that would emit a lethal dilithium ray that could cut right through you.) MacLean's image is well known for its frequent appearances in local, even national, media; he is as slick in his business and academic affairs as his erudite appearance would suggest.

No-one would call Dick Doxtator slick though he is earnest in his own way; he is a husky man in his early forties who, after several other employments, now wears the tan uniform of the Campus Security Police and, with a measure of bravado, asserts all of the vacuous authority that such a position pretends to afford.

The third person, sitting like a phantom under the gaze of MacLean and Doxtator, is Emily Allison Bean, an old woman. Her hair, a mix of soft grey and winter white, is long and scattered. She is lean, not frail but lean, and her corrugated face seems a contour map woven in mortal flesh of all that she has seen and done. Her clothes are an ancient cacophony of textures and shreds, reds and greens and browns, especially highlighted by a dun-red sweater knit with care and grace long ago.

"Good morning, officers. I am Dr. Henry MacLean, Dean of this Faculty, and we have a problem here," the Dean speaks immediately. "This is the third time that we have found this woman sleeping overnight in this building."

The transfixed gaze of the officers shifts from the Dean to a nearby row of purple benches. There, with a campus security guard hovering over her, sits an old woman, her hair long and white.

"We have caught this woman recently, on three occasions, sleeping upstairs in one of the rooms. We removed her from the building twice before and asked her not to return. And then, at eight o'clock this morning, one of our professors opened Room 2029 and found her curled up again, sleeping like a child. She is absolutely intransigent on her right to be here and does not seem able, or willing, to understand that we cannot have an indiscriminate number of mendicants treating Wilson Hall as if it were a hotel. Signs are clearly posted throughout the building that everyone must be out by 10 pm.; professors are the only exception. Obviously, stricter measures need to be enforced. So I would like you to arrest her on charges of trespassing and theft."

"Theft, as well?" Frank interjects.

"Yes. There have been break-ins to some of the food vending machines in the cafeteria and she was found this morning with a box of Kleenex that she had taken from another room."

"Kleenex? Ok, Dean MacLean. We can take it from here. We'll take her downtown and you, or someone from the university, will have to come down to the Station and lay formal charges. I'll ask her a few questions here. We will give you a phone call, if you like, once we've sorted out the paperwork."

"Good. Here's my card. I've got some other pressing business to attend to—I have a televised press announcement to prepare for this afternoon—but if you need me, I will be in my Office. That's the Dean's Office. It's through those doors over there. Good morning." The Dean turns abruptly and walks through a set of doors to the right where a small man and a very large man are standing, silently riveted by the procedures. These men, Dom and Deed respectively, have just arrived to inquire about a new teacher recruitment incentive called the Re-enter and Recover program, R&R for short.

"That's all right, sir. We will take over from here. Thank you for your help and, if we need a written statement, we will be in touch." Frank speaks to Dick Doxtator, who nods and, with a surreptitious glance at the old woman, exits out of the front doors toward his security vehicle.

"I can take the lead here, Laura. I'll be quick. ... Good morning, ma'am. My name is Frank Elliot and this is Officer Santolin. We're with the Thornton Police Department. We need to ask you a few questions," Frank says, peering down at the old woman.

"Go ahead. I guess I might have a few answers," a thin but

solid voice speaks back. "Please have a seat." The old woman pats the bench and turns her head, unexpectedly for Frank, her strong green eyes looking straight into his. He blinks and averts his gaze to a blank note pad and then back to the woman. For a moment, he is taken aback, then regains composure.

"Oh, I've been sitting all day, so I think I'll keep standing, at least for the moment. Now, what is your name, ma'am?"

"I am Emily Allison Bean."

"What is your place of residence?"

"This is my place of residence, Frank."

The sound of his name coming from this thin, dry source causes Frank Elliot to hesitate for the second time in the last moment. "But Mrs. Bean, this is the university. I mean, this is Wilson Hall. It cannot be your principal place of residence."

"I am Miss Bean, not Mrs. I have never been married and, to be honest with you, Frank, at my age I don't rightly plan on getting married. Unless, of course, you're proposing. 'Course I do see a marriage band on your hand so that's highly unlikely, isn't it?"

"Yes. Uh, yes Miss Bean, it is," says Frank, again slightly fazed by the tone, the clarity, the energy of this old woman's patter. "How old are you, Miss Bean, if I may ask?"

"'Course you may ask. Though I guess I don't have to answer. But I am not here to hide things. I am here to try to set things right, to get what's mine. Officer Elliot, I was borned on the 17th of September, in the year of our Lord, 1801."

Silence. Even Dom is wrapt at a distance. This is like a dream almost stranger than his own.

"Well, that is interesting, Miss Bean. But do you know what year this is? That would make you, well, over two hundred years old. And, well, most people don't quite live to be that old, you know?"

"Well, I don't care about most people, Frank. Caring about most people—that's probably more your job description than mine. No, I was borned in 1801. The fall of 1801. But you are right, I am not as old as you might think."

"Ok, if you say so, Miss Bean. We'll let that sit for the moment. But, could you tell me where you live?"

"I think that I already have, Frank. This is my home, right here. You are standing on my property. It's been my property for over a hundred and fifty years."

"But Miss Bean, this property is owned by the university and has been for a long time. Laura, you've taken courses here. How old is the university—they just had some kind of centennial, didn't they?"

Frank turns to look at his partner, Laura Santolin, who has been standing close behind him all the time. Transfixed by Frank's interrogation of Emily Bean, Laura is clearly taken by surprise at a question directed to her. She hesitates, her face appearing a bit whiter, pastier, than it normally should. Then she stutters out a response.

"Yes ... yes, they just did. Thornton U's over 125 years old now. And Wilson Hall, the land we're standing on right here, it was part of the original land purchase. The Presbyterians bought several farms in this area in the 1880s and it was chartered as Thornton University of the Mid-West over 125 years ago."

"Well, you see, that's just the point, Laura. Are you feeling ok, child? You don't look quite right. Why don't you have a seat on this bench?" replies Emily.

"I'm fine, Miss Bean. Now, is there some way that you can clarify your claim?" Laura's right hand brushes hair back from over her forehead. "Thornton University has owned this land for a long time."

"Yes, my dear, they have. But not for long enough. And they purchased this land from people who did not own it. And, as I am sure both of you know, if you buy something from someone who does not own it, then it is not really yours, is it?"

"Yes, Miss Bean. I guess we do know that. But you still aren't being quite clear enough here. How is it that you think you owned the property?" Frank rejoins.

"I owned the property because I owned the property, Frank Elliot. I lived on it and helped farm it from 1801 until my parents died of influenza in the winter epidemic of 1822; then it was mine outright. I was their only child—Allan and Eleanor Bean's only child. And I ploughed it and sowed it and harvested it and sweat over it and walked on it and laughed with its dirt between my fingers and toes for another forty years. I raised cattle and I raised sheep and I sang with this land in my heart and it sang with me, Mr. Elliot. I had some hired hands from time to time, but most of the time I did it myself. This land is my land; it was then, Mr. Elliot, and it is my land now, 'cause I never sold it to no-one and I never gave it to no-one. Never. It's mine."

"But Miss Bean, Emily. Try to give us a straight answer here. There is no way that you are over two hundred years old which you'd have to be if we were to believe your story. I mean you said your parents died in, let's see," Frank glances at his notes, "1822. And you worked for another forty years—so you were sixty or so then. What happened then, after those forty years? What happened then?"

"Yes. Yes, what happened then? What did happen then?" Emily's posture tenses and her eyes look past Frank, as if searching the distance for something to say, as if far would yield the words that near did not. Two men stand in a doorway where her gaze settles. One is short; the other, huge. "Well, that's the part that's difficult. Difficult to tell, and more difficult to believe. I'll give you the short version. Maybe you'll want to hear the longer version later. Maybe not. It was 1862. A time of war. The great rebellion to the south. And a time of invention. Armoured ships that could travel beneath the sea. Great balloons that could float high up into the sky. And guns that could fire bullets over and over and over again. But a good time to be a farmer who wanted to sell some of her crop. There was an endless need. And one day, it was well into the evening, I was returning to the farm with the double team, yoked, though that was going out of fashion then. I always felt more in control with a yoked team. I'd dropped off a load of grist at the train station, over east near the army base, and I was returning home. When suddenly, there was a bright light, like a thousand coal oil lamps, and the horse and wagon and the earth itself—they vanished, they were just no more. I was taken away, by this unknown power, these dark gods, and held captive for nearly, I have figured out, for nearly a hundred and sixty years, at least of my years, though it only seemed a day or so of their time. And then they returned me, a couple weeks ago, put me right down where they took me away I suppose, 'cept now it was on a big piece of cracked hard land, full of weeds and a building that said it was a dance hall, though there was no people dancing. It was all boarded up. There was no music. But I still recognized where I was, the Huron Bluffs to the west, Miller's Hills to the southeast, and I found myself, step by step, right back here. There's a grove of sycamore I planted myself still growing just over there. Used to slaughter a pig each fall for the winter, hang it from one of those trees, big kettle of boiling water just underneath. Yep, this is my land and, after a hundred and sixty years, I have returned to claim it."

"Well. Well, that's quite a story, Miss Bean, but…" Frank does not finish his sentence. There is a metallic crack from behind him, an explosion and the whistle of a bullet. He spins around to see Laura Santolin, eyes rolled up in her head, crumpling to the floor, her 9mm Sig Sauer spinning on the granite of the foyer. And beyond her, two men, one short and agile, the other tall and swarthy, throwing themselves sideways as a gunshot smashes through the doorway between them and thuds into the wall beyond.

Frank leaps up, his gun in his hand and his eyes moving everywhere. Then, partially, slowly, from brain to foot, he starts to relax—it is Laura's dropped gun that probably fired the shot. A single shot. Why that gun was pulled? Why it was off safety? These questions are placed on hold as he moves to his partner. He kneels and puts his hand beneath her head.

"Laura? Laura? Are you ok?"

He can feel a bump and some slickness where his hand touches her scalp. Probably from the fall. Her eyelids begin to flicker. She is coming back.

"Laura?"

"O. O. Frank. God. I … I'm sorry. I must have fainted." Laura's eyes begin to refocus and she looks up at her partner.

"That's no problem, kid. We better get you over to Thornton General, though. You may need a stitch or two, and probably an aspirin, and the rest of the day off." Frank has already removed a white handkerchief from his pocket and is holding it firmly to the spot where Laura's head has hit the floor. Red seeps into the cloth. "And on the way back I'll drop Miss Bean off…"

Frank pauses. He knows even before he glances back to the purple bench.

Miss Emily Allison Bean, borned in 1801, farmer, land

owner, abducted by dark gods during the time of the great civil war to the south, is nowhere to be seen. Like most of the phantoms of this earth in her time or in ours, she has vanished.

- 23 -

A bleedin' mess

On this warm and sunny Friday afternoon, Gabe and Lucky are sitting in silence at the kitchen table in Gabe's drab apartment, each with a beer in hand. Gabe speaks.

"This is one fucked-up mess, man. We ain't got the drugs, we sure as hell ain't got the money, and I've thought of everything I can. If I knew where they had Liz and Jimmy, I'd go there and shoot the fuckers holdin' them and break them out."

"Yeah ... Malley'd have the numbers but we could bring 'em down. The bastards. You know, I know how yah feel, Gabe. I been through somethin' like this; remember, I was married once. Then I came home one afternoon—actually, I guess it was morning, I'd been out all night. Anyways, I came home one morning and Tawni was gone ... just gone. No note. No trace. No nothing. Even her dancing props was gone. I looked around, everywhere, for a couple weeks or more, but never did find her. That was a low point, man. I missed her ... still do. But at least with this—we know what happened to Liz and Jimmy. We know where they are, sort of...! And we'll get them back. Here, let me give Taber another call. Sooner or later he's got to answer. Like I say, answering the phone—that's his business, man."

Lucky picks the receiver up from Gabe's old home phone on the table and punches in a number he reads from a scrap of paper, then takes another swig from his bottle. Faint in the receiver, the phone rings two, three, four times. And then a quick voice, harried, British.

"Yah, who is it?"

"Taber. Is that you, man?"

"Yeah it's me. Hey, is that you Lucky? You goddamned idiot! What a bleedin' mess you got me into, man! Do you wankers know what's going on? Do you?"

"No, man. What're you talkin' about. What's up?"

"What's up, shit-for-brains? What's up? I'll tell you what's up." The voice is frenetic, on some level, terrified. "That snow you sold me. Jesus Christ! There must be ten junkies dead in about a day and a half since I started to unload it. I cut it but it must have been pure shite, man. Either that, or just shite. Crud. Fuckin' cyanide. Two guys in the park died with the bleedin' needles still in their arms. And it's all over the bleedin' place. I even sent a whole bag east. So the cops are all over the scene, man. Everywhere! Even some Feds. And worse than that, both Dalco's boys and Malley's are sniffin' around, asking questions. They're pissed. Where the hell did you get that stuff, Lucky? Were you out of your goddamned mind? I think you sold me my head on a platter. Yours too. Just turn on the TV news—you'll see ambulances and body bags comin' from every shitty flophouse in the city. I am packin' right now and gettin' to hell out of town, man, while the gettin's good. Maybe out of the country, if I can. You and Gabe better do the same. There's a real Dalek shitstorm on right now, man, and it's goin' to get worse before it gets better. Count on it! And the next time you want to do some business, well no way, you loopy waistoid. Fuck you and the horse you rode in on! And fuck the bleedin' stable the horse came from! You hear me?"

Without a word, Lucky sits for a moment with the receiver in his hand. The other end of the line has been slammed shut.

"Gabe, I don't think we can get the dope back man. It's already been moved. And Taber seems a bit pissed. He needs some time. So we're gonna have to come up with some other plan." He pauses. "Do you mind if I watch TV for a minute? There's some news I need to catch up on. It's almost 6 o'clock. And TV always helps me think."

- 24 -

Not enough cannibals

On this warm and sunny Friday afternoon, the common room of Wilson Hall at Thornton University is buzzing with activity. With a televised announcement by Dean Henry MacLean imminent, university officials and professors have gathered and are discussing matters old and new, topics erudite and trivial. Like a spoonful of honey near a hill of ants, the nidus of this motley gathering is easy to spot—a free bar has been set up near the row of windows on one side and, as you probably know, following a longstanding tradition, professors of any merit or rank never pass on an opportunity for free liquor. TV cameras, lights, a dais and lectern are opposite. The esteemed crowd mingles and a din of conversation fills the air.

Tom Skyler, a senior English Education professor, is at the bar.

"Yes. I would like a Manhattan. But if you could use dry vermouth, please, and rum instead of whiskey, that would be perfect. O, and no bitters. I don't care for the taste. And could you put some olives in it?"

"Ok, sir. No problem. There you are. Enjoy." The bartender hands the drink to Tom.

"Thank you."

The Prince of Leroy

Connor Talbot, new to the PhD ranks and to Thornton University, joins the scene.

"I'll have a bottle of Guinness, please."

"There you are, sir."

"Thanks." He places a generous tip in an oversized brandy snifter on the bar.

"So, you are new to the Faculty, I gather," asks Tom, looking briefly at the tip jar and then back to Connor.

"Yes, I am. Dr. Connor Talbot. I start teaching this summer, in July." The two men shake hands.

"Pleased to meet you, sir. I'm Tom Skyler. And your area of study—is that journalism, communications?"

"No, no. I'm elementary school—maths and science. My research has all been in gender studies, actually. Attitudes towards the maths and sciences according to gender, where and when attitudes change, why more girls aren't going on in those fields. When they turn off. Why. The effects of role models—males, females—in teaching, in the media. The influence of occupations, attitudes at home. That kind of thing."

"Well, you have certainly come to the right Faculty for that kind of thing, I suspect. I'm sure you will enjoy yourself here. And some days, they even serve a great Manhattan, as long as you give them clear instructions."

"I guess that was quite the ruckus around here this morning, a gunshot and everything. I hadn't arrived yet. I heard that the Dean was fortunate he wasn't shot?"

"Oh ... not really, Connor. Once you get to know him better, you'll realize that the bullet would probably have slid right off."

Connor smiles. "Still a kind of bad incident though!"

"Certainly bad for the wall. But it's already been patched up, I think, hidden from view."

"Really. ... Wow. Speaking of views, the view here is wonderful. What a room this is—with this floor to ceiling glass and the old limestone! And the panels of stained glass at the top—what do they have, writing of some sort?"

"Yes, it is a marvelous room. The Wilson Common Room, to be exact. And the writing in the stained glass is all script, quotations, poems, from ancient languages—Hittite, Tocharian, Iroquoian. Dead languages. The room swims in the words of the dead, Connor. Nicholson A. Wilson was a turn-of-the-century entrepreneur, a local robber baron, of sorts, railroads and shipping—made a fortune sending supplies south during the American Civil War—and he was an amateur but dedicated linguist. He searched the world to make a record of dying languages. And, as you might guess, he was a significant benefactor to the university. Recent research is showing that his wife, Jean, was a significant factor as well, and apparently she made a superb carrot muffin."

"It is quite a remarkable space."

"Of course, that was back when amateurs regularly contributed to the academy."

"Not any more...?"

"No. It's pretty much a closed club now. You have to have the charméd letters and those are only disseminated by those who already have them. It's all about controlling the herd."

"I guess I hadn't really thought about it that way. ... Now, that's the Moira River down there, right?"

"Yes. Past the lawn and down into the woods and ravine. That's the Moira. River of fate, of sorrows. It snakes all through the campus and the town, although in a month or so, when the trees thicken with leaves and the spring run-off dies away, you will hardly be able to see it. Always a comfort, though. Always there, rarely seen, and never the same. Kind of like universities and Faculties of Education, you know."

"Yes, I suppose. And we are right near the forks of the Moira, right?"

"The forks are very close by, just to the east where Dundas crosses the river; there has been a settlement around here since ancient time. The Indigenous peoples simply called this place 'the forks'—it was revered as a sacred spot where two great rivers married and became one. And many felt that this city should have been named Forktown, not as it is after some long forgotten British military surveyor. Of course, that would have made this Fork U., but that's another matter."

"Look. Several birds just glided in."

"Ducks. Mallards, I would guess from here. Woods and Browns also nest along the river. And Canada geese. And just about every other native bird you can name. In fact, if you look over there—see that red bird—that's a Cardinal hopping about, and the group of small dark brown ones are Swallows, of course. And in the tree over there, Starlings—there are always Starlings. Aggressive as hell, they are. Foreigners. And that's a female Robin picking at the ground—carnivores, and they're bossy too. Lots of birds. I guess it must be spring, Connor?"

"I guess you know your local birds."

"Yes, in some way. ... Do you have the time?"

"Yes. It's about a quarter-to-four."

"Good. The big announcement, *aka* the press conference, won't be for another half hour or so. Time to have another drink. Or two!"

"And there they go. The Swallows. All rising in formation, in rhythm. God. Like a choreographed wind devil, or something. They really are remarkable, aren't they?"

"Yes. Yes. Pure magic, I think. You have got to wonder, though—how do they do that? How in hell do they do that?"

"Well, their bones are very light, porous, and the curve of their wings acts as an aerofoil increasing air pressure beneath…"

"No. No, Connor. Not fly. I don't mean fly. I mean, how in hell do they sing? Where do they get their songs? Where comes the courage? The unburdened art? While, here, men sit and hear each other groan. … And but to think is to be full of sorrow."

"Oh! Oh I misunderstood you."

"Well, it probably won't be the last time. But, speaking of singing birds, look. The biggest bird of all has just arrived. There's the Dean. And his family. That means that things will start to heat up a bit now that all of the key fowl are here, Connor."

Tom turns to the bartender who, on sight, has started to prepare the mix.

"Thank you, good sir. You make a fine Manhattan."

"So, Professor Skyler, you think it's a bit of a performance, do you? All an act?" Connor is caught somewhere between amused and alarmed. Wary and unsure, but also charmed.

"Yes, you might say that. Quite a shoooe! Education and politics and shoooe business, as old Ed used to say. But that's probably well before your time, isn't it? But yes, favours and grants and endowments. And perceputations, as I call them—a real song and dance. Like the birds, Connor. Only maybe more dangerous animals, fierce at times—the smaller the pit, you know, the fiercer the snakes. You'll see, when the TV cameras start to roll, just see how many professors flock behind the Dean's shoulders. Like fallen angels trying to dance on the head of a pin."

"I suppose they want to feel part of changing the world, don't you think?"

"Of course. We are all out to change the world, to storm the beaches of social injustice and bring our vision, our truth, to the lowly natives, whether they want it or not. As long as we can do it at a distance, of course, to avoid the arrows when they start to fly."

"But, it's really in our DNA, isn't it! To stand at a lectern and voice our opinions—to articulate our views, to profess our ideas to the world. Every professor has a mission!"

"Yes ... at times, though ... too many missionaries, and not enough cannibals!"

"Oh. Is that Wesley Terranian? I've heard of him. He's got some new book out, doesn't he? Getting rave reviews. What is it—ahh, *Hickory Tunes*?"

Now standing at the bar is Wesley Terranium, an old and weathered man with snow white hair. His clothes are rumpled and well-worn and might have been more comfortable in some other decade. In that regard, I suppose, he really looks like all professors are imagined to, even the females...

"Yes. *Hickory Tunes* it is." Tom responds. "And, quite frankly, it's got most of the Faculty miffed a bit, you know. It's a popular press thing, being read by a wide readership. With absurd claims—that everyone involved in education from principals to directors to deans should spend part of their day in an actual classroom, actually teaching, and that only two subjects need to be taught—Literature and Phys. Ed. And, well, speak of the devil, and who should appear!"

"*Apage Satanas* is the phrase, Professor Skyler. Good afternoon, and good afternoon to you as well Professor Talbot. Welcome to our little den of inequities, good sir. I see you are getting the lay of our land from one who knows it well. *Hic sunt dracones*, you know." Wes Terranium speaks in a raspy but firm voice.

"So, what brings you out to such a public affair, Wes? I am surprised to see you here."

"Well, Tom, I am a bit surprised myself. The simple answer, I guess, it's not everywhere you can get a free Guinness."

"It's an honour to meet you, sir. Please call me Connor."

"Very well, Connor. So I see you and Dr. Skyler deep in discussion."

"Yes, Dr. Skyler and I were talking about this and that, academic pursuits, and probing the big questions like … the role of the professor, and whether or not life has any meaning."

"A somewhat irrelevant question, I should think—life's all we have, meaning or not!"

"That … and we were discussing the birds, Wes." Tom quickly interjects to diffuse the oncoming sophistry in the air.

"Dr. Terranian, I must confess I haven't had the opportunity to read *Hickory Tunes* yet."

"Well, that'll give you something to do this summer, Connor. Actually, it's my old book, now. Though I'm still promoting it—trade edition is out in a couple weeks. But I'm on to new things."

"New worlds to conquer. I guess the guilty never rest, do they, Wes?"

"Well, you might know more about that than I, Tom."

"'A hit, a very palpable hit.' So what are you up to now, Wes?"

"I'm writing a novel. Trying to put some of my theories about English and literature into practice!"

"A novel. What's it about?" asks Connor, quite enamored of this academic star.

"I don't know yet. I just started writing and most of the pages are blank."

"But I thought, Dr. Terranian, that you are noted for saying that 'literature is useless.'"

"I did, Dr. Talbot. I did. And it's true. Literature is useless. I still believe that, more than ever, I think."

"Then, why would you be writing a novel?"

"Because my young scholar, the best things in life, the greatest things, are useless. In the purest sense of the word, useless. When you can't take some thing and use it for some menial task, some political expediency to subjugate the world, or save it, that's when that thing becomes greater than everything else around it. Larger than life. That's why stories are so important, Dr. Talbot. That's why we need poetry. And song and dance and sport and love. And the *Hamlet* you're fond of quoting, Tom, or your Keats—'Thou wast not born for death, immortal Bird.' They're the only magic we have, the stuff that dreams are made on, filling our drab world with wonder and magic and "faery lands forlorn." Like the flight of those birds you've been watching. And the songs they sing."

"And so, kids in schools should study only English and Phys. Ed., isn't that what you claim in *Hickory Tunes*, Wes?" notes Tom.

"Right you are. And with the emphasis on English writings. One thing I know is that fiction is the closest we can get to truth, if truth exists at all. Immersion in fiction is what children need. I guess that idea has touched a nerve in a few of our colleagues, hasn't it?"

"But, Dr. Terranian," Connor notes. "What about math and science? Space travel, cancer research?"

"What about them! They would all happen. You can't tell me that some dull stuff a kid reads in a Grade 10 Science text has any impact on what that kid discovers in some high tech neurophysics lab in post-doc studies or in an industrial research facility somewhere. Colleges could have a sorting out year—like the cap they use to get into Hogwarts. Let students decide what they want to study when they are old enough to do it. So they wouldn't be deadened by school like they are now, bored into drugs and death and law school."

"Ahh, at last! It looks like the crowd is gathering. It must be time," interjects Tom with a hint of relief. He knows when a Terrarium rant is swelling up like a mid-summer storm.

"Ah. So it is. Very good, then. I must get on with the business of the day, Gentlemen. All the best and we will resume this conversation later, I am sure. And read my book, Dr. Talbot. Everyone needs to read my book." Wes turns and begins to work his way through the crowd toward the dais.

"Take care, Wes. ... He is quite the character! What'd you think, Connor?"

"To be honest, I am not sure what to think. I am not sure if I have just met a genius or a madman."

"Both, I should think. Both. I never know myself whether he is full of an iconoclastic vision for the world, or just full of shit. And speaking of that, shit ... the bar's closed. But here's the Dean. And look, Connor, look at all the heads dancing behind the podium. All the buzzards have landed. And there, there's Terranium, and look what he's doing!

As the Dean speaks to the television cameras, Wes Terranian can be seen among the crowd behind him holding a copy of *Hickory Tunes* right above the Dean's head for all the world to see.

- 25 -

News Centre Now

"**I can tell you one thing,**" Gabe opens a bottle of beer and sits at the kitchen table. "Even when I get Jimmy and Liz back, our lives—yours and mine—ain't going to be worth a pinch of coonshit. At least not anywhere around here, anywhere Malley can reach. We are screwed this time. What in hell ever put it in our heads to do such a stupid thing? God."

An ad withers away as the TV pops to life, then the intro to the 6 o'clock news, a techno beat under images of local news vehicles and the station's reporter-personalities rushing from crisis to crisis.

"Good evening. I'm Trent Morris and this is *News Centre Now*. Big news on the local front, where the rash of drug-related deaths continues. Two more bodies were retrieved from the Morch Tenements today, bringing the death total to eight in the last three days. Preliminary reports indicate that all were the result of heroin overdoses. In addition, according to hospital authorities, drug-related admissions to emergency and critical-care facilities at Thornton's three local hospitals have increased by twenty-two percent since Wednesday evening. Dr. Carl Shreyer, an expert in the field of alcohol and drug abuse, suggests that an unusually pure quality of Fentanyl-Heroin must have been released into the streets recently. Its effects are just as drastic, and deadly, on experienced users as on newcomers. Police have stepped up their efforts to discover the source of this new influx and are distributing pamphlets and posters throughout the city cautioning against the use of any drugs. Especially heroin."

The visuals cut away from the News Anchor to show ambulance attendants carrying body-bags out of buildings and rolling them on gurneys into ambulances. Then a file photo of Dr. Shreyer and a cut-back to the Anchor who shifts on to a story about the mysterious murder of a truck driver.

"What a bunch of losers, eh Gabe! I tell ya, you pump that shit into yourself and, sooner or later, the reaper's gonna call."

"Yeah. It's why I want to get Jimmy out of this place. Get away from all that crap on the street. So, from what Taber said, any chance that this mess is connected to the stuff we took?" Gabe motions with his beer bottle toward the television.

"Could be. I don't know, man." Lucky speaks furtively. "Taber may behave like an idiot at times, but usually he knows his stuff, especially about drugs, how to cut it. If he cut it too rich, he'd just be burning money"

"Well, I agree with the idiot part ... as to what else he knows ... well?"

The eyes of both men shift back to the ambient hues of the television screen. A man with white hair is now speaking in front of a crowd. Immediately behind him are his wife and three children, all daughters. The man is speaking about money.

"MacLean Insurance and Real Estate is intending to match the dollar amounts of all of the donations that we are able to generate with the four fund-raisers we are organizing in the next few months—beginning with the Auction for Action Charity, then the Spring Garden Party, the July Tea at the Hunt, and the September Autumnal Ride. With the organizational support from M.I.R.E., with the assistance of our Alumni and Faculty, and with the encouragement of my beautiful wife, Kelly, and our three lovely daughters, Glenda, Rory and Carren, we expect to raise over two million dollars in support of literacy research—and M.I.R.E. will match that donation, dollar for dollar."

The image cuts back to the newsreader: "That was Dean Henry MacLean of the Faculty of Education at Thornton University announcing the kick-off to a major fundraising campaign to support the construction of a new centre for literacy research at the university. This centre should make Thornton University one of the world leaders in the research and study of literacy and related sociological and neurological discontinuities, with its findings to be regularly published in a new international journal, JOLT, A Journal of Literacy and Teaching. The journal will be supported by other corporate sponsors, yet to be announced. This project should also provide significant construction employment when ground-breaking begins in the fall..."

"Shut it off, Lucky. Shut it off. I think I got a plan that might just get us out of all this trouble. A plan—it's dangerous, risky, but it might work. And, at this point, we don't have much to lose, do we?"

"Nothing at all, man. So, let me in. Open the door, Gabe, and let me in."

"Well, Lucky, you know they say the best way to fight fire is with fire, and you know there's been a lot of fire in my family, Lucky. But not much of it ever come to any good. Well maybe that's about to change. Just maybe, it's about time we lit our own fire, and put it to use for our own good."

Lucky draws a Bic lighter from his pocket, holds it up and flicks it into flame like concert-goers used to before cell phones arrived.

"I'm with you there, man. I'm with you there. What have ya got?"

- 26 -

Hello, Mr. Dalco

The well-dressed Paul Corrino sits atop a picnic table near the parking area of Berris Thorn Park, a small inner city green space named after the founder of the city, a British army surveyor. With old mature oak and maple trees and a population of squirrels, chipmunks, a variety of birds and an occasional wino, Paul thinks, as the homeless used to be labelled, the park is a peaceful sanctuary inside the city's active hub. His blue Buick nearby, Corrino has just started to smoke a cigar, looking like someone who is nervous trying not to look nervous. A large gold-plated lighter sits on the table within reach. A black Lexus pulls up and Paul stands and drops the cigar, crushing it with his right foot. Three men in light raincoats get out of the Lexus; a fourth man, the driver, remains behind its wheel. Birds over the park seem to change their flight paths and a couple squirrels high-tail it into trees.

Frederick Dalco, a wiry man in his sixties, is the head of an east coast mob family that deals in all that is illegal under God's sun and, as is usually the case with such organizations, generally filters its gains through apparently legitimate means such as *Voyageur's End*; Dalco is a man who possesses all the power and ill-gotten prestige that a life of amoral intimidation and violence can reap.

Frederick Dalco Junior is Dalco's eldest son and is a short-tempered, malevolent individual—on an office memo of his father's identity, he would be c.c.; whether cognizant or not, he carries a vicious streak that is intent on exceeding his Daddy's darkness in resolve and reputation.

Connie Torrence is the third to egress the Lexus; tall and lean, he is one of Dalco's guard dogs, quiet and obedient until given a command, and then, brutally efficient and inexorable.

Paul Corrino steps forward to meet Frederick Dalco.

"Hello, Mr. Dalco. Good to see you in Thornton. Wish it was under better circumstances," Paul Corrino puts out his right hand and shakes firmly with his boss.

"Hi, Paul. Do you know Connie Torrence? He's in from the coast. Wanted to take a look at the operation first hand."

"Hello, Mr. Torrence. Nice to meet you." Torrence nods, but neither speaks nor offers his hand.

"And you've met Junior, my son, before."

"Yes. How are you, Frederick?"

The four men stand there for a moment, all seeming nervous now, each glancing at a different horizon.

"So, Paul, give me an update on the, uh, circumstances. What have you found out?"

"To be honest, Mr. Dalco, not a helluva lot, pardon my French. The driver for Logos is out of the picture. He never said anything, but I'm not sure if he ever knew anything, anyways. We've had some luck tracing down the old truck they used as a ram. What we've got so far is ... it used to belong to a guy named Jim Black and then, after he killed himself, fourteen, fifteen years ago—he blew his brains out with a shotgun after he killed his wife—it was used by his son, a Mike Black, but it hadn't been on the road for four or five years. It had been stored, unlicensed, in behind Black's carpet store in town here, Tom and Mike's Carpet, on Dundas, not far from *Voyageur's End*, but according to what Black told the cops, it was stolen a month ago, towed out of the lot in the middle of the night. He didn't even bother to report it, so he says, because it wasn't worth anything. It was a piece of junk and he was glad to get rid of it, for free."

"Smells like a fish story to me," grunts Dalco. "And if it smells like fish ... well, get the colatura ready!"

"Yeah." Paul responds. "I hear you. I'll get some of the boys to go see Black and check on that. As to the rest—the junky death toll is up to nine now, with three or four more in hospitals, I gather, in serious shape. Whoever cut the stuff, didn't have a damn clue what they was doing. Them junkies was prickin' nearly pure heroin—in a couple cases, they were dead instantly, before they got the needle out. The cops aren't really pushing this too hard from what I can tell—another dead junky or hosebag ain't no skin off their ass. Now if it was some rich guy's kid who was dying, that'd be a different story. But the stuff was strictly pumped in the downtown blocks and subsidy projects—it didn't show up on the rich side of town or over at the college. At least, for right now ... and I've heard nothin' for the last day or so. So maybe the pusher clued in, or maybe he got rid of it all already...?"

"But no idea who grabbed it from the Logos truck? Or who that pusher was, right?"

"No, there hasn't been a peep from the streets. I got the regular feelers and rewards out. But nothing so far on who stole it or sold it."

"Well, I think that Mike Black might be worth droppin' in on. Like I said, that smells like a fish to me. As to the cops, well, if they're not lookin' too hard, good. The more they stay the hell out of our way, the better. You don't have any guesses as to how someone would have known the smack was on that Logos truck, do you?"

"No ... no I don't, Mr. Dalco. It don't sound like the driver had any word about what he was delivering. Maybe they just got lucky. I don't know."

"Yeah," Junior barks. "Like they belonged to a reading club and needed some new books to read, right, and just happened to hit the truck with six million dollars of dope inside."

"Easy, Junior. There'll be time for you to get fired up. Paul, do you know a guy named Jerry Malley, at all?"

"Uh, no, no, not at all. Well, I guess I should say, I've heard of him. But I've never met him. He's a local contractor around town, dabbles into some different business from time to time."

"Yeah, he does dabble as you say. His name was passed along as someone we might want to check out. He's got his fingers into an awful lot of things. But, maybe first things first, the guy named Black. This is important so I want you to take care of it, personally, ok. Take a couple of the boys along, T.J. and Al, and pay this Mike Black a call. A personal call. Have a serious talk with him. Don't push it all the way but make sure that he knows what all the way is, ok. Ok, Paul?"

"Yeah ... I'll get right on it. I'll round up T.J. and Al—we'll go over there tomorrow, Monday at the latest if the store's not open on Sunday."

"Good. And I'll meet with you—what's this, Saturday—I'll meet with you Tuesday. You can let me know what Black had to say by then. And whatever else you can, find out. Keep givin' out the usual carrots. And we won't meet here. How about the municipal parking garage, level three. East side. Ok? See you there. Tuesday, around 6:00. We'll get to the bottom of this, Paul. We got to. There's a lot at stake!"

"And what about the Leroy, Dad?" asks Junior.

"Oh, yeah, that's another thing, Paul. Send out some warnings whenever you can, warnin' the locals to stay away from the Leroy—I gather from our fat doofus at the End that the little dump's been givin' us some problems. I told him I'd look into it, so we're gonna start puttin' the squeeze on them from all directions."

"Ok, Mr. Dalco. Will do."

"Good. See yuh Tuesday."

The three men turn and retrace their steps to the Lexus. It backs up and spins slightly on the gravel out of the lot. Paul watches it go and, even from a distance, you can see his body deflate and some degree of relaxation return. He turns to the picnic table, retrieves his lighter, feels its weight in his hand, flicks it into a flame that a sudden breeze blows away, returns it to his pocket, slides behind the wheel of his Buick, punches the start button and, at a safe distance, follows the Lexus out of the parking lot. Squirrels slowly re-emerge onto the greening grasses of the park and, overhead, a flock of swallows swirls through the afternoon air and coasts down toward the Moira.

- 27 -

A place called Leroy

"**I'll have a coffee, and some toast, Blue.** Coffee and some corn flakes for you, Deed?"

"Mmhmm."

Dom and Deed sit at the counter; Blue leans on it from behind and Oz stands to the side, all drinking coffee on this late Saturday morning.

Blue places a couple of thick diner mugs in front of Dom and Deed. "So what's up, boys—had any new dreams Dominic?"

"No—but that one about being dead almost came true yesterday, darlin'."

"Really ... do tell."

"Well, like we told you the other day, me 'n Deed are plannin' to be teachers. The university's offering a special plan to get regular folks, especially Natives, Indians, into the program. So we was over at the college yesterday getting the forms and we nearly got shot."

"Shot? You're kiddin'! With a gun? What are you talking about?" Blue and Oz chime in together. During Dom's flurry of storytelling, Johnny enters from the 'L' and listens from the far end of the counter.

"Well, we'd just picked up the forms that needed to be filled out, the list of certificates and stuff we need to provide, and we were standing near the front doors watchin' two cops hasslin' some old woman. Then suddenly one of the cops, a young woman, pulls out her gun and, like, I didn't know whether she was going to blow away her partner or the old lady or herself, maybe everyone, but I was pretty sure that she was gonna let loose. But then, just as she's about to squeeze the trigger, she starts twitching like she'd stuck her finger in a socket, and drops to the floor, and slam, bam, her gun goes off and the bullet went right between Deed and me. So close it whispered my name in my ear when it went by and, well, I tell yah, I won't have to see the barber this month. That's the closest I ever come to being shot and the closest I ever want to. Trust me on that! Deed, too!"

Deed nods to affirm Dom's story.

"Wow, that's pretty strange boys," says Blue. "You'd think the college'd be about the last place you'd have to worry about getting shot."

"Well, you can think again there, beautiful."

"But you guys are ok?" asks Oz. "You've both come through some tough scrapes before."

"Yeah, we're fine, ain't we Deed?" Dom nudges great Deed on the arm. "In fact, as it turns out, it was almost, kinda, a good thing. We got to meet the head of the place, the Dean. And he was very concerned about us, so concerned, in fact, that he said after the trauma of being shot at—trauma he called it—he would admit us right into the program, no interview necessary, no exam or written essay or the other stuff all the others had to do, as long as we didn't talk to nobody about the shooting. And as long as we filled in the application form and got the right documents. So there you are Blue, Oz. We're gonna be in the program. Come this fall, we start our training. And we get paid for it too, a full ride. Me and Deed. Teachers."

"Well, I am without words, boys. I don't know how in hell you do it, but you guys do get into some of the most interesting situations," Blue says with a smile, shaking her head. "And sometimes you even manage to get out of them relatively unscathed, too!"

'Well, I must admit, I was a bit concerned about this one, 'specially the interview part of it, where they ask you all kinds of things about yourself—what your beliefs are, your philosophies, about your background, life growing up in the tribe, what technological skills you got, and all of that. I wasn't so worried about myself, mind you—I figured I could string 'em along—but I didn't know if old Deed could carry it off."

"Growin' up in the tribe, Dom? Do you have to be a Native?"

"Yeah, the program's mostly for Indians, and other minorities. It's called the 'R & R' program, 'Re-enter and Recover,' sponsored by the government, as the brochure says, to try to get more representatives from outsider groups into teaching positions. And while Deed and me figure there's nobody more outsider than us, we decided that we better set that in stone, if you know what I mean. So Deed and me have this friend who owns a garage out on the Rez. He owes us a couple favours, so we're headin' out there this afternoon to pick up some certificates and signatures and stuff."

"Why does this not surprise me, little man?" Blue comments with a nod of her head.

"You are just about lookin' at two pure blooded ... what are we, Deed—Ojibwa?"

"Mmm."

"Yeah. *Me'Sherken*—that means 'teacher' in Ojibwa. Pretty good, eh, Blue?"

"You never cease to amaze."

"*Besh na geget*, boys," the Prince steps forward. Angus is at his heels but now gravitates toward Dom and Deed, each of whom provides the necessary attention a dog demands and deserves. Blue arrives with their breakfast including an extra piece of toast. "At least that's close to what they say out on the Rez when they're wishing you good luck. And like I said before, I hope this works out 'cause I think you'd be good for schools. Something a bit different."

"A bit different is a bit of an understatement, Johnny," says Oz. "I'd say the schools better count their pencils or they won't have any left; and they'll find Dom sellin' them for twice what they're worth out in the corner of the schoolyard at recess."

"Hey, Ozzy, you might just have a plan there. I must remember that. If it works out, I could let you in on the action ... for a fee, of course. That may be hard to remember, though, with an empty cup here, darlin'."

"Got you, Shorty. Here's a cup for you, too, Prince. And refills all around."

"Ahh, thank you, Blue. A little taste of heaven—what do you put in this coffee, Prince. It's like something from another world."

"Oh, as you know, Dom, that's a Leroy secret ... one of many, I suppose. If I ever told you, well, you know what might have to happen..."

"God, I hope they have Rainy's coffee in heaven, or I wouldn't want to hang around there too long."

"Oh, you probably won't have to worry about that, my

friend," quips Oz. "In fact, I'm guessing, most of us won't. Your uncle, Johnny, old Jake, always argued that most of us just ain't good enough to be saved alongside all those righteous church-goin' folk. We drink too much, swear too much, gamble too much, we got too many deals running on the side. On the road to those pearly gates, we'd probably get distracted by some sure thing and they'd lock up shop before we got inside. Dom, here, would be chippin' pearls outta that gate to hock somewhere else. The only taste guys like us will probably ever know of heaven is right here, this coffee."

"I hear you, brother. Loud and clear—pearls, eh—I can understand that," Dom chirps, tearing off a piece of toast.

"It's like, there's the good, the bad, and the somewhere-in-between, like most of us. The Leroy crowd. Jake always used to say that he figured there must be some other place, some halfway house for those of us who ain't quite good enough for heaven, but not quite rotten enough for hell."

"Yep, you're saying somethin' there, Oz. And maybe it will be right here, won't it. For most of us, heaven'll be a place called Leroy," Blue says in an earnest, wistful voice, and smiles at the end.

"I'll drink a cup to that, Blue," Johnny says slowly, thoughtfully. "I'll happily drink a cup to that."

Angus snarfs down a crust of toast from Dom and casually lays down with the deep and contented sigh that only dogs can know.

- 28 -

The games are over

A black Lexus can be seen stopping outside of Rainy's; three men get out from the back seat. The driver and another in the front seat remain in the car. The trio advances to the door. One is a large man in a charcoal suit, the general manager of the Voyageur's End, Charlie T. Walker. The other two are both handsome, well-built men, dark haired, in black suits. One appears as an older copy of the other; this is Frederick E. Dalco and the other, his twenty-something son, Frederick Dalco Junior.

On Johnny's command, Angus retreats to the shadow of the 'L' and lays down facing the arrivals; intermittently, he emits a low growl.

"Hey," blurts Dom, "I think I'm seeing double, and I'm not just looking at you for a change, Charlie."

"Well, gentlemen, welcome to the Leroy." Johnny places his hand briefly on Dom's shoulder; then steps forward, relaxed but on guard. "And what brings you to Rainy's this fine day? Did you change your mind about that cup of coffee, Charlie?"

"To hell with you and your coffee, March. Have you met Mr.

Frederick Dalco and his son, Frederick Junior? They're both staying at *Voyageur's End* for a few days and I wanted them to see you for what you are."

"Really. Well, we've just been talking about heaven, Charlie, but I guess we can change locations. Mr. Dalco and I have met, though only once or twice I can thankfully say. But we've got a ticket or two between us. He tried to buy the Leroy, Charlie, just a bit before your time, when my Uncle Jake was dying. I suppose this must be your kid, Dalco—he looks just like you, and that ain't necessarily good in a lotta ways. I hope he doesn't act like you."

"That may be something you don't want to find out," Freddy Jr. steps toward Johnny but is held back by his father's hand. Oz instinctively moves toward Johnny's side.

"Easy, Junior," interjects Dalco. "Relax for now."

"Well Freddy, looks like he's got that same edge you used to have. So," Johnny continues his thrust. "I hear there's a bunch of drug addicts droppin' dead all over town from bad dope. That some of your work?"

"I wouldn't know what you're talking about, March. No idea. But how's life around the old Leroy shithole? I see you're still hangin' around with the same bunch of hand-me-downs as your uncle used to. I guess, some creatures just never learn to crawl out of the swamp. Anyway, I'm not here to exchange pleasantries. Charlie, here, tells me that you're playing some games, billing the End for things done over here and so on. Well, the games are over, March. One more discrepancy and things will get a little rough around here, if you know what I mean. Some of the city inspectors might have to take a closer look at your operation, your kitchen, the cleanliness of your rooms. Some of the paperwork that a motel needs processed in order to stay open might not get done. You catch my drift, March? The games are over."

"Would you like a cup of coffee, Freddy? Many people say that it's the best coffee in the city."

"No thanks. I'll pass on the coffee, March."

"Well, I don't know if there's anything else I can get for you Freddy. I don't deal in fourteen year olds, you know. Little boys on leashes."

"Screw you, March. You know damn well that was trumped up. No charges were ever laid. You know it."

"How about you, Charlie, or can't you speak with your head shoved up there?" Johnny motions toward Dalco.

"What the hell are you talking about?"

"I see a lot of your thugs cruisin' around town the last couple of days, Freddy? And now you show up in this part of the country yourself. Must be something big happening? Somebody got the squeeze on you for something? One of your big buildings fall down? Well, you know what they say, Freddy, they just don't seem to build them like they used to. You can't trust a room you walk into anymore."

"Go to hell, March. "

'What's the matter, Freddy. I touch some nerve. Nudge some I-beam somewhere. Sure you won't have that cup of coffee? It might calm you down, you know. How about you Junior? A hot cup of Rainy's might melt that grim look."

"I'll show you what to do with your fuckin' coffee…"

"Park it, Junior … for now. C'mon Charlie, Junior I've seen enough here. You've been warned, March. The games are over. I'm not done with the Leroy. You can count on it."

The three men turn, move briskly out of the door and back to the Lexus. It reverses quickly and darts across Dundas to the End.

"Maybe, Freddy, maybe. Or maybe I'm not done with you." Johnny speaks quietly.

"That young man gives me a chill, Prince," Blue says slowly. "It's like there's nothing behind those eyes."

"Yeah, he is a Dalco, all right."

Oz stands at the Prince's side. Angus growls.

"He is that, Prince. He's a bold dog. But you know the old saying—I've seen old dogs, and I've seen bold dogs, but I ain't never seen an old bold dog. I can't help but wonder what the future holds for Junior! I know if I was him, I wouldn't be stockin' up on birthday candles!"

"I won't argue with you there, Oz," Johnny responds.

"Seems to be somethin' that runs in that family," Dom pipes in. "Born to swim in shit, and enjoy it."

"Yeah—his Granddaddy's the one who did in old Max," says Oz. "No proof, of course. ... But, if you got some kind of plan cookin', Prince, let me know how I can help."

"Thanks, Oz. I will."

"Count me and Deed in too," says Dom. "And Angus is willin' to help out if his growl means anything. Dogs just know, don't they!"

"Geez. You really got in their grill, Johnny," Blue says with concern. "Blunt and in their face!"

"Well, I've said it before, Blue. It's the only language guys like Dalco understand. Otherwise they'll run right over you and never look back. They get their kicks outta bumps in the road. Like Oz said, old man Bowlie tried to be reasonable with the Dalcos and take a look at what's left out back. Ashes and rubble."

"But Frederick Dalco is a dangerous guy, isn't he—you sure pushed some buttons?"

The Prince of Leroy

"Well, Blue, he's stuck a lot of buttons on himself and some need pushing from time to time. And as to dangerous—well, we're all dangerous when we have to be. Sometimes even when we don't." Johnny pauses, staring out the windows toward the End. There are thoughts. A plan that needs to be worked out. And quickly too. Dalco in town means trouble and Johnny senses a desperation about him right now, and desperation makes people do stupid, dangerous things. Especially people with power. A plan. A Leroy plan. There were things Johnny knew about the Dalcos. A situation. A trap sprung, with witnesses, cops, who knows? Timing would be the key. The exact moment. There might be a darkness to this. Danger. Even sacrifice. But maybe light too. Like Burning Day. If I could read Johnny's mind exactly, I could tell this, write it down right here, but I cannot read his thoughts any more than I can read yours. Or you mine. You know what I mean, don't you?

The Prince moves away from that darkness, for the moment, and speaks aloud, "For right now, friends, it's time for another coffee. Let's drink to forget that bunch. Pour 'em out, Blue. On the Leroy! C'mon Angus, let's you and me get to work. We got some mice to catch. Some errands to do"

- 29 -

Stale bread to feed your chickens

The restaurant is empty. Blue is making the circuit back from the eastside 'L' with a dish-tub full of cutlery and diningware that she places on the counter. She cuts around to pick this up just as an old woman enters, with long scattered hair, a mix of soft grey and winter white. She is lean and dresses in a muddy rainbow of clothes. She seems somewhat hesitant, lost, flustered.

"Hello, ma'am. Welcome to Rainy's."

"Why, hello young woman. You look like you've been out in quite a windstorm with that hair of yours."

Blue smiles. "Yep. You too, ma'am. We could probably both use a good hairdresser. Would you like to sit at a booth, ma'am, or at the counter? We have tables around the side but it's kind of dark back there."

"Oh, thank you. I really wasn't planning on staying. I … I just wondered if you had any old bread, some stale bread that you were going to feed to the chickens. I don't want to trouble you."

"Hello, there. What's up Blue? Why don't you let me take care of the lady?" Johnny P. March steps into Rainy's from the door to the Leroy's Office and nods toward the lunch counter. "Good afternoon, ma'am. Why don't you sit right over here, in this first booth. It looks like it's reserved just for you."

"Oh, well thank you. I guess it wouldn't hurt me to take a load off. I've been walking for quite a spell."

"Well then, you need to sit down and have a rest for a while. You know, I heard you asking about some stale bread. Well, we've got some soup that we were just about to throw out—would you be interested in that? And it's past the lunch hour, so I bet we can get you an old sandwich too. And a glass of milk, well, that'll be my treat, on the house. Ok, ma'am?"

"Why, yes. Thank you. Thank you very much."

"Blue, will you see what you can scare up?"

"I'm already on it, Prince."

"Scare up … Prince. My, but you people talk a strange language sometimes. Sometimes I can barely understand what you say."

"Yes, well, Prince is a kind of nickname some of the folks around here have given me. My real name's John, John March. Do you mind if I ask your name?"

"Not at all. I am Emily Allison Bean."

"I am pleased to meet you, Miss Bean."

"Please, please call me Emily."

"Why, certainly, Emily. Indeed, I shall. So, I gather that you are a visitor? You are not from around here?"

"Oh no, I am not visiting. I've come home. I grew up on these very lands. In fact, I own the land that university's built on. At least I did own it, until they stoled it from me."

Blue arrives at the table with some hot vegetable soup, a freshly made tuna-salad sandwich, and a glass of milk.

"Oh thank you, young lady."

"Now those are words I like to hear ... especially that young part."

"That's Suzie, although we all call her Blue. She's in charge of the restaurant here. Blue, allow me to introduce you to Miss Emily Allison Bean."

"Pleased to meet you, ma'am," Blue lightly shakes Emily's hand.

"The same, I am sure."

Blue returns to the counter. She leans and listens.

"So, you say stolen—do you mind if I sit, ma'am?" Emily nods and Johnny slides into the seat across from her. "Would you mind telling me your story, Emily? About how you grew up around this place and how your land got stolen? Did you live here when the army base was still located here with all of its heavy artillery and breakdowns?"

"Yup, I certainly did, son. But I don't remember any heavy artillery, as you call it. I used to drive right through the army base though. On my way to the train station where they shipped my corn and wheat south to feed those soldiers."

"Soldiers, ma'am. To the south?"

"Yup, them Union soldiers. At war with the Confederate Separationists. Them Union soldiers could eat all that we could spare and more. Say, if you don't mind my asking—I have been a little bit out of the picture for a while—can you tell me who won?"

"Who won, ma'am. Who won the war? Which war, Emily?"

"Why the only war that was being fought by the Unionists and the Confederates. The Civil War, son. The United States Civil War."

"Oh. Well, the Union forces won that war, Emily. Put a final end to slavery in North America, at least one kind of slavery. And brought all of the states back together, sort of. Like most wars, I guess, it never completely settled all things. ... So you say that you used to deliver farm goods for the Union soldiers. You must be considerably older than you look, Emily."

"In some ways I am; in some ways I am not. It's a long story. Do you have time, John March, for a long story?"

"In your case, Emily Bean, I think that I do. If you don't mind telling it, that is. Blue, could you bring me a cup of coffee, and Emily could use another glass of milk. And maybe something sweet for dessert."

"Well, John, I was borned in 1801..." Emily starts her story once again, once again recounting her tale of growing up on the farm and of the death of her parents and of the dark alien forces and, this time a new chapter, of being affronted by a discourteous Dean, of having her claims denied and her land stolen away.

- 30 -

Do Re Mi

It is Saturday afternoon. Gabe and Lucky sit at the kitchen table of Gabe's apartment, customary beers in hand.

"So it'll be like clockwork, man." Lucky speaks with some excitement. "We'll scout around tomorrow and get a sense of the lay-out, the streets, places where we can make the exchanges, and so on. Then we'll set up on Monday and as soon as we see someone at MacLean's house, we'll shoot in, grab them and be out of there before they know it."

"And you don't think it matters who it is?"

"Nah. He's got a wife, three kids, son-in-laws. He'll pay to get any of them back, and he's got plenty of do re mi, 'specially with that new campaign."

"Sounds good. And we leave a ransom note when we grab them..."

"Yeah I already wrote it—that's what I was doing with those newspapers while you were snorin' there. Here!" Lucky shows Gabe a note made up of various letters and words cut from scattered advertising fliers and pasted together:

> YOURKIL haS Been TAKeN
> WeWaNt 2 MILLIOn dOLARS
> CALL 452.4653 for INtructoNS
> 4 o CLocK TODAY

"Looks good buddy." Gabe responds. "You're always ahead of the curve."

"And the fast ball too! I used the number of the pay telephone at the corner store. They have to call us, not the other way around so nobody'd be able to trace the call. And we can hold the hostage here for a while, and then move him to my place, and then keep him in the car. Keep movin' so no-one can tell where we are. And we'll arrange for the exchange at some open place, maybe the bus station or Mason's Mall. Like I say, we can check out some places tomorrow and settle on that then."

"And the note says—we're gonna ask for two million?"

"Yep. That'll pay Malley back and give us something for our troubles. A little travellin' money to get out of here for a while, at least 'til the heat's off."

"What if MacLean won't pay?"

"We can jump off that bridge when we come to it, man. But don't worry … he'll pay. And in his kind of business it won't cost him a cent. The fucker'll just raise everybody's insurance to cover it."

"Yeah … I suppose. Well, here's to the plan, Lucky." Gabe raises his beer bottle and salutes Lucky. "Sounds good so far. This could change everything, man. A million bucks! And get Liz and Jimmy back."

"You know it will, Gabe! It's got to. There's a change comin' for us, man. I can just feel it."

"I hope so ... I'm sick of all the shit we been through. We deserve something good, Lucky. Some kind of break."

"You're damn right, Gabe. We've had a lot of crap in our lives. Sometimes I feel ... well it's like Maw used to say on those mornings after she'd really tied one on—I feel like I'm up Shaw's ass eating raspberries."

"Your Mom always had a way with words, buddy," chuckles Gabe.

"And I mean, it's not like we're bad, we're not like those other guys we met in the pen, you know, the murderers and rapists and shit."

"Well, Lucky, that young kid did end up dead in that house we jacked."

"Yeah, but we didn't plan on that it just happened. It was more like an accident than a killin'. No, what I mean is, you and me, guys like us, we ain't really bad. Like on that TV show the other day—Dr. Who-ever, they was talkin' about prisons and rehabituatin' people and stuff and they had a shrink on and he said it was sickness, not crime, small time players—guys who regularly get shafted for being involved in small time stuff, guys who do all the dirty work for the big time operators, guys who grow up in bad home situations, guys like us, Gabe. . ."

"You're reading my mail there, Lucky."

"That shrink said those guys were sick, not evil, not really even criminals. It's like those kids who can't pay attention in school, once they gave them a slap on the side of their heads, but now they understand it's a sickness, they're considered to have a disease. Remember when people used to get old and stupid, now they get old-timer's disease. And drunks, like my maw, well once they were ... drunks, but now, it's an illness, a disability, that's what the shrink called it."

"So that's what we have, Lucky? A disability?"

"Fuckin' A, Gabe. Exactly. Dr. Who even gave it a name—ASAP, he said, or something like that. It's like the flu, only there ain't no pills you can take, no shot they can give you to cure it. But it ain't our fault, man. It's just a disease we were born with and that's all."

"Well, Lucky, I guess I never thought of myself as being sick before, but maybe there's something to what you say. So, we should be treated as patients, not crooks, right?"

"You got it, pal. And though they say there's no cure, I'm bettin' a million bucks will be pretty good medicine. What do you think!" Lucky raises his beer bottle. "Hi Ho Silver!"

"Get At 'Em, Scout!"

They touch the necks of the bottles together and then take long, quiet drinks.

- 31 -

Antebellum paramours

Emily finishes her story of life in the 1800s and of being kidnapped by dark gods.

"I can only guess how you must feel, Emily. Once, a few years ago, some folks tried to steal my land from me too. But I took them to court, or nearly did, and they backed off."

"Well, I live by a law older than the law of your courts, John March; it's the law of a tooth for a tooth, and an eye for an eye. I will reap my vengeance on them, that Dean and all of his. I will get what's rightfully mine. I will."

"It's good to have your convictions, Emily. But you have to take care of yourself, you know, be careful around some of these folks. They're pretty powerful people, and they usually got the police and the law on their side. Your passion could get you into trouble."

"Oh, I know John March. I know all about passion. Passion is everywhere. There is one kind that drives the world and another that is driven by it, and both alike can make victims of their bearers. But there is also another passion, a true passion that you got to have," Emily taps her chest over her heart, and then touches Johnny's hand on the table, "that you got to seek out if you don't know it, a deep passion that shows the way for justice and leads us to truth. It's a fire inside and out and, sometimes, you got to face it. I'll be patient, John, and careful, don't worry, but I'll get what's coming to me or I'll get some satisfaction. Count on it. An eye for an eye. Say, if I may ask, where is your privy?"

"Privy? Oh, yes, just go around the corner and toward the back. It's inside. It's the first door on your left." Johnny points toward the 'L'.

Emily saunters out of sight, and for a sudden second in the stillness, one wonders if she were some phantom never really here at all. Blue steps forward to clean the table.

"You about to take in another stray, Prince? Yep, yep, yep, I can see it in your eyes. Another cast-off is about to anchor at the Leroy, right?"

"Well, Blue, this one's pretty unusual. Most of us, you and me and the rest, are cast out of space. But you know, Emily, it seems she's a cast-off of time. It's not often that I get to meet someone who's two hundred years old, you know."

"Yep, and been abducted by aliens to boot. I think she's crazy, Prince."

"Well, Blue, who among us isn't a little bit crazy, some of the time, anyway. As a matter of fact, I get a little bit nervous when I'm around people who say they're never crazy, who swear on their sanity. That's when you want to count the silverware, Blue, and sit with your back to the wall."

"Hey, Johnny, you're the Prince, man. You know what you're talking about. Should I get a room key from Benny?"

"That's the plan, Blue. It's off-season—loaning out a room for a while won't lose us any profit, will it. And I have a feeling, some good may come out of this. What do you think? Room 24 would be good—it'd be handy to the restaurant."

Blue simply smiles and nods her head—she has seen this movie before—and retreats into Leroy's Office just as Emily comes back into view. Johnny stands to meet her as she speaks.

"I see you got a dog back there to keep the coyotes at bay. That's a good thing."

"Yes ... that's Angus. And he probably could keep coyotes away, although mice are more his kind of thing. I hope he didn't bother you."

"No, no, not at all. He was friendly as all get-out. Let me rub his ears and scratch his belly."

"Good. He's a good dog. And I am hoping that you will get to know him even better. Emily, I have a proposition for you. I would like to invite you to stay over in one of our guest rooms until you can get your dispute with those folks who stole your property taken care of. You'll be able to settle in and get yourself rested."

"Well, John, thank you very much. But I wouldn't feel right, taking advantage of your generosity like that. I am not a charity case."

"Well, Emily. I am not being entirely honest with you. I do have a secret plan. The fact is, around back, I've got a garden set up, for flowers and vegetables, but it's never amounted to hardly anything. So when I heard your story, you being a farmer and all, and that garden needing to be readied for spring planting, I put two and two together. So if it's all right with you, I will turn over the Gardens of the Leroy to you and see if you can bring some life to them. Heaven knows, I've had no luck. And as for you, you'll be earning your room and board, growing food for the restaurant and raising flowers to put on the tables in here and in the rooms. And you'll be able to take Angus on walks when the rest of us are too busy around here."

"Well, well. That sounds like a very good offer. It would be nice to get my hands back into some earth, to plant some seeds and watch them sprout and rise. To be around a farm dog again. Ok. Ok, John March, you have got yourself a bargain. But only 'til I get matters straightened out with that Dean and his bunch! Then I'll be back on my own land."

"Very good, Miss Emily Bean. Very good. 'Til then. ... You got the room key, Blue? Thanks. Emily, if I may escort you? We are going to put you up in Room Number 24."

Johnny puts out his arm.

"Why, thank very much."

Emily places her hand through the crook of Johnny's arm and, together, like some flirtatious antebellum paramours, they glide out of the room.

- 32 -

Have you nothing to say?

In the northwestern suburbs of Thornton live the rich and those with the pretense of being the rich. There are some enormous mansions, built of grey stone and precious brick and set far back from cul-de-sacs and curving roadways. Gateways of rock and metal open to driveways of crushed brick and stone that lead to three and four car garages attached to dwellings that sprawl out and up. On Dover Avenue, on a lot just slightly smaller than these and in a house just slightly more modest, lives Henry Douglas MacLean, Dean of the Faculty of Education, Thornton University. Still, gates of wrought iron and large stone pillars mark the entrance and a curving lockstone driveway sweeps up to the front and curves back around to the gates. There is a large pillared portico in front of dark mahogany double doors, this entranceway flanked on each side by dense thickets of euonymus and other decorative shrubbery.

It is early evening of what has turned into a hectic day. Just two hours earlier Henry D. MacLean has made a television appearance announcing the inauguration of a multi-faceted fund raising campaign to create and support research into literacy. And just a few hours before that, at Wilson Hall, a clumsy policewoman had dropped her revolver blowing a huge hole in a wall, not to mention nearly killing two student-teacher applicants—a matter quickly dealt with. And now, to close the day, Henry has marshalled his tribe together at his residence for a secret conference.

Seven people sit around a large shining table; spaces remain for two others. At the end of this mahogany centrepiece sits Dr. MacLean, a tall man in a black suit, with everest-white hair, a deep brown tan and sharp blue eyes. At the far end opposite him, his wife, Kelly. She rests, relaxed, wearing a beaded cream-white-on-white evening gown, brindled yellow hair touching her shoulders, smooth white neck encircled by a luminous string of green stone, hands casually interlocked on the gleaming surface in front of her.

On Dr. MacLean's left, sit two of his daughters, Glenda Albane and Rory Cornel, their husbands by their sides. His third daughter, Carren, sits across the table. Glenda is the oldest daughter, in her thirties, midnight black hair and narrow face. Her expression is stern, sullen, a consequence, though, of all of the moments in her time, not just this one. She is, of course, a lawyer—you could probably tell that by her serious demeanor. Her husband, Albert, is a quiet mousy man who sits patiently at his wife's side and, beyond affirmatives, says very little.

Rory, the middle daughter, is a month or so away from concluding a graduate degree in Economics at Thornton U. and, on the exterior, at least, has a more pleasant demeanor than her sister. Auburn of hair and upper twentied, she has also just discovered that she is pregnant, something her elder sister discovered some time ago that she would never be. Just when to break this news to her sister has occupied Rory's thoughts ever since the recent visit of discovery to her doctor's. She is thinking of waiting until June, if she can disguise herself that long, when, graduated with her M.A., she would be able to spring a delicious double surprise on Glenda. For a lifetime of being second, here were two firsts. Conrad Cornel, Rory's husband, is quiet but restless during these 'family' meetings; he understands what is at stake. He knows his place and knows that his time will come. Besides, these meetings mean money for Rory and for him, money which he needs to support his wife, his gambling and his mistress.

And the youngest, Carren, sits across the table, continually scrolling and tapping on her cell phone as all humans currently under the age of thirty are compelled to do. She is scalded blonde, chopped short and spunky, nearing the end of her first year at Thornton U., and ardently engaged in texting back and forth to Andy Festes, her current male friend, thinking far more of him than of her upcoming English term paper (due in a few days); its topic, amid the recessive and random processes of her indiscriminate recollections, is something about Satan in the first couple Books of *Paradise Lost*: "Of man's first disobedience, the monkey chased the weasel, yada, yada, yada..."

"All right, everyone. This should not take long." The Dean begins, straightening some pieces of paper in his hands. "Needless to say, it is Vegas-time—all that is spoken and done here in the next half hour, remains here. This is strictly confidential information, not for public perusal. Is everyone clear on that?"

A general mumble of acknowledgement slides around the table like an exuberant wave in a drunken stadium.

"As all of you know since you were there, I announced on television today that MacLean Insurance and Real Estate, of which you are all principle voting shareholders and trustees, will match the monies raised by four charity fund raising events in the coming few months. The Auction for Action Charity will get underway in a couple days and that will be followed by the Spring Garden Party in Berris Thorn Park, the July Tea at the Hunt and Country Club, and the Autumnal Ride, out to Moira Lake and back. As all of you also know, M.I.R.E. is not in the habit of giving money away. We're in the habit of making money. Now, to get straight to the point, let me explain, what shall I call it, the darker purpose for which I have invited all of you here tonight. Yes, Rory?"

"What about Clayton Brown? He's not here and he's the other major shareholder, isn't he?"

"Yes, I was coming to that. Mr. Brown, as you know, is retiring in June from his position as superintendent with the Thornton Valley District School Board. He has had a distinguished career and has been a long-time associate and friend of mine. In fact, that's why he is a primary stakeholder in M.I.R.E., he put the initial seed money up front that enabled me to start this business. And I invested him as one of the major partners. But he has pretty much been absorbed in his own work, in education. At least, that is, up 'til now. In his retirement, he informed me a couple weeks ago, he thinks that he would like to become more personally involved with the business. Take on an active role. So, the short of it is—Mr. Brown is not here yet. That is part of the plan. He should arrive in about an hour—young Cindy will be with him. That is another part. And between now and then, let me lay out the central part of our plan. I would like to offer a divestiture scheme to all of you which would increase the individual profits of M.I.R.E. for all of us, while, at the same time, putting Clayton Brown in a less-than-advantageous economic situation. Any questions at this point? If not, I will proceed."

A mumble of understanding and interest circumnavigates the mahogany.

"All right, then. Here is how our plan will work. It begins in truth. The responsibilities of my job as Dean at the Faculty have grown enormously in the last couple years with the growth of the university, the expansion of our programs, our becoming a unitary Faculty, the new literacy initiative that we're just starting, and all the rest. I will explain to Brown and the rest of you, after he gets here, that I am in a position where I wish to alter my responsibilities at M.I.R.E. I wish to step down as CEO to concentrate on my academic obligations and, consequently, divide my labours equally among my three daughters and Mr. Brown—especially possible, now, given Clayton's desire to take on such an increased role, anyway. We will subdivide into four divisions, each responsible for an insurance portfolio and a real estate agglomeration. As an initial duty, each division will be responsible for staging one of the charity events. Glenda has already taken on the Auction, Carren has volunteered for the Spring Garden Party, and Rory, you will oversee the July Tea—that leaves the Autumnal Ride for Clayton and his division. For several reasons, it will probably be the least successful—that aside, the key is that, through our quiet redistribution of assets, Brown will also have the weakest division by far, although to an unskilled eye it will appear to be the largest—it will include our international investments. Our offshore Zeta Corp won't go belly-up for at least six months, but it will go, and when it does it will represent a huge loss to Mr. Brown and his division. And we are going to lose that land in Kananga—at first, there was some inept legal wrangling, and now, there's tribal warfare. We were going to build a resort there and it's turned into a bloody battlefield, literally. It will follow Zeta like a death blow to

Brown. But the rest of us will be entirely protected. Brown will lose pretty much everything and, if all goes as planned, we will not lose a cent. As to our declared donation to the literacy charity, there are several large corporate endowments about to be made, two will be announced at the Press Conference next week when the Auction opens, and in time we will disguise those funds to appear as our matching donations. Glenda has already drafted some of the paperwork, with more to follow. Do you have any comment on that aspect of this plan? Anyone? Glenda?"

"No, not at all. The corporate donations will be shielded to appear as M.I.R.E.'s matching gift and the rest of the plan is quite legitimate, and sensible; in fact, as you point out, regarding the redistribution, on the surface Brown's deal looks best. The fine print, of course, will make no division liable for any one of the others, but all of the divestiture will be in legalese, so almost no one will be able to read it. And, anyway, I would imagine that Mr. Brown, unsuspecting as he is, will sign in confidence. It's a good deal for him, that is, if his assets weren't on the brink of absolute failure."

"Very good, then. Let's get this wheel turning. The paper that I am sending around right now is a binding agreement that all of us will sign which negates this apportionment of M.I.R.E. one year from this day, exclusive of the events of and pertaining to the year ahead. And it is restrictive to all who sign it. What it means, my children, is that a year from now, our company will be re-unified no matter how our three divisions individually fare, except of course that its weakest elements will have been siphoned off thanks to Mr. Clayton Brown. He'll be a lost island in a great storm. So, I would be interested in hearing what each of you has to say. Glenda, let's start with you."

"As I think you already know, Daddy, I feel that it is an excellent plan and Albert and I are thrilled that you invited us to be a part of it. It is a brilliant strategy; it is going to make all of us a good deal of money, and it's going to get rid of some of the really detrimental, dead parts of this company. You are so smart."

"Thank you, my dear. Well said. And now, your turn Rory. What do you think of this plan?"

"Well, Daddy, it sounds terrific to me. Conrad and I were just looking at some of the details and they all look wonderfully thought out. I absolutely agree with all that Glenda said—it is a dazzling plan. Getting rid of that overblown and underachieving international stuff, and Brown, all in the same manoeuvre—sheer brilliance, Daddy. That's why we all love you so much, you know that, don't you?"

"Thank you, dearest one. You speak as well as your sister. And now, Carren, my youngest, what have you to say, my dearest? ... Carren. ... Carren? ... Nothing? ... Have you nothing to say? Carren?"

"Oh, sorry, Daddy. I wasn't paying too much attention; I was distracted by a message, I guess. But I think it's a great plan. There's something about old man Brown I never liked—he's too stuck on himself as an award-winning principal and stuff. He always talks down to you. Always quoting stupid stuff. I like Cindy, of course, she's always been my BFF. But she'll do fine even if her Dad is brought down a peg or two. The only thing I want to know, am I going to have to be responsible for a whole division of M.I.R.E.? I mean, I'm only in first year university. I don't think I'll have the time, and I don't really know much about the business, anyway."

"That's all right, dear." Carren's mother, Kelly, intercedes.

"You just sign the paper—I'll be overseeing your part of the business for the year, until the company reunites. Everything will be fine."

"All right. Thanks Mom. Anyway, Daddy, that's all I have to say. It seems like a terrific plan to me. Me and Cindy will get together later tonight to do some more planning for the Garden Party. We'll have fun with that."

"Thank you, Carren. And thank all of you. I couldn't have asked for a finer family. Now let's get that paper signed and let's send that dessert tray around one more time. All this hard work fires up my sweet tooth."

- 33 -

The eternal freak out of being

In Room 416 of the Voyageur's End, Angie and Bobby lie on the bed, naked but covered with bedding. Angie is holding an unlit cigarette.

"Get me a light, will you, Bobby? I need a smoke."

"Sure. I got some hotel matches over here in my pants pocket. Remind me to open the window before we leave."

"You worry too much *ma petit oiseau*. Just lay here, and relax. And next time, wear your uniform, ok? I've never done it with a man in uniform."

"Ok. Will do."

"Look at this, Bobby." Angie grabs her large black canvas purse from the floor and reaches inside. "See what I've got—over six hundred dollars. Just for you and me. I thought we could take a long weekend, go to Chicago or New York or even Toronto, live it up in style."

"Jesus. Where'd you get all that money?"

"Oh, let's just say it was lying around the apartment and then just disappeared. You know how these things happen. Some thieves must have got it, or that crooked landlord."

"So it's your Mom's. Why'd your mother have money like that lying around?"

"Oh, I dunno. She was savin' it for something. I think maybe she wanted me and her to go on a trip somewhere, you know, like Disneyland or something. Can you imagine? Being stuck with my Mom on a trip. *Mon Dieu*!"

"A trip with you would be cool, but don't you think your Mom will figure out you took it, especially if you took off on a big flippin' trip? Won't she freak out?"

"Nah, I'd just tell her it was a school trip. Besides, she's always freakin' out over one thing or another, anyway. You should've seen her when I got my tattoo. Like an atom bomb went off."

"She didn't like your dragonfly? Why … what's the matter with dragonflies? And everybody's got tatts. Even I got my chain!" Bobby points to his right bicep.

"It wasn't so much the tatt, I don't think, but the freedom, the fact that I decided to get it all by myself without asking her. I mean I've been asking her all my life. You know what I mean?"

"Yeah, I know. I have to ask dad if I want to take a dump. He still thinks I'm four."

"And the dragonfly, it's both air and land—it means change and freedom; and it's full of colour and that's what I wanted. So, yeah, mom'd probably freak out if we took a trip but she freaks out over everything. It's in the Savard blood. You get used to it. An eternal freak-out." Angie tucks the money away.

"I hear you, babe. I don't think that's a Savard thing, though; I think it's a parent thing. Maybe an adult thing. Every grown-up I know is like that—beeserk over one thing or another almost all the time. The eternal freak-out of being, of being an adult, a grown up. Sometimes, I don't think I ever want to grow up. Not entirely, at least."

"You and me both, *chérie*. Maybe we should just lock that door and close those drapes and stay in here forever..."

"Sounds like a plan ... 'cept my shift starts in half an hour." Angie sits up, grabs a pillow and hits Bobby with it.

"Hey!"

- 34 -

A right gude-willy waught

Henry MacLean, his wife Kelly, and their three daughters and two sons-in-law all sit around the living room table. Clayton Brown and his daughter Cynthia have joined the meeting. A lifelong educator and soon to retire as a supervisory officer in Thornton's education system, Clayton is a force of intellect and power in his own environs but, as is so often the case with such individuals, he is not wise enough to understand the boundaries of such intellect and power. He is, at best, a Moped that has just merged onto the MacLean speedway. Cynthia, eighteen, has been best friends with Carren for years and is now her classmate in first year university. Better with books than boys (Carren, the reverse), Cindy is more responsible and capable and intelligent than Carren but, generally, much higher strung when it comes to moments of import and pressure.

"Well, Henry, everyone, let me propose a toast: 'And there's a hand, my trusty fiere! And gie's a hand o' thine! And we'll tak a right gude-willie waught, for auld lang syne.' Here's to our brave new M.I.R.E. May it only be more prosperous than the old." Clayton Brown raises a glass of scotch in the air and motions it toward Henry MacLean seated at the head of the table. Their outstretched glasses hover in the air just short of a point where they can touch. "*Slainte Mhath*," says Clayton.

Clayton Brown sits down again, beaming and pleased, soon-to-be a retired Board of Education superintendent, he has just become the divisional CEO of a local diversified corporation with international insurance interests and land holdings—of which he and his division would principally be in charge. From local man-about-town to international maker and shaker. It has been quite a night. He is already making plans, thinking about the possibility of taking a working holiday, visiting some of the foreign sites, the Zeta Group Headquarters in Amsterdam and that development territory in Kananga—that sounds interesting. Across the room nestled in the window seat, he can see his daughter, Cindy, and the Dean's daughter, Carren, talking non-stop. Both in first year university together at Thornton, both have virtually grown up together. Cindy has entered university on a full academic scholarship in Biosciences and Clayton has no doubt that she will be a medical doctor someday—perhaps even a professor of medicine, teaching and training others to be doctors. If that were the case, this new endeavour, and the extra capital it would bring in, will certainly come in handy to help Cindy through graduate school in the best way possible. Clayton finds himself on the verge of pinching himself—all of this seems like a dream that is just too good to be true. Of course, he has decided, before he absolutely signs all of the papers he has pushed into his briefcase tonight, he would have Ezzie Lynch have a look at them. Ezzie is a trustee for the school board and one of the best corporate lawyers in all of Thornton. Clayton stares back into his scotch. It is the colour of a desert, a sandy, scotch desert and he can see the plane touching down and the natives running out on the runway to meet him, Big

Boss from over the water, Big Boss. Big Boss! Oh no, no, he is saying as his feet touch the scotch-sand, just call me Clayton. Clayton will be fine. Now, won't you take me to that beautiful piece of land where we are going to build our beautiful resort hotel? That beautiful piece of land.

"Come on into my study, Clayton, and we can finish our scotch and take care of some of the lesser details, like getting you set up with an office-space downtown. We'll let the others get on with their affairs." Clayton rises like a new-born lamb and trots ahead of MacLean as they leave the room. Conrad Cornell casts a nervous look in MacLean's direction, then motions to Rory that it is time for them to leave

Comfortably crouched into the window seat facing one another, Carren and Cindy are talking, Cindy changing the discussion to a more focused topic.

"We should talk a little bit about the Spring Garden Party. Ok?"

"Ok. Ok, Cindy. You're right. Let's firm up some things. Make some bookings. 'Cause Tampon Fuckit, you know, time flies—I learned that the other day in English."

"I love your Latin, Care-bear."

"Anyway, as you know, it'll be in Bare-Ass Horny Park downtown and for entertainment we'll have to book some bands and dancers. We'll have a couple cool groups for late in the evening but we also need some other snoring stuff, for adults and kids. I thought we could get some Celtic dancers and maybe a swing band. My Dad has some contacts with A.C.E. Entertainment Co., so it should be easy. What we'll need though is a stage of some kind for the dancers, something we can put over that old, ugly concrete patio."

"That's no problem. Like I was saying on the phone the

other day, the Board of Education has a whole bunch of plywood risers that interlock. I checked and we'll be able to borrow them, probably for free my Dad says, because it'll be near the end of the school year and nobody will be using them. And it's for charity! We'll have to arrange to transport them—that won't be a problem. The only thing is, they're kind of grubby. We will need to cover them somehow. Did you call that carpet place?"

"Yeah, I did. I'm glad you asked. I phoned Tom and Mike's, or Mike and Tom's, I can't remember what the hell they call themselves. But they said we should be able to purchase some remainders and carpet ends very cheaply and that they would do an installation for free, because it's for charity. So that sounded pretty good. And then I asked them if they sold any kind of hard flooring, for the dancers, right. They need something solid—I thought we could cover three or four of the risers with some harder flooring. And the guy said that they had some brand new stuff coming in and that we might get it for next to nothing as well, as a demonstration-type-deal. So, what's going to happen is, there's a representative from this new flooring company going to meet with us on Monday, at noon, he's coming here with some samples. I guess he's on some promotional campaign and is going to be at Mike and Tom's, or Tom and Mike's, for the whole weekend; I was going to meet with him earlier but he had some mix-up with his schedule so he's going to hang around 'til Monday—good for us. And he'll come here. Tom, or Mike, the carpet guy I was talking to, said he figured an outing would be good for the guy, especially when I told him that I didn't think I could get all the way across town on a weekday. The problem for me is, I got a Monday morning class from 9 to 11 and Brad, you know that smart kid in Poli-Sci, with the dark yellow hair…"

"And the cute ass…!"

"Well, there is that too. Anyway, he said that he would meet me at the library at eleven to show me some quick and to-the-point stuff about *Paradise Lost*. My English essay is due this coming Friday—the 29th, right—but I'm going to need next weekend to finish it. There's no way I could get it done exactly on time. So, when I drop it off to Barker in his office on the 1st or 2nd, I'll just wear something tight and low-cut, maybe that red dress. The old skank probably won't even notice that the paper's coming in late. Like they say, the shorter the skirt, the higher the mark!"

"The deeper the cleavage…"

"…the greater the average.

"A little 'T and A' carries the day…"

"… and a lot carries it further!" They laugh.

"Yeah, I've heard all about old Barker. Hopefully you'll be able to do a good paper though—that might impress him, too! I know I just handed in my last big project—the last one before exams—and I think I did ok. Of course, if you think your assignment is strange, you should've seen mine—I just finished researching hens and roosters and their mating rituals for the animal husbandry unit in Bio. Pretty hot stuff, I can tell you!"

"Maybe you can lend me that for some beach reading this summer, or not! Who the hell reads on the beach, anyway?"

"Well, it was actually better than that previous paper I had to do, remember, the one you helped me with a bit, on weeds and flowers in folk lore and in real science. I don't know where some of these profs get their ideas from—the far side of the moon, I guess. Anyway, Care-babe, I can be here by noon or a little earlier on Monday to meet with this guy. I've got no classes then. But I don't know if I want to make this decision all by myself."

"That's no problem, Cin-city. I'll be here by 12:15, 12:30 at the latest. I'll have Becka make some sandwiches and lemonade and you can sit in the summer room or out by the pool, if it stays warm, until I get here. I might even make it by noon, we'll see. And, just in case Becka has to go out shopping, or something, on Monday, here's my extra set of keys, so you can get in the house and through to the backyard. The key-tag has my name on it."

"Ok. Sounds like a plan. If you're not here, I'll wait for the carpet guy on the porch and then take him through to the back; we'll meet you there. Anyway, looks like my Dad is getting ready to go. And your new hunk has been texting you like crazy—your phone's been burping every minute on the minute. You really got him hooked."

"Absolutely. You gotta train 'em. And when you got it, you know, you got it. You know what— Andy's got a best BFF—we could double date some time."

Clayton Brown has moved back into the room and, with a beckoning wave toward Cindy, he moves towards the door, Henry MacLean like a horny shepherd close behind.

"I don't know. Remember, the last guy you set me up with. Rod, somebody? He was a two trick wonder. He talked about how much beer he could drink and showed me how to hot wire a car. And that was the entire night's worth of entertainment!"

"Well, you never know when you might need to hot wire a car. Or yourself for that matter!"

"Right! Well, send me a picture of this guy first, and I'll let you know. I want to see if his knuckles drag on the ground when he walks."

"Hey … that's the difference between us, kid. I never worry about their knuckles."

"I've noticed, my dear. Anyway if there's any change in plans, give me a call. Otherwise, I'll see you on Monday sometime after noon. Unless I see you sooner, Care-babe."

"Absolutely. Monday, Cin-city. See you later. Sleep tight…"

"And don't let the alligators bite…"

"After a while croc… what are we, in Grade Two! Safe home. Good-night, Mr. Brown. Bye bye."

- 35 -

A large coffee to go but no meatloaf

"Hey, look who's finally up and about. And lookin' like something Angus wouldn't drag in. Hey, Fruitfarm—don't you know that people die in their sleep?"

It is Sunday, near noon and a thin man in his upper-forties, or thereabouts, has opened the door. His hair is tousled and very red and he moves into Rainy's with a relaxed and provisional gait, the kind of motion with which, one supposes, he has moved throughout his entire life.

"Good morning there, Dom. Deed. How're you all doing? And gimme a break on the time—it's not even noon yet. And it's Sunday. Ain't no point in rushing things, you know. Besides, I've probably been up way before you, anyways—I opened the store an hour ago. Hey, Blue."

"Hi Mike. So, what can I get you. We got meatloaf on special today."

"Oh, that sounds good, but I can't hang around today; we're busy at the store and a bit short-staffed, especially on the experience side with big Red there. So, Blue, I think, a large coffee to go but no meatloaf—how 'bout a smoked meat on rye. That'll travel better. And maybe a couple of those cookies for dessert."

Mike 'Fruitfarm' Black points at a clear covered stand near Blue as he straddles one of the counter stools.

"Gotcha, Mike. Grease'll get that order right up. So, what's new with you?" Blue asks.

"Not much, Suzie. New York, New Jersey, as always! Got my check for that westside job on Friday. Played the ponies last night and made a little bit more, you know. Putting some new carpet in at the Eldorado this week, that is if the stuff shows up in time tomorrow. None of the companies keep anything in stock anymore—you have to order and they all claim that it will be there early on the day when you need it. But then a truck breaks down and your order sits out on the freeway and arrives ten hours late and you just sit around scratching your butt and have to pay the guys for doing nothing. And your clients get on your case for not finishing when you said you would and you have to pay a late penalty. On it goes."

"Ain't that why you charge twice what the job costs in the first place?" Dom pipes in, and all laugh in unison.

"Yeah, and I can't wait for the day I get to sell you some carpet, Dom. But, as you know, there's always something. Life don't roll out like no stretched carpet. Like this past week, for instance. Tecumseh Flooring has this big promotion on for some new product they're carrying and they want to send a representative down to be in the store from Thursday through the weekend, to give some hands-on demonstrations and talk directly with the customers, show some new samples, and so on. So I say fine, and put a small ad in the papers and everything. Well, the rep's supposed to be here on Thursday, but he phones, he's had car troubles and can't make it to Friday. So there's customers showing up to look at samples and so on, but no samples to show them—kinda makes us look like idiots. So this guy wanders in a day late and he seems like an ok guy and all, but business is business. And he sure lost us some on Thursday. So, anyways, he was supposed to leave on Sunday but, he was stand-up enough, he agreed to stay over another day. I set up this appointment for him over at the MacLean's, you know, big shots, rich buggers—he's supposed to meet with the head honcho's daughter who wants to look at some flooring for those charity events they've been planning. I thought it'd be good exposure for Tecumseh and their new stuff, and for us too. 'Course, as it turns out, the guy has spent all his expense account on the towing and a night's stay at the End—luckily, Red's livin' in a two bedroom and was good enough to put him up for the rest of the weekend. I'll stick a bit extra in Red's pay this week to thank him..."

"Now that sounds like something the Prince would do," says Blue.

"Yeah, I guess," replies Fruitfarm. "I guess a little bit of the Prince rubs off on you when you're around him enough. And that's not a bad thing. I also loaned the guy our truck today—he's out doing the rounds of some other stores. What's the word the hippies used to use—serendipity, with the emphasis on the 'pity.' But tomorrow he's gonna have to take a taxi 'cause the truck's needed for the Eldorado job, and I don't know how he's gonna get home 'cause he says he thinks his car is toast. But there's not much I can do about that. Business is always complicated, a lot like life, I guess."

"How'd you ever get into that business, anyway?" asks Blue, busy putting a sandwich and cookies into a small styrofoam container.

"Oh, I don't know. It's like anything else, I guess. You know I grew up on a farm just southeast of town, right? Orchard Valley. That's where I got this damned nick name—it was a market garden sort of place. With all kinds of vegetables and apple trees. But things happen ... me and Dad had some ... disagreements! And I grew up—I moved out. I came into town and got a job driving a furniture truck for Dray's. After a while I was delivering furniture and installing drapes for them. That's when I met Teresa—she was a niece of old man Dray. And then one of their carpet guys quit and I moved into carpet installation full time and learned the trade. And then old man Dray died and his son-in-law took over and I didn't care for him so me and Tommy Bowlie got together and rented the old barn that used to be part of the Thornton Creamery. We cleaned it out and borrowed some money, bought some carpet seconds and rejects and set ourselves up in the carpet business—Tom and Mike's, you know, paid by noon, laid by night! Then, when Tommy drowned, I inherited the business and his life insurance and a heap of hassle. Bowlie relatives nobody'd even heard tell of came out of the woodwork. The Prince helped me out then, a lot—he kept my bills paid for four or five months until all the legal wrangling got took care of. Then, when I paid him back, he wouldn't take no interest. I owe my business to Johnny, you know, probably my life, really. Eventually things settled down and I bought the new place down the road there. Managed to train a couple good installers—it's not a job for old men, you know. You got to get off the floor in the carpet business, the sooner the better. Is the Prince around, Blue? I'd like to talk to him."

"He's around somewhere, Mike. I can get Benny to take a look. There's your lunch, and the receipt for your records."

"No problem, Blue. Thanks. Maybe I'll catch him later—want to make him an offer on some new carpet for this joint. A lot of the rooms still have shag, you know, and that's not really in style anywhere any more. On this planet or any other. How about you boys? What're you guys up to? Same old?"

"Sort of..." Dom starts. "'Cept I had this dream where I was dead, and then got shot at over at the College and me and Deed are gonna be teachers..."

"Whoa ... what the hell are you talkin' about? That's a lot to take in. But I got to run. Tell you what. I'll be back over around noon tomorrow—I'll buy you and Deed lunch and you can fill me in on all the details. Sound ok?"

"It sure does, Fruitfarm. And I've got witnesses..."

"Oh you know I'm good to my word. Anyways, I better get back to the store. Red's there all by himself right now. And he's still pretty green at the job. That should cover things Blue. See you tomorrow." Mike puts some cash on the counter, picks up the receipt and food and leaves Rainy's for the short walk back to the carpet store.

- 36 -

Rats and cockaroaches

Fruitfarm pockets the receipt as the door to Rainy's closes behind him. Cradling his styrofoam lunch, he starts across the parking lot toward Dundas, then pauses. A yellow Mustang speeds into the lot, and stops abruptly in a space toward the middle where no lines are marked. As you know, there are no rules in parking lots. Fruitfarm recognizes a familiar face, turns and walks toward the car just as its two inhabitants emerge. One is a short balding man with a big nose wearing a grey windbreaker, the other a taller long haired man with a moustache, wearing a long, black overcoat even on this warm day.

"Hello, there, kid! Surprised to run into you here, Gabriel."

The two men, each at a headlight of the Mustang, stop and turn.

"Oh. ... Hi there ... Mike? Mike. Long time, no see, eh? Might of known it was you, the only person who ever called me 'kid'." Gabe squints into the sun, recognizing his older, red-haired brother coming toward them.

"It's been, what, a couple Thanksgivings, hasn't it?" Mike swats his younger brother on the right arm and can feel some metallic contraption beneath the windbreaker.

"Yeah, I guess it has. Time flies, don't it. Oh, hey Mike, you remember Lucky Burrell, don't you, from down the road."

"Yeah, of course I do. How are you doing, Luke?" Fruitfarm lightly shakes Lucky's hand noticing a blue tattoo slip into view from beneath his sleeve, strange letters of some kind; then he turns his attention back to his younger brother.

"So, how are you doing? How are Liz and Jimmy?"

"Ah, they're good, Mike. They're just fine. Everything's good. How 'bout with you?"

"Oh, Teresa's just fine—she's still working at the flower shop. And little Janey, if you can believe it, is graduating from high school this year. She's hoping to get into Thornton University—wants to be a lawyer."

"Is that right? University ... a lawyer! Good God. Well, brother, I guess it's good to know, at least, there's one smart one in the family. A lawyer! And what about Aggie and little Tom?"

"They're both ok, Gabe. Aggie's finishing Grade 9 and Tommy, he's only in Grade One. ... You know, we should try to get together a bit more. I'd like to see Tommy get to know his cousin—it would be good for him, good for Jimmy too. You know what? Tommy wants to go to camp this summer—a bunch of his friends went last year. Camp Quin-Mo-Lac, out on Moira Lake—they have a tykes' program. Maybe Jimmy could go too? The boys could get to know each other and have a helluva a time camping and hiking and stuff. And at least they'd learn how to swim, something we never did, eh? It's not very expensive for a week, or even two. I've got some extra brochures over at the store—why don't I drop by your place and give you one? You're still in the apartment on Rolph, eh?"

"Yeah. Ok Mike, that sounds like a good idea." Gabe is thinking quickly. "But, tell you what, I'll save you the trouble.

The Prince of Leroy

Instead of you comin' by, I'll stop by the store—maybe even later today we'll pull by. You're there, eh? This aft? Ok? Little Jimmy would probably really enjoy that, I bet. And getting to know Tom would be good."

"Absolutely. Hey, that's a damn nice car you're driving."

"It's Lucky's car—it's a real beaut, ain't it? It's new! You should feel it take the corners."

"So, what're you guys doin' around here, anyways? You didn't stop by for lunch, did you, parking back here to avoid getting dented by some moron opening a door?"

"No. Uh, no." Gabe is thinking quickly, again. "Lucky's got a room here for a day or two. His apartment building's being fumigated and they're puttin' everybody up at motels while they do that."

"Really. That must be a real pain. What's the problem?"

"Rats."

"Cockaroaches." Gabe and Lucky speak in unison.

"Rats and Cockaroaches," Gabe corrects. Thinking, again.

"Really. Wow. Well, I hope that works out for you, Luke. And quickly. Too bad they couldn't have put you up at the End instead of the Leroy, right?" ... There is an awkward silence between the brothers who, between them, really have only this space in common. "Well, I guess I better be getting back to the store. Red's there all by himself—he's a new guy. Drop by later, though Gabe, and get one of those brochures. Ok?"

"Yeah. Yeah, I will Mike. This aft., or maybe next day if we get tied up. And ... Liz and I are just looking at buying a home too. So we may need some carpet. If we can get a good deal, that is?"

"Hey, man, you'll never get a better deal than at Tom and Mike's. You got to know that! Talk to you later, kid. And good to see you again, Luke."

Fruitfarm turns to cross the parking lot and Gabe and Lucky move to the sidewalk of the Leroy, looking here and there. Then Gabe freezes just as he is about to speak. Fruitfarm is right behind him.

"Hey, Gabe. There's one other thing I wanted to mention to you. Do you remember that old orange Dodge pick-up that Dad used to have and I used for a long time for hauling carpet from job to job? Back when I just got started. Do you remember that?"

"Yeah. Yeah, I guess I do. ... It was an old wreck, wasn't it? What year was it?"

"It was a '74 or '75, I think, maybe older? Well, I had it up on blocks behind the store, rims in the back, right? It had been there three, maybe four years since I bought the van. I don't even know why I kept it—maybe it was the last thing I had of Dad's, I guess. Well, if you can believe it, about three-four weeks ago, somebody stole it. They must have put new rubber on it and hauled it out of there in the middle of the night, 'cause a week later the cops came by and told me that it was involved in an accident. Somebody must of got it started and then, I guess, crashed into some truck out on Highway 22—a shipping truck, I think they said. Weird, eh? I hadn't even reported it stolen—hardly seemed worthwhile. So the cops kind of gave me the once over, but I haven't heard back from them so I don't think anything more's gonna come of it. Pretty strange, though, don't you think?"

"Yeah, Mike. Really strange. Who would want that piece of junk?"

"No clue! Anyways, thought you'd like to know. Dad's old truck finally made it to the junkyard. But it got there in a kind of strange way. Kind of like the old man himself, I guess."

"Yeah, you're right there, brother. I guess, sooner or later, we all get to the junkyard, one way or another, don't we?"

"Righto, kid. So it seems. Anyways, I got to get back to the store. No rest for the working man, you know. Or the wicked, gentlemen. Take it easy and take care of yourself, Gabriel. Say hello to Liz and Jimmy. And drop by to get that camp info. Talk to you later."

With that, Fruitfarm turns, walks across the parking lot of the Leroy and vanishes west toward Tom and Mike's. This time, Gabe and Lucky wait until he is out of sight. Then they pursue their fated plans.

- 37 -

Time for a bit of Sociology and Psychology, but not too much

i

Yes. Yes. How could anyone forget her! I mean, she was a gal that needed no make-up, if you know what I mean. There I was, standin' in the Office trying to get a breath of air and when I looked up, she stood in the doorway, the light all around her. The gods would have stopped and taken a second look. It was a day in late June, I guess it'll be almost nine years ago this summer. It was a hot day, sizzling, and the air conditioner was on the fritz—those things always wait for the hottest days to conk out. So I had a couple old fans set up in the diner, purring away, only mostly all they were doing was blowing hot air around and making me hotter. So I came out to the Office to try to catch some air through the doorway. I'd only been at the Leroy a few weeks, working the lunch counter and restaurant. It was just a means to an end. I had a guitar and had just written a couple songs and was getting ready to head south, down to Nashville, where I was gonna be a country music star—but then came that hot June and Shonagh and I just seemed to dry up. The irony of things, I guess, especially for a songwriter—my music ran out on me just as she arrived bringing all the inspiration I'd ever need.

Anyway, there I was—leaning on the counter, a steaming June day, fans blowing hot air, looking at a travel brochure. And I sensed a shadow in the doorway. And she was there. Out of nowhere. She could move around like that, you know—make less noise than shade. 'Hello, you must be Suzie Greenway' she said, and stretched my name out like a glorious rubber band—SSSuuuzzzyyyy Ggrrreeeeennnnnwwaaayyyy. The sun was all around her. She was tall and thin and wore a light cotton dress dotted with small flowers that let the light rush through. Her hair was straight and golden and fell past her shoulders and her face was oval, not Hollywood glam or anything, but warm and smiling and it just pulled you in—she made you feel like you mattered. Like you were really alive. Like I said, she could turn my name and all the rest of me into a rubber band just by saying hello. 'Johnny told me that you would give me a key so I could stay a couple of days.' And stay she did, a year, almost a year to the day. With Jake's ok, of course. Johnny put her up in Number12, that's the big room round the back that has a small kitchen, and she helped out with the counter in Rainy's and the Office too. She had done some university work—had started off in sociology, but realized pretty quick, as she used to say, that sociology was the last refuge to which the desperate cling. It's the course people take, Shonagh'd say, who can't get into anything else. Anyway she switched into business and lasted there a year and a half or so, then she drifted and, like the rest of us, wound up at the Leroy. Leroy 010, as Benny calls it. Except, she was never quite like the rest of us. She was different. She was, well, like one of those spirits that the Celts speak of, a seal or silky, taken on human form and come to land for so long, but only so long. With her first step in the door, she had taken her first step toward leaving. The clock was ticking toward pumpkin-time, if you know what I mean. And, deep inside, I think she always knew it, but others didn't, of course, and you knew that was their road toward hurt. I will give her what's due, though—I mean, she pitched in and helped out around the place, waited tables and designed new menus, did the books and taxes that year, but Shonagh was, I don't know, she was … well, when you looked at her, you saw somewhere far away, and you knew she wouldn't last. It was summer but she had autumn in her eyes. Here, look at the menu. It's still the way she designed it, black background with that gold trim, and that quote on the front, Shonagh put that there. It probably says all you really want to know about her, all you need to know:

'You only begin to understand the true meaning of life
When you plant a tree under whose shade you know
You will never sit.'

ii

Yeah, when she left I helped the Prince put up that plywood, and I painted it black. But I don't really have anything much more to say. She always treated me well—she was the kind of person who brought a good feeling, a kinda light into a room whenever she entered. You don't ever forget a person like that, you know. And that's a good part of the problem, I guess. You don't ever forget a person like that. Everybody has at least one person in their life like that—and she reminded you of who that was. In some way she was everybody's. But especially the Prince's. Anyhow, that's all I have to say. The Prince don't say much about that time and I don't think he'd want the rest of us saying too much either. We probably don't know that much anyways. And the Prince, well, he's the Prince. I ain't gonna say nothing that might hurt him, you know. Nothing. That's all. That is all. Been nice talkin' to you. You have a good day.

iii

Are you kidding, of course, I remember Shonagh O'Mara. She arrived here just after old Jake had more-or-less given the place over to the Prince. In fact, it was because of the way Jake signed it over that the Prince damn near lost the joint to those guys who run the End, Dalco and his bunch. The whole thing was a mess, deeds that weren't properly notarized, surveys that were inaccurate, badly written up, everything. It was heading to the courts and then, just as suddenly, Dalco Corp. gave up on their claims and Johnny got ownership, got the paperwork all done up proper and legal. I'll never know exactly how Johnny pulled that off, but he did. Dalco scurried away with his tale between its legs and has pretty much left the Leroy alone ever since. And a good thing, too, because later on, when Jake's will was read, well, it didn't even have any signatures, no dates, nothing! But you can't really blame Jake. First of all, he really wasn't a paperwork kind of guy—he came from a different time when a word and a handshake was all that you needed. And, of course, his wife had died only a year or so before and he, himself, got pretty sick. It was a tough time, but Johnny was always there for him, you know. Jake took well over a year to die, in chronic care at T.G.H. for the last six months—the Prince used to go over at supper time every day to help feed him, although I don't think that Jake knew who the hell the Prince or anybody else was for most of that time. That's the way things go sometimes, I guess. Burn out or rust out, one or the other—and, either way, only the lucky ones'll have someone like the Prince around. 'Course, when he wasn't taking care of his uncle, Johnny worked hard to fix up the place. The Prince wanted a different kind of Leroy than the one his Uncle Jake ran. He repainted all of the rooms and put that garden in out back. He set up a bunch of rules and stuff for the people who worked here and fixed up that old incinerator, for the Burning Days, you know. And he really cut the general cost of operations around here. He chopped the laundry bills and supplies' budgets in half and, I swear to you, I haven't heard of a cable bill comin' into this place in over three years but all the rooms have a full slate of television. Sometimes you even get the pay-per-view stuff free. The Prince cleaned out most of the riff-raff who hung around here, the rubbies and grifters and hookers. But, you know, he didn't just run them off the property. No! He dealt with them pretty good, made them offers, treated them like humans. Most he put in touch with social organizations or got them jobs of some kind. Some took advantage, some didn't. But he gave them a helluva good chance, probably better than anyone else ever had. For example, there used to be an old whore who hung around here, used this place all the time. She'd pick up drunks in the bar and rip 'em off over in the rooms. God, I can't think of her name. Never mind, anyways, it will come to me, but I remember the Prince getting her into a course at Thornton Business School and now, believe it or not, so I hear, she's a secretary for some company here in town, insurance company, I think. Depending on your opinion of insurance companies, of course, some would say she just moved up in the whoring trade, but that's still pretty remarkable, isn't it? And it came just in time, 'cause she was gettin' long in the tooth for what she was doin'. The darker it was, the drunker you were, the better she looked ... but it was gettin' so it could never get dark or drunk enough, y'know what I mean! But now, I hear she's doin' just fine. Sellin' insurance with a smile.

But Shonagh, oh yeah, Shonagh used to help out in here, behind the lunch counter and waitin' tables. She was about the most independent person I ever met—you might even say stubborn. No matter how many times you would tell her how to do something, if she thought there was some other way to do it, some way that she thought was more efficient, or that suited her whims better, forget it. I said to myself more than once, 'You might as well save your words, man. Save your words. A wink is as good as a nod to a blind horse!' Those menus are still designed the way she wanted, and the colour scheme in here. She was one strong-willed young woman. 'Course she was right a lot of the time too. And, good for business. I mean, she got to know customers by name and knew about their lives, their families. People came here to talk to Shonagh first, and eat second. For a time, she made Rainy's, Rainy's. And she and the Prince absolutely hit it off. I don't know where she come from and I don't know where she went, but while she was here this place was like paradise on earth, man. Even more than normal. There was a kind of peace or harmony or something in here. A life force. A joy. I know it sounds corny but there was a feeling in the air that you could rub into your hands like soap. I don't know what it was. But Shonagh and the Prince were hot together, man. With a crowd in here on a weekend, and some band cookin' around the eastside 'L', and Shonagh and the Prince carrying on, you'd weep to see the morning come. She was goddess of the Leroy. It was all like a scene from some movie, or a book, something too good to be real. And, of course, it was—the hottest fires burn out the quickest, they say. It was pretty low around here for a long time after she left. Trust me on that. It was like Kennedy bein' killed or your last dog dyin', people just could not believe Shonagh had left. They'd come in and ask 'where's Shonagh' and you'd tell them and they'd stand there stunned for a while and then turn around and leave without even orderin' what they'd come in for. And add to that, of course, Jake died the day she left. Those were tough times. All the tougher, I think, because of the good times that had gone before. God, what a pair Shonagh and the Prince were, what a fire they lit, what a time that was at the Leroy! ... Hey, you know I've talked so much, I run out of coffee. You wouldn't mind buying me a fresh cup, would ya? Thanks.

iv

"Hmmmmm. Hmmhmmm."

v

She was *très* cool, as my daughter would say. And pretty hot too, I always thought. In fact, that's probably how I remember her best, those two things in one. *Feu et glace*. Fire and ice. Like she wanted to settle down here and make this place into some kind of kingdom, or something, but she was also being pulled in another direction. She wanted to be absolutely free, to do whatever she wanted, to go wherever she wanted. She was stranded between dreams, is what she was. I was that way once, but then I stopped having dreams. She sat and talked with me one day, it was right there, in that second booth, and she had just read about how some desert tribes in North Africa were caught in a drought and a local church, in connection with the UN, wanted donations and volunteers for relief. They were going to send a squadron of missionaries and relief workers over to Africa. Well, Shonagh was ready to sign up and go right over there to take some water and clothes and food and Bibles to help all those poor people in that desert. I told her she'd better look into it a bit closer to make sure it was all on the up and up. I'm not sure that she paid a lot of attention to what I told her, but at some point the Prince came into the restaurant and I never heard a thing about relief and those people in the desert and Africa again. Now, don't get me wrong. Shonagh wasn't, how you say, *un flocon*, a flake or anything—it's just that she couldn't latch onto something, she couldn't catch the right dream, and so everybody else's dreams caught her for a time. But they were caught too, you see. As my New Brunswick relatives would say, every fisher's greatest dream, and nightmare—the catch of your life, either you pull it out or it pulls you under. No other options. She was like some big fish who willingly took everybody's bait. The Prince came close but, in the end, she couldn't be landed by nobody. I don't imagine nobody ever will, at least, until she lands herself. *Feu ou glace*—you can't be both, or hang onto both—one'll destroy the other. And Shonagh just wasn't able, wasn't ready to decide which she had to be. In the end, *la catastrophe* ... she was the princess who didn't know what to do with her prince and disappeared with a kiss. Fire and ice.

That's really what that boarded up room is all about, you know. It's about fire and ice.

vi

Shonagh—yeah, they called Shonagh an angel. Well, she was an angel, all right, an angel of death and destruction. Of hell! She killed me and tried to destroy my world. That's the only thing I can say about her. She took that shining sword of hers and cut out my heart. Unhooked my plug. Like some butcher at Belsen. She tried to wreck everything I had spent my whole life to build. Most of all, John. She nearly tore him apart and he never saw what she was all about.

You know, I owned the Leroy and it was me and my wife who took care of John, and Matt, too, I guess ... who raised them from the time they was about seven. They were my brother's kids but when Mariah and Joe was killed—they was driving to see Matt in the hospital—he'd gotten his appendicitis out—when their car went off the road and caught fire—John escaped, but not Joe or the wife. So, the twins fell to us and we did a damn good job, if I say so myself. We inherited the boys, I guess, just like I inherited the Leroy—after my father died, my mother had to decide who got the country house, and who got the Leroy. She gave the house to Joe—and he sold it and blew the money in a year. I got the Leroy and ran it for over forty years. The boys had just turned seven when they arrived, but they was already as different as night and day. By the time he was eight John knew more about this old joint than I ever did but Matt, he never liked it here—always wanted to be somewheres else, and finally that's where he went. West—went to live with Mariah's parents on the coast. Course they encouraged that ... thought their place would give the boys a better life, but John would have no part of it. He loved the Leroy. ... Matt, well, for awhile, he kept in touch; then nothing. Like the wind. ... You know, most folk around here don't even know John's got a brother, let alone a twin. Maggie and I didn't have no children, so John became our only child—we gave him everything we could, especially after Matt left, and he was a great kid. After my Maggie died, I gave the place to John. It was his by then anyway. It was like ... that was his purpose. I know that sounds stupid to say. And I know that the Leroy's kind of an old dump. A lot of that's my fault—I didn't give it much tending to, especially after Maggie took sick. But with a bit of work, you can make a living here. Maggie and I did, and I knew that John could too. Make a living, have a comfortable life. You can be your own boss, be free here. But Shonagh, she tried to take all of that from me, and from John; she was set on changing it all, on destroying it, but I saw through her after a while and she didn't like that. I could feel my sickness coming on that year, the year she was here—I could see myself getting thinner and yellower every day, my bones rising through my skin—I knew I was on the road to dirt—but I climbed the ladder, goddamn-it, and I fought that angel of destruction for me, and for Maggie, and for John and, most of all, I think, for the Leroy. For the heart and soul of the Leroy. This good goddamned old Leroy.

- 38 -

The salt taste of blood fills his mouth

It takes Fruitfarm only twelve minutes to cover the couple of blocks between the Leroy and Tom and Mike's. He enters the squat building set back from Dundas and is greeted by a large man with shaggy black hair, Red Jackson.

"Hi, Red. Been busy?"

"Not very, Mike. One old couple came in and bought a piece of that green runner for their balcony. Other than that, nothing."

"Well, one sale is better than none, I guess. It's still early. Any sign of that Tecumseh guy?"

"No, none at all. Not since he left with the truck."

"Ok. Well, you knock off for lunch. I'll see you in an hour. Rainy's has meatloaf on for a special. I have a smoked meat."

"Ok. Good to know. See you later."

"Righto."

Red exits the front of the store just as a dark Buick pulls to a stop. Four men get out, look around, watch Red go down the street. Then they approach the store; three of the men enter while one stops and stands outside at the door.

"Good afternoon, gentlemen. Something I can do for you?"

"We're looking for some information."

"Well, I've got lots of that—flyers and brochures, and we have a computer data base…"

"No. Not rug information. You're Mike Black, right?"

"Yes, I am."

"And you owned a 1976 Dodge pick-up that was involved in a robbery?"

"Yes, I guess I did … it was stolen. You guys aren't cops, are you? I told all that I know to the cops the other day. And what robbery? I never heard about any robbery—it was involved in an accident."

"Number one, you're right, pal—we're not cops. Number two, it was a little more than an accident. And I'm betting that you know that."

The three men triangulate themselves around Fruitfarm in the centre of the showroom like the points of an isosceles and he begins to sense a danger in their geometry.

"I don't know what the hell you're talking about. Who are you, anyways?"

"You can just think of me as a messenger from God, buddy. And something very valuable got stolen and God wants it back. And your truck was involved in the heist and I don't believe in coincidences. So what've you got to say—better speak up and save yourself some grief. Maybe save your family from grief too."

"Get the hell out of my store."

Two points of the isosceles move quickly to pin Fruitfarm's arms and Saint Paul Corrino drives his fist hard into Mike's stomach. The quickness of the blow catches Fruitfarm by surprise; he doubles over and gives some of Rainy's coffee back to the world, not that the world really wants it at this point.

"Now, you son-of-a-bitch, quit playing games with us. We just saw you over at the Leroy, talking to two guys with a Mustang. Who are they?"

"That's my brother and his friend. I hadn't seen them in months." Fruitfarm struggles to regain his breath just as Saint Paul hits him again.

"Are they in on it? They looked like a pretty jumpy pair to me. What else you got to say?" Paul leans in close to Fruitfarm.

"I've got nothing else. There is nothing else. I don't know what the hell you're talking about!"

"Look. This is Sunday, buddy. I'm going to give you a day or two to think things over. But we'll be back. If you're smart, you'll return the goods. If not, well, you can't say I didn't warn you. And don't try to make a run or anything, 'cause you're gonna be watched, right!"

Paul begins to straighten up, and then remembers something.

"Oh yeah. And one other thing, from now on stay the hell away from the Leroy if you want to continue seeing the turf from the sunny side. Got it? Consider that place off limits." Paul squeezes Fruitfarm's cheeks together with his right hand and pushes his head back as the isosceles' boys let go. Fruitfarm sprawls backward on the concrete floor.

"There boys, that should do. If anyone asks you, you can tell 'em we gave him a good once over. Next time, he'll be a little looser, I bet. Let's get outta this joint."

As they vacate Tom and Mike's, the man at the door returns to the wheel of the Buick and, in a moment, car and men are gone. Fruitfarm sits and then gets to his feet. He feels shaky. He is also angry and puzzled and disturbed—he feels violated, embarrassed—and, deep inside, begins to wonder about Gabe and Lucky and the old orange Dodge and the Leroy. That man who had punched him did not believe in coincidences and, right now, Fruitfarm didn't have much faith in them either. He starts to calm down—when Red comes back, he would go home; surely the Tecumseh guy will be back soon to help Red out with the rest of the day. He would go home, make sure that his family was safe, perhaps have them stay out of town with Teresa's parents for a week. There is something wrong here, something strange. Calling the cops is an option, but it might complicate matters more than anything else. The business with the stolen Dodge is quiet right now and, somehow, he feels leaving it that way would be the best thing. Sleeping dogs, you know! Fruitfarm sits back down on the floor—that first blow had taken more out of him than he thought. He can still feel it deep inside. He will need another moment or two and then he will get up. As to the threats against him, these days there are always threats everywhere. It was an angry world—if you drove too slow, someone would threaten you, if you drove too fast, someone would threaten you—Fruitfarm felt that he could deal with the threats when the time came. Strangely, right now the idea that most fills his thoughts—the next time he sees Dom at Rainy's, he will have a story to tell that, with a few embellishments, will equal or better any of his. Right now he can see Dom jealous and squirming, and the giant Deed soaking all of it in. He smiles at the thought and then, strangely, he thinks of his long dead mother, Jane, dousing herself with gasoline and lighting that match. Something wrong, something strange. Always. And then he coughs and the salt taste of blood fills his mouth.

- 39 -

A helluva thing

Blue and Oz are standing near the end of the counter as the Prince enters from the Office. It is a bright Monday morning.

"Hey, guys. I'm going to drop by the hospital and check on Fruitfarm. Last night he was still pretty doped up. You two can keep things here under control for an hour or so?"

"No problem, Prince," says Oz. "That's a helluva thing, eh? A couple thugs bustin' him up like that, and for no reason. They didn't steal nothing?"

"No. Not according to Mike; and nothing that Red could see. Till wasn't cracked or anything. These guys just cornered him at the store, asked him some questions, and wailed away. And Mike says, just before they took off, they warned him never to go near the Leroy again. It's a strange world, Oz."

"Can you wait a second, Prince," Blue chimes in. "I'll make a sandwich and a thermos of coffee? We all know how bad hospital food is."

"Sure, Blue. Fruitfarm will appreciate that."

"So I guess it's a good thing his brother, of all people, shows up, just in time, like out of nowhere. Fruitfarm was sayin' just the other day that he hadn't seen him in months."

"Yep, I heard him say that," says Blue. "And you know Dom and Deed were some miffed when they heard. Dom says he's gonna turn the town upside down 'til he finds out who did this. He says Fruitfarm owes him a lunch!"

"Well, never underestimate Dom. He might just do that, 'specially if a free lunch is at stake," cautions Prince with a smile.

"Yeah, you're right there, Prince," says Oz. "You never know with Dom. Like that teacher thing—it really sounds like he's pulled it off. Last thing they needed was some papers to show their native status and Dom says he's off to get them today—I guess he knows some guy who owns a garage out on the Rez. Who knows with Dom—he never stops talkin' and good old Deed never says nothing."

"Yep ... great Deed never speaks, does he?" Blue adds quietly.

"No, not that I've ever heard, Blue," says Johnny. "I guess he was a normal kid 'til both his parents went out to a community dance one night and just disappeared. Without a trace. Children's Aide took care of him after that, at least until he met Dom, and now they kind of take care of each other. According to Dom, Deed stopped talking and started growing—within a year he was almost as huge as he is now, and all in Grade 6. And never said a word since."

"How curious!"

'Our Prof says its psychosomatic trauma, to use his words, and not some physical thing—it's like his body has trapped his words inside. Like a spell that needs to be broken, a dream he needs to wake from ... some magic word or great act—that's all he needs. Or a shrink. So says Benny. In the meantime, he is one awesome guy—our silent friendly giant."

"Well, it's damn good he's friendly," Oz interjects. "Can you imagine what he could do if he ever got riled? That time the jack was broken, he held up the back end of the van while I changed the tire. All by himself. I wouldn't want to get him pissed at me! And sometimes silence ain't so bad either. I figure Dom talks enough for both of them!"

"You have never spoken a truer word, Oz. ... So, I see you working with Emily. How's she doing?"

"She is settling in like she was born here, Prince."

"Well," Johnny says with a smile. "She may have been, Oz—a long time ago, so she says."

"You should see her work ... I mean, she must be twenty years older than me and she's out there hoeing and raking—she can't figure out why we don't have a team of horses and a plough. I told her that I could rent a roto-tiller but I kind of get the sense that she doesn't know what I'm talking about. So, I just let her hoe and rake and chop. She seems happy doing it ... with me and Angus watching and getting her whatever she needs."

"Well, I guess she's got a lot of energy stored up, a lot of mojo..."

"I picked up some stuff for her—I gave Benny the bills. A new shovel and a hoe and some chemicals—calcium oxide, phosphates, potassium—although she just calls them lime and potash and says they're good for the soil. She's got a great big garbage can of this stuff all mixed up back there, toxic as hell if you ask me, and several pails full of it. She claims she needs to mix it into the soil before she plants. She keeps saying she's waitin' for the right moon to get the crops in? And she wants a load of cowshit, boss. So I told her I'd speak to you about that."

"Sure, Oz. It's good to know I'm cowshit central around here. I have this strange feeling that the End is about to buy some bags of cow manure—I bet Emily'll find cowshit-in-bags a bit of a trip."

"No doubt, but I bet she adapts to it. She's quite a character. Kind of a trip, herself."

"You said a mouthful there, Oz."

"And right on topic, here's the food for Fruitfarm, Prince," Blue interjects.

"Thanks, Blue. You, too, Grease." Johnny shouts to the unseen cook in the back. "I'll get going then. I'm not fond of hospitals—I don't s'pose anyone is, but Fruitfarm's a good soul. Sometimes, we gotta do what we gotta do. See both of you in a couple hours or so."

"Tell him Oz says hello. And I'll try to get by later."

"Give him our best, Prince."

Johnny exits back into the eastside 'L' and, for Oz and Blue, the day unfolds as usual.

- 40 -

The Leroy sounds fine to me

The bright yellow Mustang is parked on Kent Street, a side-street that leads into Dover Avenue just in view of the Henry MacLean residence in northwest Thornton. Sitting in the front seat, Gabe and Lucky pass a paper-bagged bottle back and forth. Lucky is talking to Gabe.

"So, your brother's gonna be ok?"

"Yeah, I called the hospital this morning and they said he was doin' fine. But that it was good he got there when he did. His wife and kids were with him this morning."

"I still can't get over finding him like that yesterday. He was damned lucky we cruised round there when we did."

"No kiddin'. He was in pretty rough shape. And no idea who attacked him, or why. Makes no sense, man."

"You got that right." Lucky takes a long swig of the bottle. "You saved his life, bro., calling the ambulance just in time."

"Yeah, that should get me a better seat on the ride to hell?"

"Shit, man, for that, you get to drive the bus." Both men laugh.

"But you know what I forgot, I forgot to get the damned

pamphlets for that summer camp, and that was the reason we went there in the first place."

"Hell, man, when things work out for us, you'll be able to buy your own summer camp. Fuck the pamphlets."

"Yeah, I guess. Anyways ... so, Lucky, we still need to decide where we make the trade. What about the Eldorado Mall? In the Food Court? I thought it looked ok yesterday."

"Yeah ... but no. No to the mall. It's too far to walk to get out, and the parking lot's a zoo. Might get trapped. We want someplace we can drive right up to, get the loot, dump the person we grab, and hit the road."

"What about the bus station?"

"Too busy there. And it stinks. All those people ridin' the buses and sweatin'."

"So, what does that leave ... Barry Park is too wide open—no cover? ... The Leroy, I guess?"

Lucky takes a swig. "Yeah, I think it's the best. We know the place. We take a room, get the money and just leave the sucker we kidnap behind. Lay low for a day, make arrangements with Malley, get Liz and your boy, and then take off. Get outta town for awhile. Split the profit and let the good times roll. And all the summer camps your kid will ever need."

"Ok. That sounds solid to me, buddy. 'Though I got to admit, every time I get near the Leroy I can't help but remember ... oh, what in hell was her name? Remember, the old black whore, the night before that house job fell apart and we got sent up?"

"Oh God, yeah. ... Grace. Old Amazing Grace. Right? We were having drinks at Rainy's, getting primed for the job and she picked us up."

"Yeah, and you passed out and I was too drunk to do

anything, but she wanted her money anyways. We had that big argument. You woke up and went for her but she booted you in the balls."

"Yeah, the bitch was a fuckin' soccer queen, and she was packin' a big old colt '45 too, which kinda tipped the argument in her favour."

"Gimme that." Gabe takes the bottle and a long drink. "She took all the cash we had … I remember we had to walk all the way across town, and arrived late, and that meant we were all out-of-sync. And that's really what screwed up that job. That and you sending that kid to the promised land."

"Mostly I just remember Grace kicking me so hard in the nuts I could see next Tuesday."

"Anyways, that's the past, buddy. This is the future. And the Leroy sounds fine to me."

"Yeah, and maybe we'll have a drink at Rainy's before the deal goes down to celebrate that future. Only this time I'm gonna let my nuts skip the party."

- 41 -

Let's go Larry

A blue and white taxi enters the driveway that curves in front of the Maclean house, deposits a man with several sets of carpet and floor samples at the front portico and then moves away. The front door opens before Dave punches the doorbell.

"Hello. You must be from the carpet place?" A pleasant-looking, young blonde woman greets Dave. Dave puts his samples down and they shake hands.

"Yes. I'm Dave Bryden, from Tom and Mike's Carpet although I actually work out of Elliot City. I'm here to see Carren MacLean."

"Yes ... er, 'no' actually. Carren is delayed for a few moments. But I'm Cindy Brown, her partner-in-crime. You and I can get the business started. Carren's detained but should be here shortly. We can go through the house ... there's some sandwiches and lemonade out back ... Whoa! What is that?"

The shrill screech of a car's tires is close. It is a yellow Mustang and it careens out of a side street, slows briefly on Dover Avenue and then twists sharply into the long drive that horseshoes toward the MacLean estate. It comes speeding right toward them, then skids to a precipitous halt. A short man in a light windbreaker jumps out of the passenger's seat. And he is waving a huge revolver.

"Get in the car. Both of youse," he shouts and pulls the front seat forward. "Get in the damn car. What's the matter with you? Are you both deaf?"

Gabe shoves his gun in his belt, grabs the petite blond woman by the shoulders and pushes her into the backseat of the Mustang, her head thumping off the door frame. Then he turns to the man who is advancing toward him.

"C'mon. C'mon." The man wearing a long dark coat behind the steering wheel is shouting.

"Wait a minute. You can't..." Gabe hits the salesman hard in the stomach and doubles him over. Then he grabs him by the collar and belt and throws him sprawling into the car. The man crashes over the woman who has just started to struggle up, knocking her down again. Gabe leaps into the front seat and slams the door.

"Let's go Larry, let's go!"

The Mustang lurches forward, ripping down the drive and turning right onto Dover.

"I'm goin' to take her easy through here, Curly Joe. Wouldn't want to get pulled over for somethin' stupid. Have those two keep their heads down, or else."

"Yeah, both of youse. Get your heads down. Lay down. You mac, on the floor, and you lady, lay on the seat." Gabe brandishes the revolver over their heads and both of the back seat captives comply with assorted grunts and whimpers. A degree of incomprehensible terror is settling in.

"Let's go Larry. Get at it, Scout!"

"You got 'er, Curly. Hi Ho."

- 42 -

Ah shit!

The Mustang slows.

"Ah shit!" the driver says pulling a piece of yellow paper out of his shirt pocket. "We forgot to leave the god-damned note."

A car's tires squeal in braking and a yellow Mustang twists through a U-turn on this otherwise quiet suburban street in northwestern Thornton. It accelerates, then slows briefly and sharply twists again into the long drive that curls in front of the MacLean estate. It stops abruptly in front of the portico and, this time, the wheel man gets out and strides up to the heavy front doors. He pulls a dispenser of Scotch tape from his coat pocket along with a folded up piece of yellow stationery; then he tapes the paper to the entrance and returns to the car. The Mustang jolts into gear and quickly retraces its previous exit out of the driveway. As it disappears, a light gust of wind flutters the paper, the tape releases and the yellow note lifts gently into the air and wafts down to concealment among the branches of some waxy euonymus clustered beside the entranceway. A young chipmunk scurries over to inspect it but, not yet able to read, and the note being tasteless, the striped rodent quickly loses interest and turns to other concerns of its day.

- 43 -

Waiting in the dark

The Mustang eases to a stop in a parking space near the entranceway of a rose-coloured apartment complex on Second Street. This is Lucky's castle, at least, a dank lower studio apartment half below ground is.

"Gimme my gun, Curly. Ok." Lucky turns to the back seat. "Now listen to me, and listen good. Nobody needs to get hurt here. Just cooperate and everything will be fine. I'm gonna escort both of youse into an apartment here—I'll have a gun on you all the time, and you can see the blade my partner's carrying, right. Don't look at nobody, don't talk to nobody. We'll get you inside, we'll make the deal, and you'll be outta here in a couple hours. All right. Nobody says nothing. Now, let's go."

The four, huddled close together like the forlorn phalanx of some lost and dysfunctional Roman legion, moves awkwardly across the weedy asphalt and into the apartment building. They pause as one steps out of the group.

"Shit, man," Gabe whispers. "You can check your mail later. Let's keep moving!"

The party moves on to a splotchy brown door marked number two, and then inside.

"Ok. Both of you, keep moving. Into this bedroom here."

The captives move as told into a small room with a small bed and a number of scattered magazines and articles of clothing. The curtain on the small window of the room has been sealed tight with silver duct tape. Now the hands of each captive are tightly secured behind their backs, legs wrapped tight and a piece of tape secured over the mouth. Both are pushed into a sitting position on the bed and Lucky flips on a bedside radio. A strange country-sounding tune is playing: "O on the day the dead awaken, I think that I'll just sleep in…"

"Just be patient. This won't take long and then you'll be outta here." Lucky flicks out the light and shuts the bedroom door cascading the room into a void.

"Damn." With the pungent earthy smell of the room enveloping him and Cindy Brown bruised and shivering beside him, the thought enters Dave Bryden III's head: "I left my samples laying against one of the pillars at the front of that house. The boss'll kill me if I don't get them back."

Dave turns on his side. There, there, he feels the paper in his pocket. At least he hasn't lost that, the receipts he's collected from the towing and the garage and the night at *Voyageur's End*; his suitcase and other personal stuff are still at Red's where he'd slept the last couple nights. But at least he hadn't lost the receipts. When he twists back into a sitting position, he brushes up against Cindy Brown and, feeling the firmness of her left breast, he can't help but feel a slight wave of arousal. But then he can feel her shaking. He starts to try to say something but can't and realizes he can't at the same time. And so he sits calm and steady in that pose hoping that he can give Cindy, and himself, whatever it is that Cindy, and he, need. From the moment America had hiccoughed on the freeway, time has made no sense. And it continues that way. And so Dave Bryden III continues that way. Silent. Waiting in the dark. Waiting.

"All right." says Lucky. "With that radio on in there, they won't be able to hear us, and it'll make the time pass more quickly for them anyways. So ... so far, so good. They didn't put up much of a fight did they?"

"Nah. If that was me or you, we'd still be scrappin' back there in that driveway, wouldn't we?"

"Damn right. Nobody'd pull up in a car and take me away. 'Course I think we surprised them—they weren't expectin' it. But still, they was pretty soft. Rich people—got more money than muscles. Here's the woman's purse. She's only carrying about fifty bucks—but here's her keys and ... yep! Carren MacLean. Her Daddy's the rich one, all right. But he's gonna be a little bit poorer soon. Right, Gabe? And the guy must be her husband, or brother, or something."

"Yeah, probably. He sure as hell wasn't her security! We pretty well had to take both of them, I guess, them standing there together, seeing the car pull up, seeing us. It may turn out for the best anyways. They'll be gettin' two back for their money instead of one. It may make them hand it over a bit quicker. 'Course it may also take them a day or two to raise the money. You know that, right Lucky—probably be Wednesday before we get it?"

"Yeah, I suppose! But it'll be worth waitin' for. And you'll get your wife and kid back. So, Gabe, now what?"

"We wait—a bit anyway. Somebody'll find that note and know what's up. The note said to call that number at 4 o'clock, right?"

"Yeah. I'll go over there just before four and wait. You can keep a lid on things here, right?"

"No problem."

"And then we'll stay here for a while, then go to your place … move around so no-one can zero in on our location. We'll outsmart 'em, man, keep a step ahead of 'em."

"Sounds good to me. You got any beer here?"

"Beer! Hey, man. Does the Pope take a shit in the woods? I got a whole case in the fridge just for the occasion. Bring me one too, there, will you Curly Joe? All this kidnap stuff makes me thirsty."

- 44 -

Nature commits no errors

It is an unseasonably warm March Monday.

Dom and Deed wander about Wilson Hall. They have thirty minutes to kill before the Registrar's Office opens. The requisite forms and all of the other criteria necessary, including special approval by the Dean, himself, have been completed to enroll in the government's Re-enter and Recover Educational Initiative. They just need to hand in the last of this paperwork.

"C'mon Deed. Let's see if we can get a cup of coffee. They must have a cafeteria around here somewhere."

The two men turn down a long hallway. On their left, an imposing Gothic doorway with large brass letters announces The Nicholson Archibald Wilson Memorial Library; to their right, the Wilson Study Hall. And directly in front of them, at the end of the hall, Nick's Café.

"There's a cafeteria down there, Deed. We should be able to get some coffee there."

They enter the cafeteria, a large bright room with banks of long empty tables and a wall of windows that offers a view of a parking lot and a student residence. The cafeteria is empty, however, and the serving area, normally bustling with all the fare

The Prince of Leroy

that students can be enticed to consume, is fenced and locked down. It is that time of the year when the Faculty of Education's students are out doing their practice teaching in regular schools and, since this building serves this Faculty alone, campus food services closes here for these periods of the year. However, along the left-hand wall where they enter are several vending machines. One offers soft drinks, one, juice and bottled water, one, an array of potato chips and other snack foods and one, Delicious Coffee. Fresh ground as you order it. Through a glass partition, you can even see a pile of dark brown beans.

"Well, Deed. I guess this will have to be our coffee. I got a buck seventy-five—have you got a quarter. That'll get us two. ... Great. Thanks brother."

Dom feeds the change into the great machine which groans into life, whirrs for several seconds, makes grinding-like noises which suspiciously sound like an old recording, then drops a cup down a chute and fills it with black liquid.

"There's yours, Deed. I'm having mine sweet and lite, just like the sign says."

The two men, carrying their full cups of coffee like unpinned hand grenades, walk slowly across the cafeteria and sit at a table buttressed against the windows. Then, each sips his brimming cup and, just as quickly, places the cup on the table. They look across at the other.

"Holy shit, Deed! What the hell do you think that is? It tastes like some swamp water Hitler farted in. Delicious Coffee, my ass."

Deed smiles.

"Good morning, gentlemen. I see you have been introduced to one of the seven wonders of the modern world, our vending machines. If it says its coffee, you know, it must be coffee."

Dom and Deed both look up to see a man standing over them, dressed in brown corduroy trousers, blue denim shirt, with a shock of white hair and a great amber beard.

"Do you mind if I sit down and join you? I'm waiting to meet a person over in the Library and for a call on my cell phone—the cafeteria is the best place in the entire building for reception. I'm Wes Terranian. I teach English here."

"Have a seat, Wes—the more the merrier. I'm Dominic, this is Deed. We're going to be students here in the fall. We have some papers to drop off but the office isn't open yet."

Terranian sits, puts his briefcase on the table and loops a brown tweed sports coat over the back of another chair.

"Indeed. Ah, the paperwork—ah, the auguries of bureaucracy! The world is still greased by ink and parchment, I'm afraid. And, as you've noticed, this time of the year everything is a bit slow around here. ... So what makes you want to be teachers?"

"Oh, I don't know," says Dom. "I suppose the same thing that makes you want to be a professor."

"That's a very good answer, good fellow. The great diversivo principle of debate—respond to the question with the question."

"So, what does make you want to be a professor?"

"Oh, lots of things, I guess. Some of it simply has to do with the standards, the old creature comforts, keeping warm and dry and fed. But there's also a kind of unstructured freedom to this sort of life. Much of the time, you can do what you want, when you want. And you get to explore lots of interesting ideas and concepts, challenge yourself intellectually, engage in some fascinating discussions with colleagues, maybe make the world a better place."

"Sounds just like what we do at the Leroy, eh Deed? The

Leroy's a motel, Professor, that a bunch of us hang around at, do small jobs for. But most of the time we just do what we want to and have long conversations and arguments with our friends, sometimes our enemies. I don't know if we make the world a better place—maybe, maybe for ourselves sometimes. I know the coffee's better there than it is here. A helluva lot better! ... What are you carrying there—looks like three books, all the same?"

"Yes, they are. It's a recent book that I have written. It's called *Hickory Tunes*. It offers my views on education today, some of the things that I think should be changed, some redirections that need to be considered. That kind of thing. Here, have a look at one." Wes hands one of his books to Dom.

"So, you wrote this. A whole book?"

"Yes, it had been a lifetime dream of mine to summarize and clarify my own ideas and conclusions in respect to my experiences in education. To codify all of it in one place. And part of it is a personal reflection about my own a-progressive education, the generally deleterious effect it had on me and my generation. As to why I am carrying these around, I just found out that our Library has not yet stocked any copies so I came down to talk to the head librarian and offer to sell her two or three but, not unlike your intended destination, the Library is not open yet—won't be in until after 10:30. It's the off-season, so-to-speak, around here. By the way, this would be a good book for anyone just entering the profession. They're only $65.00 a copy. You might think about it. It would be a good summer read for you."

"Thanks, it looks like quite a book. It's thick. Here Deed, why don't you take a gander. So what did you say that you profess at here?"

"English—English education, actually. Training people to be English teachers."

"God, I remember English in school. I hated that subject. Remember, Deed? No offense, Wes, but it never made any sense to me."

"No offense taken, Dom. It is a challenging subject for many, as are the maths and sciences for others."

"Well, to be honest, I wasn't crazy about them neither. But I still found English the worst. My teachers would read out some poem or something, and then go through it and find all kinds of hidden meanings and stuff. I never could see any sense in any of the things they was saying. I don't know whether it was all just beyond me, or whether them teachers was just making all that stuff up to try and impress. Either way it made no sense."

"Well, perhaps in the coming year you will get a chance to read some literature again, some poetry, and you'll reassess your views. It is a wonderful thing, you know, it can lift the spirit and the soul. I talk about poetry a bit in that book your good friend is holding. Poetry and vision. You know, "a vision, or a waking dream. Fled is that music," especially in our crazy contemporary times? As I say, that book, itself, has been a kind of lifetime dream of mine."

"A lifetime dream, eh? I've been a little bit shy of dreams, lately," Dom responds.

"Ahh, no, you mustn't be shy of dreams, my friend. Dreams are part of what make us human. Dreams are the language our subconscious uses to tell us our own story. Some would say that to understand our dreams is to know ourselves. Though often it's not easy—dreams are elemental tales, often blunt and fragmented, like the stories a young child might tell, or some old folk tale. Or maybe like some of those poems your teachers read to you?"

"Really? So ... you know a lot about dreams, Professor?"

"Well, I am not a psychoanalyst, or a fortune teller with a Tarot pack, but I have read some of the historical experts, Freud and Jung and the like."

Dom jumps on this, sensing a chance to solve the mystery that has been annoying him for the past week. "Did those guys ever say anything about a dream where you dreamed you was dead, 'cause I just had a dream like that and it scared the bejesus out of me?"

"Well, yes. ... Yes, Freud certainly had a little bit to say. Old Brücke's dream, and all of that. A great deal of Freud actually has to do with the inevitable but painful riddle of death. Looking at his works in the library might show you how to carry off a Freudian analysis of a death dream such as yours."

"OK. Sounds good. I should write those names down ... you wouldn't have a pen and a piece of paper, would you?"

"Sure, here's a post-it note and my pen."

Wes snaps open his briefcase and hands Dom a yellow note and a gold pen.

"Thanks, Professor. That's a heavy pen."

Dom takes the paper and gold pen and prints the names very carefully: Fraud, Young.

"So do you remember anything in particular about what these guys say about a dream where you're dead?"

"Well, yes, if memory serves me," Wes speaks slowly, carefully rummaging out old recollections as if it's a test. "Freud comes to the general conclusion in such cases that the dream may not be about death *per se*, but probably concerns change, some irrevocable event that is about to happen in your life. It may mark a point of metamorphosis for you—as if you were about to emerge from a chrysalis, be changed into a butterfly."

Dom's facial response is somewhat incredulous. "Specifically, as an example, it may show you that, through such change, you can achieve more in life than you have done thus far, more, say, than your father did, although what Freud calls a replacement may need to occur, you may need to substitute another strong and respected figure for your father in order to carry on a satisfying and healthy growth, or perhaps, at least initially, to enable you to actualize the change itself, to break through, to break out of the cocoon of your life."

"Ok—well, I don't know about butterflies but my old man cut the scene when I was ten. Left a bar to get a newspaper and got run over by a cab. I'm pretty sure that I can beat that. So the guy that's dead in my dream is my father, and not me. Wow."

"Maybe. Something like that. Or maybe it's your old self. The person you used to be. Of course, there are other ways to approach the topic, to see dreams more as archetypes of truth and reality, and not wishes as Freud did. The things of your dreams are personal symbols, psychic realities. The dream is the utterance of the unconscious, the doorway to your innermost soul. Carl Jung says that nature commits no errors—so, if you can come to terms with the meanings of those dream symbols as they manifest themselves in your life and determine how they might connect to the lives of others you've encountered, then you should understand your dream, and understand yourself a bit more."

"OK ... well, that's something for me and Deed to chew on. One other question for you, Professor..."

Wes's cell phone chimes a Baroque tune.

"Oh, sorry. Excuse me, gentlemen. I really must answer this. It's the call for which I've been waiting. And I really should talk privately..." Wes rises and moves farther into the cafeteria.

"No problem, Professor. As a matter of fact, Deed and me got to be going too. That office'll be open by now. Thanks for the info. See you in the fall."

"Yes, gentlemen, yes. Hello. Wes Terranium speaking…"

Dom and Deed drop their empty cups into a large garbage pail as they exit the cafeteria and Wes Terranian, the large room now empty, walks back and forth listening intently to the caller on his cell phone.

"I still have a full carton; I even have three copies with me, but just a minute … let me write that down. … Oh? … Oh!" Reaching for his gold pen, Wes realizes that it is gone, and, in the same moment, that three copies of *Hickory Tunes* have devolved into two.

- 45 -

What the hell's the matter with these people

"**Nothing, Gabe. Nothing.**" Lucky slams the door of his apartment. "Absolutely nothing."

"There was no call?"

"Nothing. I can't believe it. I waited over a half hour at that phone near the corner store and nothing. What the hell's the matter with those people?"

"Christ, it's after five o'clock now. Somebody must of got home there and found the note. And I know the phone number was right. Something's fucked, man."

"Rich assholes is what they are, Gabe. They're different. They don't care about nothin' the way we do, not even their kids. And the kids, well, like we said, if that was me or you back there in that driveway, we'd still be fightin'. Nobody'd pull up and just throw me in the back of a car."

"Damn right there, Lucky. Like you say, rich people—more money than moxy. But, the woman's purse ... her keytag says Carren MacLean. Henry MacLean, the real estate guy, is her father. And that was certainly his house."

"Well, maybe nobody got home yet."

"Maybe, but we can't wait. I already phoned Malley and told him we'd have his million by Friday and make the trade then. So we got to get this show on the road. Hand me the telephone book, will you?"

Gabe takes the old house phone from the counter top and puts it on the table as he sits down in a chair. Lucky pulls the thick, dust-laden book of numbers from the top of the refrigerator and gives it to him.

"What're you goin' to do?"

"I am going to phone him at the university. I know he has a big office there. Let's see … ok."

Gabe dials and then sits intently, cradling the receiver of the phone like a baton of nitro on a hot Rockie afternoon, Coolies drilling just around the bend.

"You have reached the Main Switchboard of Thornton University. For service in English, press one. For service…" Gabe hits one. "If you know the extension number for the individual or department you are trying to contact, dial that extension now. If you would like to speak with an operator, please wait on the line." Gabe waits. Some torturous classical music invades the earpiece. Then, startling, a voice, "Yes, good afternoon. Thornton University. How can I help you?"

"Yeah. Yeah, I would like to speak to Henry MacLean."

"That is Dean MacLean, I presume. I will put you through to the Faculty of Education." Gabe waits as electronic reverberations enact a coup d'etat along the line.

"You have reached the Switchboard of the Faculty of Education, Thornton University. For service in English, press one. For service…" Gabe hits one. "Business hours for the Faculty of Education are Monday to Friday, 8:00 am to 4:30 pm.

Although the Main Offices are closed at this moment, you may leave a message in the voice mail system if you wish. You have two options. If you know the extension number for the individual or department you are trying to contact, dial that extension now, and leave your message at the tone. If you do not know the extension but would like to leave a message which will be forwarded on the next business day, please press pound and …" Gabe hangs up.

"Damn it. Look up MacLean's home number, will you Lucky? Maybe he left work and got home by now."

Lucky fumbles through alphabetic fog for a while; Gabe gets up, grabs a beer from the refrigerator and returns to his chair.

"There ain't no number, Gabe. It looks like he don't have a home number listed, at least not for that address on Dover."

"Yeah, it figures—he's probably unlisted, or only uses a cell…"

"Hey, but you know what is here … the number for MacLean Insurance and Real Estate."

"What the hell … gimme that. We'll get through this one way or the other." Gabe squints back and forth from book to phone punching buttons as he goes.

"Good afternoon, M & J Communications. My name is Grace. How may I help you?" The voice holds a curious familiarity which catches Gabe for a moment, then he presses onward, suppressing an old memory.

"I need to speak to Henry MacLean."

"I'm sorry. MacLean Insurance and Real Estate is closed for the current day but will re-open tomorrow at 9:00 am."

"Well, listen lady. Listen good. This is an emergency. Life and death, do you hear me? I got to get in touch with Henry MacLean as soon as possible."

"Well, sir. If it's an emergency, I am sure that I could patch you through to one of the other agents who is on-call..."

"No. Listen. I need to speak to Henry MacLean, and only Henry MacLean. It's a personal matter. An emergency. And now, if not sooner."

"Well, all right. Please hold, but be patient. This may take a few moments, that is, if I can contact him at all." The controlled anarchy of jazz music now riots sorely in Gabe's country rock ear.

Both men take long swigs of their beer.

- 46 -

Any quadruped can get a degree in those

Henry Maclean is sitting at the kitchen table surrounded by shining marble tile and monstrous aluminum appliances. MacLean is drinking a tall glass of dark liquid and intently reading a journal, on occasion retrieving a pencil from the table and making notations in the text. His daughter Carren sits at the opposite end of the table sipping on a glass of Coke and staring at a thick variorum edition of *Paradise Lost*.

"I got to be honest, Dad, I really have no idea what the front door this guy is talking about. First of all the English he uses is, like, written in smog and the story he's telling is just as confucius. It's like he starts in the middle or something, and all the characters have stupid names. Like Moloc and Beeline and Mammary and Sneezy and Grumpy! It might make sense if I'd been dead for five hundred years … I don't know why they make us read this old crud…" Carren shakes her head, exaggerating her frustration even as she is revealing her sloth.

"So the girl who is apt to send a message by writing lol, btw, qfk, wtf, r, and u can't decipher an old poem? I am shocked … really!" Henry smiles.

"Oh, Dad, you know...," Carren rolls her eyes at her father.

"Well, my dear, give me five minutes to finish this article and then maybe I can help. All you really need to do is pass this first year survey credit and then next year you can still go on in English but choose all the bird stuff in the department—Canadian Literature, Children's Lit, Modern American or British, even some loopy creative writing class. Because from what you're telling me about your reading of Milton and Shakespeare and other Renaissance stuff, you're a modern gal, and you really don't want to slip out of English into something like Theology or History, where the language might be worse and the ideas even more confucius, as you say, or maybe even laozi! And, surely, you mustn't descend into something like Soc. or Pysch—any quadruped can get a degree in those. Oh, it's my cell..."

A muffled buzzing is heard and MacLean fishes his phone from his pocket.

"Hello. Dr. Henry MacLean speaking."

"Good evening, Dr. MacLean. This is Grace at M & J Communication. I apologize for contacting you at this number and this time of day but we've got a curious call and, before I dismissed it, I thought I should run it by you."

"Certainly, Grace. Not a problem. What is it?"

"Well, I have a gentleman on the line who phoned M.I.R.E after hours and, of course, was forwarded here. This man claims that his call is an emergency and that he has to talk to you personally, and he sounds really agitated."

"Ok Grace. That does sound curious. Put the call through, but mask this number. I may not want to talk to this person twice. ... Hello. Dr. Henry MacLean here. I understand you have some urgent business with me?"

"Yeah, I do. Here's the deal MacLean. I've got your daughter and son-in-law. And if you want them back, I want two million dollars, in small bills. Tens and twenties. And I want it delivered by Wednesday. You got that?"

"You … you've got my daughter? May I ask with whom I am speaking?

"You can ask all you want. But I want two million. And we'll arrange the drop site later."

"My daughter? Are you sure? Which one?"

Gabe whispers. "Pssst, Lucky, er, Larry. What's the name on that set of keys? … Ok." He speaks loudly. "Yeah, Carren. We got Carren. That's C.A.R.R.E.N! And her husband."

MacLean replies in an incredulous tone. "Well, to be honest, sir, I do not know what you are talking about. Carren, that's C.A.R.R.E.N, is sitting not a metre from me in our kitchen. And, she is not married, at least not that I know of. And my other daughters, with their husbands, are all here as well."

"What?" Gabe descends to silence.

"So I have no idea about what you are blabbering. If this is some kind of crude prank, it is in poor taste. Please do not bother me again. Good day."

- 47 -

A knight without armour in a savage land

Dave Bryden III had not slept well last night at the End in spite of the relatively luxurious room. He wasn't used to being alone in bed, and he wasn't used to drinking as much as he had. And of course the disorder of the day preyed on his sleep as well. So it had been a restless slumber. And so here in the dark, in spite of the ludicrous danger of the situation, maybe because of it, he had lain back and drifted away. And dreams had come, three of them in rapid succession and then they had repeated themselves like television programs after a sweeps month, over and over. Encore presentations as reruns are now called. In the first, Dave was a gunslinger riding his sturdy golden horse across the dusty plains with no true direction or purpose that he could discern, just riding, searching, like the old TV show, a paladin, a knight without armour in a savage land. And then he arrived at a one-street five-saloon town and there was a hasty trial convened and he was the defending attorney. Atticus the Kid! His clients, two shifty greasy-haired fellows, were accused of horse stealing and rape and were probably guilty, but he defended them with every argument he could muster, but when the verdict was read, it was Guilty As Charged, and they were sentenced to be hanged by the neck until dead as soon as a couple ropes could be found. Except when the ropes were found, which was instantly, it was Dave on the gallows around whose neck they had strung the reaper's string and, there, next to him, with a noose for a necktie as well, was his horse, looking as surprised and pissed off as Dave was. Dave's greasy-haired clients were nowhere to be seen but as two were guilty, so two must hang. And, as the hooded hangman shifted his anxious grip on the polished lever, the last thing Dave saw, as the trap door opened and the rope snapped, was his horse wagging a front hoof at him and cleverly turning into a red and white Omni which, according to a recent local bylaw, was pardoned of all sins. And then, before the gallows took his breath away, the second dream. Dave was in charge of the carpet store—Eddie DiGenero had put all of his trust in Dave to open the store and manage the cash and deal with the big corporate buyers while Eddie was taking care of some secret business elsewhere. And so Dave had dressed up—he had rented a striking black tuxedo from Terry the Tuxedo Man, collar trimmed in sable silk and a dark scarlet cummerbund, although the suit did have to be back by five o'clock that day. And the store was filled with customers and every customer was placing a gigantic order so that by noon Elliot City Carpet had made more in one day than it usually took in for a whole year. But then the carillon in the top of the City Hall tower struck twelve, each great bong vibrating across the city, and a customer tried to exit through the front door but it was locked. As Dave started to move toward the door to help, he saw another customer pull on the end of one of the great rolls of carpet that lined the sides of the showroom and as the customer pulled on that green carpet, it turned to water and a green sea flooded across the showroom. And another customer touched a burgundy carpet and there was a burgundy flood whose waters sat atop the green waters like some kind of delicate cocktail. And then there was a tacky orange flood and then an Axminster flood followed by a cheap wash of plaid waters. And all about him customers were crying and screaming and drowning and somewhere a dance band seemed to kick in, playing upbeat hymns, and Dave realized, to his horror, that his tuxedo was getting wet, damaged beyond all repair in this rainbow flood and Terry the Tuxedo Man would make him buy it and that would use up all of the profits of the day and besides a sculptured plush peach flood had just raised the waters to the ceiling of the showroom and then, just when there was no hope, the third dream took over. Dave was still in his tuxedo but he was in a narrow confined space and was moving, slowly, horizontal, down a crowd-lined street. He could just twist his head sideways enough to see hundreds of people, maybe thousands, waving and cheering and weeping, and then there was an echo and a ricochet and everybody scattered, that is, almost everybody, except for one small boy who looked intently at him as he passed, stepped forward, stood at attention, and raised his right hand in a perfect salute. And then he was on his horse again, riding and riding. And the endless plains stretched away for miles, offering a freedom open and inviting and terrible.

So when the two men who had kidnapped and bound him abruptly opened the door and re-entered the room, Dave was almost overjoyed to be released back from his cycle of sleep into his nightmare of waking.

"Who the hell are you people? Gabe—I mean, Joe—take that tape off their mouths."

"Sure thing, Larry. Let me get my knife out."

- 48 -

Something's coming, don't know when

A short stump of a man eases on top of the auburn-haired prostitute and conducts himself through a symphony of movements from syncopated bass to steamy slide trombone to timpani thunder and then slides off like an unread concert program discarded in the rain. A few moments pass.

Sugar Chaque is a hooker; by all accounts, so people tell me, a nice person, too. She is, one might conclude, a nice hooker, exactly the kind that you would choose, not of course that you, like me, would ever choose to entertain a hooker. To be duly noted, though, Sugar is probably not her real name any more than auburn is likely the real colour of her hair. She is one of Jerry Malley's regulars.

"There's your money, honey. Now I got some other business I got to attend to. No need for you to hang around, ok?"

"Ok, Mr. Jones. You knows how to reach me when you wants to see me again."

"Yeah, I'll be in touch, Sugar. You be a good girl."

Sugar quickly dresses and, just before she disappears out of the door, holds her right pinky finger to her lips, then waves it several times at Malley. The way she always says good-bye to him; he nods. Malley slips back into his underwear and a pair of fine light wool trousers, dark blue. He scoops his cell phone from the night-stand near his wallet and hits a memory button.

"Hello. Yes. Is Paul Corrino there? It's, uh, Divine Delivery Service—he'll want to take this call."

Several seconds pass. Then the static breath of a receiver being hoisted.

"Hello, Paul Corrino here."

"It's me, Paul."

"P?"

"Oh, yeah, P. Safe to talk, uh, Q?"

"Yeah, I guess. I thought you was gonna use the burner I gave you."

"Oh yeah ... sorry. No, I guess I left that in another coat. Should I hang up?"

"Nah, I'm alone right now. Duwayne took the call and then he stepped out to get a Coke. We should be ok. As long as we make it quick. So, how's it goin'?"

"Not too bad, I think. I'm phonin' from a room at the Leroy Motel. You know where that is?"

"Yeah, it's a flea bag, isn't it. A dump. Over on Dundas, across from the End? What are you doing there?"

"Oh just some regular business. Wanted to get you up to speed. I've started to move the haul, a bit at a time. And those idiots that ripped us off phoned me to say that they wanted to make an exchange—they can't get the heroin back but they got a million bucks to pay for the wife and kid. They want to make the trade this Friday."

"Really ... do you trust them? How in hell would those guys get a million bucks?"

"I've had them tailed since we grabbed Gabe's family and they got some kind of cock-eyed scheme going down—looks like they're holding someone themselves. But racing around in a flashy, yellow car, it's like they've been holding up a sandwich board, look at us, we're up to somethin', 'cept right now the cops are so busy with dead junkies they haven't bothered to read the sign."

"Really—that sounds like it could complicate things…"

"Maybe, maybe not … Gabe's buddy, the guy named Luke Burrell, is one to be careful around. He's always packing and can be a bit of a loose cannon, you know. He's the one that beat that kid to death on the spur of the moment and did time for Dad."

"Ok, good to know. Like you said, they ain't the brightest stars in the sky, and when you mix in firepower with stupidity, well…"

"That's why I'm keepin' an eye on 'em."

"So, what's your plan, P? Are you holding the guy's wife and kid around your place?"

"No. They're over at the cottage on the lake. I gave Gabe 'til the end of the week—if he hasn't produced by then, the wife and kid'll take a swim. It's all being done on the slide, real quiet. I don't want to get caught in some kind of blown up shit-storm, especially with Dalco's rabbit ears up."

"I hear you. So, at least for now, we hold the course."

"And if the idiots come through with the bread, I'll let 'em go. There's no real profit in doing them, at least for now. After things quiet on the Dalco front, then all bets are off. Eventually, it's good to sew up all the loose ends, you know."

"Yeah, I hear yah."

"Besides, I need to keep a clean profile, being a public benefactor and all."

"What do you mean?"

"Well, Q, my company just gave a big donation to the M.I.R.E. literacy foundation, that big new charity they started here in town. It was really the first payback on the Logos deal—I laundered some of the profit through their charity—got some good publicity and advertising in return, not to mention a hefty tax deduction."

"I am impressed, P. I got to tell you, though, Dalco's not a happy camper. He's come to town—in fact, he's staying right across the road from where you are right now, at the End. And he's got his son with him—now talk about loose cannons, there's a real one. Freddy Junior, he gives me the shivers. He's also got one of the east coast guys down here, a guy named Connie Torrence. Do you know anything about him?"

"No, never heard tell of him. But there are always lots of east coast guys no-one's ever heard of. I do know of Dalco Junior, though, and he is one dangerous mother. He wants to take over from Frederick and from what I hear is willing to do—in fact, has done—just about anything in order to prove himself to the old man. I heard he cut a guy's hand off, a butcher who owed a bit of protection coin, and sent it to his home by Fed-Ex, overnight delivery. Stay clear of him, if you can, Q."

"Yeah, I know the boy's reputation. Most of it's true, too. So, believe you me, P, I'm trying to stay clear of all of them as much as possible. And say as little as I can. Except that Dalco sees me as his right hand man. I just had a little interview, yesterday, you know, with Gabe's brother, Mike. About nothin', really, 'cause I know he don't know nothin'. I'm meeting with Dalco tomorrow afternoon at the old parking garage, to tell him what I found out. He's a sly bastard, you know, never meets with anyone in the same place twice. I'm going to tell him that the theft of the truck is simply a coincidence, as far as I can figure—that Mike Black has no connection to the Logos heist. I hope he buys that—it's the truth, you know. But guys that deal with lies all the time, like Dalco, they don't often know what to do with the truth. At any rate, I figure that we don't want Dalco connecting Gabe and his pal to things, through that truck or Mike or anything else, 'cause that might lead them right to you. They're both fairly well known as a pair of your grunts."

"Yeah, I suppose. And, you know, if they get linked to me, I might just get linked to you, right?"

"No problem P. Just relax. Everything's cool. Dalco still has no idea what went down—he still fingers the Asian boys for it. I think he's going to hit the Ng gang just on suspicion. And all hell may break loose if that happens—although in some ways it might be good, it would probably add to our cover."

"Yeah, yeah. Ok, Q. Well, good to hear that things are still under wraps. Let's us keep it that way. Ok? Stay the course and don't do nuthin' stupid."

"You got it, P. Anyway, I better go—I can hear Duwayne coming back. You let me know what the idiots do. And use the burner next time, ok? I'll be in touch—let you know how tomorrow's meeting with Dalco goes. Talk to you later."

"Yep."

As he flips his cell phone closed, Malley finds himself rapidly snapping his fingers as if *West Side Story* has just broken out in his right hand. It is a nervous reaction he has had ever since he was a child, ever since he learned to snap his fingers. Jerry is thinking. Things are not quite as clear as they should be, like the thick spring fogs that creep in regularly this time of year. There seemed to be a lot of blurry moving parts and it wasn't always clear in what direction they were moving. Maybe he shouldn't have kidnapped Gabe's family; maybe he should have let that go for awhile. But he hadn't. There was a lot of money at stake, and their lack of loyalty, and their stupidity—it really pissed him off. Not only did they need to pay, but they needed to know they was paying. Malley puts on his white shirt and moves to the window where he pulls an end of the curtain askew. He can see the fog lugubrious, slowly enveloping the great Leroy sign like some giant boa. Absent-mindedly, he snaps his fingers several more times. 'Something's coming, don't know when, but it's soon; catch the moon' was a lyric he could have sung but didn't.

- 49 -

Our brother's keeper

Nearly every surface is white where Henry MacLean sits in his kitchen peeling a peach, the juice oozing out, running over his fingers and dripping on to the pristine plate below. All in all, it has been a good week. Three large corporate donations for the new literacy foundation have materialized already—two had been expected, but the third, from a successful local contractor, Malley & Son Enterprises, had come out of the blue. They must have come into some big money recently to contribute what they did. In addition, last week's press conference had gone off reasonably well, in spite of old Terranian's antics, and a meeting with the University president had been mostly congratulatory. All was good. Henry slices a section of peach and sucks it into his mouth from between blade and thumb. His phone, sitting in the middle of the table in front of him, starts to vibrate like a bug rethinking its landing on a barbeque grill. Henry reaches for the device, silences it by punching a button and puts it to his ear as he swivels his chair. Carren re-enters the room and opens the refrigerator with a mute wave to her father. A gruff voice barks into Henry's ear.

"Hello again MacLean! Is that you? Listen to me and listen

good. I got a friend of your family, Cindy Brown. If you ever want to see her again, I want two million dollars in small bills. Call this number at 7:30, that's a half hour from now, and I'll give you more details—435-4653. You got it. And no cops, you hear. And that's a pay phone so don't bother trying to trace a location."

"Who are you? What…" The line goes dead, hollow, I suppose, as a poem T. S. Eliot could have written.

"What was that, Dad?"

"To be honest, Carren, I don't know. It's the second time today someone has phoned me with some sort of kidnapping ransom threat. Remember earlier tonight? This time though he didn't claim to have you, he said he had Cindy. And for some strange reason, he didn't give me any information—he wants me to call him back. But he said the number so quickly, I didn't get it anyway. Curiouser and curiouser!"

"Oh! That is curious. Creepy. But, you know, I was supposed to meet Cindy here this afternoon but I was late, doing more research on that stupid assignment for English, you know the one you helped me with earlier, Milton and Satan and their hot and horny gang. I still really don't know what I'm going to write about—I just can't get into the right frame of mind. Like, I need to be involved in something, kinda know it from the inside, before I can start to write about it, you know. Anyway, I was supposed to meet Cindy and some carpet salesman here at noon but it was two thirty before I got home and the only thing here was some carpet samples left out front. I figured they left those for me to have a look at so I stuck them in the side door of the garage and then I had to dress and meet Andy and his friends."

"Why don't you give Cindy a quick call to see if she's home?"

"Okay. Will do." Carren, with a can of diet Coke in her left hand, palms a smart phone in her right and routinely thumbs an encoded number—no response—she taps a second.

"Hello. Could I speak to Cindy, please? It's Carren." She takes a long sip on her Coke as far away words are spoken.

"Oh. Ok. Well, I haven't seen her, I'm afraid. Not since a couple days ago. Could you have her give me a call though when she gets in—could you, Mrs. Brown? Thanks. Bye."

Carren pockets her phone and takes another long swig of her soft drink. "No. The Browns haven't seen her either. And they were having some big, special dinner at home tonight for friends to tell them about her Dad's big news and she was supposed to be there. So I think little Cindy is in for some big caca when she gets home. You don't think there could be anything to that call you got, do you Daddy? What did they say, anyway?"

"He didn't say much at all. ... No, it couldn't be. It was just some stupid person's idea of a prank or something. If he calls again, I'll get the phone company to trace him. And Cindy, she'll show up. Besides, Carren, I don't suppose that it's really any of our business anyway, even if she were being detained, right? We are not our brother's keeper, are we? Or our sister's! How would your Milton put it—it's not up to us to justify the ways of young women to God, now is it?"

Both Henry and Carren smile, Carren awkwardly, as if she sort of understands the joke, though she may not.

"Dad, that's bad. Almost as stupid as my assignment. Maybe I'll quote you in my essay, ok? Regarding Satan, the Dean of the Faculty of Education says ...! But, if I get what you're saying, it's also sort of true, isn't it. It's the world we live in—you mind your own business, and to be honest, I think, that's the way most people want it. People in suburbs or high rises never even know their neighbours, neighbours who might live only six inches of concrete away, and they've never talked and they're happy with that arrangement. They might not say they're happy with it but they never do anything to change it. Like, they don't start a rebellion or anything! And if their neighbour comes to visit, they speak through a four-inch gap with their safety chain latched, and next time, they look through the peep-hole and walk away silent, pretending they aren't home. Most people spend their spare time on Facebook or Twitter or other Soc-sites and you don't really even know the people who are called your friends there. We're really all alone in our own worlds. O, I suppose there are a few tree huggers around and people who collect some cans at Christmas, or something, but it's a phase they grow out of. And, besides, with Cindy, she can take care of herself. She's pretty smart, and athletic. And she knows how to hot-wire a car—I took care of that. Besides, knowing her parents, the dinner was probably some big snore and she's managed to find a way out of it."

"Yes, I'm sure. It will all sort itself out. Everything does. Hey, I know what you need. A slice of peach to go with that diet Coke, while you explain what you said about hot-wiring?"

"Don't mind if I do. Can't beat peach-flavoured Coke, you know!"

- 50 -

A mad jigsaw puzzle

Dalco, Junior and Connie Torrence get out of the black Lexus after it parks at the rear of the Voyageur's End. A dim outside light illuminates them and casts their shadows. Dalco talks over the roof of the car in low voice, serious and private.

"So ... according to T.J., the yellow Mustang is owned by a guy named Luke Burrell. He just bought it—where a wastoid like him got the money, we can only guess. His buddy is Gabe Black, and it's his brother that owns the carpet store, where the old Dodge came from. T.J. said that Corrino went pretty easy on Black yesterday and didn't really push him much on anything, not even the brother angle. But T.J. said that, when he and Paul was tailing Mike, they saw him and his brother and Burrell having a long talk just across the street here, out in front of the Leroy."

"It all smells fishy, Mr. D.," Connie pipes in.

"Yeah, no shit ... like a beached whale in August, if you ask me. And T.J. says that Luke and Gabe have been part of a local clan, run by the Malleys, for a long time. They even did some time for one of old Duffy's muscle deals that went south. And they've worked off and on for his son, the one they call Stump, ever since they got out. Now, given how clueless they are, I'm guessing they wouldn't have hit the Logos van on their own—it was part of a larger operation."

"It's, like, a mad jigsaw puzzle..." says Connie.

"But at least we're starting to find some of the missin' pieces."

"So ... at least one question that remains, Mr. D., is how did dey know to hit that partic'lar truck? To hit the guap, the jackpot? That's still a missin' piece."

"Yeah, but I think that missin' piece is close to bein' found, Connie" replies Dalco. "And I think we all know the answer—there's some piece of shit on our side mixed up in it. Someone who knew what truck, and when. And there ain't that many who had that inside jack. You know, it's kinda interesting, isn't it, how T.J. can come up with more information in a half a day than Paul Corrino did in a week? As you say, something stinks, Connie, and it's beginning to smell like the Saint."

"Yeah, I'm bettin' Corrino, too, Pops. He's been pretty quiet and then takin' it easy on Black when we know that the brother was involved..." Junior is priming up.

"We'll see, Junior. You and Connie and T.J. will be meeting with him in the parking garage tomorrow. In the meantime, I want you to get going on the Leroy shake-up we talked about. Do everything you can to fuck them up. Connie, here, can help you."

"Already on it. I got some ideas that'll make them wish they'd never messed with us. Like seeing that mangy mutt of theirs has an accident and a bunch more stuff. You'll see." Junior is almost giddy in his anticipation.

"Good. I know you'll do a good job," his father responds. "As to Corrino, I got taps put on the phones since Sunday—at his home and all of them at the office—Duwayne's been keepin' an eye on him and he's goin' to check the recordings later tonight and give me a call. And I got a couple other feelers put out, one with some guy named Bruce, one of Malley's goons—money's always where true loyalty lies, you know. I'm guessin' Corrino knows more than he's been saying, and may turn out to be the key piece to this jigsaw. So, Connie, Junior, by the time you meet with him tomorrow, you may have some real interesting questions to ask. Ok? Good. Now c'mon, we still got things to do. The night is young."

- 51 -

Fruit goes before the fall

It is nearly ten o'clock when the doorbell rings and then rings twice more before Henry reaches the foyer, glances at the security monitor and pulls open the right side of the heavy maple portal.

"Well, good evening, Clayton. What in heaven brings you over at this hour?"

"I have to talk to you Henry. Some crazy man has Cindy … I mean, he kidnapped Cindy. He phoned me—told me that he'd phoned you but you never called him back—twice. It's bad, Henry, it's bad. He said he wants a couple million dollars or he'll…"

"Whoa, whoa. Come on in, Clayton. Come on in, and have a chair and calm down. Can I get you a drink?" MacLean leads Clayton into the plush living-room.

"No. No. Well, yes maybe some water."

After a brief moment Henry re-emerges from the kitchen with an Aqua Madonna.

"Let me get you a glass. So tell me, what's this all about?" Henry opens a dark, stenciled China cabinet and retrieves a crystal highboy which he hands to Clayton.

"What time is it? Yes, ten o'clock. Well about an hour ago I got a phone call and it's this crazy man who says that he kidnapped Cindy and that if I don't pay him two million dollars I'm never going to see her again. And he said that he's talked to you…"

"No, no Clayton." Henry sits on the cranberry-coloured leather sofa opposite Clayton's chair which is etched in deep green palm fronds. "I can't say that I know what he's talking about. Nobody's talked to me. Are you sure he's got your daughter? Has she been missing?"

"Yes, she was supposed to be home for supper but never showed—we thought she might have been hiding out at the library, studying and missing our dinner party on purpose. Or even over here, but then your Carren phoned. You know how these young kids are—but no, he has her. I heard her on the phone. She was crying and said 'Daddy' and it was her. And he said that he had talked to you…"

"No. I never talked to anybody like that. I would certainly have called you if I had. So, have you called the police?"

"No. No. Absolutely not. He warned me that if any police show up anywhere then all bets are off. And he said, 'you know what I mean by that.' And to be honest, Henry, I'm not sure if I want to know…! Do you think he'd really…" Clayton Brown's voice descends into an occlusive mumble.

"Well, Clayton. I suppose it's difficult to know what to do."

"I know what I've got to do, Henry. I've got to give this guy what he wants. It's only money he wants for Christ's sake. He's got Cindy."

"Yes, I guess. That's a lot of money though."

"What the hell are you saying, Henry? What other option is there? You tell me. And that's why I'm coming to you 'cause I know that you can get that kind of money. And get it quick."

"Well, Clayton, I don't know ... I ..."

"My God, Henry. We've known each other for forty years. I gave you the loan that got your business started, that allowed you to pursue your academic career. You can't have a second thought about this..."

Carren steps around from the kitchen into the living room.

"Henry, if ... if it were your daughter and you came to me, I wouldn't think twice. Think if it were Carren. You have got to help me, 'cause by myself I can't raise that much money, not that soon. The guy wants it by day after tomorrow, at the latest, by Wednesday, Henry, or, or he says 'then all bets are off'—you know what he means by that.'"

Henry MacLean glances toward his daughter.

"Ok, Clayton. Ok. Maybe I can help. You wait here—I'll get on the phone and make a couple of calls. We may be able to do something. Is there anything else I can get for you?"

Clayton collapses back into the large soft armchair, slightly, hopelessly nodding his head from side to side.

"Ok, then? I'll be right back. Carren, could you come with me, please?" Henry, unseen by Clayton, puts his finger across his lips signaling his daughter's silence.

Henry MacLean and his daughter retreat through the kitchen and into his study, where Henry closes the door. They speak in whispers.

"So, Dad, was Cindy really kidnapped?"

"Yes, I guess so, although I didn't let on to Clayton that I knew anything about it. It wouldn't look good, especially if things don't turn out, well, you know ... perfectly?"

"O my God. ... but yeah, I get the picture. So what are you going to do? What about Cindy? You can't just let the kidnapper keep her? But, you really just can't give him a bunch of money, either, can you?"

"Well, while Clayton was blubbering in there, I started thinking that this may all turn out for the best and even speed up our little coup. Just listen—we had liquid donations, just today, of nearly two million dollars, a half a million right out of left field from that Malley group who, to be honest, I hadn't actually heard tell of before. In total we've got nearly eight million lined up already. With some of your sister's creative paperwork, those funds will easily allow each of our proposed divisions at M.I.R.E. to match the monies raised in our charity events and, being deductible, make a little profit as well. Each, that is, except Brown's. What I think I can do is partition the donations collected to this point to each of our new divisions so that Brown can liquefy the amount that he thinks he will need from his own division's allotment. Of course, he'll be responsible for that sum—if he manages somehow not to lose it to the kidnapper, fine, but in the more than likely scenario that it does disappear, Brown is responsible and the fault lies with him. One more cruel zephyr to help push him off his cliff, I should think. For the rest of us, no risk, no foul. Not a breath. Nothing ventured; nothing lost. Nothing from nothing."

"Wow, that sounds perfect, Dad. Can you actually do all of that? And Cin-city will be ok too?"

"Just a simple phone call should take care of it. By tomorrow, Clayton can probably give that kidnapper two or maybe even three million dollars for dear Cindy, if that's what he wishes to do. In that case, your Cin-city may turn out to be dearer than he ever dreamed."

"And all the rest of us will come out of it looking pretty good, won't we?"

"Count on it, sweetheart. Count on it. Now, why don't you go back in there and see if Mr. Brown would like anything. Tell him I'm making some phone calls and everything should be fine. Here take him a peach—maybe he would like a piece of fruit. You know what your Milton would have said, don't you—fruit goes before the fall. Right?"

With a muffled laugh, Carren quickly snatches the offering from her father's hand. And in the muted light of the study, as she turns, father and daughter look unsettlingly alike. And in that instant she also realizes, sharp and sudden as a serpent's sting, that writing her essay for English will be no problem at all. Cast among serpents and gardens, she knows exactly what she will write about.

- 52 -

The hydro man

Today, it is new. Eighteen floors of cement and steel and tinted glass. Pristine and shining in reflective sunlight. Proudly built by Regent Construction, subsidiary of Dalco Corp., and happily inhabited by the Thornton Hydro Commission, at last a place in which to consolidate all of its scattered offices. But in time, in fifty or maybe seventy-five years, it will no longer serve a purpose, it will be worn and used and need to be replaced. Perhaps they will do it by implosion. Where charges are placed and crowds gather at a safe distance and television cameras whir and the switch is thrown and puffs of smoke and dust roll out and, suicidal, the building abruptly sinks into itself like a distraught maelstrom. Perhaps by then, they will use some different method for demolition, perhaps some laser device that disintegrates cement and steel and tinted glass floor by floor so they can turn around and instantly build again. Perhaps, as some kind of publicity stunt, they will do a retro demolition. Truck in some great crane on loan from a museum with its huge metal ball stretching from a great steel cable smashing into the building again and again, blast after blast from the past.

Perhaps they will have to bring in trucks to carry away the

concrete debris. And if they do, possibly as they near the end of the job, as they begin to truck away some of the cement and steel that composed the foundation of the building, perhaps one of the workers will notice something curious about one of the foundation blocks and take a closer look. There the worker may see, inside the broken concrete form, small open spaces and tubular channels, and inside these, old brittle sticks that, upon closer inspection, appear to be bones. The bones of a human body. A complete set of bones. Perhaps, like some homage to victims of ancient Pompeii, they will fill these spaces with plaster and flush out the form of a man from an earlier time. Possibly some poor worker trapped in the haste of erecting this old building. In all likelihood, some bored forensic anthropologist will be called upon to examine these bones, to flesh out their DNA and extrapolate a cause of death and a time of life. Perhaps he or she will find traces that indicate the onset of arthritis in the joints, and evidence of a left arm that was once fractured. No doubt, he or she will find the small hole in the back of the skull, perhaps even the small lead pellet still rattling around in the cranial cavity, which would suggest a violent death. Surmises will be made, and a cursory data check will ensue, and speculations will be uttered about famous people who went missing long ago—there will probably be Jimmy Hoffa jokes—and the case will be passed along to the homicide division and given a label and a number—the hydro man, unsolved case #313. A brief and intriguing curiosity. But then a pimp without a head will show up in an alley, and an eviscerated child in a yellow kimono will be pulled out of the river and the curious bones found in the old foundation will be set aside. A cold case. Filed away. No more time to be given.

There will be no record of the game winning home run he

hit in Grade 8, of strawberry-haired and Irish Ramona Stewart, the first great love of his life, of the broken arm he suffered during that smash and grab at O'Neill's Jewellery Store (the glass in that case was a hell of a lot harder than it looked), of the six men he killed while working for Frederick Dalco, of the sad, sick feeling deep in the pit of his spine when Dalco Junior and his men cornered him on level three of the municipal parking garage and he knew that they knew something they shouldn't, couldn't, of the brief second of disbelief beyond understanding when the muzzle touched the base of his skull. Of the hydro man, #313, beyond his DNA, and a probable cause of death, of Saint Paul Corrino as he had once been named on the street, who many years ago double-crossed his boss, Frederick Dalco, and got caught, nothing more would be known. Cold cold case. Filed away in concrete and then in paper. No more time to be given.

- 53 -

Corvid scarlet

Trace sits behind the desk in the Office of Le Roi Motor Inn, sets down the *Entertainment Weekly* she has been glancing through, picks up a cup from the surface and takes a sip of her coffee. She replaces the cup carefully in exactly the same spot.

She glances beneath the counter where Angus is gently snoring at her feet. She likes that, doesn't know why but, somehow, there is a comfort there. She likes the dog and he seems to like her. She pulls up her purse from a shelf, opens it, takes out a bottle of Corvid Scarlet nail polish and places the purse back in its precise spot beneath the counter. She glances at the clock and at the strange plaque below it on the wall—a stick with a bracelet. Then she unscrews the cap and places her left hand on the counter, spreading her fingers.

Trace sweeps a layer of scarlet over the nail of her pinky finger, and admiringly looks down at the change she has made. Cool. It is Wednesday evening.

- 54 -

Above us only sky

Lucky watches intently as a mosquito nestles into the hairs on his left forearm and begins to suck itself fat. He watches its opalescent wings flutter and its right front leg move up and down and he watches as its belly slowly expands. Then, with his right middle finger, he slowly reaches over, the Enola Gay descending on Hiroshima, and squashes it. A puddle of bright red blood coalesces like an atomic kettle lake in the hairs of his arm.

Lucky turns his attention to the other occupants of the room. Gabe sits on the end of the bed and is watching television—the Cartoon Channel, where an animated Batman is tied to a nuclear warhead that is about to land on Gotham City. Evident, as well, Superman, his friend and super confidante, is on the way. The young woman, Cindy Brown, is laying on the bed, eyes closed, hands tied behind her with yellow nylon rope, a piece of duct tape over her mouth. The carpet salesman, Dave Bryden III, exhibits similar restraints but is propped in a tub chair in the corner beside the windows, drapes closed.

"Joe."

"Just a sec, Larry." Superman is catching up to the rocket

and with one hand, tears the ropes free from Batman, with the other, redirects the rocket toward the sun. In the split seconds of cartoon denouement which follow, which include a quick round of fisticuffs in which the villains are overcome and their weapons confiscated, the world is saved once more. Batman, too.

"Yeah, Larry, what's up?"

"It's getting close to the time, isn't it?"

"Yeah, what is it, 7:45? We got a few more minutes. I don't want to take it out there too early. Like I said, I told MacLean and Brown there'd be a suitcase under the sign of the Leroy between 8:00 and 8:15, that they should fill that suitcase with the money and return it there by 8:30. I didn't want to take their bag directly from them, you know—it could be bugged or primed with that explodin' blue shit, or somethin'. So we're gonna use this trusty old case. It's sturdy and it's be easy to see at night." Gabe holds up a silver aluminum case.

"Where'd that come from, anyways?"

"Don't know—it was around the old house. It had a foam rubber lining that I ripped out so there should be room enough for lots of dough, right!"

"Absolutely. Lots of loot. We'll be rich as Arabs, have anything we want. Paradise, man ... no hell, no heaven, like the Stones said—just the sky above us. So..." Lucky lowers his voice. "We get this money and then head back to your place?"

"Right. After we get the money, we get the hell outta here. We'll count it at my place and make the trade with Malley...," Gabe whispers, "... on Friday across the road at the End like we discussed. Around supper-time, when the rush hour traffic has died. Then me and you and Liz and Jimmy will get outta town and get out quick, for a while anyways."

"And we just gonna leave this pair here?" Lucky mimes the whisper.

"Yeah. Brown or somebody'll find 'em. That sound good?"

"It does to me, man. I'm getting restless to get this over with. That chick is starting to freak me out—I mean she's quiet for hours on end and then, suddenly, she goes nuts, rolling and trying to scream and stuff, and then she goes quiet again. And the guy stinks. I will be glad to see the end of them. The only thing, they'll be able to recognize us, won't they? Give our descriptions to the cops and stuff."

"Well, they don't know our names, right. I figure we get away to some other part of the country, maybe change the colour of our hair. I'll grow a beard, you shave your moustache…"

"No way, man. This moustache is part of who I am. It's like my tatts. I ain't shaving it … no way."

"Well, whatever—grow a full beard then or something. Wear some different clothes, you know. Lay low. And in a few months, little Cindy there will be back living in her big comfortable world and she won't remember that any of this ever happened. And the other guy, well hopefully he'll forget all about us too. "

"Yeah. Maybe. Let's hope anyways. "

"We'll give both of them a good talking to before we scram. And we'll clean up the room—make it look like we never been here. Take the garbage, straighten the towels, wipe everything down. Nobody will know nothing. Nothing."

"Ok … sounds solid."

"Anyways. As you say, it is about time that I put this case in place. Hand me my knife from over there, will you, Larry? I better take that with me."

Gabe hoists the aluminum case in his right hand, cracks the door open, pauses and turns toward Lucky to get his knife which is laying on the bureau. And Dave Bryden chooses this moment. He springs from the tub chair and thunderously charges, driving his shoulder into the full of Gabe's back, rocking the smaller man heavily against the wall. The case flies out of Gabe's clutch and he crumples to the floor. Unexpectedly, though, for a moment, the blow stuns Dave too. And just as he regains himself and puts a foot in the small gap before the door can close, about to kick it open, Lucky strikes like that old tobacco jingle. He has grabbed the first weapon he can find, the aluminum suitcase, and swings it hard across Dave's forehead. The poleaxed salesman drops in his tracks and Lucky slams the door shut. Cindy rocks her body, then rolls across the bed, nearly tumbles off, then rolls back again, and is silent.

"You, settle down," Gabe loudly to Cindy, then to Lucky, "Hey, man, you dented the case."

"You ok?"

"Yeah, that son of a bitch. He's out cold, is he? Bastard. Let's tie him up good, and put him up there on the bed next to her. Damn it, my back hurts. And let's take his goddamned clothes off too. Then he won't be so quick to go running around."

"He's out of it, Joe—I'll take care of him. I don't trust the bastard. Here's the case—you better get it planted out there so we can get our money."

"Yeah, ok. I won't be too long. Though, like I said before, I'm not going straight to the sign—they might be watching. I'll go back through the breeze-way and circle around. Don't want them to know where we're staying, right. It's also gotten pretty foggy out so that'll help too. See you in a bit. I'll knock twice, wait, and then twice again."

"Ok, man. Take it easy. I'll take care of this guy. And I'll bag his clothes."

Gabe looks back at Lucky and raises his right hand giving him a big thumb's up as if the movie were good. Then he disappears with the aluminum suitcase into the dark now filling in with thick spring fog. Lucky closes the door and looks at Dave Bryden who lays heaped on the shaggy yellow carpet. From the bed Cindy opens her eyes and starts to roll back and forth again and make desperate sounds. This is complicated enough and is getting worse—it is starting to get on Lucky's nerves. And worse, still, there on the bureau sits Gabe's knife. He hadn't even remembered to take it with him into the night. That is not a good omen. Lucky steps over and picks up the long slim blade. It is as sharp as a razor.

- 55 -

Tom and Dick Grill

"**You know, I haven't been down** in this area for some time, Clayton. The land around here has some real potential—that's a huge open space out back of this place. It would be a natural space for development—mixed housing, a couple high rises, some town house complexes, maybe some semis. I must come back and take a closer look, and do a search on some of the deeds."

"Yeah, sure Henry. But I got to tell you that's about the last thing on my mind right now. I don't see anything out front—that damn fog has gotten as thick as pea soup. What'd he say—we're supposed to pick up a suitcase between 8:00 and 8:15, from under the sign? God, I can hardly think straight."

Clayton sits on the edge of the bed and, with his right hand, nervously eases his wedding band round and round the third finger of his left hand.

"Try to relax, Clayton. You need to be cool here. Calm."

"I know. I know you're right. I hope that we've done the right thing. Not involving the police. And me, borrowing all this corporation money. It's like *zugzwang*, you know, like they say in chess when you're forced to make a move that weakens you …

but I've no real option. I've got to tell you, Henry, I really appreciate your support in this, and coming down here with me. Deciding to rent a room here this afternoon was a good idea. It's made it easier to focus, get collected. Molly wanted to come but I thought it would have complicated things even more. She's worried sick, of course, but..."

Clayton stands and paces back and forward in the small room.

"Yes. Just you and me, Clayton. That's best. Tom and Dick Grill. Brothers-in-arms."

"Oh, oh yeah, the registration. How did you come up with those names?"

"The last time you called me, yesterday afternoon, I was out getting the barbeque ready. And, as you know, I've been doing some research in onomastics—Tom, Dick and Harry used to be the most popular male names, at least up to the middle of the last century. So, when I knew that we needed to conceal our identities, *voila*."

Clayton steps into the bathroom, picks up a small soap and puts it down again. He re-enters the room, opens a door in the wall behind which there is another door, locked, an entrance to the room next door.

"Well, it's good that you've been able to do some clear thinking 'cause I am just a ball of nerves. Why do these rooms have double doors like this—I've never really figured it out?"

"Pass-through doors. I think it comes from an earlier custom—when adult couples frequently used to vacation together. Adjoining rooms—connected but separate. Some families probably use them now. Parents on one side; kids on the other. ... So, how much money did you withdraw, Clayton?"

"Just what he asked for. Two million. And I got it mostly in fifties and twenties. I'll get the money back into the fund as quickly as I can—even if the police are not able to catch this bastard. I can re-mortgage the house, sell the cottage if I have to. Don't worry. Neither my division of M.I.R.E. nor the literacy charities, neither will suffer. On my word, Henry."

"Oh, Clayton, don't worry about that—not at a time like this."

"Thanks, Henry. You are about the only person who could have managed all this, getting those funds together and all—what's the phrase for it—you're a fellow on whom I have built an absolute trust? That is a quote from somewhere, isn't it? I can't remember where … some play, I think"

"Yes, maybe … I don't remember right now. Anyway, it's about ten after eight. Time for you to go and get the case for the money, don't you think? Get this show on the road."

"Yes. I guess it is. Wish me luck, Henry. I'm afraid my brain is as thick as this fog is right now. As soon as I get Cindy back though, you're are going to contact the police, right?"

"Absolutely—I've got my cell phone in hand. We'll bait them with the money and as soon as you have Cindy, I'll make the call. We'll do just fine, Clayton. Just fine."

"Ah, what's the room number here?" asks Clayton squinting at the emergency information on the back of the door.

"It's 23, I think."

"Yes. Good. I don't want to get lost. Back in a bit."

Clayton opens the heavy door and the fog leans forward like a hungry creature of the night and takes him in.

- 56 -

You know I always like seein' youse too

Jerry Malley grunts in pleasure as the auburn-haired Sugar Chaque rides him like a skint cowpoke on a spirited bronco at the fall rodeo. The bronco's energy dissipates; Sugar dismounts and awaits her score from the judge.

While Sugar dresses, Jerry sits on the side of the bed, lights a black Cuban and blows a great cloud of blue smoke across the room.

"It was nice to see youse again so soon, Mr. Jones. It's like you owns this room or somethin'."

"Yeah, well, sometimes I got a lot of business in this part of town, Sugar, and they let me have this same room. They kinda reserve it for me so usually I don't gotta sign in or register or nuthin'. And it's nice to have some company. And you, baby doll, are the best company I ever have."

Sugar Chaque genuinely giggles, "Aw, thanks, Mr. Jones. You know I always like seein' youse too."

"Anyway, kid, there's your meal ticket and I'll see you again

The Prince of Leroy

soon, ok." Jerry hands her some bills. Theirs not to know, but had his pecker been omniscient or her cooch clairvoyant, they would have understood this to be a final and poignant star-crossed parting. Such a sweet sorrow, Romeo and Juliet could probably have taken notes.

"Sure Mr. Jones. Thanks." Sugar presses her pinky to her lips in the accustomed manner, waves it at Jerry and slips out the door into the meagre glow of the yellow Leroy lights. A lost billow of fog wanders into the room to take a look around like a lonely ghost on the dole.

As he dresses Jerry wonders what he should do now. He has trailed Gabe and Lucky to this place, of all places. Their yellow Mustang sits directly across the parking lot from his room. And they are definitely up to something but just what, well that is anybody's guess. Perhaps he will try Corrino again. He has tried to get in touch several times since late last night, this time using the burner Paul gave him—Paul was supposed to meet with Dalco, and Jerry wants to know what Dalco knows. He also wants Paul to know where the two idiots are and that something's about to go down. Malley flips open the phone and taps the button. The line rings six, seven, eight times. Nothing. He decides that maybe the memory of his phone is on the fritz, checks a carefully coded directory in his pocket and dials again. Same movie. Short and silent. Not even a one-reeler! He pulls the curtain back and peeks out the window, and speaks low but aloud to himself.

"Well, the Mustang's still there. But the damn fog is so thick, it's like, if you was suckin' on a nipple, you couldn't hardly see the other tit." Jerry smiles at his own dim wit and snaps his fingers a couple times. He decides to wait just a little bit longer.

- 57 -

The road goes on forever

Without lights, the black Lexus rolls to a quiet stop at the west side of the Leroy's parking lot; its engine silenced.

"Jesus and Mary, Boss, that was the craziest short ride I ever took. I thought we was gonna get creamed for sure slippin' across the road there in the dark."

"You ain't seen nothing yet, Connie. We're just getting' started—and the road goes on forever, man," croons Junior.

"Well, your idea of coming over here unseen may be a good one, Junior, but I'll be damned, the view here isn't a hell of a lot clearer than it was from the End. What a hell of a night for fog." Frederick Dalco mutters.

"Yeah, well, I can get out and do some scoutin' around if you want, Dad."

"No, just wait, Junior. Maybe in a bit. Let's sit here for a second. There's certainly something goin' on though. That's the yellow Mustang over there and there's a dark Beamer, along the side here—I can't imagine why anyone who could afford to drive a Beamer would stay in this dump. Something ain't straight."

"The Mustang is their car, isn't it?"

"Yeah, Junior, and somehow they're at the core of this. Ya

gotta wonder about that Beamer, though. Maybe finding out who owns that might be smart…"

"I can find out who owns that car in a minute, Dad. I'll just go knocking on the doors over there and ask real polite. We'll find out."

No, Junior. I think we should sit tight and see what's going down. We don't want to make any more mistakes. Like popping the Saint before he gave us squat! We need to sort out this "Ps and Qs" nonsense. We need to find the fuckin' dope and we need to fuck the ones who stole it. And it feels like we're real close here. Real close! So let the fog sit and we'll see what crawls out of it. See what the game is before we force the ante. We'll get the plate numbers on the BMW and we'll know who owns that car before the sun rises. And we'll take down yellow Mustang and his pal when we need to. And the downtown Yellowman too. This business is mine, my time, my money—I want you to get on with the Leroy, Junior. Rock their world.

"Yeah, I got you Dad. I'm already on it. Things are in motion—you'll see before the end of the week."

"Good. I know you'll do the job."

"Hey, look Dad. Somebody just moved out of a door near the Mustang. Under that yellow light." Frederick Dalco Junior punches a clenched fist into the side of the driver's seat as he turns to Connie and his father in the back.

"Hey, Connie? Can you feel it? Can you feel it? The road goes on forever. And the party never ends."

- 58 -

Beyond the gift of reason

Dave Bryden III is stretched naked and unconscious on the bed. He is on his right side facing the door and curtained windows, hands taped behind, with a mustard-coloured blanket tossed over him. In the middle of the bed, with her back to Dave, is Cindy Brown, quiet and motionless, hands loosely tied behind her with yellow nylon rope. She is still wearing the beige dress that she had carefully chosen and put on first thing Monday morning. Only now it is marred with stains and wrinkles and a small tear in the right shoulder seam. Lucky circles around to her side of the bed and sits on the edge. Something is stirring deep inside him which he would not fully comprehend even if he tried; in fact, a thousand Harvard psychologists probably wouldn't fathom it either. Shadows slip in quick succession through his thoughts: little helpless Archie in Grade 3 sitting, crying, in the wet marsh, a black thing with a long scarf hanging from a playground slide as fire engines sweep past, an old drunk with a look of surprise and a shard of glass in his throat, a young girl trying to get to her phone. Other shadows come and go too. Lucky stares not so much at Cindy as through her. Cindy takes a deeper breath.

"It's all right little girl. No-one's gonna touch you—you're worth too much to us just the way you are."

Lucky lays down facing her and shifts closer until his entire body borders itself along hers. He can smell the faint traces of shampoo and lotion that still emanate from her hair and skin. Then, with his right arm, he slowly reaches under her head and across to Dave. He has not really thought this through any more than he has thought through most things in his time on this earth. His hand curves around the salesman's head, the way you would touch a small baby, until he gently holds Dave's forehead in his hand above the pillow. Lucky's left arm encircles Cindy—she cringes slightly—but the hand moves beyond, upward, as if to join his other in some kind of prayer, some ritual benediction. But it stops just short, pauses and then makes an easy twisting motion, softly drawing the razor-like blade across Dave Bryden's exposed neck. Then Lucky retreats, sits up, and moves off the bed. He circles around. Neither Cindy nor Dave move. Lucky has done what he had to do, that's all he knows in a kind of knowing that exists beyond the gift of reason, and now he has already started to move on to something else, to clean the knife. But, then there is a gurgling sound, and a noise of air, a kind of strange whistle, and the convulsive clicking of teeth. Lucky doesn't like this noise, looks for something to stop it, looks for the first thing he can find. He reaches the night stand near where Dave's eyes have opened, grabs the television remote and forces it into the salesman's mouth, as deeply as he can. And it works. The sounds stop. And Dave stops. As if he has decided to skip his own funeral. And Lucky, moving on now, grabs another beer, and moves to the bathroom where he rinses the knife. Then he returns to the tub chair in the corner and sits down.

There are two knocks at the door. Then a pause. Then two more. Gabe has returned. Like the vast universe, itself, the plan is unfolding.

- 59 -

That's a lot of Pérignon

Clayton Brown steps back into the room. He is carrying a large aluminum case which he flings on the bed and clicks open.

"So the suitcase turns out to be that?" says MacLean. "Looks like an old photographer's outfit. Though that's quite a dent in its side."

"Yes. It was sitting right between the posts of the sign, just like the guy said. The only thing I could think—that means Cindy's not far away. Let's get it filled. I want to get it back as soon as I can."

"Ok, Clayton. I'll hand you the bundles of cash and you can pack them in."

The two men go to work. Henry MacLean removes the money from a large nylon gym bag and hands pack after pack across to Clayton Brown who stacks them into the aluminum case.

"This thing is sure going to be heavier going back than it was coming over, I can tell you that."

"So, Clayton, the deal is that you just leave the case under the sign. You're simply supposed to trust him to release Cindy?"

"Well, Henry, the point is—what choice do I have? You tell me."

"No. Ok. Ok, I hear you. I hope ... I'm sure ... she'll be all right."

"The kidnapper let me talk with her on the phone last night. She said she was still ok, but, understandably, she sounded pretty down. Scattered. The guy said that he would release her right after he counted the money. I guess that I have no choice but to trust him. ... There! Is that all?"

"That's it. Two million. That's a lot of Pérignon!"

Clayton flips the lid of the suitcase closed and presses each of the locking flaps in place.

"Yeah! Well, I guess I might as well get this back to the sign. Be back shortly..."

- 60 -

Another bug on the windshield

Two knocks. A pause. Two more. The door opens and Gabe steps in.

"Hey, Larry. That's so damn foggy out there I almost didn't find my way back..." Gabe stops, all utterance suspended. He is transfixed in what he sees. "Holy shit, Lucky. What happened here? What the fuck happened?"

"It was wild, man. That dude woke up and went crazy, Gabe. Knocked me over. Grabbed for your knife. You left it there on the dresser. He almost got it too. It's all I could do ... wrestle with him back there and take him out. Here ... here's your blade, man. I cleaned it."

Gabe takes his knife, shining clean, from Lucky. "Holy shit. So ... so are you ok?"

"Yeah, I'm fine. Like you said, anyways, he wasn't no use to us, or anyone else as far as I was concerned. He was just getting in the way. Things'll be fine without him. The deal's still good— it's for her, right?" Lucky lowers his voice. "We'll just leave him here when we get the coin. I got his clothes and stuff in that garbage bag. We'll take it with us when we go. He'll be nobody."

"God, I hope this doesn't screw stuff up any more than it already is."

"What's screwed up? Nothing's screwed up, Curly. This guy is just another bug, man, another bug on the windshield. He got himself in front of the wrong truck on the wrong road at the wrong time. Nothing's screwed up, man. It's business as usual."

"Ok. We'll play it your way, Luc ... I mean, Larry. Not much choice now, anyways. And maybe you're right. This guy was a nuisance, and he did piss me off—my ribs are gonna be sore for a month. One of them may be cracked .... anyways, another ten or fifteen minutes and I'll go back out and get the suitcase. I..."

Cindy groans. Loud. She has shut herself, her thoughts, her feelings, her senses, to the terrible sounds she has heard and the tremors of a life leaving so close to her—this couldn't be real—real had taken a vacation somewhere else for the last couple days. But as the warm, wet liquid trickles from Dave's pillow and pools around her neck, real has made a homecoming complete with a high-step marching band and somersaulting cheerleaders and she can take no more. With a strength that she did not know she had, she rips the cords from her wrists, tears off the duct tape gag, and screams. Loud. Horrible. Edvard Munch would have blushed. She screams again, leaps over Dave's still body and bolts to the door that Gabe is still holding open and into the fog. Lucky and Gabe, frozen, look at each other. Then, instantaneously, each turns to the door and, like their favourite television heroes from long ago, their current namesakes, they arrive simultaneously, collide and, for a moment, are stuck in the passageway. Then they are into the night, the door slamming closed. And Dave Bryden III is left behind, quiet, silent, smiling grim for none to see. America, indeed, will never be the same.

- 61 -

The phantom slips away

Clayton leverages the aluminum suitcase from the bed.

"Jeez ... like I said, this is a lot heavier now than it was bringing it over."

"I guess so there friend. Old Midas would be jealous…"

There is a distant scream. And another. And the sound of a door crashing open. And another scream, this time louder, outside, and the sound of someone running. And then others running.

"Henry! That's Cindy. My God, Henry, that's Cindy. C'mon."

Adrenaline becomes principal. Clayton drops the aluminum case back to the bed and is at the door; Clayton tosses the gym bag down and is just behind him. The fog billows into the room as the two men burst out. They rush into the murky oblivion, punctuated only by distant noises and the diffused splotches of orange light above each of the motel's doors.

The door to Room 23, itself, swings wide behind them, bounces from the rubber stop screwed into the floor and clicks shut on its return. Silence. Then, the far pass-through door moves and a phantom slips into the room. It is a phantom with long flowing hair, a mixture of soft grey and winter white. It is a figure who has recognized a voice and who has a score to settle. And the opportunity has graciously presented itself. Emily moves to the bed, quickly flips open the suitcase, smiles, and closes it again. In only a few days here, she already knows a great deal about this place, more than some who have been here far longer. She pushes the bed to the side. As it slides away, it nudges the night-stand. With a pocket knife, she quickly slits the frail shag carpet and tugs on a trap door that lies beneath. On her third tug, it releases. There is a dark space down there. She pulls the heavy case from the bed and lets it fall into the dark. It hits the dirt below and flops on its side. It will be there to retrieve, if she decides to do so. That is not really the point, is it? Emily quickly closes the trap and pulls the carpet back in place. She does the same with the bed and straightens the night-stand as best she can. There ... the first sortie back at the man responsible for stealing her land. Fort Sumter perhaps. She can return later if she wishes. It looks like a lot of money. Perhaps, she thinks, she will be able to use his money to buy back her land. Wouldn't that serve him just right. At any rate, they will not find their money—even if they figure someone next door has taken it. They would not find it there or here, or anywhere. It's as if the dark gods have swooped down once more. And so the phantom slips away, pulling the double door nearly shut behind her as she goes. The click of the lock on her side is as satisfying a sound as she has known in many years.

- 62 -

On a foggy night

"Ok, boys," Dalco speaks from the back seat of the Lexus. "We ain't seein' diddly here. Let's go for a stroll around this shitheap. Pete—take a piece of paper out of the glove box there, or use your phone, and go over and get the licence on that Beamer. I think knowing who owns that car will be good info for us to have … maybe not so good for the owner, but good for us. Then get back to the car and wait for us here. I want to be ready to get the hell out of here, and fast, if we need to. C'mon Connie, Junior—let's wander around on a foggy night and see what we can see, maybe nose that Mustang. Let's go."

The three men get out of the Lexus and amble on to the sidewalk that leads around the Leroy. Pete, the driver, momentarily follows their exit with pen and paper in hand. Connie and the Dalcos stop for a brief moment outside of the rooms on the west side to look at the BMW and across at the Mustang on the far side of the lot. Then they move on.

Frederick Dalco Junior's right hand shoots inside his jacket.

"What, are you jumpy or what?" his father asks.

"Nah, Dad. I just saw the curtain on that room move—that's all. I guess it's nothing, but I like to be ready, you know."

There is a faint scream, and then another, and across the way a door bursts open and a figure flies out, shortly followed by two more. And then two more from another room. The Dalcos stop and wait. Along the sidewalk, an apparition approaches and then turns and sprints away. Then, in the far dim light, there is a confrontation of some kind, a splash and a man screaming.

The fog is muting all in sound and shape. Wrapping tighter and tighter. A vague but palpable tension.

"You might want to get a hand on that heater now, Junior. Something's up. Let's take a bit closer look. But careful, very careful."

- 63 -

Holy shit on the sepulchre

There is not a helluva lot of sense in just staying in here. Jerry takes another long drag on his cigar. If you could of seen something across the parking lot, then that might of made sense. But with the darkness and the fog, you couldn't see the end of your dick if it was painted neon red and whistlin' Dixie. Jerry smiles—he is probably his own best audience. Then he hears a scream, and another, and the faint but certain sound of people running. Something is up. Jerry moves to the window and pulls back the curtain.

"Christ Jesus, Mary and Joseph!"

He quickly lets the curtain fall and staggers back across the room. Standin' right outside his goddamn window was Frederick Dalco, with two or three of his boys.

"Holy shit on the sepulchre!"

That is the last thing he needs to see. The guy he has just ripped off for six million dollars in drug money, standin' right outside his room. What the hell is goin' on here? If I had some fuckin' cheese in my mouth, I'd sure as hell spit it out, he thought. I feel like a fuckin' rat in a fuckin' trap.

- 64 -

When hens are made of clay

In the thick and dark, Clayton and Henry go in separate directions and then, in a few moments, regroup beneath the light outside Number 12 toward the back stretch of Leroy rooms.

"I wonder why in hell this one is boarded up," says Henry.

"Did you see her? I haven't heard a sound in five minutes. I went all the way around the place. In front of the restaurant. Everywhere." Clayton is verging on frantic.

"No. There were two or three guys standing outside of a car over there. But no sign at all of Cindy. Nothing. 'Course you can't see two feet in front of your face when you get away from these lights."

"Wait. Wait a minute, Henry. What's that? Someone just ran out of that breezeway down there. Coming this way. They're walking slow, now … aren't they? And carrying something. A bucket or something. My God, Henry. It's … yes … it's Cindy. Cindy. Cindy. Over here. Here." He starts toward her but stops as the young woman quickly moves toward him, then stops, clearly visible beneath a yellow light.

Cindy stands near Number 14, one room away. Her long hair is twisted and curled. She puts down what she is carrying, a heavy pail of some kind, and steps toward her father. Wheels are turning.

"Sweetheart? Are you ok? What's that you've got in your hair. Sticks? Dry weeds? Cindy ... say something. Cynthia! It's your father!" Clayton reaches out to touch his only daughter but she recoils a step and puts her arm up as if to fend off a blow.

"No. No. My father's quit and gone to play. That's what they say. That's what they say. Left me alone with sticks and clay. You know, roosters like hens, but that's ok. ... And my best friend too, et tu, et tu."

"Cindy. What's the matter? You're safe now, safe. Dr. MacLean and I have come to take you home. It's all over."

"He smiled on me. Smiled on me and set me free. But O O O O ... a bloody smile it was." She stands directly in front of Henry. "But you, you know all about bloody smiles, don't you? You're the king of bloody smiles, aren't you! 'Cause that's the only smile you own. Magic smile, twisty smile. Turn clay to clay. You with your rusty crown. Here's fennel for you." Cindy pulls a weed from her hair and flicks it at Henry. Then she steps back toward her father. "And rosemary for you. That will do. But only pansies left for me. And what remains to be. At least, that's what they say. Don't they. Don't they. 'Cause when hens are made of clay, roosters cannot play. Only pray." She couples her hands as if in prayer; then turns them to fists. "Prey. Prey." Cindy steps quietly back again and retrieves the pail that she had been carrying. "Can they? No. No. No."

Henry MacLean is one of those men of instinct. Whether it is researching some esoteric topic at the National Archives or Library of Congress or wooing some prospective philanthropist for the Faculty of Education or debating some indignant miscreant at a University Senate gathering, Henry MacLean always has the instinctive sense to do or say just the right thing at just the right moment. And so, as Cindy quickly steps forward, Henry steps back and turns away. The cascade that comes from the pail that she empties, aimed at him, catches Clayton Brown directly in the face as he reaches out toward his daughter. It is a thick white liquid and drenches and coats him, and burns. Clayton sings out in pain, agony, and claws at his face.

"Jesus. Jesus. I'm blind. Help me Henry. Cindy. Help me. I can't see a thing."

Cindy has already dropped the pail and sprints out of sight—"No ... No..." into the night. Into fog. Henry, dry as a desert, stands still against a black piece of plywood nailed over a door to one of the rooms of the Leroy. Strange thing, that.

Henry does not move. He is waiting just a little while longer.

- 65 -

Holy Mother of God

"**Ok, boys,**" Dalco speaks. "We ain't seein' dick-all here. And this crazy shit's gonna bring some cops. I'm guessin' our local losers fucked up again. Let's get." Dalco, Junior and Connie begin to retrace their steps around the Leroy toward the Lexus.

Pete straightens up from taking down the plate number of the Beamer and peers into the dark. He can sense something coming. He turns to wander back to the car—he has been told to be ready—when he hears some odd sing-song noise, like a child would make, and a figure flies past him. He hears the door of the Lexus open and slam closed before he realizes exactly what is happening. He stuffs the piece of notepaper into his pocket and rushes to the car. There, sitting behind the wheel, as near as he can see, is a young woman. But a strange young woman, with sticks and cakes of mud matting her hair. And she is bent down doing something under the dash. He grabs the door handle but it is locked; so is the back door. He raps on the driver's side window and the woman looks up and stares at him.

"Get the hell out of there, kid. That's not your car, and you have no idea what you're messing with."

With a blank response, the young woman in the car returns to the task she was at before Pete arrived. Then, remarkably, the Lexus fires up and lurches forward. And Pete can only now feel the key-fob in his pocket and put his hand on his head and wish to Christ that he was anywhere but where he was.

"Holy Mother of God! I am fucked twice up the ass on a Sunday morning."

- 66 -

Rat in a trap

"Looks like time to get the fuck out of Leroy!" Jerry Malley mutters. He quickly releases the side of the thick blue curtain he has pulled back. His fingers snap repeatedly. Rapidly, he tucks in his shirt, pulls on a windbreaker, takes a quick look around the room to make sure that he has left nothing, and opens the door slowly, quietly, and shuts it behind him in the same manner. He can see the Dalco bunch moving under an orange light still toward the back of the motel complex and he hears another voice screaming in pain in that general direction. Malley looks left and right and then moves to his BMW. He presses the remote fob, hears the door click, and gets in. In a split second, he eases the car to life and swings out intending to avoid the great Leroy sign; then it'll be straight ahead, toward the Office and the southeast exit of the lot. Yes, he is going to get out of here unseen, unnoticed. A close call. But there are no rules in parking lots. Another car just now screams at him from behind and clips the tail end of his Beamer, sending its nose to the right, out of control and crashing straight into the innermost post of the Leroy sign. The sign does not move, nor does the Beamer; it stops abruptly, the hood crumples, steam erupts from the radiator, the air bag explodes, and Jerry curses as his cigar is plastered against his face. He is covered in tobacco and ash and spark and talc.

This other car, a large dark vehicle, barely misses a beat and plows on, racing into the night. The squeal of tires and brakes on Dundas suggests that it holds no more respect for other vehicles than it has for Malley's. As Jerry spits the cigar and ash and other crud from his mouth in short, bitter bursts and as he squints through the tinted windows to see men approaching through the fog, indeed, he does look ever so slightly just like the very rat in a trap that he had proleptically envisioned.

- 67 -

Bird and fish and stone

Cindy puts the petal of the Lexus to the floor and soars out through the fog on Dundas past the obfuscated forms of cars and trucks and buses until, as she nears Confederation Bridge, the fog breaks and, spotting a flight of silver birds circling down to rest on the river, Cindy regains her sanity but loses her concentration. The Lexus, almost of itself, veers to the right, slices through the guardrails and, along with Cindy, becomes a bird for a time and then a fish and then a stone. And then sand and silt and blackness, as all settle in to rest below the ever-swirling eddies of the Moira, that old river of old sorrows.

- 68 -

Everything's been quiet, Mr. Prince

Trace takes another sip of her coffee. It is very good coffee. That makes this job worth something just by itself. And the quiet nights. The fog. The fog is really thick, but to be expected—it is the time of year for fog. With the heat trying to return and the cold hanging on—they fight it out for who is going to control the world. For domination. Each spring and fall, these two great universal forces work themselves into a white frenzy, panting and sweating and steaming—that's where the fog comes from, Trace's Grandmother had told her when she was very young. So Trace has known fog for a long time—in fact, she considers herself a bit of a fog expert. Like everything else, there are many kinds, many categories. Advection and Radiation and Freezing and Steam and Evaporation—those are outside fogs, the London soup variety, like tonight, and they aren't too hard to take. Quiet. Still. As long as you keep them outside. But when they get inside, now that is something different. That is the fog that can get you. Tease you. Hold and trap you. Rape you. And it comes in all kinds of pococurante shapes and sizes and colours. Sometimes it rubs you, coats you ... makes you feel just right. But most often, well, you ain't so lucky. It rises up and pulls you under; swells up in your throat, closes the breathing down and cakes the eyes. Steals your teeth. Makes nothing seem worthwhile. It suffocates all that you are or might be. Pins you to the table. You can never ever escape the fog—Trace knows that—but here, now, at the Leroy, she is starting to convince herself that, maybe, just maybe, she can manage the fog and get by. Just get by, that's all she really wants for now, the possibility of fog control ... not that murky absence which the other way around inanely annunciates. If there is to be sacrifice, a crucifixion of some kind, shouldn't there at least be the vain hope of salvation.

Trace is finished with the nails of her left hand and now turns to her right. She spreads her fingers. There is something in the fog that sounds like a scream. She sweeps a layer of scarlet over the nail of her right pinky finger and that old nail is reborn. Then another scream and another and the sound of running footsteps. The fog. She sheathes on another layer, this time, her ring finger. There is a man screaming now. Another nail glistens in the light. And then the sounds of cars crashing and a large black vehicle swoops past the Office and out into the murk of Dundas. The scarlet bathes another nail. And then her thumbnail too. Trace stares at the regenerated hand splayed on the counter. Yes, she thinks, possibilities are alive here at the Leroy. Fog under control; salvation, well, who knows about that. But, here, one coat at a time, at least a kind of separate peace for the moment.

The door from the apartment above opens, and Johnny descends three or four steps. Angus continues to sleep but his tail thumps the floor a couple times.

"Hi, Trace. What's all that noise I'm hearing down here? Out in the lot? People running around and that just sounded like a car crashing?"

"Noise? No? No. I'm sorry. I didn't hear anything. Everything's been quiet, Mr. Prince. All quiet."

- 69 -

Taking charge of change

The morning sun etches rainbows over the grey cement as Oz works along the back rooms of the Leroy, spraying the sidewalk clean. The colours dissipate as he finishes, no leprechauns, no pots of gold apparent. He begins to wrap up the sweaty hose as Johnny emerges from the eastern breeze-way.

"G'day, Prince."

"Mornin' Oz."

"God, this weather's sticky for this time of year—feels like a storm's comin'."

"Yeah, it is close. Maybe a storm is just what we need around here, to clear things a bit." Johnny stretches and yawns.

"You're lookin' a little beat down, Prince."

"Yeah, maybe a bit. I didn't get much sleep last night."

"Quite a ruckus, I gather."

"Like your storm already blew through, Oz. That dense fog and some rowdy stuff, people shouting, cars taking off, crashing, and then, just like somebody turned a switch off, absolute quiet."

"Kinda sounds like a normal night at the Leroy, if you ask me, Prince!"

"Yeah," Johnny smiles. "I see you washed that stuff away—some of Emily's concoction got tossed?"

"Yeah, looks like. In your storm! So, first night on the job, how'd Trace handle all the commotion?"

"Like Trace handles everything, I think. From far away. She didn't flinch a finger."

"Well, whatever works. Good thing she's on desk, not watch, I guess. So who were the hellraisers?"

"From what I could tell, just the regular run-of-the-mill ghosts, cash, fake names and addresses. Same old. But other than that bucket being thrown, I don't see any real damage. Jackie'll be here soon and she'll give the rooms a once over." Johnny turns to leave, but stops. "Oh, and Oz, in case I forget, Dom and Deed will have the van tomorrow afternoon—Friday—to run an errand for me, pick up some boxes from the Flying J down the freeway. Got a deal on some stuffed toys. Gonna donate them to the Children's Hospital—make their new CEO look good. Good PR and it's not costing us a thing."

"The best kind of charity ... you know, free... and that hospital has lots of sheets and towels, too!" Both men smile; then Oz hesitates a moment before he speaks again. "This old board covering 12 is lookin' pretty shabby ... I was thinkin' ... I might paint it..."

"Yeah, that's fine, Oz. Go ahead. It won't hurt."

"This board ... you know, it always reminds me of your Uncle Jake, and of the time Shonagh was here. They never really got along, did they?"

"No, they were oil and water. Of course, Jake was in his decline when Shonagh arrived. Aunt Marg had just died from the brain tumour and Jake just wasn't looking after much of anything, including himself. He never really read the signs. I mean if he had taken care of his health, gone to the doctor's earlier, he might be here today."

"It was odd, I always thought. I mean, everybody else thought the world of her? But not Jake…"

"He didn't mind when Shonagh waited tables, or redesigned the menus, or did the taxes, the web-site, but when she tried to get him to take care, eat right, take his meds, no…! To be honest, Oz, I think then she reminded him too much of Aunt Marg. She cared too much and that reminded him of all that he had lost."

"Yeah, that makes some sense, I guess. In some ways, Prince, I always thought Shonagh and Jake were too much alike."

"How's that?"

"Well, both saw that the world was broken, like, and both had pretty clear ideas about how it should be fixed. In many ways, 'though they would never have admitted it, their ideas were the same. They wanted a world filled with honesty and fairness—a world where you could be free to do the things you wanted, and when … where people worked together and helped others, and trusted each other. A world that included kindness and craziness; fun and joy. It's just that Shonagh felt that it needed to happen everywhere, all at once, and now—her world was the planet. But Jake's world … well, it was the Leroy. And in the end, neither of them seen those two worlds was the same place, and they wanted everyone they knew to make a choice— one or the other. No compromise. Shonagh, God love her, never saw that the way to save the planet was to embrace the Leroy. And Jake never saw that the things he could do here could shape the world."

"Yeah … you may be right, Oz. And I guess for a while I kind of got caught in the middle, but then I inherited Jake's side. He was dying of cirrhosis and a hundred other things and he gave this world to me. Shonagh had my heart, but the Leroy, this old shithole and all of the people who drift in and out of it, my old friend, well, it had my soul. Still has, I guess, though there are a lot of days, and nights—like last night—I really don't know why. Shonagh stayed here as long as she could but her world, as you say, was calling and, it sounds stupid, but I think I understood her too much, cared for her too much, to try to keep her here. Or maybe I was just too damn stupid, or stubborn—too much like Uncle Jake. I don't know. But Shonagh was smart, you know that, and in the end, I think, the Leroy would have destroyed her, in the same way somehow, it seems to save so many others. To give them shelter—what do you call it ... sanctuary?"

"Yeah, Johnny, it's the glue that puts a busted world back together for a lot of the busted people around here."

"So, as you already know ... one thing led to another; Shonagh threatened to leave, had to leave, and I knew I couldn't stop her. She wanted me to go with her, but Jake needed me, though he'd never admit it. And then he died—the machines that were keeping him alive just stopped working that night. It's like the great clock of the world hiccoughed and he was gone. He finally just let go. And so did Shonagh. By that time, even with Jake in his final days, she had come to realize that I would be tied down here even more. She knew I just couldn't leave. I was caught between two worlds, Oz, like a two-ring circus and I was a clown doing a juggling act between them. And all in a time when clowns don't entertain anybody anymore," Johnny waves his hand at the space across Dundas Street and speaks quietly. "Uncle Jake always told me that the land over there was Thornton's original circus grounds, near where the old army base was, and carnivals would set up two, three times a year, and he said that, when the circus came to town, it was like a dream come true for a kid. Fortune tellers and elephants and tigers and candy-coated apples. A world of magic. But that was a long time ago. Now it's the End and Shonagh's gone."

"And so we boarded up Room 12, the last place you saw her—the heart of the Leroy. Keep it waiting for her. A beacon and a tomb. Do you think she'll ever come back, Johnny?"

"We did what we had to do, Oz. What I still need, I think; so yeah, paint the board. Make it blacker. But … nah! Shonagh's gone. Everything changes. It's all we know. The circuses have left town, Oz, and taken their wonder and joy with them. And I seem to be left here to keep on juggling. A couple of times, I've thought about going after her. Of course, I've also thought about going to the moon—you can't do everything you think about. And God knows where she's got to anyway, how different she might be, what it would take to find her. The last I heard she was in Alaska but, now, well, she could be in Belleville or Beijing for all I know. Besides it would be like travelling into the past and I'm bound to the present, Oz, to the Leroy. It would be a fool's quest. I'd just get caught between two worlds again, in time and space. No, Shonagh and Jake are both gone. Circuses too! But the Leroy's right here. It's where some of us belong, I guess. Forever. And sometimes, Oz, like last night, it's kind of a circus itself."

"Well, as I always say, Johnny, there are three sides to every story. Did you ever think, maybe the fool's quest is staying here, boarding up this room, burying yourself in this place like some kind of out-of-joint … well, clown? Like you say, everything changes. So, refusing to change, refusing to take charge of change, is a game of clowns. 'Cause, if you don't take charge of change, Prince, it'll take charge of you! That's what hell is!

Growing old in the same place. Never really making a choice. You wake up one morning and suddenly your joints ache just thinkin' about gettin' up. Maybe you need to do for yourself before that happens? Maybe that would make what you do for others around here matter a bit more? Maybe this room's been boarded up long enough…"

You can't catch the future, Oz, any more than you can free the past.

"…maybe the last circus has left town, Johnny. And maybe nobody really can change the world, past, present or future, but we can all change ourselves, or try to. Maybe it's what we're born for … to try."

"You mean, just say 'to hell with it, Clem,' and turn around in the night like Uncle Jake in that dream of his?"

"Yeah … to hell with it Johnny. And live our lives running at the dark, humans trying."

"By God, old man, aren't you the poetic one this morning. You must be hangin' around the Professor too much. Or is Blue writing songs again? But, you know, I think you're right, Oz. That board could use another coat of paint and there is a storm comin'. I better check some of the windows around back. Maybe do some fresh caulking."

"Hell, Prince. I can do that."

"No, you keep helping Emily with the Gardens. I'll do it. Gettin' ready for the storm before it gets here is something I need to do. And like you say there are some things that have to be done, that you just need to do by yourself."

"Yeah, I know Johnny. What's the old phrase—live as long as you can, close your own eyes when you die!"

"Yeah! Something like that. Sometimes it's easy and sometimes it isn't. But maybe it's really the only way to live your life, to save your world. It's how you know who you are when you get up in the morning, aches or pains, like it or not, have a cup of coffee, talk to strangers checkin' in at a cheap motel. You gotta be who you gotta be, Oz. It's just that, sometimes, it takes a while to figure that out, sometimes a lifetime, maybe longer. Like Uncle Jake used to say, we're the sum of all we hide. That's life at the Leroy, isn't it? Sometimes a blessing, sometimes a curse, sometimes just a hole, a black board. Life at our Leroy! But it's the life we know. Heaven on the slide. Secure, safe, here. And, when all is said and done, I think it's enough for a clown like me, Oz. See you later, old man." Johnny squeezes Oz's shoulder with his right hand, turns from his gaze and moves away toward the Office. "Errands to do."

"Ok, Johnny. But let me know whenever..." Oz pauses, thinking carefully about what he wants to say, then shrugs his shoulders, "... whenever I can help."

Oz turns and heads out through the breezeway, and the Prince, close to the Office, notices a city bus pulling away and Jacqueline Savard walking into view.

"Good morning, Jackie."

"*Bonjour*, Prince."

"*Comment allez-vous?* ... How was that? Did I get it right?"

"*Perfectionner mon prince.* You got it perfect. Sad to say, though, the honest answer is—not so hot! *Tabernacle!* Angelique is driving me crazy. *Toujour du coq à l'âne.*"

"Really? So what's our little angel up to now?"

"Mostly, more of the same. Her marks aren't great, she's coming in late almost every night. I tried to talk to her this morning, but she just blew up and ran out. And you know that money I've been saving for a trip, well, I checked this morning and it was gone. All gone, over 600 dollar, and there's only one person who could have taken it."

"That doesn't sound good."

"No, it's pretty serious, and it's just going to set up another fight. And she's runnin' around with that Walker kid ... and I'm not too sure about that..."

"Oh yeah, Bobby ... well, I know him a bit. She could probably do a lot worse."

"'Cept he's a moron. *Un crétin stupide.* A lot like his father."

"Well, that may be so, Jackie. I won't argue with you there. But don't give up on her Jackie. Angelique's a good kid at heart. You got to keep trying to bring her 'round. She needs you, relies on you more than she knows. That's probably part of the problem."

"*Oui*, but she doesn't get that, Prince. I'm just about at my wit's end. I'm afraid she's gonna do something stupid, something big and stupid, like get pregnant, or run off with someone. And that's not good—I know. I been there."

"Well, not that I would wish it on her—but who knows, maybe she needs some kind of wake-up call, something to make her give her head a shake, to make her see what she has..."

"*Oui. Oui.* You might be right. I'll think about that, see if I can figure something out. I was hoping to take a trip with her, but now that money's gone."

"Well, I might be able to help out, Jackie..."

"Oh, *non*, thanks but I'll talk to her, Prince. You've done enough for me. We'll get this straightened out. Like you say, she's really a pretty good kid, just sometimes she doesn't think things through. *Parfois, elle est un ouragan.* In the meantime, these *chambres de motel* aren't cleanin' themselves, are they? I better get to it."

"Ok, Jackie. See you later. I guess I got some 'gettin' to' to do as well…"

Johnny turns into the Office and Jackie heads toward the cleaning closets near the eastside breeze-way.

- 70 -

The heart of the problem

Frank Elliot removes his cap and sits behind the steering wheel of the blue and white Dodge Charger. It is Thursday morning but it feels every bit like a Monday. Damn those west coast basketball games, especially the ones that start at ten and go into overtime. And then his head was so filled with bees anyway, from all the things that happened recently, he didn't really get to sleep, he figured, until nearly three o'clock. And then there was the long and involved debriefing this morning on a couple more junkies in bad shape, on a body found hanging in Berris Park and on a bad accident that happened out on Confederation Bridge last night. Wild times in Thornton. But Thursdays had a tradition of being kind and gentle—a sort of interstice between the tying up of what happened last weekend and the unravelling of what was to be this weekend—he hopes that will be the case today. With the recent spate of dead and dying junkies all over town, though, he knows the odds are not in his favour. First thing, as soon as his partner arrives, he needs a coffee and he needs it quick. He glances at his watch. Nearly 8:30. It is time to be rolling.

"Hi, Frank. Sorry I'm a bit late, but the Captain wanted to

ask me a couple questions and gave me some forms to fill out." Laura Santolin gets in and closes the door, setting her cap next to Frank's on the seat.

"G'Morning, Laura. Good to see you again, partner. Ready for bear?"

"Yeah. Let's get at it. Coffee before bear, though, I hope?"

"It's the only way to start the day, isn't it?"

The blue and white fires into motion, pauses at the curb to look both ways, and then shoots to the right. Traffic along Dundas is sparse this early; perhaps it is a sign of a peaceful day to come.

"So, how are you Laura? How are you feeling?"

"I'm fine, Frank. I had a bit of a headache on the weekend but the doctor gave me some Tylenol, the stuff with the codeine. She's going to take the stitches out next week. I think I've got more pain from thinking about the forms I've got to fill out than from bumping my head at Wilson Hall. Wow, they want you to write a novel when you get hurt a bit."

"Yeah, they sure do. All the city's legal eagles perk right up when anybody gets scratched and a cop's around. Even if it's the cop! They'll make you dot every i, cross every t, and do it twice just to be sure. It's not that they care that much about you, you know—it's just the city don't want any lawsuits."

"I kind of gathered that. But I've got to thank you, Frank. For sticking your neck out like you did."

"What do you mean, Laura?"

"You know what I mean. Writing up the report the way you did. And calling me at home to make sure that we told the same story."

"Well, there's no sense in blowing a little accident way out of proportion. And the Dean of the college, he seemed very happy to go along. The fewer waves that rock the boat the better. And the two guys who nearly got hit, the Dean's already met with them; he made some kind of deal. And from my brief conversation with them, I'm not surprised they went along with it—they looked to me to be workin' some angle. ... And so, that's the end of that."

"I know the kind of grind they can put you through when you discharge your weapon, especially in a place as public as we were last week. And me, still new on the job. Writing it up to make like that old woman, that she... she..."

"Hey, partner. It's simple. That old gal lunged for your gun, it de-holstered, hit the floor and went off. Then she high-tailed in the confusion. End of story."

"I know ... it's just ... just that it sure takes the pressure off, Frank. It's one I owe you, big time." Laura turns her head to the window and puts her hand to her face. She is trembling.

"Hey, it's ok, partner. It's nothing you wouldn't have done for me. Right? Accidents happen, to all of us."

"Yeah, I guess they do, but ... oh, there's Stanley's. Coffee time."

"I'll just use the drive-thru. You know I always like this time of day, Laura. Streets still wet with dew. That old sun just starting to fire itself up. And most of our troublemakers are deep into sleep right now, having nightmares about what they were doing last night, and they haven't dreamed up today's bad news yet. ... Two medium black, please. ... Husbands and wives still aren't awake and ornery enough to start fighting and the stores are still closed so they haven't discovered last night's break-ins or caught any of today's shoplifters. Most peaceful time of the day. ... Thank you. ... The only really bad thing about this time of today is this coffee. God. Remind me not to go back to Stanley's ever again, will you?

"Frank, you say that every time," Laura gently chastises him.

"Well, I don't know. They're handy, I guess. And all over the place. But their coffee is an arrestable offence. There must be some place in town you can still get a decent cup of coffee. I don't know…"

"Frank, there's something … something I need to talk to you about."

"Yeah. … Ok. … What is it, partner?"

The cruiser swings out into traffic again. The two officers balance their coffees in their hands as they move casually through the mostly vacant streets.

"Well it's about last week. Last Friday, at Wilson Hall."

"Ah, why don't we forget about that, Laura. Nobody got hurt. It was just an accident. It's over with."

"Yes, but I think that you know that it was not just an accident!"

"Ok, partner. What do you need to say?"

"Well, you know, I was standing there, backing up your interview. I mean, you're so good at it so I was listening closely like I always do. And that old woman, surrounded by you and the Dean and that security guard, those two other guys just standing back there watching, that old woman just looked so sad and pathetic. And she was telling you that unbelievable story, about being two hundred years old and getting kidnapped by, what'd she say, dark gods, and claiming that the university stole her land. She was just so, I don't know, isolated, vulnerable. Alone. But genuine, honest somehow. And when she said her name, Frank—Emily Allison Bean—something just started to churn up inside of me. I don't know what it was. Did you know that I had a great aunt named Emelie? Maybe that was it? It just seemed to be too much, too much of a coincidence, too much of a … a trap. It was like she was some sorry, innocent creature caught in a snare who didn't know why or where it was. It was like … like it was me! Like all of time and circumstance had conspired to bring me to this place, this moment. It's the way I've felt sometimes in this job, as a rookie. I looked down, Frank, and I swear to God, for the first time, I saw that gun in my hand. I don't ever remember taking it out of the holster. Flipping the safety. But there it was—it just appeared, just like that old woman, out of nowhere. And that's when I went down. That's when I dropped the gun and it went off. It was the only thing I could do. My only response. The choice I made."

"That is curious, partner. Maybe the old gal put you in some kind of trance or something. One thing you learn in dealing with some of these perps, don't pay too close attention to them. Some of them are real snakes—they can charm you, intentionally or not. Lull you into a false sense of security. Always look away for a split second every now and then. Never stand directly in front of them. Remind yourself to breathe regularly. With some, you have to be real careful not to get sucked into their weird worlds, into their darkness."

"Yeah, maybe that's what it was, Frank. I don't know though."

"So you don't remember pulling your weapon. Do you remember what you were planning to do with it?"

"Yes, Frank. I think that's the heart of the problem. That's what's really bothering me. I think that I do know exactly what I was going to do with it."

Laura looked straight across and her unblinking eyes caught Frank's as he glanced at her, away from the road.

"Well, partner, maybe we each did one another a favour then. ... You also did old Emily a good turn, of course. She escaped. In fact, she has absolutely disappeared. Maybe those dark gods got her again! Who knows? The point is, it's an incident that's over. It'd be best just to forget about it, let it go, don't you think?"

"I guess so, Frank. That may be more easily said than done, though. 'Cause, you know, she got into my head somehow. I had a dream last night, Frank, and she was in it. We were a team, like Butch and Sundance, or maybe more like Thelma and Louise. And the world was against us and there I was, with my Sauer, about to shoot my way out of a trap. About to go down in a blaze of glory, Frank, 'cause the bastards had done us wrong and they were closing in. No. I don't think I'm going to forget Emily Allison Bean for a while. And you know what, and maybe this is what troubles me the most, I don't think that I want to forget her. And, strangely somehow, that makes me feel as good as I've felt in a long, long time."

There is silence in the squad car.

"I've got a lot of doubts, Frank. I think maybe, at the end of the day, I'm going to ask for another couple days off. Maybe longer. I think I need that."

The radio crackles. The two officers balance their coffees and casually attend to the sound. Probably another lost cat or dog. Or maybe another dead junky.

- 71 -

*A*ssez *propre*

Jackie pushes her cart past Number 17 and stops at 18. The rooms run backwards at the Leroy, from Number 1 on the farthest side to 24 next to the Office. She twirls a set of keys into her left hand with a neat spin of the chain attached to her waist and opens the door—the move would make any gunfighter jealous. Jackie winces as a somewhat peculiar smell drifts from the darkness of the room. She doesn't spend any time trying to identify the odour—she's been doing this job long enough to be smart enough not to think about it. She flips the switch and pulls open the curtains to ease a mottled light across the grey room. She moves through and into the bath, pushes the shower curtain back, twists a water tap on for a count of three, turns it off and looks at the tub. *Assez bon*—good enough.

She picks up four towels of various sizes scattered about the room and deposits them in the laundry bag on her cart. She repeats her tap manoeuvre at the sink, wipes the vanity with a cloth, drops two semi-used bars of soap in the toilet and flushes it—good enough. She deposits two motel-sized bars of soap near the sink and places fresh towels on the rack. In the main room, Jackie pulls the bedspread off the bed, quickly decides that these sheets have to go, rolls them up and remakes the bed. She glances at the carpet—*assez propre*. It is not that Jackie would ever do a poor job here. Far from it. She holds great respect for Johnny P. March—he is a fair man and treats her well and has paid her several times even when she did not show for work, like when Angie was sick last fall and when she had to go back east for her mother's funeral. He has never tried to take advantage of her like most of the rest—in fact, he has even sent her home in a taxi that time after the big football party when she invited him to take some advantage. He is too good. Like they say, he is the Prince. *Il est le prince.* But still, when you are cleaning rooms at the Leroy, there is only a certain level of excellence to which one is compelled to strive. That is Jackie's view of life and she's been around long enough to be smart enough not to think about it too much.

Jackie locks the door, leans on the window sill and pulls out a pack of cigarettes, DuMarier Lites. Two more rooms to clean and then she'll put on her other Leroy hat, working in the kitchen and waiting tables at Rainy's. She has lots of time today, only the six rooms to clean before she is needed for the lunch hour rush, which on an off-season Thursday will probably be about five people, and two of those will only have coffee and a piece of pie. Jackie drags the last sweet smoke from the DuMaurier and tosses it to the parking lot. She pushes her cart away from Number 18, past 19 and 20 and stops at 21. There is a squeal of tires in the street behind her and Jackie glances over toward the End where a yellow Mustang has just hit its brakes and swerved in—some idiot out doing what idiots do. She ignores them and turns back to the task at hand. She flips the keys into her hand in the accustomed manner and opens the door. A slightly unpleasant smell cascades over her from the darkness. This time though it is not an odour that Jackie can be smart enough not to think about. It is a smell beyond that of perfume or after shave or sweat or pot or sex; it is a smell that moves something inside Jackie and she knows it is a wrong smell, a foreign smell, even before she reaches for the light switch, before her right foot touches a slickness in the carpet.

"Oh, *pardonnez* ... excuse me, sir. I thought that the room was empty. I..."

Jackie stops. There is a naked man on the bed. But the naked man is not responding. He is not awaking in surprise and frantically pulling covers around himself. He is not cursing the motel maid for her interruption. He is not some pervert intentionally involved in some creepy act of indecent exposure. He is just there, arm over the side of the bed, face sideways on the pillow, with a big, sad smile, looking straight at Jackie's silhouette in the morning door.

"Excuse me, sir. *Allo!* Hello?"

She pulls open the curtains. She doesn't scream. Women like Jackie don't scream. But her breath catches somewhere deep inside her body and she freezes. That smile. O that smile. She cannot really believe that she is seeing what she is seeing—that's what she said many times later when she was asked, by the police, by her friends, and by those others too.

- 72 -

You can check out any time

The two police officers attend to the crackled radio voice that enunciates with all the clarity of a subway loudspeaker.

"Did you catch all of that, Laura? I sure as hell didn't. Could you repeat that Beth—there's a lot of static here today?"

In a slower, carefully articulated manner, the Dispatcher repeats the message: "Emergency at the Leroy Motor Inn. 2545 Dundas East. Proceed immediately. 911 call. Probable 10B54."

"'Copy.' Hell, partner. Another emergency at the Leroy. Probably some pissed-off spouse caught some other pissed-off spouse again. Anyway, Laura, hit the lights. Might as well try to part the seas and give 'em a show when we arrive."

The Charger, lights flashing, assuming its own moniker, leaps into speed and roars through the city for a several blocks. Some cars slow and pull to the right; others are oblivious as Frank flashes lights and manoeuvres around them.

"Assholes," he mutters.

Then the cruiser turns onto Dundas, slows and slides left into the parking lot of the Le Roi Motor Inn. The car rolls to a stop in front of the Office and the two officers get out, putting on their caps as they do so. They are met by Benny.

"We received an emergency call," Frank speaks to the lean twenty-something with the scruffy beard who is approaching from the Office. "Do you know what's up?"

"Yes, come with me, please," replies Benny, and turns toward the eastern row of rooms.

The door to Number 21 is still open and a maid's laundry cart sits outside its window. Frank glances at the walk in front of the door. There is the partial outline of a dark footprint on the cement and a couple more are just discernible, heading toward the Office. Avoiding them, Frank takes a quick look inside the room; his attention is diverted as an ambulance roars into the parking lot. The yellow-shirted lean man waves it toward the area where they are standing.

"Laura, you better call for back-up. Tell them to notify S.I.— we'll need their help … and homicide, I think. Vance will need to be informed. And the medical examiners. Thursday just got a lot busier, partner—I think that we got us a murder at the Leroy."

"Oh. Ok, Frank. I'm on it."

"And I know that's just what the Coroner needs right now, another stiff!"

The two attendants from the ambulance, each carrying a large black satchel, arrive at the door and are stopped by Frank.

"Easy boys. I don't think from where I'm standing there's any need for a rush. How about just one of you coming in with me, and bring a stethoscope. Come on."

Frank, followed by a tall man in white, steps into the room. The walls are covered in a dark burgundy wallpaper, its design composed of Ionic columns wrapped in olive-coloured vines with small faded purple clusters of what must have been intended as grapes. The ceiling is a light grey stucco; the floor, a matted, golden copse of shag, carpet that has endured far too much for far too long. There is a dresser and mirror along the right wall with a small cathode-ray television anchored to the far end and, on the left, a regular-sized bed with a night-stand holding a wooden lamp and heavy black telephone. The ceiling light is on and the curtains on the window, drawn back. Grey light swims through dust particles that fill the room. To the right of the back wall is the open door to the washroom; to the left, a small closet with no door. On the bed there is a naked male—he is lying on his stomach, his head resting on a pillow with face turned toward the window. One arm is languishing off the bed and touches the floor as if it were part of an incomplete Sistine fresco, the other is perpendicular to his body. As Frank surmised from the doorway, and knew even before he reaches the body, the male is dead. The discolouration of the sheets, the thick coagulation in the carpet around that side of the bed, the seven to nine inch slit in the throat which, with the head propped on the pillow, exposes a crevice-like gap nearly three inches wide at its apex below the left cheek. Yes, this guest has checked out for good.

"If you could be careful to disturb as little as possible here, I would like you to check this fellow's pulse. I just want to be sure that a fast trip to the hospital isn't going to do this chap a lot of good! Ok?"

Frank stands aside while the ambulance attendant kneels and touches the naked man's wrist and then gently places the stethoscope under his arm on the exposed left side.

"No. Nothing here, Officer. He's deceased. For some time, I think."

"Ok. I guess I sort of knew that. Thank you for your help. You and your buddy can move on out now. I imagine there's some livin' people out there that need your help a lot more that this fellow ever will, at least at this point. We'll contact the Coroner for transport. We've got a bit of looking around to do before we move him. Thank you—please be careful on your way out."

As the attendant exits, Laura returns.

"Help's on the way, Frank. O ... my God. *Dios mío*. That's brutal."

"Yeah, it ain't a pretty sight, Laura. You better get your gloves on. If you could round up the witnesses and then come back and stand guard here at the door, I'm going to take a quick look around. Ok? Unless you'd rather do the 'prelim' talks?"

"No, it's all yours partner. That's why you earn the big bucks, right! But, hey, you want to know something strange, other than this, I mean. A real coincidence. When I walked down to the corner there, you know who I saw, I think, I'm sure, and she was pushing a wheelbarrow around to the back. I swear to you, I saw Emily Bean, you know, the old woman from the university. The one who disappeared."

"Really. Well, it is a small world, isn't it? So maybe the dark gods didn't get her, after all! Curious. Or maybe not—this is the Leroy, you know! Some dark gods probably have permanent residence around here! Anyway, one thing at a time, for now. This mess needs our full attention."

"Yeah, I hear you, Frank. I'll tape off the scene and make a list of the employees who were around, and get the registry for last night." Laura moves back toward the cruiser.

"Thanks, Laura. I'll give the room a good once over." Frank steps through the room and into the washroom, snapping on a set of latex gloves as he goes. Towels are all in place and the soap is still in its wrapper. The vanity and the tub are bone dry, the shower curtain is pulled to one side, the toilet seat is up—it might have been used, but the rest of the place looks like no-one has ever been there. He'd have to talk to the maid and the other

Leroy people, of course, to make sure things hadn't been disturbed. Frank looks around the room. The bedspread and sheets have been pulled to one side and the body is stretched out on the other. There is no sign anywhere of any luggage or clothes or personal effects. No watch, no rings, no visible jewellery of any kind on the corpse. No natural marks or tattoos to be seen. And there is nothing hanging in the closet. Frank gently opens one of the drawers in the dresser—empty. The same with the other three and with the nightstand, except for the requisite *Gideon's* and a battered, three-year-old phone book. Frank kneels and shines his flashlight under the bed—nothing but more shag, a bit lighter shade of gold than the rest, a slight, rectangular indentation in the floor under the middle of the bed, and a light patina of dust. The maids of the Leroy did not vacuum under the beds every day, maybe any day, he guesses. Couldn't blame them either he thought. A large bug of some kind scurries through the light and Frank gets up. As he turns to go, he glances at the body one more time. Male. Caucasian. Late thirties, maybe early forties, he figures. Perhaps a bruise to the left side of the head, some matted hair. Some contusions on the wrists. Hard to tell from this angle, though, if there are any other significant wounds or bruises. Of course, a slit throat is enough. It is as if this fellow was just sleeping here in the buff and someone crept up behind him and slit his throat. Eyes open though—guess you didn't sleep with your eyes open. But I suppose he could have opened them just as the knife went in. Blue eyes. Dark brown hair, a bit greasy. He probably could have used the shower. He'll get that in the morgue, Frank supposes. And he did seem to be smiling—wait. What is that? His mouth is open at a strange angle. There is something in his mouth, jammed in by the looks of it. But Frank isn't going to mess with that—no. Beyond his pay grade, as they say.

That is enough for a preliminary investigation. With this kind of a case the suits would take over as soon as they arrive, anyway—and after all, that's why they got paid the bigger bucks, right? He would tell them to have a closer look at the mouth—there was something there. Who knows, maybe that would be the clue that breaks the case. He glances one more time at the corpse and moves to the doorway. There is something deep within based on his many years in the force that is telling him that this is a case that may not get solved.

"God, Laura. I got the feeling that this is going to be a strange one. There is absolutely nothing in there except the body and a lot of blood. Heaven knows who that poor soul was."

"Well, Frank, I guess it's livened up Thursday for us, whether we needed it or not. That dark-haired woman by the Office door, the one in the green uni, she's the one who found the body. She's a maid here. I told her that you would probably want to talk with her. I got her background info—address and such. Her name's Jacqueline Savard."

"Ok. Thanks Laura. I imagine the second battalion will be getting here soon. Then we'll get to stand around for a while with our nightsticks up our asses. I'll have a quick talk with her."

Frank walks past Numbers 22, 23, 24.

"Excuse me, Jacqueline Savard? My name is Frank Elliot. Could I have a word with you?"

A pretty woman with raven-dark hair turns to him. She lowers a cigarette, a half-smoked DuMaurier.

"Sure, Officer. But I don't think that I have much to say," Jacqueline steps toward him. "Do you mind if I smoke?" She takes a long drag on her cigarette. "I got to tell you, I'm a little bit shook up. I don't run into that kind of thing every day, you know?"

"Yeah, I can imagine. To be honest, I'm thankful that I don't run into that very often myself. Anyway, I understand that you found the body, right?"

"*Oui.* I was just doing my rounds, cleaning the rooms, and I opened 21 and there he was."

"Did you touch anything, or change anything in the room?"

"No. I just opened the door and looked at him. I told him I was sorry for barging in, but he didn't answer. When that happened, you know, my first thought was, he's smiling at me, that sick bastard is getting his kicks by having me walk in on him like that. I've heard of that kind of thing happening to maids in other motels, you know, but not here at the Leroy. 'Course I supposed, there's always a first time. But then, when he didn't move, he just kept smiling, and my foot touched something slippery inside the room, I knew there was something wrong. I flipped on the lights, and I pulled the cord on the curtains, and I knew he wasn't smiling, Officer. I knew he wasn't ever gonna smile again. I got to tell you—I really could not believe that I was seeing what I was seeing. I'm not sure that I believe it now. So then, I just stepped back out of the room, came back to the Office and told Benny to call 911. That was about ten, fifteen minutes ago."

"Did you know the man in the room? Had you seen him check in or anything?"

"*Non.* Never saw him before. I finish here, most days, by mid-afternoon; usually don't see anyone check in."

"Mrs. Savard, did you see anyone else enter the room today while you were around either before or after you left it?"

"No, I didn't and I know that I'm not going back into that room for a while either, I can tell you that. And it's not Mrs. Savard. That was my mother. Call me Jackie."

"All right. I have one further question and I hope that you will not take this the wrong way. I have to ask you this. Did you, or did anyone else that you know of, take anything from the room?"

"Do you mean, like, did I rush in and steal all his wallet or watch, or something? That is a shitty question, but the answer is no. The Leroy may be a bit run down, but it's an honest place. And so are those of us who work here. The Prince wouldn't have it any other way, you know! Now if you want your pockets picked, just go over there to the End." She gestures across the road. "They'll steal you blind right across the Check-in counter and smile at you all the while they're doing it. And then they'll put a chocolate mint on your pillow to thank you. There are no mints at the Leroy; it's an honest place. Just talk to the Prince."

"Where is the Prince?"

"I'm not too sure. I don't think I've seen him today."

"Well, I'm sure he'll show up, sooner or later, to take care of things. He always does, doesn't he! Thank you very much, M ... Jackie. For right now, I think that those are all the details that I need. Please wait around though. They'll be some detectives arriving—in fact there they come right now—they'll want to talk to you too. Probably ask you the same questions I just did. So please try to be patient with them. And thanks."

A light bronze Chrysler pulls sharply into the parking lot, stops near the cruiser, and shuts off its engine. Two suited men get out. Right behind them, an SUV cruiser arrives with three occupants inside, a uniformed driver and two more suits.

And the events of the day evolve. Events that would stretch late into the afternoon. Details to be checked again and again; questions to be answered over and over. The first two men are senior detectives, Earl Vance and Phinny Lowe. They converse briefly, perfunctorily, with Frank and Laura—this is their third motel corpse this morning and its barely 10:30—then proceed to Number 21 to look around.

The second pair of suits carry large rectangular briefcases into the motel room. They are the S.I. team and will scour the room for all of the macro- and microscopic clues that contemporary forensics dines on. The flash of digital cameras has already commenced.

Earl and Phinny glance around a bit but mostly leave the scene to the forensics guys, Alf and Bill. Earl motions with his arm, pointing to the head of the corpse.

"Alf, take a look in the guy's mouth, will you? The prelim guy says he thinks that something might be stuck there."

"Ok Earl. Will do! You done with the first round of photo ops, Bill?"

With an affirmative nod from his partner, the man adroitly turns the corpse's head ceiling-ward and, with his thumbs, moves the jaws open.

"Ah shit, Earl. Look! I think the head just came loose." Alf's voice is animated, then with a chuckle, "Nah, just kidding!"

"You are a riot, my friend, a riot … you should give up the day job and hit the comedy clubs," Earl responds with sarcasm and a smile.

"Well, there certainly is something in the mouth all right. It's jammed right down the throat. Let's see—maybe I can get it. Yes, it's loose. Well, what do you know! You know what, Earl, it's the goddamn TV remote. And you know, he could have choked to death on this remote, maybe before he was cut. Very interesting. Let's see."

There is a popping sound and hissing and the television comes on, casting a blue haze into the greyness of the room and cracking its silence. Across a barren desert a small bird flies in a cloud of dust toward a mountain-shadow. There, next to an empty carton, perched on an Acme Atomic Pogo-Stick and ready to pounce, is a wolf-like beast, but one who is not quite wolf-wise enough.

"Hey, it's the cartoon channel. He must have been one bored son-of-a-bitch to watch that, or maybe there was a child here."

"Alf, turn that off," says Bill. "It's weird enough in here right now without that thing playing. And put the remote back in the mouth, as close to where you found it as possible. You might be right about choking or suffocation. The medical examiner folks will want to have a look at that. That'd be a new one wouldn't it, death by remote control."

"Ahh, I don't know, boys. Not to wax philosophic, but most of the world seems dead by remote control these days, if you know what I mean. Come on, Phinny," says Earl. "Let's leave these guys alone in their warped little world. You can talk to the maid," he lowers his voice and elbows his partner lightly in the arm. "I hear she's pretty nice lookin'—maybe you'll get to stay over at the Leroy tonight. Maybe make you forget old Bonnie, eh? Anyway, I want to see the desk clerk, get the names of the people who stayed here last night. And I want to see Johnny March, too. You never know what the Prince is up to—it wouldn't be impossible to imagine that he might just know something about all this too."

Earl and Phinny turn back to the Office. Phinny introduces himself to Jacqueline and both go into Rainy's and sit in a booth. Earl speaks to Benny.

"Been a kind of busy morning, hasn't it? What's your name, son?"

"Benny, sir, Benny Alamo. Just like the fort, or the car rental company! And yes sir. It has been busy, too busy."

"I need to see the register for yesterday."

"I'm ahead of you, sir. Actually, we use these old registration cards. Here's the one for 21." Benny hands Earl a white 5X3 index card. "We also transfer this info into a data base, so I can give you a print-out if you need one."

"Yes, that would be handy. So, somebody named Howard registered in 21, and paid cash. And he claims to be a doctor? Staying here? And didn't fill out any of the rest of the registration form? Licence plates, or anything? Do you normally allow that?"

"Yes, yes we do. We don't normally push for info whether they use cash or credit. This is the Leroy, after all! People are looking for a private, comfortable stay. A discount stay. That's usually why they choose here. There's nothing to steal, and the rooms are pretty-much indestructible, so we never need to contact anyone after they check-out."

"Yeah, but I guess some of the people who stay in them aren't so indestructible, are they? The ones who check out but never leave?"

"Like the song says!"

"Yeah. Like the song. Do you remember anything about the person who rented 21 last night? Were you on duty?"

"Yes, I checked them in. But I don't remember much. He wore a blue coat, I think, and had brown hair and a moustache. His friend never left the car."

"Friend? Them? You mean there were two of them?"

"Yeah, there were two. And they were driving a kind of sedan. Black, a Chevy, I think. Yeah, black Chevy."

"Are there any other details that you remember? Anything particular or peculiar?"

"Not that I can think of, sir. Except maybe that they arrived early to take a room. They were here around lunch-time. Most people don't come around until late-afternoon, or later, you know. So yeah, I thought arriving that early was a bit peculiar."

"Yeah, you may be right. Anyway, tell me, Mr. Benny Alamo, just like the fort, how squeamish are you? If I took you down to Number 21 before the Coroner's van gets here, would you be willing to look at a dead man and tell me if he was the man who paid for the room yesterday, or his buddy in the car?"

"No problem. I can certainly try, sir."

Just as they turn to exit the Office, the Prince of Leroy steps in. He seems calm but alert as though some antediluvian instinct has cut in.

"Hi, Benny. What's up with all the commotion? Hello there, Detective Vance. What brings you to our fair establishment? We got some more marital discord going on?"

"Hello, Johnny. A bit more than some marriage counselling this morning, I'm afraid. What brings me here is a stiff in Number 21 who's got a slit in his neck big enough that of all his blood leaked out. I was just about to look you up—wondering if you knew anything about any of this."

"No, can't say that I do, Earl. Sorry to hear about it though—among other things, it's not exactly good advertising, you know when it shows up in the papers and all. And sure not good in any way for the guy in 21. Was it a suicide?"

"No—cut throat. Pretty sure he had help with that. It's a homicide, Johnny. Is there anything else I should know about? Any other unusual happenings around the place yesterday, or last night, gentlemen?"

"No. None that I noticed, Earl. Except the fog. It was pretty thick."

"Yeah, well it's always kind of thick and foggy around the Leroy, isn't it? I presume that Benny, here, doesn't work 24 hours, so I'll have to talk to your night clerk. Who's that?"

"It's Tracey Walters. I can get you her number, although she didn't say anything when she went off shift. Of course, Trace doesn't say too much anyway."

"Tracey Walters—I think I know her. You employ some real first class citizens around here, don't you, Johnny. Anyway, first

The Prince of Leroy

things first. C'mon, Benny, let's take a walk—your desk-hop here's going to have a look to see if he recognizes the deceased. Why don't you come along too, Johnny?"

"I think I'll pass, Earl. I never saw anyone who checked in yesterday. I did notice a car parked out there last night—a red Toyota, I think. But, to be honest, I'm not too partial to corpses. So I'll stay here—the Office needs someone on the phone anyway."

"Did you say red Toyota? I thought you said it was a black sedan of some kind? A Chevy?" snaps Earl looking at Benny, then at his notes.

"Well, I don't know. I could be wrong, I guess. I'm not much of a car person."

Earl just shakes his head.

At the room, the forensic men have turned the body onto its back and are snapping more pictures.

"Anybody wants some prints, let me know. Maybe some 4x5s for your wallets? What do you say, fellows?"

"Forget Alfie," quips Earl. "He works around a lot of embalming fluids and other chemicals. It's rotted away what little brain he had. So, Benny Alamo, is that Dr. Howard? Is that the man who rented this room yesterday?"

Benny steps into the room and glances uneasily at the corpse; he turns back to Earl with a negative shake of his head.

"No, Detective," adds Benny. "Howard was short, shorter than that guy. I never saw him before. ... You know, Detective, I do not envy you your job, dealing with this kind of thing all the time. I'd end up in the looney bin."

"You're right there, Benny. It's never easy, and you never really get used to it. Or if you do, well, then you got some real problems. Real looney bin problems! Like Alfie in there, right! Anyway, thank you. I suppose even if you had said that it was the infamous Dr. Howard we wouldn't have been much farther ahead. I suspect that your man Howard checked in and out of about a dozen motels around town the last twenty-four hours. Anyway, I need to get the names and addresses of all of the others who stayed here last night. Can you get me that print-out? We'll have to try to contact them to see if anybody saw anything. I got to tell you, this is starting to look like one of those hunts for a needle in a haystack after the haystack has been fed to the herd."

They move back toward the Office where Johnny is standing. Benny slips inside to get the print-out as Johnny speaks.

"You can do me one favour, Earl. Move that guy out of here as soon as you can, will you? And these cop cars. You'd be surprised how many people don't turn into a motel when there's half a dozen cop cars sitting around with their lights flashing. Know what I mean?"

"Yeah, I do Johnny. We'll move as quickly as we can. I'll get the boys to turn off the lights—we don't need to make this anymore of a circus than it is. We'll have rubber-neckers out there plowing into each other. But it is a murder you know. That guy didn't slit his own throat. And if this thing ever gets to court, we got to have all the details right."

"Fair enough ... thanks."

Jackie and Phinney return from the restaurant. Jackie's body language suggests that she has now landed somewhere between tired and ticked off.

"Earl, I told Jacqueline that she'd have to stay around for a while, that you might want to ask her a few questions. Is that right?"

"Yeah, that's right, Phinney. I know it seems like we ask the same questions over and over, ma'am, but that's how we get our evidence, cross-check it, and so on. So if you don't mind staying put, it won't be that long."

"What can I say? I'll be here. I still got to finish my cleaning anyway. I didn't get to *vingt-trois* yet. That dead guy got in the way, I guess."

"No, Jackie," says the Prince. "You've finished your cleaning for today, maybe tomorrow too. Why don't you go in and keep Blue company. She'll be dying for all the gossip anyway, so she'll be able to pass it along to Dom and Deed and the rest of the regulars, right? I'll do 23 later myself. Ok."

"Johnny, you don't know how ok that is. I got to tell you, I really do not feel like opening another of those rooms today. *Merci beaucoup. Vous êtes le prince.*"

"As soon as the officers are done, I'll give you a lift home, too. By the time these guys clear out, you're not going to feel like waiting for any bus."

Jackie moves away to the restaurant and Earl interjects.

"I'll be in and talk to you in a bit. But right now, where is that register print-out?"

As he speaks, Benny steps from the Office. "You can keep this, Detective Vance. Unless you need to see the people's handwriting?" Benny hands a computer print-out to Earl:

"Thank you. This is good. But I will need those registration cards for all of these people, too—for handwriting, signatures, verification, and the like. We'll make copies and return them to you. Man, this won't be easy. Getting in touch with these people may take a while, especially since most of them that aren't fake are likely on the road. And by the time we do contact them, they probably won't even remember staying here, or they may not want to when they find out what went down. You guys hang around. We've got some paper to do and maybe some other questions."

"This is where I live, Earl. I'll be here," says Johnny.

"Hey, a quick question. There doesn't seem to be anything

	Le Roi Motel	Invent: <u>28/03</u>
Room	Name/Address	Payment
9	Cliff Marion, 4 pers, 1 ngt RR4 Sheffeld 412-687-4142	MC 4234-3876-9889 02/24
11	Robert Henry, 1 pers, 1 ngt 17 Ross St. Apt 313, Newton 282-3769	$
18	Eve Bigelow, 2 pers, 1 ngt Belleville 613-962-2473	V 4551-3902-2978 03/21
21	Dr. Howard, 2 pers, 1 ngt ///	$
23	Tom and Dick Grill, 2 pers, 1 ngt 75 East 43rd, New York 212-459-3972	$

but the body in the room but what do you do when people do leave stuff here? Like these other guests? Personal effects and stuff, when they haven't filled out a return address—what do you do?"

"Same thing we do if they have filled out an address. Nothing. It's the policy of the Leroy, Earl—most hotels for that matter. We save the stuff in that walk-in safe over there." Johnny gestures toward the Office. "But there's nothing in there from last night yet. It'd still be on Jackie's cart down there if there was anything left behind."

"I'll check that out. And if somebody does leave something…?"

"If they can describe it, what it looks like, what's inside, it's theirs. We never open up suitcases, or wallets, or anything. Leroy policy, no ifs, ands or buts. Too much trouble if you do. You flip open a wallet, empty a purse or open a suitcase and somebody'll say you stole something. You're a cop, you know the way some people are. So we bag all the stuff we find, jewellery and so on, and store it here in the safe. Except food, of course. Or booze. We throw that away. Every six months, I get rid of it—all of it, no questions asked. In fact, we just had a Burning Day, as we call it around here, last week."

"Oh yeah. You use that old furnace that belonged to the abattoir, don't you?"

"You know it, Earl. You don't really have to ask any questions, do you? You know it all."

"I wish I did, Prince. It'd make this job a damn sight easier."

"Yeah … I suppose it would."

"Anyway, I've got some paper work to do here. I'm going to sit in the restaurant. You guys stay around until we let you know you can go. It shouldn't be too much longer." Earl turns to the Office and restaurant.

"Yeah, no problem, Earl. Have Blue get you a coffee, if you want one. On me. … Benny, my man, I think it's going to be another slow day in the motel business. Especially at the good old Leroy."

- 73 -

Back on the saddle

The old blue Econoline eases out of the Leroy parking lot, turns west on Dundas and then, a couple blocks later, right onto Victoria, angling toward the northeast end of town. Johnny is driving and Jackie, looking tired beyond her days, sits on the passenger side. She holds her purse and has set a large purple nylon gym bag beside her.

"I guess you want to go home today, Jackie, and not to the gym," Johnny asks.

"Ah, *oui*. Straight home if you please. The gym can wait. I feel like I've already had enough of a workout today. Those cops just asked the same questions over and over. Then the smile of that poor bastard. He looked so lost, so alone. That's going to stay with me, Prince."

"Yeah, I hear you. Grisly stuff. Sorry you had to deal with that. Anyway, like I said, I don't want you back to work until you feel like it, next week at the earliest—take longer if you need. Just call and let me know. It's the slow season and we'll be ok…"

"Thanks, Johnny. I'll take 'til Monday but sitting around and waiting won't change what happened to that fellow today, or how I feel about it. It's better to, how the *anglais* say, get back on the saddle."

"Yeah, maybe. Anyway, see how you feel by first of the week. You'll have some time to relax, some time with Angelique ... maybe sort some things out...?"

"Maybe ... though she's already told me she's got plans. Basketball tomorrow, and she's gonna meet that Walker kid at the End around 4:00 on Saturday and head out to Stokes Point. It's that spring tradition the seniors have—*un feu de joie*, a big bonfire with music and dancin' and stuff. I said that was ok, but I wanted her home by midnight, and I was gonna phone Charlie Walker to make sure his son knew that too. Well, I got to tell you, giving Angelique that *couvre-feu*, that did not go down so good."

"Ah, well, Jackie. I think at heart she's a good kid. You've raised her well, but ... well ... she's a teenager. Driving parents crazy is what teenagers are put on this earth to do, right?"

"Well, she's certainly doing her part good."

Johnny smiles, and Jackie continues.

"But, Johnny, I will give her credit ... when I phoned her today to tell her about what had happened over here, she said she'd cancel the plans she had and come right home after school. And she said she'd pick up some, how you say, *la restauration rapide*. So sometimes *ses intentions* are good—like when she learned to speak French *pour sa grand-mère*—but sometimes, like you say, she's a teenager."

The Econoline turns into a parking lot and stops at the door of a twelve-plex.

"I hope you and Angie eat well, Jackie. You take care. Get some rest and the world will feel better tomorrow."

"Maybe ... for some of us, Prince. For some of us. ... Thanks for the ride and I'll see you on Monday. *Au revoir.*"

"I'll watch you into the building."

Jackie shuts the door of the van and, carrying her gym bag and purse in her left hand, she traverses the sidewalk to the small portico and pulls open the door with her right. She holds it open with her left shoulder, waves a tired farewell to Johnny and disappears inside the walk-up.

The blue van motions forward, pulls into the street and disappears south heading back toward the Leroy. A half a block back down the street, a yellow Mustang slides to the curb and parks.

- 74 -

The prosaic detritus of the day

By the time Johnny returns to the Leroy, the last of the police vehicles has departed, including the charcoal grey Medical Examiner's van bearing away the unknown victim of Room 21 in a black body bag. No crowds line the route. No salutes are given. Johnny enters the Office where Benny is busy carrying some items into the walk-in safe.

"Hey, Benny. I see the Heat's lit out, eh."

"Yeah, Prince. Getting close to supper time, you know. I been putting all of the prosaic detritus of the day from Jackie's cart into the safe—not much stuff and pretty pedestrian, I think, but that's the norm, I gather. Of course, the place was pretty empty last night, though not quiet I guess. Or uneventful. I left the cart outside 23."

"Thanks, Benny … 'prosaic detritus', eh? But yeah, there was more going on than I'd like to think about. Give me the key to 23, will you? Jackie didn't get to it. I'll give it a once over. Just promise me … I won't be finding a dead body in that room, will I?"

"Let's hope not Prince. I've seen all the flashing lights that I need to, for today at least! And enough bodies like that one for a lifetime. I'm still jittery ... in a state of disbelief, I think." Benny hands over a set of room keys ringed to an oval tag with the motel's name stenciled on one side and the phrase "Plant a Seed" printed on the other.

The Prince leaves the Office, turns right, moves to Room 23 and twists the key. The lights and opening of the curtains reveal a bed still made. He would have to check the sheets anyway—curiously, some travelers remade their motel bed; some to erase their presence, some to cover up their sins, some from old habits taught to them when they were kids, he guessed. An empty nylon gym bag lays against the wall, fuel for the next Burning Day. Johnny tosses it toward the door, notices the unlocked pass-through door and locks it. The washroom needs some fresh towels and new soap. That done, Johnny turns to a quick check of the sheets. They are fine, but it is then that Johnny sees one of the night-stands is at a strange angle and that indentations in the shag show that the bed has recently been dislodged from its usual position, the carpet moved. Johnny bends down, sees that the carpet beneath the centre of the bed also seems twisted, torn.

Instinct drives his next move. Johnny turns and shuts the door carefully and pulls the drapes closed. Then he moves the night table and pulls the bed sideways. The carpet has been moved; in fact, a flap of it has been cut and torn and then hastily replaced in its former position. Johnny knows that someone has accessed the crawl space. He moves the bed to the side and peels the flap back to reveal a trap door, two feet by two feet, ringed with a metal lip. Long ago, it was carpeted over when the shag had been installed. Each of the units is the same. The entire Leroy had a four by ten-foot crawl space underneath and trapdoors were originally installed to allow access to the electric and water utilities that ran there. At some point this sort of access was deemed unnecessary, not used and eventually carpeted over.

Johnny lifts the trap door. It releases easily from the floor; obviously it has just been used. He lays down and looks into the darkness; he can see nothing. He reaches to the night stand, grabs the wooden lamp, pulls the shade off, turns it on and thrusts its barren bulb into the cavity. Quiet, level dirt, an assortment of wires and pipes—the crawl space stretches away in both directions—but there, laying on its side directly below him, an aluminum brief case. A large dent in the side that faces up, clearly visible.

"Well, well. What is this?"

With some effort, Johnny pulls up the case—it is surprisingly heavy. There must be something inside. He rests it on the bed and stares at it in bemused curiosity, divining what its contents could possibly be. For once, it seems, the Professor might be wrong—the so-declared prosaic detritus of the day might have some significance after all.

- 75 -

One toke over the line

Inside the door of her apartment, a wave of exhaustion sweeps over Jacqueline. She hangs up her coat and moves to her bedroom where she drops the gym bag on the floor. She changes into a nightgown and slippers, tossing her work clothes on to a bedroom chair, and pads to the kitchen. Just as she is pouring a glass of Sandbanks' Cabernet, keys rattle in the door and Angie arrives, her knapsack and a pizza box in hand.

"Hey, *maman*. How are you?"

"Oh, I'm fine, *ma chèrie*. *Très fatiqué*. Let me get some plates out and I'll tell you about it ... a bit of it, anyways. How about you? Did you have a good day?"

"It was fine ... you know high school. Another day, another hundred assignments to do. And sorry about stormin' out this morning but ... you look tired. Here let me help. You sit."

"*Oui*. That may be the best offer I've had all day. There's some salad from yesterday in the fridge ... it should still be all right."

Angie pulls a salad container from the refrigerator, puts in on the table, then flips the pizza box open and serves her mother a large slice. She takes one herself and sits opposite.

"Ok, *maman*. Tell me about today. What you said on the phone sounded pretty wild."

As the two eat, Jackie runs through the events of the day, most of them anyway, leaving out some of the more sordid descriptive details, emphasizing the repetitive inquisition by the police and the extraordinary kindness of the Prince. By the end though she has noticeably started to slow down with weary overcoming her narrative energy, yawns punctuating her exclamations.

"Oh, *pardonnez moi, ma chèrie*, I think that my night is over. Let's just leave this stuff in the sink ... I'll clean up in the morning."

"Sounds good, Mom. You look like you need some sleep. I'm jealous, 'cause I gotta do one or two of these assignments, especially that math homework. *C'est sacrément difficile.*"

"I can imagine. And I am afraid that I cannot help you *ma petite fille*. It is not my strength ... far from it."

"Good night, Mom."

"*Bonne nuit*, Angelique."

Angie grabs a Coke from the fridge and heads to her bedroom, shutting her door firmly. Jackie finishes her wine with a long swallow, puts the glass in the sink and slips down the hall to turn in. She tucks under her covers and drifts off almost instantly. Deep, far away sleep takes over.

Then, soon, too soon, there is noise. Not inside sleep noise, but something else. Outside of sleep. A bell going off. A knocking on the door. Steady. Repetitious. And it is—what the hell—Jackie squints at her bedside clock radio—it is just after two in the morning. Too early to hear the crows piss as family elders used to say. But then worse ... a muffled scream that she knows is Angelique.

Jackie rocks out of bed, throwing her arms into her nightgown and driving her shin into the corner of the bedroom chair as she does so. She staggers into the hall and heads toward the living room just as lights flash on and nearly blind her. She limps her way forward. And then she stops—the ominous sound of a revolver being cocked drowns out sense and reason. What the hell is going on?

The moment is unreal, dreamlike. But Jacqueline knows that this is no dream—Jacqueline doesn't dream. But there, in the middle of her living room, stands a living nightmare. Two men. One is standing behind her daughter, holding her around the throat with his arm. Angelique looks terrified. The other has just cocked a huge chrome revolver and is pointing it straight at her. The one holding Angelique is a stocky man and wears a greasy light-coloured windbreaker. His hair is speckled with grey and thinning on top and a large pock-marked nose dominates his face. The other man, the one with the gun, has the face of a weasel, moustached, and he wears a long dark coat, the kind Keanu Reaves wore in that old movie about the future—that curious image flashes in Jacqueline's mind. *Matrix.* She wishes that she had just a bit of the firepower that Keanu had in the lobby scene in that movie.

"Who are you? What do you want? Money. What? There's an old stereo. We haven't got much but..."

"Shut-up lady," the long coat spits. "We'll ask the questions. Sit down on the couch. And, Joe, put the sweet one in this chair."

Jacqueline hesitantly moves to the sofa, tightly holding her nightgown about her. The windbreaker man twists Angie around and puts her forcefully into a chair that faces Jacqueline. The long coat presses the gun to her daughter's forehead; Angie's shoulders shake and she begins to sob.

"Shut up, kid, or I'll blow your damned head off. Now, bitch, we want the briefcase."

"You want what...?" Jacqueline stammers. "What do you want?"

"You know goddamn well what we want. Where is it? Where's the briefcase?"

Jacqueline is a survivor. She knows these men, these kind of men. Driven by a life of fatigue and dead ends, they are now on the verge of something. Or they think they are on the verge of something and are just desperate enough to do some dangerous and unthinkable thing that will finally make living pay off for them. Maybe they are even a step or two past the verge, one toke over the line of civilisation and sanity. Of course they will never get where they think they are going, but these kind of men, they never know that, and that makes them all the more desperate and forsaken in a way they will never ever understand. But Jacqueline knows it, she recognizes it in the glare of the living room light—she has seen it many years before in the eyes of a man going out early one morning to buy a pack of cigarettes. But Jacqueline is a survivor. She knows another question is not the answer.

"O you mean ... the briefcase! You think I got the briefcase."

"We're not here to have a debate lady. You went through all the rooms. We watched from the hotel across the road and then the cops arrived. They didn't take nothing but a dead body out of there. But you, you left with that bag. We know what's in it. The briefcase, the metal one. Now, let's have it. That's the last time I ask." He pushes the gun tight to Angie's head.

"Ok. Ok, it's right over here." Jacqueline hesitates. "When I saw that briefcase, that room, I got to tell you gents I did not believe I was seeing what I was seeing. Can I get up and show you? I got it pretty much hidden."

"Yeah. No problem, lady. No sudden moves, that's all." He motions to his partner, "Watch the little bitch, Joe."

Jacqueline stands up from the sofa. She isn't sure if she will be able to walk at first, but she can. She moves toward the short front hallway, and slides back the large aluminum sliding door from the right side. The long coat with the gun stands close to her side—she can see a strange tattoo that resembles something like *un ancien hiéroglyphe* on his neck, like an inky language labyrinth where a person might get lost, where a monster might hide. But now, she will need to focus and she will need her courage; now, she will need strength and quickness. There will be no second chances. From somewhere deep inside, she hears a voice: fly on my beauty, fly on.

"It's right down here," Jacqueline says, bending and releasing the cord on her nightgown at the same time. Her breasts swing free and shine free in the glare of the living room light. The slight but audible inhalation of long coat is her cue. Using both hands, from deep within the closet Jacqueline swings the old fire extinguisher hard and deep into long coat's groin. His libido transmigrates from one extreme state to another. And Jacqueline does not stop. Her motion regains itself and continues around like an Olympic hammer thrower to bring the full force of the extinguisher into the side of long coat's face just above the tattoo, just as vomit spews out of him. Flesh and bone crunch, disgorge and blood flies, the close air fills with the dire odours of a smorgasbord of bodily fluids, and a grunted curse accompanies the sound of the gun hitting the hard parquet of the hallway. Jacqueline is not sure which of her actions directly precipitated the releasing of the revolver, but she moves like a nursing cat with another mouse in mind. She grabs the gun and walks straight toward the windbreaker.

"*S'éloigner de ma fille* ... get away from my daughter."

The windbreaker raises his hands and backs away.

"Hey, take it easy lady. We weren't gonna hurt anyone." He begins to lower his arms and Jacqueline sees the glint of a blade as it slides into his right hand.

Without a thought, she fires. Luckily for windbreaker, this is the first time in her life that Jacqueline has ever fired a gun. He screams as the bullet sings past his right ear and he bolts past her to the door. Jacqueline turns and fires again and the hallway light shatters in a shower of sparks and glass. Long coat is also up and moving, hobbling, skipping—it is hard to describe exactly—but he too is out of the apartment brushing the door into motion and a third shot splinters wood directly where the peephole was. Her aim is improving. And Jacqueline stands there with the gun just pointed at the doorway for a long time. The faraway sound of an engine ignites the night and the squeal of tires ensues. Jacqueline steps though vomit and glass and over Ray's fire extinguisher and closes and locks and places the chain on the apartment door. She drops the revolver. Her body starts to quiver in short quick spasms and is still moving uncontrollably when she takes her daughter in her arms. They stand there as the sound of a distant siren races closer and the howl of another, the one wailing inside Jacqueline's head, subsides into a dull silence.

- 76 -

On the road again

The yellow Mustang is parked on the far side of Berris Thorn Park under a large silver maple that overhangs the Moira. It is Friday March 29th, just after noon. This will not be a good day for several citizens of Thornton. A short man in a grey windbreaker crosses the park and gets into the driver's side of the car while another pops up from the back seat.

"Here's your food, Lucky." says Gabe. "There's ketchup for the fries in the bottom of the bag."

"Thanks, man. I am starving."

"How do you feel? That broad really laid you low this morning, didn't she? What'd she hit you with—looked like an old torpedo or something? And she almost blew my fuckin' head off."

"Yeah, no shit! She surprised us pretty good. But I'm okay, though I might not be dancing for awhile, or fucking. I'll tell ya, though, she had a nice set of tits. ... Worst thing, I'm still some pissed off losing my gun like that—it was an awesome cannon, best thing I ever bought. Next time, I'm just gonna shoot first and ask questions later."

"I'm with you there, buddy. But at least we got some

replacements pretty easy. Like you said, Gord's Bait 'n Guns 'n CDs was a piece of cake."

"Yeah, I told you Gord's would be an easy jack, that side door popped open like a crack whore with overdue rent. Half the shit in there's stolen and bein' fenced anyways so Gord's ain't too close with legit security, or with the cops, legit or not. I just double-checked the two heaters we took and they'll do, solid Colt semis; of course they ain't no hundred caliber Glock."

"Yeah, I know. But at least we loaded up on ammo. We got enough to make Waco proud. And those Colts'll be trusty friends enough, plenty to have when we meet up with Malley's guys, though I hope we won't have to use 'em."

"I only wish I coulda found one of those rocket launchers. I know damn well Gord's got a couple of them somewheres. But I didn't really have time to look…"

"That's probably just as well, pardner. They'd be pretty heavy to lug around, and hard to hide. Besides, Lucky, I can only imagine you with a rocket launcher! Holy shit!"

"Yeah," Lucky smiles. "You may be right."

"Anyways, I just got off the phone with Stump's office. They haven't seen him in a couple days or so. They say it's unusual—he's generally around all the time. That just adds to the weirdness of the last couple days, I guess."

"Yeah, last two nights have been pretty crazy, haven't they? Nearly out of control."

"No shit. Wednesday, with that fog and crazy people all over the place. The Leroy was like a fuckin' zoo at feedin' time with all the cages open. And then last night, runnin' into that goddamned kung fu wonder woman. One thing, then another. What's your take, Lucky?"

"Well, like they say, when it pours, it rains!"

"You never said a truer mouthful."

"Pretty wild, Gabe. Pretty wild. All of it. That girl we kidnapped, she went nuts. Dumped that pail of crap on the guy, blinded him and then took off in that big car. There was no way we could of caught her. And I swear to you, you may think I'm crazy, but that guy those others dragged out of the Beamer, the one that crashed into the pole, to me, that looked like Stump Malley. Short and mean, cursing and swearing. I think that was him."

"You might be right. So maybe somebody got him—he's probably got lots of enemies—and that's why he hasn't been around his shop. Anyways—a lot of crazy going on! And I got to tell you, buddy, those other cars sure arrived in a hurry to pick everyone up—it couldn't have been more than a couple minutes. I think one just went across to the End but the other, the one they threw that short pissed-off guy in, it took off down Dundas like a bat."

"Yeah, whoever all those guys were, they sure drove some nice wheels. And then that tow truck arrived just as they was leaving—I'll bet it was their call. Swept that Beamer right out of there, gone like a fart in a windstorm. Those guys must have some real pull with their auto club! As to the money, I thought Stevie Wonder and his buddy had the case in their room. But they left with nothing, and we checked, right? There was nothing there!

"Yeah, and no case under the sign. You got to figure those guys were Brown and MacLean, don't you? And I know that somebody took the aluminum case. But where it went, no clue!"

"I still think that damned maid got it. The 'hoor de France. We watched everything yesterday, the whole show. Never took our eyes off the place, right? Cops all over but they only took the dead guy, nothing else, no metal case, nothing that I could see. And those rooms don't got back doors. I think the maid put it somewhere when she cleaned the rooms, in her cart or something. And I think we was right in trailing her to her apartment. She carried that big bag in and everything. And then look at the way she fought ... like you said, who would of guessed that she was some kind of freakin' martial arts maniac..."

"'Course maybe one of those others got it. The other ones who work there, or even one of the cops—you can't trust no-one these days. But I didn't see it go. So, maybe it's still somewhere at the Leroy. Or maybe they didn't bring no money at all. I don't know. I think it's time for 'Plan B.'"

"What's that, pardner? I didn't know we had a 'Plan B.'" Lucky mumbles through a mouthful of fries.

"Well, when I went to get the food and called Malley's Office and couldn't get him, the secretary put me through to another of his guys ... I think maybe she knew why I was callin'. I told this guy that I wanted to get Liz and Jimmy back today. It was Stump's original deadline and I wanted to keep it that way. Whether Stump was around or not! So, we're set up for this aft., 6:00 pm, the Lobby of the End. The guy said he'd bring Liz and Jimmy there for sure and we'll make a trade right in front of the main desk, where everyone checks in. That way everything will be in the open, clean and clear."

"What about money, man? Where're we gonna get that? Go back to the maid's place? There'll be cops all over..."

"No. What I'm thinkin', Lucky, is to hell with the money. We got us these guns—and I got an old suitcase at home; we'll fill it with some sand or newspapers or something, I'll put a couple five dollar bills in it so they stick out, and it'll look like we're ready to make a trade. We'll drive the Mustang to the front door and walk in with the case. Drop it, grab Liz and Jimmy, and get the hell outta there before Malley's men know what's goin' on. Wham, bam, and we're gone."

"Shit, man, now you're talkin'. That sounds good to me, Gabe. This kidnappin' thing we just been through, it put a lot of stress on me, man. It wasn't good for me. Too complicated! A simple plan like this will be a lot better. Ride right into the place and do what we got to do. You deliver the suitcase and I'll cover you. I'll have your back. You know, don't you, man, that I'll always have your back! Always. So, yeah, this sounds good. Hi Ho Silver, Gabe. Hi Ho." Lucky and Gabe fist punch across the seats.

"Get At 'Em, Scout. Lucky, you are the man."

"And, how about this, Gabe? What if I go into the End an hour early or so—maybe go in at 4:00 or 4:30 and sit in the bar or something. As soon as you get there, and I see Liz and Jimmy, I come out from hiding and we'll surprise the shit out of them. That way it won't be a stand-off of any kind—we'll have the edge. And we'll be out of there before they know what's goin' on. Simple, straightforward. What do you think?"

"Yeah, well. ... Ok. That sounds ok. It would surprise the hell out of them, wouldn't it, and it's gotta better the odds for us? Might be dangerous though ... for you. Are you sure?"

"Ah, no problem, man. Anything for Liz, and little Jimmy."

"... and I can drive the Mustang right up to the doors, park it there. If there's any shootin' though, we gotta be careful. I don't want Liz or Jimmy hurt."

"No, no. That would kinda defeat the purpose, wouldn't it!"

"Yeah, it would. Anyways ... all right, then. I'm thinkin' this may work out after all. It's a clear plan. No complications. Quick and to the point. We just gotta stay cool and stick to it."

"You got that right, man. We need to keep cool. Use some stealth. Like those bombers—nobody sees them comin' 'til you're fucked. Man, this burger's good. I was starved..."

Around them, there is a still silence in the car; in Berris Thorn Park the chipmunks and squirrels hold fire as if the universe is waiting for what's to come next. Lucky breaks the calm.

"So what do you think, Gabe? When you think about everything. All the things we've done. It's been a pretty good ride, hasn't it?"

"Yeah, I guess, Lucky. All in all, not too bad. Better'n a kick in the nuts on a frosty day. Except maybe for the prison part. I coulda done without that. And I coulda wished better for my Mom and Dad. And this mess right now, for Liz and Jimmy. But beyond that, we've had some good times."

"Yeah, we sure have."

"Remember the time you got into Coach Williams' locker and filled the toes of his shoes with Plaster of Paris from Art— he damn near broke his foot trying to put them shoes on."

"Yeah. I'd filled his jock too, but I guess that didn't have no effect." Both men laugh. "God. Hey, you know what I thought about the other day that I hadn't remembered in a long time. Right after I got the new car, I was takin' a cruise out near the old home, 'round the Valley—do you remember how we used to hide down in the ditch when old man Robbins would bring his loads of peas by, heading for the Co-op pea-viners?"

"Oh hell yes. And we used to race up and grab a handful of fresh peas from the wagon. I don't think anything ever tasted as good. But then, that one time we pulled the peas out and the back ladder broke right off. And he just kept on going— spreadin' his peas all over the damned highway. Was he ever pissed when he looked back and saw what had happened! I think he would of killed us if he knew what we did. Remember, we circled back around and he ended up paying us five bucks each to help him pick up his peas. What a day!"

"Yeah, I got a red handerchief and tried to direct traffic out of the way. I was the pea police for a day! What a joke! And God, speaking of jokes, remember that trip to Brownsville, and 'cross the border to Mucho-moron, or whatever its name was, remember, to pick up those drugs for old Spender, from the, what was it we called them, the los bandittos? Taco-benders. Shit, we got drunk in that little Mexican place and paid for four whores, two each—what'd we call them, our mucho tac-hoes—and spent three days pissed to the gills, drinkin' and smokin' cheap dope and bangin' a couple tac-hoes every time we wanted."

"Hell, yes. Fucked-up in Mexico."

"Yeah. The days of weed and pussy, man."

"Who can forget? 'Though, to tell the truth, I think I forgot more about that trip than I can remember. Lost some brain cells there, buddy! And we used up all the money Spender had given us to buy the drugs so, when it came time to make the deal, we got the los bandittos drunk and let them take on our whores and we just took their dope and drove back home. How stupid could those guys be? God, what a trip that was. You had the old convertible back then, didn't you? Do you remember? ... What a trip! We roared across the countryside, taking the back roads so's we wouldn't be seen, breeze in our face, watching the sun set and the sun rise, throwing empty beer bottles at road signs and stray dogs. Trading old Spender's drugs here and there for food and smokes. And, remember the evening we raced that silver ambulance across the high plains all the way to Abilene."

"Hell yeah, we'd of beat the fucker too if those semis hadn't cut us off."

"Man, it was one glorious time! The best days of our lives!"

"You know what? I think we need to do one of those trips again, Gabe. Once this situation is cleared up. Get ourselves out into some space, where it's not so closed in. What do you think?"

"Sure makes sense to me, pardner. We need a break, and we've earned one after all this mess—you don't need to be a rocket surgeon to figure that out. Right after I get Liz and Jimmy back. You and me, Chemo-savvy—on the road again."

"You said it, Tonto. Things are gonna turn around, man. Fuckin' rainbows are gonna be chasin' us. I can feel the electricity in the air. Just the sky above us, man. Just the sky. What d'yu say? Hi Ho, Silver. Away."

"Get At 'Em, Scout. Get at 'em!"

- 77 -

Let me see your gun

Angie opens the drapes of suite 503, the top floor of Voyageur's End. The view sweeps to the north. Far below, it seems, and just slightly west across Dundas Street, is *The Le Roi Motor Inn and La Reine Restaurant* where *sa mère* has worked for years. The solid, little Leroy, still point in her mother's universe. And behind it two old abandoned buildings, one that was once a Dance Hall and, the other, just the foundation of who knew what. Beyond that, an open field strewn with weeds and junk leads to the empty K Mart which now has a white cross stuck on its roof. Beyond that, across Simcoe Avenue, low rise apartments and residences sprawl into northern and eastern suburbs—Angie thinks maybe she can make out the apartment building in which she and her mother reside—and beyond that, trees and farmer's fields and a whole world that is not Thornton. She turns back into the room.

"This is a great room, Bobby. It even has a stocked bar."

"Hey, leave that alone, Angel. They check the stock in those things every day."

"O, come on, Bobby. One little drink each won't hurt anybody. And they probably won't even check until somebody else stays in the room for a night. They'll get charged and probably won't even notice. Here ... here's a Drambuie for you, and, yes, a Bailey's for me. Here, take it."

"Well, ok. I guess one drink won't matter that much. I can probably sneak back and replace it, anyways, from the bar stock downstairs."

Each of them snaps the miniature cap and downs their bottle in a couple swigs.

"Mmmm ... So how's your Dad doin', since my Mom dumped him? She really blew up at him, didn't she!"

"Yeah, I don't know. He's pretty pissed off, I guess. For a while, he was trying to figure out some way to get her back, but now I think he's trying to figure out how to get back at her, through the Leroy, maybe. He called those Dalco jerks in to look at the situation. And that has just made everything worse around here with those creeps prowling around everywhere, all hours of the day and night. Dad expects everybody to kiss their asses the way he does. What a pain! So it's not very comfortable around here right now. But I think Dad really liked your Mom and thought it was going to develop into something."

"Yeah. What do you think about that Bobby? I mean, we could have been brother and sister, right? Now wouldn't that have been cute? In some way, you know, I think that's the big reason why Mom cut it off with your Dad—she found out that I was seeing you. And she wasn't too pleased about that. Still isn't. Too complicated, too creepy. That and the fact that your Dad was always giving Mom things, asking her out, but then he'd spend most of the time talking about getting her a job at the End. Mom said she wasn't sure whether he liked her because she was a woman or a workhorse."

'Yeah, well, that's Dad. He's got this place in his blood."

Angelique leans over and gives Bobby a tender kiss and speaks quietly:

"I think there must be a course somewhere that all parents have to take on 'how to be screwed up'."

"Yeah, you may be right there, Angel."

"Where love and having fun gets replaced by worrying about everything from utility bills to your daughter's period…"

"Ahh, anyways … so you're ok, though, after last night … sounds like some weird shit went down."

"Like I said, I'm fine. I was scared, though. My Mom really stepped up on those two creeps. Who knew! She knocked that one guy senseless and grabbed his gun and just started shootin'. But, like I said, Bobby, I was pretty scared."

"That must have been bizarre. And they came right out of nowhere. So the cops came and…"

"And did dick all. Except take the gun as evidence. And warn my Mom that she could have been charged for discharging a firearm in public. Can you believe that shit? They told her that if she'd hit one of them she would have been arrested. *C'est quoi toute cette merde*—someone breaks into your apartment in the middle of the night, with a gun and a knife, and you'd get charged, put in jail, if you hurt one of them? What a bunch of crap!"

"I can believe it. We covered some of that legal stuff in the Security course I took at the college. A lot of it don't make much sense. So the cops don't have any idea who it was. Or what they was after?"

"Nah, the cops don't have a clue. Cops never have a clue, do they, Bobby?" Angie takes Bobby's hat off and gives him a long, slow kiss on the lips.

"Whatever you say, Angel."

The Prince of Leroy

"Mom wanted me to stay home today. The Prince gave her the day off after yesterday, longer if she needs it, he said. But I needed to get out of there. ... I put that money back—you know, the money that *maman* had saved, that we were going to use to get away. Keeping it after last night didn't seem right."

"Well, that's ok. My Dad laid the law down to everyone. With these Dalco guys around here right now, everyone needs to be on their toes—I won't be able to get away for a while anyways."

"Hey. Let me see your gun? It looks something like the one that the crooks had. I wanted to keep it for protection, but, like I said, the cops wouldn't let us."

"Yeah, here it is. It's a Smith and Wesson 29. A classic. The safety's on, but be careful."

"You mean this little thing here." Angie flips the safety off and casually points the revolver directly at Bobby, who frantically springs off the bed to the floor.

"Jesus, be careful. That's fully loaded, with full metal hollow points. It'd take my goddamn head off."

Angie giggles, low and deep.

"I know. Believe me, it's a lot nicer on this end, holding it rather than having it jammed in your face. And there's something carved on the handle?"

"Yeah—R W W—my initials. I didn't want nobody stealin' it."

"So, Robert Walker ... what's the other 'W' for?"

"Webster ... it was my Mom's maiden name."

"Cool. We're always tied to family, aren't we—whether we like it or not. I'd like to learn to fire it, sometime. Will you teach me?"

"Yeah, we could go over to the range someday. It's fun..."

"Cool." Angie turns, opens the night stand drawer and drops the revolver on top of a golden *Gideon's Bible*.

"There, that can keep in there for a while." She closes the drawer, turns back on the bed and, in the same motion, removes her t-shirt. "Right now, I'm more interested in another gun that you're carrying, Officer Bobby Walker. Does this help you get the safety unlocked on that one? Or should I say uncocked...?"

"O yes, I think that it might, Angel." Bobby stands and removes his belt and holster and his shirt.

A shadow of light flits across the room. And glare from the hallway blares in like the egotistical stereo of some teenager's beat-up convertible, trembling at a red light. Then the light changes with a click and the hall glare roars away; the door is shut and it is dark and quiet again. But it is a changed quiet. A changed dark. Two men are inside, one dark haired and handsome, the other, a shadowy appendage.

"What the hell?" Bobby grunts.

- 78 -

Time for a bit of Meteorology and Archaeology, some Mythology too, but not too much

Late on this Friday afternoon, the day is close, the volatility of the sky, rising. It has been unseasonably warm for this time of year and something has got to give. In this case the something is a dark massing of clouds to the west of the city with occasional sheets of faraway light and a low grumbling. A storm is about to break, and, ominous, it looks like a big one.

Johnny walks along the sidewalk from the back of the Leroy and turns into the Office, Angus at this side. It is a small space, with a couple of upholstered chairs and a rack for tourist brochures in front of the counter, a plastic schefflera in a wooden washtub in the corner near the entrance to Rainy's. Windows compose the two front sides and main door of the Office. Behind the counter to the left is a stairway up to a green door and private apartment above; to the right is the grey metal door to a large Mosler walk-in vault. On the wall between the stairs and this grey safe, a small round clock ticks away and, below it, a wooden plaque displaying what looks like a copper-coloured stick encircled by a black metal band.

"Hi, Benny," Johnny speaks to the slight young man behind the counter who is wearing a white shirt, or a yellow shirt (we have spoken of this metamorphosis before). "How goes the day?" Angus brushes up against Benny's legs and stretches out behind him.

"So far, good, Prince. Hey, Angus! ... Seven registers, and it's still early. Feels like a serious storm coming, eh? People may be getting off the road."

"Yeah, maybe a good thing. A bit of rain to wash things down, you know, cleanse the place."

"Hey, Prince, I got a question ... in my six months here, I've never asked—what is that, up there?" Benny points to the plaque. "That stick on a wooden plaque with a metal hoop?"

"Oh, I'm surprised someone hasn't told you, Benny. That is Leroy, himself!"

"Leroy?"

"Yep. At least that's what the regulars named it over the years. It's a fossil that was unearthed when the land for the Le Roi Motor Inn was first being excavated nearly eighty years ago; the stick is actually part of a human arm, an ancient fossilized humerus, or so I'm told, and it was found inside that bracelet which, itself, is covered with odd signs and symbols scratched into its surface. Probably something the old chap was wearing when he died. Comes from a time long before there were any white settlers in this area, I suspect."

"Really."

"The original owner of the motel simply mounted the bone

and metal band on a plaque as a souvenir and placed it on the Office wall where it's been ever since. So for the regulars it became the last remains of Leroy, or so it's been christened and, like so many things christened around this joint, Benny, the baptism stuck."

"And you know today, Prince, construction would have been halted and archeologists summoned in, and Indigenous representatives, and there would have been all kinds of red tape. Who knows, this motel might never have been built at all."

"Well, that would have been a shame, wouldn't it?"

"Yeah ... where would all of us be, I wonder? And who would we be"

"I wonder, too, Professor. You should take it down sometime, maybe do some research on it. It would be interesting to know what the message on the bracelet is, what old Leroy's trying to tell us."

"Really ... Maybe I'll do that, have a closer look at it. Maybe take it in to the university sometime, but I'll be careful. The Archeology Department might be interested in latching on to it, though they probably have thousands like it ... but I wouldn't want it to get claimed by them, or to get lost among all the other bones, all the other artefacts, like the Ark at the end of Indiana Jones."

"No, it has its place here, I think, like a lot of us bones. It is kind of a sacred thing to some ... every now and then when there's a full moon, and the regulars get in just the right mood, they'll cram in here and drink a toast to old Leroy. Sometimes even light a candle or two. You'll see that someday—it's quite a thing!"

"Ah, there's no end to the charms of this place, Prince. No end. And so just now I realize that Leroy's been looking over my shoulder all the time I've been here. Was he the original Prince, maybe? You think? Paying heed and offering his daily benediction. And all in silence. Quite a thing, indeed! All the outcasts, all the stories, and you, the Prince ... you know this is a mysterious and mystical place, full of wonder. Old as time, young as each breath we take. Quite a place you run, Johnny P. March, innkeeper of the living and the dead, the devious and the damned, the forsaken and the anointed. The light of this world."

"Ahh, you're turning poet on me now, Benny. Save it for your epic! I've got some bookkeeping to do upstairs. Trace should be here to take over soon. Tell her to let me know if she needs anything."

"Will do, Prince. She phoned in a few minutes ago. Said she just got on the bus and should be here in fifteen or so, depending on the Friday traffic. In the meantime, I will give this remnant of Leroy some thought, do some research. And maybe I'll light a candle."

Behind Benny, Angus rolls over in his sleep. He occasionally thought of Leroy too. From time to time, he would stare intently at that bone and plaque, I suppose imagining what it would've been like to be alive in Leroy's distant time, to lope along on the primal hunt, but then, if dog could shrug, Angus would shrug and turn back to the doggy matters of his doggy day. In any case, the bone and piece of wood to which it was attached were too high on the wall for further thought or action.

The telephone on the desk spits out a loud and angry snarl; it reminds one of the heavy black phone your Great-Grandma once had, connected across the breathy party lines of long ago, nosy and sordid, not cute and candied as so many of the dancing ring tones of today.

"Good afternoon. Reception desk of the Le Roi Motor Inn. Benny speaking."

- 79 -

She is loud and has a tongue like fire

In the hallway near Room 503 on the fifth floor of the Voyageur's End, two men wait quietly, pretending to chat when others walk by. They are waiting for the right moment, and now and then speak in very low, very serious voices.

"So, yeah, I got a phone tip said she'd be here Saturday afternoon around four, but then Pete saw her with fatso's kid in the Lobby today. He followed them to this room and called me."

"And you said the guy who phoned you originally wanted you to call him back…"

"Yeah, he said 'give me a heads-up' before I did anything. But that sounded screwy to me … some kind of game or something … and anyways, she's here a day early."

"Good."

"For us! Not her!"

"The coast looks clear, kid"

"Ok. Let's hope this key card works."

Junior Dalco slides the plastic card into the slot and removes it as the light blinks green, and he and Connie are in the room.

"What the hell?" Bobby speaks and then doubles over,

without wind. He is propelled into the washroom and the door slammed shut. The shadow slips a chair under the doorknob to secure his confinement.

"Wait outside the door, C-man. Here's the key card. Make sure there's no surprises. I can take care of the rest." Connie quietly exits and closes the door. Frederick Dalco Jr. turns to the topless girl on the bed. "What's your name, Cutie?"

"It ain't Cutie, that's one thing asshole. Who are you, and what are you doin'?"

"In a minute, you, sweetheart."

Angie instinctively grabs her t-shirt and begins to move off the bed, but the suddenness of the assault and a quick ounce and a half of booze alter her reflexes. He is on her. She flails out with her arms but he is big, too big, and his blows, one, then another, and one more which is unnecessary, knocks her back down on the bed. Blood dribbles from her lip. Then he slaps her once more.

"Now, what's your name, you little bitch. Tell me, or else."

Angie is sobbing. "It's Angelique, Angelique Savard."

"And your mother, she works across the road at that shithole, the Leroy Motel, doesn't she?"

"Yes, yes she does. What of it, asshole?"

Frederick slaps her again, hard across the left cheek. "Well, I got a message for you to take back to your mother and all of the others at the Leroy. The message, little Angie, from my me and my Dad, is this—pay attention, you little whore—you fuck with us and our place, we'll fuck with you and yours." Frederick tears at Angie's jeans, jerking them to her ankles and then jerking them free of one leg. And his own belt is loose, and he is on her, right hand grasping a full fist of dark hair, left hand occasionally slapping her across the face, back and forth, whenever her hands try to push at him, and his entire body driving in and up, in and up. And Angie takes him and takes his weight and gasps and gasps but her crying has stopped. She beholds the white stucco on the ceiling, the way it catches the light and invents penumbrae, like the distant surfaces of the moon, like a great white ocean, dark and sweeping over her world. And then he is done and, for one brief moment, he collapses to the side, his right side, the wrong side. And closes his eyes. Angie slips from beneath the dark wet hair of his chest and the sweat of his labour and stands, naked with one pant leg twisted about her ankle. She feels the *Gideon's* in the night-stand—no, that is not what she wants at this moment in time. Maybe later. She hoists the revolver, its safety already unlocked. And, here, now, she is Savard, her mother's daughter.

Frederick Dalco Jr. opens his eyes. He looks up. This spunky little bitch has climbed off the bed and, with the drapes open, she is a black silhouette against the darkening afternoon. And moving. Now she is standing close, at the foot of the bed. He swears. She won't be standing quite so easily, so defiantly, when he leaves the room, or his name isn't Frederick Dalco Jr. He can hear someone pounding on the bathroom door. That stupid Walker kid, that curious phone call—both had led him right here, the perfect way to get back at the Leroy. At least to start. He couldn't wait to tell his father. But now, right now, the little bitch is speaking. What is she saying? She is loud and has a tongue like fire.

The first bullet hits Frederick Dalco Jr. directly in the sternum—that would have been enough. But the second takes off his lower jaw, and the third, fired from closer range, although a moot digression at this point, decrees that he will father no children. Connie Torrence, the shadow, is one and a half strides inside the room, with his gun drawn, when an explosion hits him in the right side of the head and the pattern of the wallpaper near what was once his left ear takes on a new design. He drops like a terminal lawn dart. Angie shuts the door and sits on the bed. Until two days ago she had never heard a gun fired up close, but now, now, look around.

In a moment she hears the thumping on the washroom door and goes over and removes the chair. Bobby, breathless, steps out and immediately falls over the corpse of the shadow. His face comes to a stop inches from the remains of Freddy Junior's head. He stumbles to his feet, scrambles to find the shirt that he had discarded what seems like hours ago and looks at Angie.

"Holy shit, girl. What have you done? And with my gun. I'm screwed."

Angie looks straight into Bobby's open eyes. Her grip on the gun tightens. "Get out of here, you asshole, you chickenshit…"

Bobby steps back and falls over the shadow again. He scrambles up, pulls the door open and is gone.

Angie shuts and locks the door. She tosses the gun on the bed and walks over to the window. Naked she stands, except for the tangle of blue jeans around her left ankle, and she looks out across Thornton and shivers. Dark clouds billow—a storm has arrived. Sheet lightning bathes the far horizon and, now, large droplets begin to hit the window. A childhood memory surfaces. Twitch, blink—but nothing is altered. No witches or genies to the rescue—life is not a sitcom. And then tears swell up from deep within and Angie weeps with the rain. She weeps for herself, but there is an immeasurable honesty in these tears, so she also weeps for her mother, and for her father whom she has never known. She weeps for her picnicking ancestors in that dream her mother once told her about. And she weeps for all the foolish things that she has done and for all the good things that she has not done. She weeps for the sun and for the moon, for the stars and for the sky. For things that change and for things that do not. And when she looks down from the End, most of all, deep inside, she realizes that she weeps for the Leroy and the overwhelming emptiness of things. And in the end she weeps because she realizes that her weeping does not matter.

- 80 -

Hurricane Angel

"**Good afternoon.** Reception desk of the Le Roi Motor Inn. Benny speaking."

"Hello, Benny? Benny, this is Jackie. Is Johnny around? I need to speak to the Prince. *Très important!*"

"Yeah, hang on ... he's right here." Benny turns to the Prince and holds out the receiver. "Prince, it's Jackie ... she sounds upset. Says it's urgent."

"Hello, Jacqueline. What's up?"

"*C'est terrible!* It's Angelique, Johnny. *Voilà du propre!* She's got herself in a helluva mess. I just got off the phone with her and..."—the vacuum of silence fills the line—"and I didn't know what to do. I don't know if anyone can help this time, but you're the only one I could think of ... I'd asked her to stay home today but she wouldn't. Now, she's in a big hole..."

"I thought she'd be at home today too. Talk to me, Jackie. What's up with little Angel this time?"

"It's bad, Johnny. She's in ... let's see, I wrote in down ... in Room 503 at the End. She just phoned me. And she's shot somebody—she thinks it's Frederick Dalco. She says he's dead. And some other guy. That's a pretty big hole this time, Johnny."

"She's at the End today! I thought you said she wasn't going there 'til tomorrow."

"She was going there tomorrow, too, for that beach thing, but she told me she had to see her Bobby today, especially after yesterday. We had a break-in, a couple thugs, the cops were here … I'll tell you about it later…"

"A break-in?"

"Yes, but right now…"

"Ok … right now. Room 503, right? And you say there's two dead…!"

"Oui. I've got a cab on the way. I'll come right down. But … you're right across the road—I thought you could get there quick…"

"Ok," Johnny's large exhalation is noticeable. "Jackie, listen. Why don't you stay where you are. We—all of us—may need you there more than here. Phone Angie back. Talk to her, keep her on the line and in the room. Door locked. I'll go over and see what the situation is, and get her back here. Then I'll get her to your place, ok? Tell her I'll be there in ten minutes, or less. 503, right?"

"*Oui. Merci.* Thank you, Johnny … so much."

Johnny has regained a closer-to-normal composure; he is sorting things out.

"I'll talk to you on Angie's cell as soon as I get to 503. Don't worry. We'll get this sorted out. One way or another!"

Johnny puts the receiver back in its cradle and shoves the telephone across to Benny. As he turns toward the door, he finds that Oz has been standing there for some time.

"Got some trouble, Prince? Sounds like the real magilla this time."

"Yeah ... sounds like a real mess, Oz. Our favourite troubled teen is up to her ass in it. But it's not something I want to get anyone else involved in..."

"Well, Johnny, when I signed on here it was for the whole ride not just the sunny weather. I'm guessing by the look on your face that this ain't a clear day, that you could probably use some help and, you know me, that's what I do."

"Well, Oz ... to be honest, there are a couple things you could do. Bring Angie back here from the End, for one. And get her home, somehow..."

"Let's get to it then." Oz turns and pauses half-way through the Office doorway.

"Benny," Johnny speaks to his desk clerk?

"Trouble, Johnny?"

"Sounds like it, Benny. Hurricane Angel at it again. But, there may be a rainbow here, too. We'll see. Dom and Deed aren't back with the van yet, are they?"

"No, they're still out on that run for you."

"Ok. Can you hang around until they get here and, when they do, keep them around? Feed them, give them coffee. At least until Angie gets here—Oz is going to bring her back; then have Dom and Deed use the van to run her home ... you too. Trace should be able to manage things after that."

"Absolutely, Prince. Sounds like this might be another verse for the great Leroy epic."

"No shit, Benny. It could be that, and more! Thanks for hangin' around for a bit—shouldn't be too long." Johnny turns to Oz. "Let's go, Wizard. It's going to take some magic to calm this storm."

Johnny and Oz exit the Office and walk straight toward the

great sign of the Leroy. Angus arrives with a whimper at the Office door just in time to see them depart but too late to lead the journey, or follow.

"No truck to camouflage us this time, Oz. And World War III may just have started … and this battle's for more than dirty linen."

"Hey, hey. No matter. It's the war that keeps us alive, Prince. Let's be quick—it's dark enough, nobody will notice."

With greater consistency, drops of rain begin to pelt down. The two men hook the much-removed cover away with their fingers and, in a brief moment, cover replaced, they have disappeared, working their way through the subterranean trenches towards Hell's Boulevard and the End.

- 81 -

The fox is trapped in the henhouse

Unencumbered by the usual load of ersatz laundry, Oz and the Prince are through the Leroy trench and into Hell's Boulevard quickly. Dropping down in the furnace room, they furtively navigate through the storage area with its racks of supplies and cleaning materials. The open-mouthed canvas carts beneath the laundry chutes are partially-filled and, in cast shadows, appear like a nest of young birds yearning to be fed by the cavities above. The Prince and Oz quietly round a basement corner and, with no one in sight, move across a dark hall to a service elevator. They board and Johnny presses five, the top floor. With a painful grunt, the elevator lurches into motion, disinterestedly hoisting another middling cargo upward. With a jolt it stops and the doors grind open. Johnny looks both ways—the hallway seems empty.

"Let's go, Oz. 503?"

"That way, kid," says Oz motioning to the right.

They move down the hall and three doors around the corner to their left, an outside room, 503. Johnny tries the handle but it is locked. He knocks twice and whispers.

The Prince of Leroy

"Angie. It's me and Oz. Angie."

He knocks again, louder, and on the third rap the door opens. Angie stands before them, in t-shirt and jeans, her hair disheveled, face red and swollen. She folds herself in the Prince's arms and all move inside quickly and lock the door. Through the window on the far side of the room they can see a torrent of rain slashing down.

Both men make a quick survey of the carnage. The beige carpet is soaked and lubrous. The bodies lie in opposite directions, each face down but each missing a significant portion of its skull. As Jackie had foretold, this hole is deep; it is going to take a long ladder or maybe an old tunnel and some trenches to get out. And a lot of, what was the word he'd heard Fruitfarm use, a lot of serendipity.

The Prince is visibly struck, pale; he holds Angie while Oz steps past him and breaks the still silence.

"That one's Freddy Junior. Who's the other one, Johnny? Johnny?"

"I'm not sure, Oz," Johnny hesitates and takes a deep breath. "But if he was hanging around with Junior, he probably wasn't much. One time, though, both of them probably had hopes ... people that cared. ... How are you, Angie?"

"I've been better, Johnny. That son-of-a-bitch raped me." She nods toward Junior. "He busted in on Bobby and me, and Bobby, he did nothing. Nothing."

"Yeah, well, I can't say I'm surprised. Apples don't fall far from their trees, you know. But don't worry about that right now, Angie. Give me your cell, will you? Your Mom's on the other end, right? Hello. Hello, Jackie. Jackie?"

"No. She hung up a while ago. Told me you'd be coming, to wait here, then hung up..."

"Ok. It's dead, disconnected. Well, we'll get in touch with her later. First thing, I want to get you out of here. Angie, put on your socks and shoes and go around the room and pick up everything, everything, that might be yours. OK?"

"Ok, Prince. Thanks … thanks for…"

"That's all right, kid. There'll be time later. Oz, can you come in here for a minute?" The Prince motions Oz into the bathroom.

"Look, Oz. This is a mess. A helluva mess. Dicey, and dangerous. It's not just dumping our dirty laundry at the End. I can't ask you to get involved in this any further."

"Too late for that, old friend…" Oz nonchalantly holds up a plastic dry-cleaning bag that already contains body parts. "Junior's jaw, I think, or part of it anyway. What are you lookin' at me like that for? This shit don't bother me—remember I did a tour and then I worked for Bowlie's before I hired on at the Leroy. Besides, you think I'd let you leave me out of this. Like I said, I signed on for the full ride, Johnny—and you know and I know this kind of thing ain't in your comfort zone. But trust me, these guys got what guys like this deserve. It's not the first blood splashed on them, but it'll be the last! And if we don't get this cleaned up perfect, we're all in for a shit-storm. All of us."

"Well. I won't lie. I can really use your help here. This is a mess. Angie's always a ticking time bomb, and that damn Dalco kid—like father, like son, I guess."

"What do you mean?"

"Oh, you know—their brains are behind their zippers."

"Not all of them, Prince. Some of Junior's are back there in the closet."

"Yeah, I see that. But, back when Uncle Jake was sick, you remember, Dalco and his company tried to squeeze the Leroy away because of Jake's sloppy books and everything. Well, I happened to come into possession of some rather intriguing photographs, Freddy Senior doing his best Jerry Lee impersonation. He had already paid off the 12-year-old's parents, but me having the photos convinced him to back off the Leroy deal. And real quick, too."

"I always figured you had some angle there. Scum begets scum, I suppose."

"I guess it does. Anyway, I appreciate your help. All of us do." Johnny puts his hand on Oz's shoulder. "Thanks old man. ... Now, first things first. We need to get Angie out of here. Can you take her across to the Leroy? I'll get some cleaning supplies and try to get started here."

"No problem, Prince. I'll use the back stairs and get her out that way. And I'll bring back some of those large garbage bags and a couple carpet knives, too. This floor's a mess—we're gonna have to get rid of some of the carpet."

"Good idea." Johnny turns into the room. "Angie. You ready? Time to get you home."

"Yeah, Prince. What should I do with this?" She holds the Smith and Wesson in the fingertips of her left hand.

"Ah, Angie, I think maybe you've already done enough with that. Just give it to me and I'll take care of it." Johnny takes the handgun from Angie and checks to see that the safety lock is on.

Oz cautiously checks the hall, then he and Angie exit and quietly move to the rear stairway and vanish. The Prince uses the large handgun as a stop to keep the door of 503 slightly open. He traverses diagonally across the hallway to a nondescript door opposite, the maid's closet. Surprisingly, it is unlocked. Johnny repockets a paperclip and quickly retrieves a pail, solvents, rags and a mop. He returns to 503, tosses the handgun back on the bed, locks the door and places the cleaning supplies in the bathroom. He runs some hot water and mixes in a large portion of the solvent in the pail. Dampening a face cloth, the Prince sits on the edge of the bed and wipes the Smith and Wesson clear of prints. He notices initials carved into the grip: RWW.

Suddenly the electronic lock of the door clicks, dim light from the hallway cascades into the room, and a pudgy hand swipes all of the lights on. Charlie T. Walker stands in the doorway.

"What the...? Well holy shit. Oh, my, my. Bobby told me I'd find something here. If it ain't the Prince of Leeeeroy, with blood all over his hands ... and a couple corpses to boot. Finally, the fox is trapped in the hen house. Oh my, my..."

- 82 -

If his brains were lard

"Oh, hi Charlie." Johnny coolly glances at Charlie as if he's holding a royal flush in a million-dollar buy-in. "You better close the door, Charlie. You don't want your guests seeing this."

"What, seeing that the local god of all losers in a trap! You're a Bowlie burger now, my friend."

Charlie shuts the door.

"Take a closer look, Charlie."

"Holy shit," his voice lowers. "Is that Dalco's kid? What the hell did you do?"

"Not me, Charles." The Prince stands and moves toward Charlie. "But this might look familiar." The Prince holds out the Smith and Wesson for Charlie to see. "This pair had their heads blown off with this. And the owner was so proud of it, he even carved his initials into the stock—R.W.W. Now I wonder who did that? Let me see ... the R could stand for ... hmm ... Roy? ... Ronald? ... Robert, Bobby...?"

"Shit! You got to be kiddin' me!"

"And wait 'til Dalco finds out!"

"But Bobby wouldn't have done this...? That boy's dumb as toast—if his brains were lard, he wouldn't grease a pan—but even he wouldn't be stupid enough..."

"Well, good luck convincing Dalco of that when he sees what's become of his kid. You and I both know, Charlie, that it will not matter, for Bobby or you or anybody around this mess, if Dalco gets wind…"

"Shit. Shit. Shit. Shit. Shit."

"You can say that again, Charlie. In fact, you can say that all the way out of here. Look, I got a plan to take care of this. And it will keep your son, and you, and the End, too, out of the wind. All you have to do is calm down, stay quiet, get out of here, and all of this will pass. Leave this to me … it's something I can do. I think I can, anyway."

"Shit. Shit. Shit. Shit. Shit. Damn it, March. Damn that stupid kid. Damn you."

"You're welcome, Charlie. Here, take this thing with you." Johnny hands the revolver to Charlie which he takes and holds like the proverbial hot potato. "Now, go, and don't say anything about this to anybody, or we'll all be Bowlie burgers."

Charlie opens the door of 503 and leaves, closing it as he goes and shoving the Smith and Wesson out-of-sight in his pants pocket. As he jams the down button at the main elevators, he does a double-take as Oz casually turns the corner with garbage bags and other indistinguishable devices. Oz nods in passing but Charlie just turns and looks straight ahead until the doors divide like the Red bloody Sea and Charlie can escape to a more promised space. He shakes his head slowly, but it is at this point that he begins to hear some commotion from below echoing up through the elevator shaft. Perhaps it is just thunder from the storm outside but somehow it seems different; it sounds like the popping rhythm of guns being fired. Involuntarily, his hand touches the revolver in his pocket—it can't be Bobby this time, can it?

- 83 -

The soup was good, man

At five minutes to six, Lucky wakes from a quick sleep. He is still tired and sore from the chaos of yesterday. He is sitting in a booth in the *Coureurs Bistro*, the restaurant situated just off the foyer of the Voyageur's End. It is a multi-purpose space serving everything from the so-called free continental breakfasts in the morning, mostly all-bran muffins, stale cereal and watery orange juice, to elegant overpriced meals in the evening, each table lit with a votive and served by a waiter in a crisp blue jacket with gold piping. There since just before 3:30, Lucky has been drinking boilers—using lite beer with the whisky though so he can keep his head straight—and sampling the food, mostly chicken fingers and some milky-white soup.

He has just been memory-dreaming about Sheri Lynn Frazer, the most beautiful and desirable girl in his Grade 7 class. She is the Laura Petrie of New Rochelle come-to-life in the public school of Orchard Valley where he grew up. And on one cold January morning he is walking to school and there has been a tremendous ice storm the night before and as he passes Sheri Lynn's house, where Mrs. Convoy used to live before her stroke, Sheri-Lynn emerges in a pink winter coat with matching mittens and they walk to school together. The convexed gravel road is coated with an inch and a half of ice, slick and treacherous and sloping to each side. And he and Sheri Lynn walk down the middle of that crystal way, one on each side of its apogee, holding hands to keep from sliding apart, to keep from falling. Holding hands with Sheri Lynn Frazer and the crisp blue world shimmering all about them. Grade Seven and the glistening future stretching out before them. And then Sheri Lynn's pink mitten slips off and she and he start to slide slowly toward opposite ditches and they can only turn and watch each other glide away and wave a cold farewell, her mitten in his hand. And laugh at the silliness of their predicament. Their lives. And Sheri-Lynn got pregnant in Grade 10 and disappeared from the visible world in accord with the social morays of the time. And Lucky, well, here is Lucky. Awakening in the *Coureurs Bistro*, he checks the clock over the bar and quickly beckons to the waiter.

"What's the charge, man? I had the Special, those chicken things with the Roman lettuce salad, and two or three drinks. And some soup. The soup was good, man."

"I have your check right here, sir." A young, fair-faced blond man presents a piece of paper to Lucky on a plastic tray stamped American Express in faded gold lettering. "I am pleased to hear that you enjoyed the soup."

"Is it ok if I just sign for that and add it to the bill for my room?"

"Not a problem, sir. Just sign there and put your room number in that box." The waiter points to a rectangle on the check.

"Ok." Lucky hesitates, then signs with a flourish. "There you are, man. And I added a good tip for you, too."

"Thank you, sir." The waiter takes the tray and the bill but only moves a step or so away. "Oh, wait. Excuse me ... ummm, Dr. Howard? I am sorry, but I do not believe there is a Room 7-11. In fact, *Voyageur's End* only has five floors."

"Oh, sorry ... I thought that was the room." Lucky, from the consumption of time lost and alcohol found, is a bit flustered, but more annoyed.

"Not a problem, sir. The numbers are easy to confuse. Would you mind coming over to our computer at the bar; just give me your room card and I can quickly verify your room number for you."

Lucky stares at the waiter for a brief moment, and glances at the clock over the bar, which reads 6:02.

"Shit, man! I'm late. And I gave you a good tip."

He draws his revolver, puts it directly to the waiter's stomach, and pulls the trigger.

- 84 -

Je ne suis pas fait de sucre

Oz knocks twice, then once more and Johnny opens the door to Room 503.

"I just saw big Charlie prowlin' around. Is that trouble for us?"

"No, don't think so, Oz. Nothing that his son's smoking gun didn't fix! I think he's on our side for this one. He knows Dalco!"

"Anyway, Angel is over with Benny and Blue right now—they're waitin' for Dom and Deed to get back with the truck. Blue's feedin' her some salad and fries and, you know, all things considered, she seems ok. More of her mother in her maybe than I would have guessed…"

There is a hurried knock at the door and Oz looks bemusedly at Johnny.

"You expectin' more visitors, Prince. Must be nice to be so popular. Let me see." Oz squints through the peep-hole. "Well, hell. It's Jackie. I didn't think she was s'posed to be around."

Oz opens the door and Jackie enters.

"Jackie! What's up? I thought you were going to stay at

The Prince of Leroy

home." Both Oz and the Prince stand just inside the doorway, shielding Jackie from a view of the room.

"Ah! You know me better than that, Johnny." She tries to look around the men's shoulders. "I took a cab. It dropped me off right at the side door and I used the back stairs. Nobody saw me."

"This is quite a mess in here, Jackie. But Angelique's ok. A bit bruised, but ok. Oz just took her over to the Leroy. She's with Benny and Blue—they're trying to feed her some food and a coffee, I imagine. I hope she doesn't need a visit to the hospital—it would probably be better if she didn't. Questions might be hard to answer. And they follow some pretty strict procedures. You need to talk to her about that."

"I will. Thank you, both of you." Jackie pushes past the men. "Oh, *mon Dieu*. This is what she did? *Jesu, Marie et Joseph*." She puts her hand over her mouth. "*Vu des cadavres*. This is starting to become a habit for me."

"Yeah, I suppose. Like I said ... a bit of a mess ... but if we get it cleaned up, get the bodies out of here, cut out the ruined carpet—we'll take a sample and get one of the guys from Tom and Mike's over here first thing to replace it—we can cover it up, I think, make it go away—protect Angelique."

"Ah, yes, *mon petit Ange*. You know I told you about that money that had disappeared, our trip money—well, I looked this afternoon and it was all returned. I don't know, Johnny, if I will ever understand my little girl."

"Growin' pains, Jackie." Oz mumbles. "Growin' for the kid, pains for the parent."

"Anyway, I got rid of the gun, I think, and I got some cleaning stuff mixed up in the bathroom. We need to get at it, Oz. Get the bodies out of here and clean up. No need for you to be involved, Jackie. Why don't you go over to the Leroy and Dom and Deed can drive you home with the van as soon as they get back?"

"*Non. Non.* I am already involved, Johnny. By blood. In more ways than one. And, in this light, tonight, you look so old—I know how this is for you. I know. And besides, I am a cleaner. It's what I do. And I'm her mother. I wiped her ass when she was *une bébé*; I guess I can wipe up this mess now."

"Are you sure, Jackie? After what you've just been through … I mean you're welcome to help, but…"

"I have never been surer, Prince. But, you know, someday, someday, the wipin's got to stop!" Jackie's eyes tear up. … "Now. You and Oz, get these bodies in the garbage bags—it's where they belong anyways—and let me get to work."

"Ok. Ok. Oz, it sounds like the boss has spoken."

"I hear you, Prince."

While Jackie gets the pail and cleaners from the bathroom, the two men pull garbage bags over the corpses, one bag from each direction—double-bagging as your corner grocer might say. Oz is careful to pick up what bone splinters and itinerant bits of flesh he can find and throw that in the bags, too. And to complete the gift wrapping, silver duct tape is used to bind the packages, the same way they do for Christmas in hell, I suppose, that is, were they to celebrate Christmas in hell. Then, as Jackie starts to wipe the walls in earnest, they check to see that the hall is empty, hoist the dead weight of Connie Torrence between them and move as quickly as possible out of the room.

"Right here, Oz. The elevator's too risky, too public. Let's use this."

Balancing the corpse in one arm, Johnny twists the knob and a door swings back to reveal the open mouth of the End's central laundry shoot.

"It's small, but as long as we get our aim right, he should go straight down. Let's just hope there's no-one down there—it's late enough, there shouldn't be."

Johnny starts the feet into the opening and, within a moment, Connie Torrence's remains are hurtling on their last amusement park ride, dropping with a definitive thud into the laundry cart waiting far below. A moment later, Frederick Dalco Junior pays for the same ride and is tipped into the chute. And shortly after, a large piece of newly cut carpet follows; then its blood-soaked under-pad.

"Oz, I'll just see if Jackie's done, help her put stuff away and make sure she gets out of here. Meet you in the basement."

"See you down there, Prince. I've got a sample for Tom and Mike's. We better get those stiffs out of the laundry bins before somebody tries to dry clean 'em."

Jackie is just stepping out of the room as the Prince returns. She stows the cleaning equipment in its cupboard as Johnny takes one last quick look around. With the exception of a large section of carpet missing, exposing a section of grey concrete floor, the room, clean with bed expertly made, looks ready for its next guests.

"*Assez propre*," Johnny says, loud enough to bring a smile to Jackie's face. The Prince places the "Do Not Disturb" sign on the handle and departs, with Jackie, down the back stairs. They arrive at the ground floor and Johnny pauses at the door.

"Why don't you head back to the Leroy, Jackie … Oz and me'll take it from here. Check on Angie, and Dom and Deed can give you a lift home. And thanks so much…"

"*Non*. No. It is me that owes all the thanks. *Merci, Prince. Merci* … it's all I can say. I…" She hugs him and he holds her in the dim light of the barren stairway. Johnny pushes the release bar of the door and guttural torrents of rain gypsy-dance all around them.

"I know, Jackie. I know. ... We'll talk first thing tomorrow. ... I wish I had an umbrella to give you."

"Bah ... *Je ne suis pas fait de sucre.* You know that, my Prince." Jackie hesitates, her hand resting on his shoulder, then slides away and exits. The Prince slowly turns and moves on down the stairs toward the basement. The storm is not over. There is still much to do.

- 85 -

Magic carpet ride

As the Prince arrives, Oz has already wrestled a garbage bag enclosed corpse on to a push cart, but Johnny can see that he is agitated.

"What's up, Wizard?"

'Shit, Johnny. One's missing … there's only one here. Somebody must of taken one … unless he got up and walked away?"

Oz turns and starts to look about the room.

"What? No. Wait, wait a minute, Oz. The carpet and under-pad—they're not here either. I thought it didn't sound quite right. I don't think Freddy Junior finished his ride. He's stuck up there in the chute somewhere."

"God. So, what do we do now, Johnny?"

"You stay here, Oz, or maybe roll that one into the furnace room, near Hell's Boulevard. I'll go back up to fifth floor and see if I can figure something out."

Johnny moves off quickly, catches the freight to fifth floor and opens the maid's closet. He emerges with his arms full of a quantity of bedclothes and a pillow. These he stuffs into the laundry chute, using his right foot to force the last of them in.

"Well, this should be interesting. Here goes nothing."

The Prince puts his left foot into the chute and eases in most of his leg. Then, twisting sideways, he does the same with the right. With the cushion of bedclothes falling away under him, Johnny forces himself into the tin passage. There is room for him to press his back to one side with his knees and hands on the other; he tries to ease his way down. But that doesn't work all that well and, after a moment, he slides, then falls. About halfway between floors two and three there is a stutter in the descent as he collides with underpad and carpet and corpse and then a release, and a straight fall toward the basement.

Oz stands there in awe as the entourage arrives, first garbage bag Freddy, then carpet, then underpad, then bedclothes, and, at last, the Prince. The laundry bin rocks, one of its wheels twists and bends and it tips sideways. The living and the dead dance across the floor.

"Jesus Christ, Johnny! Are you ok?" Oz rushes to the Prince to help him up.

"Yeah, more or less, I think. But I'm betting that I'll be sore tomorrow. That chute—I imagine what a coffin must feel like. A long narrow one at least. And a crowded one, too. But I'm fine. Looks like a torn shirt and a little scrape on my side, but generally, never felt better, Oz. Just like the water slide out at old Lake Park, without the water. Remember that?"

The Prince stands and arches his back.

"Your hands look a little roughed up, too."

"Just a scratch or two. Quite the magic carpet ride!"

"No shit, Prince. Too bad, it's probably not a story we can tell."

"No doubt, old friend. Come on, let's get this mess cleaned up."

The Prince of Leroy

"Sounds like some kind of ruckus upstairs. If I didn't know it was thunderin' out, I'd think those were gunshots."

"All the better for us, maybe ... as long as they stay upstairs. Even this storm, though ... it's a distraction. Just as if we planned it."

Oz and the Prince put Junior's body on a rolling cart, replace the laundry chute receptacle in its place and toss in the odds and ends of bedding Johnny used for his ride. Then they negotiate the rolling cart through to the furnace where its shadow awaits. The bodies are lifted into the entrance to Hell's Boulevard, then the carpet and under-pad. They complete a once-over of the basement so that, more or less, it resembles its former self, then replace the tunnel grate and move on their way, carrying one of the dead. They arrive at the trench that turns toward the sewer grate and the Leroy's sign and Oz pauses, but Johnny whispers.

"No, Oz. Not that way, not back to the poles this time. Keep going straight ahead. We'll take a different route this time."

The trio moves on until another large opening appears, this one to the west and about two feet above the lower level of the Boulevard.

"This is a new hole, isn't it Johnny?"

"Yeah. It's not as old as some down here. Let's leave this one and get the other."

A few minutes later the second corpse makes an appearance, doing its finest impersonation of a stretcher for some stained carpet and under-pad.

"Ok, next leg of the journey, boys. Put one up here, Oz."

Like a sad bale of straw on a weary August wagon, Connie lands on the ledge of this newer trench. Johnny hops up and, bent over in the confined space, drags the body out of sight. The act is repeated for Freddy Junior and the waste carpet.

"This is the old crawl space under the Leroy, isn't it? You

have access to all the rooms from here. And ... ah, I see said the blind man. This is where the End's cable comes in! All that free cable! You're always full of new tricks, aren't you Prince."

"Gotta keep at least one step ahead of the bastards, Oz. You taught me that. That's a lesson, I guess, these two didn't quite learn, did they?" Johnny pauses—this is as close to a eulogy as these dead would ever receive. ... "Come on. I want to pull these two guys down under 17, close to the breeze-way. Ok?"

"After you, Johnny. As always, Prince, after you."

In a few moments, the sewer cover next to the Leroy's sign nudges itself up and over and two men quickly emerge in the pounding rain. They look around; they replace the cover and rapidly move across toward the Office of the Leroy. There is some commotion going on across the road at the End, yelling and popping sounds and, far down along Dundas, a cascade of sirens seems to be approaching. Trace is looking down at the counter and does not see Johnny as he enters. Oz waits in the doorway. Angus is preoccupied, intently staring out the windows across at the End and uttering intermittent growls.

"Hi, Trace. How are you tonight?"

"I'm good, Mr. Prince." Trace looks up. "Real good!"

"Glad to hear that. Did you see Benny, and Jackie or Angie?"

"Yes. They were here. Well, in the restaurant. But they left. In that van. That little guy and that big guy, they came and took them in the van. The blue one. A little while ago."

"Ok, that's good. Could you give me the room key for 17? There's no one booked in there for tonight, is there?"

The Prince glances at the sign-in register. Then he scribbles a name down.

"No. It's vacant. I think. Or was. As far as I know. ... Here's key number seventeen."

"OK. Thanks Trace. I have an errand to run, then I'll be around later. If there's anything you need, let me know."

"Sure thing, Mr. Prince."

"And consider No.17 booked for a couple of nights."

"Sure thing, Mr. Prince."

Angus briefly looks at the two men but then resumes his wrapt vigil. There is danger afoot just across the road.

Inside Room 17, Oz and the Prince pull the bed to the side, slit the carpet and pull open the rusted trap door. Then, requiring more exertion than either expected, they hoist the two heavy and stiffening bodies into the room and lay them on a sheet on the floor. Johnny fetches up the carpet and under-pad. They shut the trap door, replace the shag and the bed to previous positions, and leave the room, a 'Do Not Disturb' sign on the door.

"Ok, Oz. We'll store these guys here for now. That's all you can do for tonight, I hope. Thanks. That's another big favour that I owe you, old man."

"Bah! Who you think you're kiddin'? Me owe the Prince favours—never in a lifetime. See you tomorrow, Johnny. We'll get this cleaned up then. Get rid of these guys somehow. And get the carpet guys to the End. You get some sleep—you look pretty beat down."

"I'm feelin' it too, man. Like the devil at the crossroads."

- 86 -

Jesus

Outside the rain is pounding down, thunder and lightning strutting a cosmic hoedown. The spacious foyer of the Voyageur's End glistens with a faux marble floor, fake pillars, tropical foliage and pleather sofas and chairs. A long registration and check-out desk stretches along the rear with a hallway to the left leading to exercise rooms and the pool. On the far left side, glass-paneled doors lead to the *Coureurs Bistro* which serves both as bar and restaurant. To the centre-right of the foyer, a hallway leads to elevators and ground floor rooms.

Gabe parks the Mustang on the curved drive to the east of the main entrance, leaving the key-fob behind the sun visor as planned; he enters and sits a heavy briefcase on the floor near the end of one of the sofas. He nods at another person who seems equally out-of-place here. This man, a Malley thug named Frankie, ambles toward Gabe, cautious as a stray dog chewing on a bumblebee. Both men stand uncomfortably in front of one another.

"So, where's my wife and boy? I don't see them." Gabe speaks quietly.

Frankie replies curtly. "That was never the plan, friend. Give me the money, we count it, and then your wife and kid'll be released. We'll tell you where."

"What the hell do you mean? That wasn't the deal, man."

"Well, with the boss not around, that's the deal, the one me and the boys decided on, like it or not."

"I don't care if your boss is out takin' a shit on the freeway. I got the money right here. Now, I want my wife and kid?"

"Mr. Malley said that when we got the money, we would release them. Gimme that, we'll get outta here, count it, give you a call. That's the deal. Your wife and kid are fine and they'll get released, but after we count the bread—that's the deal."

The thunder rumbles from outside the front doors; then more thunder roars from the direction of the bar; it is followed by a large commotion and people yelling. And like some gunslinger of old, Lucky backs out of the saloon, weapon in hand, and there is more furious noise, and he fires his gun in the air and turns. Frankie instinctively reaches beneath his coat and Gabe hits him with his right fist. His gun fires before he has managed fully to draw it and a bullet tears out through his jacket and shatters a mirror along the far wall. Frankie swears and hits Gabe hard in the left eye and, weapon now drawn, Gabe fires back at close range and Frankie screams and drops. Gabe sees a flash of fire from beside the reception counter and feels it too. And that fire is returned by Lucky who is suddenly right beside Gabe and, seeking cover for both, piles into him. They tumble into a large flower-splattered sofa which tips over and the right side of Gabe's face cracks into a faux-marble plant stand. And then gunfire erupts, it seems, from all directions. There are at least four people shooting at them and the foyer of the *Voyageur's End* is filled with smoke and screaming and the rending of glass and furniture and plants.

"Where's Liz and your kid? I don't see them anywheres."

"The lying bastards never brought them, Lucky. They broke their end of the deal."

"The bastards. God-dammit! Anyways, Gabe, they got us pinned down pretty good. We got to get out of here."

"No shit, man!"

"Fuck, I wish I had that rocket launcher. Anyways, come on. Like the Ranger said, sooner or later, gotta settle with the world, man! Let's give 'em hell, Chemo-savvy."

"That's me, pard!"

The two look up over their sofa bunker and let fly. There are already at least two guests on the floor, checking out when they had expected to be checking in. And a curious old man who pokes his curious head up from the reception counter loses a curious ear and one of Malley's thugs takes a slug in the knee and goes howling off toward the elevators. Lucky and Gabe leap to their feet—easier said than done, Gabe realizes—but then there is another hail of gunfire and a chandelier comes crashing down, and one pane of the large windows at the front of the End blows out and, nearly to the doors, Lucky and Gabe drop down again, this time behind a trolley piled with expensive luggage that soon starts to resemble the empty eyes of Swiss cheese. And when Gabe looks up amid the dust and smoke and bedlam, Lucky is gone. Nowhere to be seen—he has just vanished. Without a word. Like Queequeg in the wake. And Gabe struggles up and feels something like a wasp sting his upper chest and then he is outside where the rain cascades in sheets. He cannot see the Mustang parked where he left it, although with his face swollen as it is, he cannot see much anyway. But he does sense the two men exiting behind him, after him. So he rushes across Dundas and past the Leroy and the

Roosevelt and out into the deteriorating parking lot beyond. Somewhere, far off, he thinks he hears a dog bark, and briefly thinks of Scotty, that rough and tumble farm mutt of his childhood, but no time to think about that. Running, hobbling, doing his best. Winded, he stops. And in a clear strike of lightning above and close, he sees a white cross hovering in the air, and a great light floods over his face. He drops, awkwardly, painfully, to his knees.

"Jesus."

And then it is dark again. Perhaps the heavens have smiled on another lost angel found. Or perhaps not.

- 87 -

Silent as lightning, stoic as thunder

The rain continues to pour although the thunder and lightning have started to slide a bit toward the east. A blue van pulls into its customary parking space behind Rainy's, its lights go out and Dom exits the driver's side in the pitch dark. He stares across the street where all hell seems to have broken out at the End. Sirens can be heard in the near distance. He can hear a dog he recognizes as Angus frantically barking and clawing at the back door of Rainy's and he can also hear voices off to his left across the desolate parking lot of the old K-Mart. Before he can open the door to greet Angus, two men emerge abruptly from the storm, one of them complaining to the other.

"Where the hell'd he go, Bruce?"

"I don't know, Bruce." A second like-named thug speaks (hereafter designated 'Bruce-Bruce'). "Damn rain's so hard, I can't see a thing."

"Well, I say to hell with it. I can hear the heat getting closer. Let's head back. This is suicide out here anyways—we could be picked off before we ever saw what hit us. ... Hey, wait a minute! Over there—you. Don't move."

The two men, guns held straight out, both see and move toward Dom at the same instant. Bruce-Bruce speaks:

"Okay, Buddy. The game's up. Drop the gun."

Dom instinctively understands the inherent danger here. These guys are at the tail end of something; they look tired and edgy and, worse, hard to read. His dead-dream flutters briefly to mind.

"Whoa, hold on there, boys. I ain't got no gun. You got the wrong guy."

"Is that him, Bruce? He looks short enough."

"I dunno, and I don't really give a fuck. Everything was flying in there. I really couldn't see shit. But let's take him back anyway. He'll do."

"Yah, he looks short enough to be that dumb fart who blew Frankie away. Let the boss finish him. Or should we just waste him right here and skip the trouble."

"I know what you're saying," quips Bruce.

Bruce's expression changes suddenly from a satisfied comfort to a grunt and a painful wince; he shudders as a vice grips and raises the wrist of his gun hand. Audibly, bones crunch. His gun clatters to the pavement and he is lifted up screaming into the storm, his shoulder dislocating. Before he can process the situation, Bruce-Bruce also rises up as a huge hand grips his shoulder and inside of his neck; then searing pain as muscle is mulched and tendon from bone lets go. And his weapon drops, and he swings around in confusion like a broken weather vein on an abandoned barn. A giant of a man stands between them, silent as lightning, stoic as thunder. And the lightning slashes again and they sway in the frieze like forsaken thieves on an ancient tree.

And then, they are released, trivially cast away, weeds left broken but not severed by an indifferent mower. And, as much as anything else, that indifference strikes deep, horrifies them. They scramble up from the pavement and hurry back in pain towards the light of the End.

"What the hell was that, man?" Bruce grunts as he runs. "Lightning or thunder? My wrist. My shoulder's gone."

"I don't know. Mine too." Bruce-Bruce stammers. "It could of been an angel of God or the devil hisself. I don't know. But either way, I thought it was gonna crush me like an insect. Like we just didn't matter."

"The only thing I know—it was big. Fuck ... even if I got to go straight, man, flip some burgers or something, I don't never want to meet that thing again. Never."

"Let's just get the fuck outta here. Nothing good never happens to nobody around this old Leroy shithole!"

And unseen in the dark as these two stumble away, another, a newcomer who carries no name, takes all of this in.

- 88 -

The implacable weight of knowing

Dom and Deed, appearing a bit ruffled, wander into Rainy's to take their accustomed stools at the lunch counter. The Prince, sensing their arrival, steps through the door from the Office. Angus comes barreling in from the eastside 'L' and all but ploughs into them in his excitement.

"Hi, boys. Everything go ok."

"No real problems, Johnny. Just like clockwork. Aside from being a little on the damp side. We followed your directions. Timing was perfect. The semi just pulled in as we got there. And we got ten boxes, not eleven, not nine, ten—just like you told us. And I didn't say hardly nothing, just like you told me. Ask Deed, he'll vouch for me. And then, when we got back, we took Jackie and Angie home—Deed even got out and walked them right to their apartment door, just like some kind of gentleman—I didn't know he had it in him"—Dom lightly elbows the gentle giant—"and then we dropped Benny off at his place, as requested. Anything else you need for tonight, Prince?"

"No, no. You did great, guys. Just perfect."

"We left the boxes in the van. It's locked. And I think it's fairly waterproof. Here are the keys. So, as you say, Prince, errand accomplished."

"Good." Johnny smiled. "The boxes can wait until morning. That van is as watertight as anything else around here. Here's a little bit extra for your extra troubles." Johnny gives Dom and Deed each an envelope.

"Whoah, no need for that, Prince. But thank you."

"Hmmmmm."

"So, looks like it must of been quite a ruckus over at the End tonight, flashing lights and cops and people running around?" Dom inquires.

"Yeah, quite a ruckus, I guess. Sure got Angus wound up—he is not fond of fireworks. I'm not sure what went down—haven't heard a word. But things seem to have settled—almost back to normal, boys, whatever that is. I'm sure you'll get it sorted out for us, won't you Dom, and let us all know by tomorrow?" Johnny teases Dom.

"Yeah ... probably, Prince. You know me. I got the nose for news!"

"Anyway ... for now, time to get some supper, boys. It's on the house tonight. Whatever you want? Grease will set you up. Just remember our slogan, 'if the service is slow or the steak's tough, speak to Lou.'"

"Yeah, I know, and Lou don't exist. I seen this movie before."

"Can't fool an old dog, can we ... and Jackie and Angie seemed ok?"

"Yeah, Angie seemed good, Prince. Quiet, but good. I gather she had a bit of a rough afternoon. But she's a gutsy kid, and that'll either save her or kill her. One or the other. And Jackie, well Jackie's Jackie. Tough as nails when she needs to be ... so I think she's all right, too."

"Well, thank you gentlemen for all of your good work today. Enjoy your supper. I've got a couple more errands to do before the night is over. This rain looks like it's letting up a bit, so that's good. The clouds are still keeping things dark, though ... and that's good too. For some errands, I guess, darker is better. Goodnight all. You stay, Angus—Grease'll fix you something special, too. G'Night." Johnny says these words quietly and leaves the restaurant as a chorus of 'good nights' echo in reply. Angus utters a brief and soulful whine.

And for a brief second, in the feeble and distorted light of the doorway, Johnny's face looks like something an old master might have fallen to late in the day, ancient and wrecked and full of the implacable weight of knowing. But the others, turning to their labours and menus and thirsts and the stroking of Angus, take no notice and, silently, the Prince passes into the rain.

- 89 -

A beautiful friendship

By Saturday afternoon, the storm front has passed and more seasonable weather has taken occupancy, spring cool and calm and humidity free, the kind of air that gives you deep and vitalizing breaths. Johnny has just arrived back in the Office where Benny Alamo is leaning against the counter, doing his monthly weekend shift. He speaks in an upbeat way.

"How's it going, Prince. You're still looking a little tired."

"Last night was a long one, Benny. And I ain't getting any younger, you know."

"I hear you. Jackie and Angie all set?"

"Yeah. We had a good talk and they're on their way. Both of them seemed pretty relieved—I think the time away will do them good. Probably do some good for everything around here too."

"And Oz was saying that we had some visitors today … early?"

"Early doesn't say it. Just after six this morning Oz saw them comin' in—lookin' to do some nosin' around when he intercepted them. According to Oz, they were from some retirement home out in the Valley, The Last Resort, I think he said it's called."

"Oh yeah, I've heard their jingle on the radio—you know the one:

'The first resort to turn to,
The best resort you'll see,
The only resort to lean to,
The last resort you'll need.'

It ain't exactly great poetry, Prince. Especially done as it is in a kind of upbeat fake Irish patois, like some drunken leprechaun on crack."

For the first time in a while, the Prince smiles in an easy way.

"Well, I guess they had a couple patients wander off this past week and have been looking around for them since. Someone told them they'd seen somebody old wandering around over here and so they wanted to check it out. And Oz told them, in no uncertain terms, that there was no old person wandering around over here except him, and that was on his good days."

"That sounds like Oz."

"I got the names they're looking for … Oz wrote them down." Johnny fishes a paper out of his shirt pocket. "Ahh, here … they're missing an Alpheus H. Thompson and a Harriet Ostrom. From what Oz tells me, based on the creepy pair he talked to and their crappy van, old Alpheus and Harriet might be better off wherever they are. Food for thought, anyway Benny."

"From the jingle alone, I'm not surprised. I'll keep an eye peeled, Prince, for the searchers, not so much the escapees."

"You're starting to get the Leroy way of doing things, Benny. For better or worse, you're starting to get it."

Like the iconic beaver slapping its pond, Blue's slight whistle from the restaurant is a warning to everyone. Angus appears out of the kitchen. A shaggy fat man with a greying beard and thick glasses chugs down the remainder of a cup of coffee, dumps some money on the counter and, taking a half sandwich with him, heads for the rear exit. At least three other patrons do the same. A couple more hunker down in their booths and start to eat faster. A bronze Chrysler and a white Cadillac pull up together, stopping with authority just outside the Office.

"Heads up, Johnny, Benny. We got company." Blue quietly reports through Rainy's doorway.

"Thanks, Blue. We got it."

Detectives Earl Vance and Phinney Lowe get out of the Chrysler; Charlie T. Walker and Frederick Dalco emerge from the Cadillac. All four men walk briskly into the Office of the Le Roi Motor Inn. Angus sits in the doorway to Rainy's and growls intermittently.

"Hello, Johnny, and it's Benny, isn't it? Johnny, we just need to speak with you and your staff for a couple minutes. It's about a missing person. We'll be as efficient as we can." Vance takes the lead. "Phinney, why don't you pull Benny aside here and then check on the employees in the restaurant and anyone else you can find. Ok? And if somebody would calm that dog down, we'd all be better off."

"Yeah, I'm on it, Earl. Hi there, Benny." Phinney and Benny move sideways to the restaurant doorway, where Benny quietly strokes and calms Angus while Lowe asks a couple questions, making notations on a small pad of paper. Then he leaves Benny and moves out of sight into Rainy's. Benny stays with the alert dog.

"Yes, Earl, gentlemen." The Prince moves in front of the counter and looks straight at the trio in the room. He leans gently back against it. "What can I do for you? That was a helluva rain last night. Except over at your place, Charlie. It looked like the fourth of July with all the fireworks and lights flashing."

"We ain't here to talk about the weather, March, or what happened last night at the End," Dalco growls.

"Enough gentlemen, let's not get into that." Vance is blunt, affirmative, like a man who has put up with enough in the last few days and just wants to get home, tend to his lawn, play with his dog, watch some meaningless game on TV. "Just a couple questions for you, Johnny. I know you're always on top of things around this neighbourhood."

"Sometimes, Earl. Sometimes."

"Mr. March. Mr. Dalco's son is missing, has been since yesterday morning. Mr. Dalco reported it today and we're doing some preliminary investigating. He says it's not like his son to be out of touch for any length of time. He thinks that you might have some knowledge about Frederick Dalco Junior and/or his whereabouts and wanted me to talk to you."

"Well, I don't know why he would think that, Detective Vance. I only saw Freddy Junior once or twice in my life, once being last Sunday when these gents dropped over to offer me some friendly neighbourhood greetings. Remember?" Johnny glances toward Dalco and Charlie.

"I want you to search this goddamned place from pen to pig." Dalco barks. "Where's that tramp that works here, the one with the daughter?"

Charlie's eyes can be seen to wince at this.

"Easy, Mr. Dalco. Please, let me do the questioning."

"That's not a problem, Detective. Search all you want; clean some rooms if you want—I can get you a master key. Now, if you're referring to Jacqueline Savard and her daughter, Angelique, they've gone on vacation for a couple weeks. It's been a long time coming. And a long time in planning. Jackie's been working overtime to save enough money and next week is Spring Break at Angie's school—so they left this morning. Be gone for a couple weeks. But I don't see what they would have to do with Freddy Junior being missing. I'm pretty sure he didn't hang around with them—they don't even know him, do they?"

"I remember Mrs. ... uh, Jackie Savard. Mr. Dalco, do you have any reason to believe that your son would be linked up in some way with them, connected to them or their vacation?"

"Uhh ... no, not really, I guess," Dalco grudgingly accedes, knowing it is a place he cannot go.

"Jackie's been at home ever since she found that body the other day. And her daughter's stayed with her all the time. Quite a shock, as you can imagine ... and then on top of it, there was some kind of bizarre break-in at their apartment,...," the Prince adds quickly.

"Yes. I read a report. Curious to say the least—coincidences almost always are. Sometimes when it rains, I guess, it rains every day. So, Johnny, you have not seen Frederick Junior at all, at least since last Sunday? And you haven't been over at the End in the last twenty-four hours?"

"No, not at all, Earl. I don't visit the End very much, unless I get an invitation, and that doesn't happen very often. Look, I'd like to help—we sure don't want someone like Freddy Junior running around off his leash, but I haven't seen him since last Sunday when he was here and left with his father, and Charlie there."

"Walker," Dalco blurts. "You tell him, Walker. Tell Vance what you said to me. Something about March. Something you'd seen. You were mumbling about something this morning, when you was whining about the mess at your place. Your kid or something."

Charlie T. Walker stiffens and glances at Johnny and Vance and then he holds his gaze on Dalco. Finally, he looks directly at Johnny again, then to Vance.

"Well, Detective Vance, I guess maybe I was just mumbling this morning. After that mess yesterday, I was pretty shaken up. So—that's all it was—mumbles. Nothing, Detective Vance. I saw nothing. And I haven't seen Freddy Junior since yesterday morning when he was having breakfast in the coffee shop at the End. What's left of the coffee shop now..."

Johnny returns Charlie's stare and, ever so slightly, each nods his head at the other as if a beautiful friendship were beginning and the *Marseillaise* about to break out. Then Charlie stares straight at Frederick Dalco who looks away.

Phinney returns from Rainy's and shakes his head in the negative to Earl. "Nobody remembers Freddy Junior around here, Earl, at least not since last week when he and Mr. Dalco visited together, and left together."

"Well, Mr. Dalco, it doesn't look like there's anything here. I think we had better go. I'm sure your son will turn up. It's only been a little over twenty-four hours and you know what young men can be like."

"Goddamn it. He's my son, Vance. My boy, and he's missing. I just feel it. I know it. I expect you to put more men to work on this, and now. He's my son for Christ's sake."

"We're already doing that Mr. Dalco. Sorry to trouble you, Johnny. If you do see or hear anything, please let me know. I believe you know how to reach me."

"Yes, I do know that. Good afternoon, gentlemen."

The quartet retreats to the cars and, after a brief discussion over the roofs of those vehicles, the cars, in turn, retreat out of the lot, one to the End and one west along Dundas.

Angus watches the cars leave, then retreats to the kitchen.

"You know, Benny," Johnny speaks quietly. "You know that fertilizer we were just going to bill to the End's accounts. Let's give Charlie's stamp a rest this time and pay for that ourselves. Give the End a break on that one."

"Sure thing, Prince. I get it. That'd be a Leroy way of doing things, wouldn't it?"

- 90 -

Yes

"Morning, boys. You look a little beat down today." Blue looks up from a Monday morning newspaper spread across the lunch counter as Dom and Deed amble in.

"Morning, Blue. Yeah, we're movin' a bit slow today. We had a couple late days on the weekend; had to take care of some errands."

"I thought maybe you'd floated away in that flood we had the other night."

"Yeah, could have, Blue. It rained so hard, I hear some fish drowned."

"I believe you, Dom," Blue smiles. "Just like everything you say. What can I get you?"

"I'll have a coffee and some toast. How 'bout you, Deed? Coffee, and some corn flakes?"

"Mmhmm."

"And where's my favourite Leroy canine this morning?"

"Sleeping somewhere, I think. He's been on edge so much all weekend, he tuckered himself right out. But he'll probably surface sometime soon, especially when he smells that toast."

Dom pulls a roll of bills out of his pocket. Blue pours out the coffee and sits a bowl of corn flakes in front of Deed.

"Set 'em up, Blue. Extra toast, too. I'm payin' today."

"The toast will be just a sec, Dom. That's quite a little roll you got there. What'd you do ... knock off the other six dwarves?"

"Not quite, Flo the beautiful! At least I won't have to waste any of this on tips."

"Really ... I don't remember when you ever did that before anyway, my little one."

"But, yeah ... me and Deed found a couple of items just laying on the pavement the other day. Took awhile but we turned a nice little profit on them."

"Must of been some pretty valuable items."

"Yeah ... the kinds of things there's always a good market for, somewheres, Blue! Always somebody who wants one. Somebody with a dream. So what's up around the Leroy?"

"Things have settled down a bit after the big shoot-out across the road on Friday—there's still news in the paper about it and buzz all over the web—people are calling the End the OK Corral these days."

Dom smiles. "Maybe change those paddles on their sign to long rifles, and break the canoe in half. I heard the place is in quite a mess, two or three people dead, twice that many wounded."

"Yeah, they're calling all of it storm damage and got some big discounts on there now, almost as cheap as staying here. Trying to claw some business back."

"So there might be a few slim nights ahead for the Leroy, then."

"Ah. The Leroy always survives, you know that, Dom. It always makes it through."

"And thank the stars for that, Blue. I hear there was a big firefight downtown too—started early yesterday afternoon and continued off and on through the night—I guess one of the Vietnamese gangs was involved. A regular massacre. Feels like Thornton's becoming a real big city."

"The radio news this morning made it sound like some kind of mob thing."

"Yeah. Dalco and his crew was probably mixed up in it."

"He was in here again the other day … with a cop."

"The perfect alibi, probably. What'd he want?"

"Oh, something about his kid gone missing or something. The Prince said it didn't make any sense to him."

"Hey Blue, speaking of things that don't make any sense, I got to tell you, me and Deed saw a couple things the other night, late Friday, that didn't make much sense either, after we took Jackie and her kid home and ate here and was leavin', just after the ruckus at the End had died away and most of the cop cars had left."

"What was that, Dom?"

"Well, when we left, we went out the 'L' at the back, just to double-check that we had locked the van after we'd parked it. And, of all the weird things, we saw the incinerator on. We stood right there by the van for a couple minutes, just watching as the furnace door was opened and closed and that fire blazed in the night. Somebody—and I swear to you, it looked a lot like Johnny—somebody had the old cooker going full blast. It looked as hot as I've ever seen it, like a bit of hell had leaked right through the earth. Maybe because of the darkness and the drizzle, I don't know. It felt like some real tragic magic, but not our business, so we went on our way. Right, Deed? I was surprised, you know, 'cause Burning Day was over. And I've never seen the Prince get near that fire."

"No kiddin'. That does sound strange. You sure Deed and you weren't just into a bit too much of our Kickapoo Joy Juice?"

"No Blue, we were both dry enough to be fartin' camels. Trust me on that! It had been a tense night, you know, pickin' up that load in the storm, and gettin' Jackie and Angie home, and then all the fireworks. People running around, and whatnot!"

"Well, I don't know ... I was off-shift by then and nobody said anything Saturday. Maybe there were things left over from the 21st, or something? Beats me! Ask Oz about it if you get a chance. But I doubt it was the Prince. He doesn't do fire."

"Yeah, I know ... he always has Oz own the match."

"Yep ... that's Burning Days. And you know, since you mention it, it always amazes me how much stuff gets left in the rooms even after a slow night or two. It's like everybody leaves the Leroy in a rush..."

"...'cept those that never leave at all..." Dom chips in, "the living and the dead."

"I get your point, Dom. That poor bastard from the other day. I guess they still don't know who he is."

"That ain't no way to go, Blue. All alone in an old motel."

"You said it. It still gives me the shivers."

"Mmmm." Deed nods his head.

"Makes a person think a bit, doesn't it, about just being alive," continues Dom.

"Indeed. Indeed. And so here we are, I guess. All the human remains."

"Sounds like there might be a song there, Blue."

"Oh, there's a song everywhere, Dom. The words are written

in the air we breathe, but you've got to be in the right state of mind to copy them down. And that state is never easy to find, or hold on to. Trust me on that, gentlemen." Blue is silent for a moment. "But anyway, like I was saying, on Saturday, even after these last slow days, I saw Johnny putting a ton of stuff in the safe, just a couple night's leftovers—a pair of women's shoes, perfectly new, an overcoat, a green gym bag, a couple books, a big silver case, dented in one corner, a pair of expensive shades, an umbrella, and a plastic bag full of cosmetics and some other stuff. And that was only for two off-season nights. Wait'll summer gets here. ... There's your toast, Dom." Blue places a plate of toast in front of Dom and moves a metal basket of jams and jellies within his reach.

"Thanks, beautiful. Anyways, as I was saying, Friday was a curious sight. That fire in the dark—must of made a long work day for somebody. But the night wasn't over, Blue, and Deed can back me on this. As we turned and headed for home, just down the street here, we looked up and saw the strangest thing, maybe, I've ever seen. There was a damned bright light—I swear to you—a bright light that come shooting across the sky, from the west, just over the treetops…"

"Some of us call that lightning, Dom," Blue smiles, "or streetlights!"

"That's what we thought, too, at first. With that crazy storm around and everything. Something strange, rare … like, horizontal lightning. But then the son-of-a-bitch of a thing stopped, I swear, a dead-stop, right there over the old *Holy K*. Just hung fire right there in the middle of the sky. And then it reversed and took off like a flash right back where it came. Outta sight. Isn't that right, Deed?" Dom nudges the quiet giant.

"Mmmhm."

"Well, who knows Dom? ET was a short dude ... maybe he's back looking for a friend?"

"Well ... make fun of it if you want, but it pretty much capped off one of the strangest nights on record for me. Sent a freakin' chill right down my spine, I can tell you. Almost as bad as dreamin' you're dead."

"Well, I gather it was a strange night, I'll give you that. But it was probably some new Air Force gizmo, a drone or something. There's no telling what the military is experimenting with these days. Meanwhile I was home having a long bath and drinking some herbal tea—nothing strange about that."

"Well, that beats seeing hellfire and ufos, I guess. And a gunfight at the End. Or getting' shot at. I guess any day you don't wake up in a body bag's a good day."

"I won't disagree with you there, Dom."

"Anyways, I wanted to ask, on our way in, I seen Trace out there pushing one of the room cleaning carts. And there's someone else with her. I guess Jackie has the day off?"

"Yeah. Trace is adding to her repertoire here. And Jackie, actually Jackie's off for a couple weeks! I think it's a good thing too—finding that body really spooked her. It spooked me enough and I didn't even see it. And she's needed some time off, anyway. And Angie, too, I gather—she got into some kind of mess last week. So she and her daughter are away on a trip. Hopefully she can get that kid sorted out a bit. But what's really cool is where they went."

"Man, Blue, that coffee was good. Where'd she go? Back home—east coast?"

"Refill comin' up, since you're actually paying today! No, she and Angie went to Paris. For two weeks, if you can believe it. Paris!"

"Paris? Paris, France?" Dom asks incredulously. Blue nods. "Wow! She must be making some real coin somewhere. Paris! ... Unless the Prince had something to do with it?"

"Well, rumour is he might of. I know that he and Jackie had a long talk early Saturday and by noon, she and Angie were on a commuter flight to New York to catch a first class flight. Can you believe it? She's probably sitting in some nice street café, right now, drinking a glass of wine. Paris in spring, you know. It's gotta be nice. And she and Angie are going to stop off on the east coast on their way back and spend a few days with her Dad. Gotta be nice."

"Hell yes, gorgeous. Good for Jackie! You know, Blue, if you weren't so good lookin' and outta my league, with the bundle I got right now, that's where I'd take you…"

"Dom, you are full of lot more than toast and coffee! As usual!" All of them chuckle a bit; some like-noise even comes from Grease back in the kitchen.

"So who's the other woman out there, the one that's helping Trace with the rooms. Is she new?"

"As far as I can tell, that's just another stray, Dom, another one of us. You know, the lost and the lonely who end up stumbling out of the desert and into this oasis."

"Really! I do feel a song comin' on, don't I?"

"Well, stranger things have happened, I suppose. Especially with all the stuff that's been happenin' around here lately. Maybe I will try dusting off the old quill and Birdseye again. Or maybe not!"

"That woman looks familiar."

"Well, you might have seen her somewhere. It's another of those strange things that seem to happen around here all the time, something like your Friday night lights, Dom. Her name's

Laura Santolin. She's a cop—at least she was one. She was actually here last week with her partner, investigating that body Jackie found. Anyway, she came wanderin' in again Saturday and I recognized her and asked her if she'd come back on some official matter. And she said no, that she wasn't a police officer any more, at least that she had taken a six month leave. And then she had a long talk with Johnny, and, wouldn't you know, he set her up in one of the rooms and she's goin' to help Trace out with some of the cleaning and fill in for Jackie in the restaurant for the next couple weeks. After that, we'll see! 'Round and 'round it goes at the Leroy, you know."

"I think me and Deed have seen her before. I'm pretty sure. I hope she's not packin' a gun when she's cleanin' rooms."

"I don't think so." Blue smiles. "Anyway, as I say, after Jackie returns, who knows? A lot of the time, Dom, we have more strays in this motel than paying customers, but that's the way Johnny likes it—it's what makes the Leroy, the Leroy, I guess."

"Well, I'll have to say hello to Laura, and I haven't really met the old gal yet, you know, the one who owns the university, the one the aliens abducted!"

"Yeah, so she says, but she seems like a sweetheart. If she's the end result, maybe aliens should abduct everyone!"

"It could never happen to me, Blue. I got Deed to fight them off. The aliens wouldn't stand a chance. They'd put their tails between their legs, even if they didn't have tails, or legs, and go rollin' back to Pluto or Krypton or wherever the hell they come from." Deed is smiling through a mouthful of corn flakes.

"You are probably right there. But I got to tell you Laura and Emily certainly hit it off; they sat in a booth back there for over two hours on Saturday and talked and talked. I guess maybe that's what both of them needed."

"We all need that from time to time."

"I guess you're the expert on that, aren't you, Dom? Isn't he, Deed?"

"Mmhmm!"

"I'll let you know when I need your two nickels, big fellow." Dom playfully elbows Deed. "Is the Prince around today?"

"No. He's gone too. Took off late Saturday. Told Benny and me that he might not be back for two or three weeks, maybe longer, if you can believe it. That Oz was in charge—that, if there were any problems, just see Oz."

"Wow, that's strange. I've never known the Prince to be away for more than a couple days at a time. And he was just away. I'll bet you he shows up again before mid-week."

"Normally, Dom, I wouldn't take that bet, but I don't know. There was something in his voice when he talked, something in the way he looked. I think he might just be away for a while this time. Of course, I haven't told you the biggest news of all. Just before he left, he told Oz to open up 12, can you believe it, take the black boards off and air the place out. He told him to have it cleaned up and ready to use again by the time he got back. What he said, I think, was mostly for Oz to hear but all of us were there. 'Time to take charge of change' he said. 'It's been closed up long enough.' And he repeated that—'time to take charge of change.' And then he said something about 'true passion' and running at the dark. He slapped Oz on the shoulder, nodded to us and walked away. Loaded up a small backpack, gave Angus a handful of treats and vanished in a cab. To the airport, I guess."

"Wow. Maybe you're right. Might be a sign, Blue, a sign that there's some change in the air. But I don't know—the Prince is the Prince. Where was he going?"

"He didn't say. He just roared out of here like a river in spring."

"Probably off to Atlantic City ... toss the bones and skin the rabbits."

"I don't know. I don't think so this time. It felt like it had more legs than that. I mean, like you said, he was just there a week or so ago. No, I got the feeling that the Prince was up to something bigger this time, off on a grander errand somewhere. Something real big."

"Ah, so he's off to slay some fiercer dragon. He's always got something bigger going on."

"Maybe."

"Maybe it has to do with that shipment me and Deed picked up for him Friday. Now the Prince told us it was just a deal on some of those small stuffed toys that the kids are crazy about, that he was going to donate them to the Children's Hospital, public relations for the Leroy. As if the Leroy needs any public relations! Donate, hell! No, the Prince is up to something, Blue. He's probably somewhere right now waking up some sleeping beauty with a kiss, about to score a pot of gold and jewels. The holy grail. That's why he's the Prince."

"You may be right, Dom. He usually has something on the go."

"He sure does, always. No rust on him. Never! And nobody never puts one over on the Prince, either. It's like the world is a book and he's the only one who can read. He's always there, always ahead of them all. And mark my words, the day somebody around here needs him, that's the day he'll come walkin' right back through that door. Yessiree, Blue. Thank you. Damn, Rainy's coffee is good. Best in the world, gorgeous." Dom raises his cup. "So here, here's to our Prince, wherever he is!"

Blue touches two fingers to her right brow and drops them

in a quick salute. "To Johnny P. March, gents. The Prince of Leroy."

Deed raises a spoon filled with sugary corn flakes and milk and gently touches Dom's thick mug.

"'Course when I say that about the Prince, Blue, about people needing him and him being there, I may not mean myself anymore."

"Really, Dom? What do you mean?"

"Well. I think I'm on the verge of something, Blue, of some big kind of change myself. I can feel it in the air, like spring—ever since I had that dream, you know, that dream about me being dead. The money Deed and me just came into, and the teacher thing, and gettin' shot at, and that downpour on Friday—it's like everything old has been washed away in the last couple of weeks. Burned-off like a Leroy fire. Did I tell you about that crazy professor we met over at the university? He gave me a book and a nice pen and he told me about a shrink named Young—yeah, same name as the old quarterback, the southpaw—well this Young wrote all about dreams like mine. And I've thought about it an awful lot. And this Young claims my dream's not negative at all—'course he wasn't the one havin' the dream—nevertheless, he says the dream probably means that I'm on the brink of change, on the road to becoming something new. Like a butterfly, I'm just about to break out, discover my new self. It's my past that's dead, not me. And I think he may be right 'cause you know what's weird, like I said, I can feel it. It's like, my wings are greased with Leroy's coffee and I'm about ready to fly. For the first time, maybe ever, I feel like I'm ready to do something different, to change. Like, maybe, I won't need the Prince anymore. Like, who knows, maybe I'm gonna be a prince myself! Now, what do you think about that?"

"I don't know, Dom. Sounds pretty strange. Like your light in the sky. But I suppose anything's possible. When the End can become the O.K. Coral and cops start cleaning rooms at the Leroy, who knows! Maybe I should pick up my old guitar again? Does that mean we won't be seeing you around the Leroy as much? Do you really think you're ready? Do you think the world's ready?"

"Beats me! But it better be, Blue, it sure as hell better be. 'Cause, whether it's ready or not, here I come."

Angus pokes his head out from the Office; he stands in the doorway waiting.

"And you Deed, what about you? Are you ready to join your good friend? Ready to change your world?"

There is a moment of silence as great Deed pauses, stares at an empty bowl, and then, casually, he looks across at Dom, then straight at Blue, nods his head and speaks.

"Yes."

The dream is the liberation of the spirit from the pressure of external nature, a detachment of the soul from the fetters of matter. ... As everyone knows, the ancients before Aristotle did not consider the dream a product of the dreaming mind, but a divine inspiration, and in ancient times the two antagonistic streams, which one finds throughout in the estimates of dream life, were already noticeable. They distinguished between true and valuable dreams, sent to the dreamer to warn him or to foretell the future, and vain, fraudulent, and empty dreams, the object of which was to misguide or lead him to destruction.

—*Sigmund Freud*

Knowing your own darkness is the best method for dealing with the darknesses of other people. One does not become enlightened by imagining figures of light, but by making the darkness conscious. The most terrifying thing is to accept oneself completely. Your visions will become clear only when you can look into your own heart. Who looks outside, dreams; who looks inside, awakes.

—*Carl Jung*

Trust in dreams
For in them is hidden the key to eternity

—*Kahil Gibran*

And if my thought-dreams could be seen.
They'd probably put my head in a guillotine.
But it's alright, Ma, it's life, and life only

—*Bob Dylan*